HANGING ON

GREAT LAKES BOOKS

HANGING ON

Or
How To Get Through A Depression
And Enjoy Life

BY EDMUND G. LOVE

WAYNE STATE UNIVERSITY PRESS   DETROIT

To Joe Bourdow

This is not a novel. The events described herein really happened, but in order to protect the privacy of some of the individuals it has been necessary to change names and otherwise disguise certain events.

Foreword copyright © 1987 by Wayne State University Press. Great Lakes Books edition published 1987 by Wayne State University Press, Detroit, Michigan 48202. All rights are reserved. No part of this book may be reproduced without formal permission.

91   90   89   88   5   4   3   2

Library of Congress Cataloging-in-Publication Data

Love, Edmund G.
    Hanging on, or, How to get through a depression and enjoy life.

    (Great Lakes books)
    Reprint. Originally published: New York : Morrow, 1972.
    1. Love, Edmund G.—Biography—Youth.   2. Authors, American—20th century—Biography.   3. Depressions—1929—United States.   I. Title.   II. Title: Hanging on. III. Title: How to get through a depression and enjoy life.   IV. Series.
[PS3562.084Z5   1987]   818'.5409   87–18897
ISBN 0–8143–1931–9 (alk. paper)
ISBN 0–8143–1932–7 (pbk. : alk. paper)

Printed in the United States of America.

Foreword to the
Great Lakes Books Edition

Edmund G. Love, the author of this book, is a member of a once-common species in American society, perhaps not yet extinct but definitely on the endangered list: a natural-born storyteller. Before high-circulation magazines, radio, movies, and television came along to preempt people's imaginations and recreational hours, they had to provide their own diversions. Every community, almost every family, had a yarner who could make a trip to the county seat as suspenseful and engrossing as any episode of your favorite television serial. Edmund Love is that kind of writer.

The good storyteller is not held to the demands of accuracy in every detail, especially the inconsequential detail. His product is fiction, not autobiography. But such "fiction" can reveal more *truth* than what often passes for factual reporting. Mark Twain was not a factual reporter in *Life on the Mississippi* or in *Roughing It*, yet he gave the reader a true and vivid sense of how steamboating on the Mississippi or the mining-era West appeared to a young man in the 1850s and 1860s. Here Edmund Love shows us how a young man confronted the Depression in the 1930s.

Refer to "the Depression" today and most listeners will have to stop and think a moment before recalling the 1930s, a period they probably read about in a high school history textbook. Oh, yes, they may say, that was the time everyone gambled on the stock market and lost their shirts. They seem to remember massive unemployment when millions of people lost their farms and homes and had to go out on the highways or live in Hoovervilles. There were strikes, and the country was on the verge of revolution until Franklin D. Roosevelt was elected President and promptly ended the Depression.

Such an amalgam of some fact and more myth stems mainly from John Steinbeck's *Grapes of Wrath*. That classic work depicts the plight of a particular group of Depression victims. But the

"Okies" who left the drought-ridden Midwest for California were a tiny minority even of the Oklahoma farm population. Most Americans—the great middle class—had not played the stock market; they lost jobs but probably managed to hang on to their homes; they never thought of taking to the roads because they knew conditions were as bad or worse elsewhere. Instead, with courage and ingenuity and a variety of expedients, they found ways of "hanging on."

Edmund Love was a youth, little more than a boy, when the story begins. A member of a prosperous family in the thriving industrial city of Flint, Michigan, he could look ahead confidently to college and a career in whatever direction his inclination might take him. Instead, an economic tidal wave swept over him and over every other American, even including some of the super-rich. This book shows how the pressures continued month after month, year after year. It shows the fortitude, the ingenuity, the endurance, and the simple courage and good humor with which people responded to the Depression, month after month, year after year.

Given half a chance, youth is always more or less irrepressible, even in the midst of a great depression. Some families were shattered, but others held tightly together during that trying period. Some parents managed to find a way of sending sons and daughters to college. College students still joined fraternities or sororities, engaged in or frustrated idiotic pranks, got drunk, fell in love, and may even have graduated and found a job. But all jobs then were "temporary." Employers were also "hanging on."

In what was a stroke of good fortune, Love got such a temporary job as timekeeper in one of Flint's auto plants. Here he had a ringside seat where he could observe a great transformation in American society, one which led to the emergence of the modern industrial labor union. Flint was a major arena in the birth-struggle of that movement. Those who have heard a union official blast greedy employers may be surprised to learn of an earlier time when even automobile plant workers felt great pride in and loyalty to those same employers. What brought about this profound change of loyalties, especially among those who were lucky enough to hold jobs so many others were futilely seeking? This too is part of Edmund Love's story.

Alistair Cooke once commented that each generation always believes it is the first to have a truly enlightened attitude toward sex. This was true even in the Depression. The Flapper of the 1920s had set the pace and although the miniskirt was then undreamed of (well, perhaps *dreamed* of), nubile high school girls still found ways of flashing a bit of thigh to attractive young teachers if so disposed—and, of course, some were disposed. Perhaps an ancillary thought emerging from this book is the simple truth that while the forces of society are in constant flux, the fundamentals of human behavior throb ever onward, much the same from one era to the next.

Still, outlook, attitude, trust, and faith may all be permanently affected by how one is tossed and thrown in the currents of life. Those born between 1900 and 1928 were forever marked by the Depression, and far more deeply than by any war. Younger people may wonder why their elders shake their heads over present-day prices and wages, why they are distrustful of banks and other financial institutions, why no chicanery from Wall Street ever surprises them, why they sniff at "high" unemployment figures of 6 percent, and why they are surprised if a politician's promises and prophecies are ever fulfilled. All these are marks of the 1930s left on those who lived through them.

Those "children of the Depression" (even those of advanced years) never forgot a time when unemployment was 33 percent, counting only "heads of households," and they never viewed a job as a "right." They remember banks closing, with no insurance of any kind for depositors. The only unemployment insurance they knew was a personal savings account, unless it had vanished in a bank failure. They never forgot a time when one simply had to "hang on"—which is what Edmund Love and the great majority of Americans did throughout the 1930s.

A further word must be added. A story like this could suffer if a reader empathized too much, felt too powerfully the hardship and misfortunes described. But time tends to soften all things, especially the adversities suffered when we were young. Edmund Love's extraordinary narrative skill takes us back to the trials of his youth, but always tempered by a good-humored and sensitive perspective on the hardships he and others somehow overcame. It is actually astonishing that such a fundamentally unpleasant subject can, through the writer's art, be distilled into enjoyable as well as informative reading. In short, this book offers a skillfully written and fascinating narrative.

People may wonder if a 1930s-type depression can come again. We do not know the answer to that question. We do not know if a modern, efficient, industrial society can operate in peacetime so that virtually all of its members may be gainfully employed. The 1930s Depression was ended by the successful depredations of Adolph Hitler, not by political genius in this or any other country. Since 1945 the United States has never reverted to the isolated, peacetime conditions of the prewar era. Our military forces and our military expenditures have continued to equal or exceed wartime levels. America has not, since 1940, had a true peacetime test of our modern political and economic structure.

If such a severe test ever does come, as it very well may, the best hope we can give the twenty-first century is that people then may have the strength to "hang on" as courageously as did Edmund Love and his contemporaries in the 1930s.

Theodore R. Kennedy
Professor Emeritus
Michigan State University

Introduction

There were two shaping forces for my generation. They were the Depression and World War II. To my mind the Depression is still largely an unexplored period despite the millions of words that have been written about it. The literature of the period seems to have developed its own set of clichés so that whenever the word "depression" is uttered we immediately call to mind soup kitchens, breadlines, and Okies. If we don't hear about that side of it, we are likely to be presented with a Washington's eye view. All of these things were part of the scene, and Washington certainly was one center of the unfolding drama, but it seems to me that the full meaning of the Depression escapes when one concentrates on those aspects.

My generation came to the Depression governed by a set of principles deeply rooted in the past. We emerged from it with an entirely different set of principles. A whole way of life disappeared in those years—a whole set of attitudes. Much is written these days about the new American revolution. It is, of course, a revolution in human rights and its roots lie back in the Depression years. It stems not from anything my generation did, or has done, but from the attitudes that were more or less forced upon us during our youth. Young America of the 1930s emerged from the Depression more liberal and more open-minded than had any generation before it. Although these past thirty years are not notable for any of the great breakthroughs that now obviously face America, the beginnings go back to the Depression years. My generation learned to look at things as they were, not as they were supposed to be, and it was the desire and the necessity to search out the real truth in things that constitutes the most important legacy to the present younger generation.

I think that the Depression was a revolution. Almost every man, woman, and child was affected in some way. For eleven years the average American was flat broke. He lived from day to day with no cushion against disaster when it came. There was no place to which a man could turn for help or encouragement because the family next door and all one's relatives were in the same situation. There were no rich uncles. Out of this travail, as discouragement followed discouragement, Americans began contriving ways to meet the emergencies. It became obvious that the old truths—such things as complete self-reliance and the childlike belief that virtue always triumphs—were not enough. Things like collective bargaining, unemployment insurance, and social security were born. More important, a new kind of American was born—an American who was willing to accept the fact that his world was not the perfect place he had been led to believe it was, an American who was willing to actually do the things needed to make it better. The development of that kind of an American was the product of our revolution.

In order to try to bring a better understanding of this era, I've resorted to autobiography. I don't think Edmund G. Love as an individual is very important, but as a young man who graduated from high school in June, 1929, and whose first eleven adult years were spent in the Depression, his experiences might help others to understand better what the period was really like.

Part I

I

One Sunday morning when I was seventeen my father and I were sitting under the awning on our back terrace, reading the papers. On a sudden impulse I turned to him.

"Are you worth a million dollars?" I asked him.

The question obviously took him by surprise. He let the paper fall to his lap and gave it some thought. When he finally looked at me, there was a trace of a self-satisfied smile on his face.

"I suppose I am," he said.

I know, now, that he was not worth a million dollars. Most of his fortune was on paper and mighty flimsy paper at that. It is not important, anyway. What is important is the fact that in that summer of 1929 our family was living as if we did have a million dollars. Parked in the driveway, not fifty feet from where we were sitting, were three shiny new automobiles. One of them belonged to me. It had been my high-school graduation present. Our house had gay awnings, a carefully tended yard with a picket fence around it, and a new paint job. Inside the house everything was new. It was kept immaculate by a housekeeper and a maid.

Walking over to the picket fence, I could look five blocks up Welch Boulevard and see other houses with new cars sitting in the driveways and the ostentatious trappings of wealth. I could see the house of Jim Wiesner, but Jim wasn't there that summer. He was touring Europe. The trip had been his graduation present. I could see the house of my best friend, George French. He wasn't home, either. He was out at the country club which his family had just joined. I could see the house of Hank Feller. He was out at the family cottage exercising his new motorboat. The peculiar thing about all this affluence was the fact that none of our famiies had a tradition of wealth. Opulence was new to all of us.

We all lived in Flint, Michigan. We were at the very end of the era in which the United States changed from a rural into an urban society. Practically everyone had come to Flint from somewhere else in the last twenty-five years. My own family had moved there from the small village of Flushing, ten miles away, in 1924. Jim Wiesner's father, a plumber, had moved into their house in the same year. He was now a plumbing contractor. George French's father had been a mechanic in the locomotive shops of the Burlington railroad somewhere west of Chicago. He was now master mechanic in one of Flint's auto factories. Hank Feller's father had been a farmer near the small town of Tawas. Now he was a partner in an auto-haulaway company. In 1904 the population of the city of Flint had been ten thousand. Now it was 156,000. I had no trouble visualizing what these figures meant. When we moved into our house five years before it had been the last house on the street. From my bedroom window I could look out over the rolling country to a farm about a mile west of us. Cattle still wandered around the barnyard. I hated that farm. Shortly after we arrived in Flint, I got a paper route that covered our neighborhood. It had forty-three customers, and I got it on condition that I would deliver a paper to the farm. In rainy weather the lane that ran out there became so muddy that I couldn't ride my bike and I had to trudge a mile each way, always ending up soaking wet. In winter it was worse. I'd have frost on my eyebrows before I got home. The only good thing about that farmhouse was the fact that it marked the western limits of my route. Everything between it and my house was my territory. I held the paper route until the spring of 1927, slightly more than two years. Every single day someone would start digging a new basement on my route. When I left it I had 883 customers which I served with the aid of four helpers. By then I could see only rooftops when I looked out my window.

A great many people who flooded into Flint during these years came to work in the auto factories, but the teachers and the shoe clerks came, too. Prosperity touched everyone. It was a poor man who couldn't make money in Flint. There has been a tendency to call the prosperity of this period a phony prosperity, but I've never thought it was. It was based on solid growth. Every one of those new houses that were built on my paper route had new things inside them, new not only in chronological age but in technological terms. Electric refrigerators, vacuum cleaners, radios, toasters—these and dozens of other new products were purchased by people who had never seen them before. Someone had to make all these things, and all over the United States people were leaving the farms and the small towns and streaming into the Daytons, Tulsas, and the Birminghams to do the work. Flint was just one such city and its product was automobiles.

The new American society was a peculiar one in many ways. The 1920s have long been known as the era of the flapper and flaming youth—the Roaring Twenties; but this phase of life scarcely touched us in the midlands. My family and the families around us were still basically oriented to the farms and small towns from which we had so recently come. It was a conservative society, and by 1929 its conservatism more nearly matched the general temper of the country than did the high life which was supposed to be lighting up the sky. Events in my family tended to make us a little more conservative than most. A year after we moved to Flint my mother died. During the next five years the dominant influence in my life was furnished by my Grandfather Perry who ran the house, aided and abetted by Freda Williams, a crotchety widowed aunt who was brought in to be our housekeeper after my mother's death. At the moment of our tragedy my father was in the midst of starting his new lumberyard and he found an outlet for his grief by burying himself in his work. Most mornings he was up and out of the house before the rest of the family stirred, so it was Grandpa Perry who presided over the breakfast table, who questioned my brothers and me about our plans for the day, and who gave or withheld permission for our various projects. At the evening meal he occupied my mother's place at the table and it was he who corrected our table manners and supervised our dress.

This dominant position of Grandpa Perry—my mother's father—was bound to have a good deal of effect upon me. He was in his middle seventies then. He was a man of the nineteenth century and the ideas which he firmly implanted in my mind were nineteenth-century ideas. A good many of his beliefs and quite a lot of his personality brushed off on me. He was a courtly man who never used profanity in the presence of the younger generation and he insisted upon propriety in his grandsons. He never came down to breakfast without being shaved and properly dressed. Neither did my brothers and I. He never smoked a cigar in the presence of ladies. As a matter of fact, in his book, women were a breed apart, people to be put a notch above everyone else, always to be deferred to. In the age of the flapper, quite naturally, I'm afraid I was something of an anachronism. I was in awe of women.

Grandpa Perry had been retired from business since before I was born. He had very little to do but travel and poke his nose into things that interested him. His great passion was the lawcourts.

Every morning after my brothers and I departed for school, he would walk the two miles downtown. If the county circuit court was in session and if there was an especially interesting case, he would retire there and listen in. Every two years he would volunteer for the February panel of jurors. His favorite court, however, was the Municipal Court. In Flint the Municipal Court was the small-claims court, dealing in cases that involved sums up to $300. Grandpa would sit on the back benches or wander around the hall. Whenever a litigant demanded a jury trial, the judge would send the bailiff out into the hall to round up the six men needed for a petit jury. Grandpa always managed to get himself picked. It is amazing the amount of litigation he had a hand in settling over the years. From 1924 until 1939 there were very few days when he didn't sit on some kind of a jury. I have known him to sit on four cases in one day. When one stops to consider the fact that he got three dollars for every case he sat on, it is not hard to realize that Grandpa had a good thing going for him. All through the Depression years he came home every night with his three or six dollars. Grandpa was never one of the unemployed. On some occasions he had more money in his pocket than all the rest of the family combined.

It should not be assumed that my brothers and I were not influenced by my father. He was a thoroughly modern man in every respect, entirely different from Grandpa. He was a big, rough-and-ready man with a tremendous sense of humor. He was a born salesman with an outgoing nature, and our house was always a popular meeting place for his friends, who dropped by at all times of the day and night. Above all else, my father was an openhanded man, a person given to the grand gesture. I never recall that he asked the price of anything. When he bought shoes, he bought the best shoes. When he bought lamb chops, he insisted on the best lamb chops, and plenty of them. It never seems to have occurred to him that anyone would cheat him and I don't think anyone ever did. The trouble with my father was that he simply didn't know how to bring up three sons. During my mother's lifetime he had left all the household details to her, and that included our upbringing. After her death he was bewildered. He didn't know what to do, and not knowing, he did very little. Not being a person given to the enjoyment of the young, he assumed an aloof position and let us make the first move. If we wanted advice, he was always there, but there was none of this "buddy-buddy" business with him. Even his advice, when he gave it, was apt to be vague and couched in general terms. The phrase that he used most often to me was "be a man." I soon came to realize that this ruled out any complaining, dishonesty, shirking, or flightiness. It was a phrase wide enough in its connotations to include practically everything. If my brothers and I really wanted to know how it was to be applied in any particular instance, all we had to do was watch him and draw our own deductions. Fortunately, he was man enough to be a good two-fisted example. We grew up emulating him, or trying to, rather than listening to him.

There were other influences that prepared me for the years ahead. One can't overlook education with all it implies. In one major way, my education was flawed. In Flint, where new families were arriving every day, it was impossible to build schools fast enough. Between 1925 and 1928, I went to four different schools, each one of them brand new. When I was in the ninth grade I entered Emerson Junior High School. Although the ground for this school had been broken only a year before I entered, it was overcrowded before it was ever finished. The city had placed it at the extreme northern city limits, a good mile and a half beyond the nearest houses. It was intended to accommodate 1,800 students. In one short year the city built out and around it, and the city limits were moved five miles further north. On the first day I entered the school, I was one of 2,500 students. In the tenth grade I entered Central High School, finished in 1922 to accommodate 2,200 pupils. By the time I got there it had 4,200 students. In the middle of the eleventh grade I moved to Northern High School, an edifice that was hurriedly opened before it was finished. As it stood it was supposed to accommodate 1,100 students. Some 1,800 showed up the first day. By the time I graduated it had 2,500. In an atmosphere such as this, attending classes that rarely contained fewer than forty pupils, almost always on half-day sessions, the formal part of my education was bound to be slighted. I was inclined to be a daydreamer and I simply got lost in the crowds. Somehow I managed to get through Julius Caesar, Ralph Waldo Emerson, and trigonometry, and at the end I was somewhere in the upper third of my class, but I never distinguished myself as a student. I certainly had no firm grounding in much of anything.

Probably the one teacher who had a lasting influence on me was Guy Houston, the lean, ascetic, hawk-nosed man who became the head football coach at Northern High School in the fall of 1928. Although I was not an athlete myself, I was the student manager of both the track and football teams, and as such, I was thrown into close contact with Guy Houston from the very beginning. Furthermore, my three closest high-school chums were on the various teams that he coached and they were as much influenced by him as I was, so that we all lived by the code that he set up for us. No one who ever had the opportunity of Guy Houston's guidance could help but be a man. He demanded toughness, perfection, and a high sense of responsibility on and off the athletic field. In that first fall he was coach he took an untrained and untried group of former scrubs from Central High School and won the city championship. In the next seventeen years, as long as he was coach, he turned out more state championship teams than any other coach in the history of the State of Michigan and in the process he turned out an extraordinary number of high-minded citizens. The qualities that he demanded of the young men who crossed his path, whether as athletes, students, or just friends, were much the same as those my father talked about in his vague way. Perhaps the only difference in the two men was that Guy Houston was more articulate and that he was better able to explain what it meant to "be a man." Whatever the case, almost from the first moment I met him, I tried to live up to him. His principles have stayed with me all my life.

My friends—George French, Jim Wiesner, and Hank Feller—had as much to do with shaping my attitudes as anyone. We first met each other in the eighth grade when my family moved to Flint. Because we lived within a few blocks of each other, we were in the same boy-scout troop, walked to school together, peddled papers out of the same substation, and generally chummed around together. In our high-school days, George French was always the leader of this group. He was a little like Frank Merriwell, or perhaps it was Sir Galahad. He was a tall, handsome boy who lived a good, clean Christian life, and a Spartan one, on and off the athletic field. He was the star end on the football team, the star center on the basketball team, president of our senior class, and an all-A student. He never swore, he never drank, and he had nothing to do with anyone who did. He had one quirk that annoyed me a little. I would call it a "proletarian" streak. God knows, I don't think he knew the difference between Karl Marx and Groucho Marx, but he always referred to Jim's family and my family as "you rich folks" as though there was something the matter with it. On the other hand, he was the most gifted mechanic I have ever known. He was always going down to some junkyard or other and buying a car for ten dollars, then bringing it home to his backyard to dismantle and rebuild it. When he was done his cars ran like tops.

Jim Wiesner was a little different. He'd always been something of a mama's boy, a big, hulking crybaby type who seemed clumsy at everything he did. For some reason that I could never fathom, Guy Houston gave him a football suit and set out to make a tackle of him. Quite early in the season we played Lansing Eastern High School and Jim went in as a substitute. Lansing had a big bruiser of a fullback, and the minute Jim got in the lineup, every play was aimed at him, with the fullback carrying the ball. Lansing was making five or six yards at every crack. Guy Houston watched carefully and soon discovered that Jim was backing up three or four steps every time the ball was snapped, to brace himself better for the coming onslaught. A lot of coaches would have gotten Jim out of there, but Guy Houston looked along the bench and beckoned to Hector Ring, the toughest, nastiest boy on the squad. He told Hector to go in at fullback—the equivalent of linebacker today—which put him in position directly behind Jim. Hector wasn't to pay any attention to the Lansing fullback. He was to pay attention to Jim. Every time Jim backed up, Hector was supposed to kick him in the pants. Jim backed and Hector kicked. After the third kick, Jim was sore in a very vital spot, and he began turning around to take the kick on a less vulnerable part of his anatomy. When he did that, Hector slugged him. Jim backed and Hector slugged. Jim turned around and backed, and Hector kicked. At half time Jim came into the locker room with both eyes blackened, a tooth missing, and a bloody nose. I had to fix him up, and he was a mess. It made no difference to Guy Houston. At the beginning of the second half Jim and Hector were right back in there again, but by then a miracle had happened. Jim wasn't backing up anymore. He was a lot more afraid of Hector than he was of anyone on the Lansing team. Lansing never made a foot over his tackle for the rest of the afternoon. Nobody made a foot over his tackle for the rest of the season. He became our first all-state football player, but he became more than that. He became a man in that one afternoon, one of the best men I ever knew, and for the rest of his life he used to talk about it as the turning point in his career.

The fourth member of our group, Hank Feller, was a different sort of boy entirely. He was a small, wiry boy, almost devoid of any sense of humor. From the time I first knew him, he'd always known exactly what he was going to do with his life. He was going to the University of Michigan, take a degree in biology, and then come back to Flint and teach it in the public schools. Like the others, Hank was an athlete and, because his father didn't believe in paying his way through college, Hank was determined to make it by way of an athletic scholarship. Every morning, for as long as I knew him, Hank would tuck his books under his arms and run all the way to school—a distance of two miles. Each evening he would run home again. It was Hank who got me my managership. That first semester we went up to Northern High no provision had been made for any athletic teams, and we had no gymnasium, so that Hank had to go all the way across town to Central High to practice. He needed someone to hold the watch for him, and I often went along. Other boys soon joined us, and I ended up as student manager without realizing it. Guy Houston made it official the next fall. Hank went on, in his senior year, to be the best miler and half-miler in the state. Some of the records he set in 1929 stood for more than thirty years. Needless to say, he got his scholarship at Ann Arbor.

As anyone can see, this was a masculine world that I lived in during my high-school years. Although Freda Williams was a fussy, frilly woman who filled our house full of lace curtains and doilies (she even put a flowered slipcover on the box where my brothers and I kept our baseball gloves), I don't recall that she ever made any impression on me at all. Among the group with whom I chummed, girls were as alien as they were at home. Because George and Jim and Hank were busy following Guy Houston's ascetic code of conduct, none of them ever had dates. As a matter of fact, I seem to recall that most of us were disdainful when the subject of girls was brought up at all. We were a fine bunch of clods.

Privately, during this period, I had come to have an ambiguity in my thinking about women. My father never discussed the facts of life with me nor did my grandfather. To my father, sex was a very private matter. For him to have had any talks with me on the subject would have been an admission that he knew something about it. He wasn't going to admit that to his sons. Grandpa, being a true Victorian, wouldn't admit that there was any such thing as sex. As a consequence, whatever I learned about it I learned from my friends. They didn't know any more about it than I did. Still, it was an interesting and amusing way to learn about a subject that was so important. Most boys I knew—even my own group—had at least one dirty joke in their repertoires, and these stories were traded back and forth as a later generation traded bubble-gum cards. The heroes of these stories were all traveling salesmen and the heroines were all farmers' daughters. They were titillating stories, so sex was a titillating subject. It has always seemed to me that this is exactly what sex should be.

I had only one firsthand experience in this aspect of girls, and it wasn't much. In my tenth-grade year I took English from a teacher named Mabel Parks. It was one of those unwieldy classes of forty or more students, and in the process of alphabetical seating I had ended up in the back row. Miss Parks wasn't able to keep track of everything that went on, especially in the remote parts of the room.

This was at the very peak of the flapper era, and on my immediate left sat Phyliss Hahn, the real genuine article. She had a yellow slicker with snappy sayings written all over it, she never buckled her galoshes, she tried to look like Clara Bow, her skirts were short, and her stockings were rolled just above the knee. Every day when Phyliss came to class she would flounce into her seat, very deliberately pull up her skirt, and cross her legs. As the class hour progressed she would hitch the skirt up a little higher. By the end of each class hour her whole thigh would be bared for my pleasure. I paid very little attention to Miss Parks and quite a lot of attention to Phyliss. In the end it was Phyliss who came to grief not me. For some reason or other, the idea never seemed to get home to her that I was scared to death by this whole performance. I was fourteen years old and I had no idea what to do should this ever go beyond the stage it had already reached. I do think that I had carefully mapped out a route of escape if she ever made an overt move. After some weeks of this, piqued by my lack of a positive response, no doubt, Phyliss did take steps. She owned a dress made of some fish netting which I'd seen on several occasions, but on one bright afternoon she came to class with it on and thoughtfully left her underwear at home. Fish nets without slips underneath them don't hide a thing and when she took off her coat she was sensational. I tried not to look at her, or rather I tried not to let Phyliss know I was looking at her, but every time I surreptitiously rolled an eyeball her way, there she was, winking at me. Just what the outcome of this would have been, I'm not sure, but I was saved. Every boy in the room had his head buried in his arms peeking under his elbows at the back of the room, and even Miss Parks was bound to notice the distraught air after a while. When she discovered what it was all about, she marched Phyliss right out of there. Phyliss was suspended for two weeks for that little episode, but she still didn't seem to sense the truth about me. A little later in the year, while Miss Parks was putting adverbs on the board one day, I felt someone pull the sleeve of my sweater and I looked across the aisle. Phyliss was holding up a flask, obviously wanting to know if I wanted a drink. When I vigorously shook my head in the negative, she took a pull for herself. She took another drink during the conjunctions and still another during the prepositions. By the time we got down to the interjections, she was quite drunk. All of a sudden she jumped to her feet and lurched across the aisle to give me a kiss. I dodged and weaved around like a prizefighter, trying to avoid her. After a moment she gave me a disgusted look and dumped the contents of the flask over my head, then stumbled up the aisle and plopped herself down on Paul Lovegrove's lap. Paul dumped her on the floor and ran for his life. That was the end of Phyliss, but the experience took about two years off my young life. I had to go to the principal's office and explain that I was a victim, not an accomplice, a pretty hard thing to get across with all that whiskey smelling up my hair. Of course, it was the easy way out, because it postponed my having to come to grips with the subject for some little time. I still hadn't had a date with a girl, let alone grappled with one, as I approached my graduation from high school.

As I have said, there was an ambiguity in my thinking about girls. I was an avid reader. From the time I was nine years old, I had read everything I could get my hands on. I usually read by authors. When we took up the *Idylls of the King* (expurgated edition), in the tenth grade, I waded right through Tennyson. When we studied *Tess of the D'Urbervilles* in senior English, I went to the public library and swept the shelves clear of Thomas Hardy. By the time I finished high school I had waded through Dickens, Scott, Hugo, and Dumas, *pere et fils*, among others. Most of my reading was unguided and it was therefore hit and miss. Along with Dickens and Hardy I had managed to finish off James Oliver Curwood, Jeffery Farnol, and Clarence Budington Kelland. I was a real sucker for a romantic love story, and I always fell in love with the current book's heroine. Some of the women I read about were incredibly voluptuous and unbelievably beautiful, not to mention pure, noble, and unattainable. Long before I reached maturity I had made up my mind that I was going to have one of these paragons some day, and this resolution never quite left my subconscious. I usually went for the biggest busted, most exquisite woman in any group and I don't think I was ever equipped for that sort of thing, with the result that I failed to achieve more often than I achieved. The peculiar part of it is that I never fully equated these dream girls with the Phyliss Hahns of this world. It never entered my mind that they were the same kind of creatures. I wasn't clear in my mind for a long while just what I'd do with one of those beauties if I ever got one. I certainly had no idea that she might stand up on her pedestal and do a striptease.

I read other things besides fiction. I was especially fond of history and biography. Unfortunately, there is a good deal of difference between information and knowledge. I was long on the information and short on the knowledge. I had no real understanding of life at all and I was about to enter a period when I would need all the knowledge I could get.

II

The most important single event of this part of my life was my father's second marriage, which occurred on my seventeenth birthday, February 14, 1929. Although my father had evidently been courting his new wife for some time, neither my brothers nor I were aware of it and the news of his elopement stunned us. Good, gentle Grandpa Perry set us an example by welcoming our new stepmother with open arms, however, and my brothers and I soon accepted the new order without resentment.

Gladys Russell was a divorcée who worked in the bank where my father did business. She was a tall, attractive woman who dressed well and had great charm. She was used to good things and she came from a background that included wealthy and cosmopolitan friends. Up until the time she came into our lives, my family had always remained close to its small-town roots in Flushing. Now we moved into a new world. Glad went through our house with a magic wand, changing everything. She threw out all our old clothes and dressed us new from head to foot. She redecorated the house inside and out. The picket fence and the awnings were her ideas. A battalion of landscape gardeners swooped down on us every Friday afternoon and manicured the lawn for the weekend festivities. She made my father join the country club. That led to new golf clubs for me and lessons from the club pro. She undertook to undo all those years of neglect under which my brothers and I had labored since my mother's death. Our personal habits and our manners were carefully scrutinized and corrected. We took a crash course in etiquette and the social graces. The lessons included not only golf but tennis and bridge. And to my great disgust we were enrolled in dancing school. The old pool table disappeared from the basement and a croquet set blossomed on the close-cropped backyard.

Glad had a great influence on our neighbors, too. As the spring arrived and they could see the transformation that was taking place in our household, other people realized they were prosperous, too. Jim Wiesner's father bought a new Buick to match my father's new one and he put awnings and a picket fence around his house, too. George French's father joined the country club, an action that caused the proletarian George as much distress as the dancing school did me. The Fellers got a new car and had a formal garden planted beside their house. It was as though our family were the Joneses and all the rest were keeping up with us. Actually, it was an awakening. People simply realized that they were big-city folks now and that they ought to take advantage of the prosperity which they enjoyed. It is no wonder that I always think of that summer of 1929 as a gay and happy time. It was like Camelot with the pennants flying from every tower.

My stepmother wasn't responsible for everything that happened. There were some rather astounding changes taking place that I had a little trouble adjusting to. There was the matter of the senior play, for instance. It was chosen especially to provide a large number of parts. Disdainfully I turned down the part that was offered me, only to find out that the whole football team was going to be in the cast. I was further surprised to learn that Hector Ring, our slugging fullback, had taken the lead in our production of *H.M.S. Pinafore*. He had a beautiful voice, and it didn't embarrass him at all to get up in front of people and show it off. The final blow came a month before graduation. Listed under the program for commencement week was a formal dinner dance. I immediately crossed *that* off. I had no sooner done so than I learned with dismay that George French was going. He'd even gotten up the courage to ask a girl for a date. Then, in rapid succession, Jim Wiesner, Hank Feller, and Hector Ring all announced that they were looking forward to the affair. It was incomprehensible. I was being deserted, but it slowly dawned on me that I was going to have to go to that dinner dance. That presented problems. I was afraid to ask a girl for a date. Moreover, I was having trouble at the dancing school. This was my own fault. I'd been mortified when told that I would have to go and I approached the whole business in a stubborn, obtuse way. I just refused to learn to dance. I learned the steps all right but I just marched around the floor counting to myself, never realizing or caring that there was any connection between the music and what I was doing. I might just as well have been in a drill hall. By the time the senior dinner dance approached and I began to worry about it, it was already too late to salvage anything from the school. I took the matter up with my stepmother, and she was quite pleasant about it, volunteering to help me.

Getting me ready for that dinner dance was a desperate undertaking in our household. Every evening after dinner the rug was rolled back and the records were put on the Victrola. My father and Glad demonstrated. My brother Walter glided about effortlessly, trying to show me what I was doing wrong. Even Grandpa Perry took a hand. It all did no good. Just a week before the dance I was still stalking around the living room, stiff-legged and dangerous. At that point I was rescued. A few doors up the street from us lived a delightful little redheaded girl named Monta Wascher. Monta was two years younger than I was, a sophomore at Northern High School. She'd only recently become a girl. For all the years I'd known her she had been an irrepressible tomboy. She climbed trees and hung from the limbs by her knees and she played baseball and football with us in the evenings. Now she ran around with my brother's crowd. The important thing about Monta was that I wasn't afraid of her. I was used to seeing her everyday and I could relax with her. One night in the midst of my trial she came down to the house to play croquet and, spunky girl that she was, she volunteered to take a hand. To my surprise, I discovered that I could dance with her. It was just that I wasn't self-conscious in her presence. On the first try I managed to get through three whole records without stepping on her feet. It should not be assumed that I became a graceful and accomplished dancer. I had simply reached the stage where I wasn't maiming my partners, that's all. We tried it again the next night and I finally reached the conclusion that I could actually dance. I could now consider the next move—getting a date. There was no problem about that. Glad was already remarking about what a beautiful girl Monta was, and I took a good look. She was beautiful. She was a picture. There was one big drawback. She was in the tenth grade and I would risk losing face by taking a sophomore to the senior dance but I soon overcame that objection. She was the only girl I *could* take because she was the only girl I could dance with. I blurted out the invitation and Monta accepted. We all heaved a big sigh of relief. Monta went down and bought a bright-green evening dress and I was fitted for the tuxedo which Glad had bought me. I was now ready for the biggest thing to happen to me in my young life. I was about to fall in love for the first time, but not with Monta Wascher.

In addition to dressing our family up and adorning our house, Glad brought a lot of new people into our lives in those first few months. Her best friend was a woman named Louisa Flexner, but in that first week of June, 1929, none of us had met Mrs. Flexner. The Flexner family was wealthy by any standards. Mr. Flexner was in the auto-parts manufacturing business and was president of one of the large companies in that field. He had his principal residence and offices in New York and he had a palatial home in Palm Beach. Just at the time of my father's remarriage, Mr. Flexner had decided to take up farming as a hobby. He didn't intend to plow the ground or milk the cows. He just intended to own a farm. To that end he had come out to Flint—his hometown—and had bought six hundred acres about five miles west of the city. He had stocked it with tenant farmers and a large herd of Guernsey cattle. As an adjunct to this farm, he built a beautiful summer house.

While I was having my difficulties with the dancing, Glad announced at dinner one evening that Louisa Flexner was on her way north from Florida to occupy the new house. Almost in passing Glad also mentioned that Louisa had a daughter, Molly, "about your age." Molly would be spending the summer in Flint. This bit of information piqued my interest. I was prohibited by the code from asking any questions, but I wondered about her and I generated a good deal of anticipation. I was ripe and ready to be plucked.

The Flexners traveled north with a large entourage that included several cars and a household staff. They did not arrive in Flint until the evening before my dinner dance. At about eight that evening the telephone rang, and I answered it, then turned it over to Glad. At the moment of that phone call I was deeply involved in an argument with my father. I wanted to borrow his car the next day for I had many errands to do. For some unexplained reason he had said no and I had pressed him until we were both getting angry. When Glad came back into the room from her conversation, she calmed me down.

"That was Louisa," she said. "Molly is coming by the first thing in the morning to pick up some decorating material I have here. I'm sure she'll be glad to give you a ride downtown so you can do your errands."

Molly Flexner was fifteen years old that summer. To a person who has reached the old age of seventeen, fifteen is pretty young. I might not have been so enthusiastic. Luckily, I didn't become aware of this blemish until it was too late. Molly certainly didn't look fifteen. She looked eighteen. She was a tall girl, almost voluptuous of figure. She had long brown hair and big soft, brown eyes. The thing that set her apart from every other girl I had known was her air of sophistication. It was a genuine sophistication, the product of New York, Palm Beach, and exclusive girls' schools, yet there was a touch of shyness about her, a shyness that just matched my own. This was the fifteen years showing through the veneer. On that first morning when I saw her come bouncing up our front steps, I knew I'd been presented with a real prize. She was the beautiful princess out of all those books. When I opened the door at her ring, she cocked her head quizzically and then smiled warmly, lowered her eyes, and lifted them again. In her moment of shyness, all of my own shyness and awkwardness dropped away.

The decorating swatches were brought out and arrangements made for Molly to drop me downtown. I followed her down the steps without the faintest trace of self-consciousness and got into her neat little roadster. As we drove off up the street I hoped that George and Jim and Hank would see her. My first thought, after she let me out, was about that dinner dance. Here was the girl I really wanted to take. I thought about it all morning and then I almost ruined the whole thing by asking Glad whether Molly might like to go.

"I'm ashamed of you," Glad said. "You've asked Monta. If that's all the sense of decency you have, I won't let you see Molly at all."

It was fortunate that Glad was distracted at that moment. My father came turning into the driveway with a brand new Chevrolet Six sport coupé. It was a beautiful car, dark blue, with disk wheels and a rumble seat. My father got out of it, bowed low, and presented me with the keys. Now I knew why he hadn't let me borrow his car. This was my graduation present. I spent the entire afternoon carefully wiping the dust off it and admiring it, tearing myself away at the last minute to go up and change into my tux. Monta got the first ride in that new car but the poor girl didn't know that she was sitting in the seat reserved for Molly. Molly and the car and the future all went together, somehow. I was in a supremely happy mood and the dance went off very well. I didn't step on Monta's feet once.

The day after the dance was Commencement Day. What an aptly named day, it seemed to me. I had fulfilled my obligation to Monta and nothing stood between me and Molly—my future. I had visions of myself snatching up my diploma and running out into the June night to jump in my car. Molly would be there and the three of us —Molly, the car, and I—would all start out together.

It wasn't as easy to put this dream into operation as I thought it would be. When I came down to breakfast at eight o'clock, I found my father in a rare philosophical mood. He was inclined to dwell on the meaning of this important day in my life. I was impatient, wanting to get to the telephone, but my father kept on talking. At the very end of our conversation he informed me that he would like to see me at some time during the day. He had a summer job for me and he thought we ought to talk it over. I told him that I had graduation rehearsal at nine thirty and that I would come over to his office afterward if he liked. At last he left, and as I turned to the telephone Glad came down the stairs. She sat down and began to talk about the importance of the day in her turn. I couldn't talk to Molly with anyone standing around to listen in and before I knew it, nine fifteen had come and I had to rush off to rehearsal with the important call still unmade. At school I couldn't find a telephone. Noon came and I had to jump in my car and rush to keep the appointment with my father. Several drugstores with pay telephones loomed up as I drove across town, but by then I was losing my nerve. As I drove up in front of my father's office, I steeled myself. Now I would make the call.

My father's lumberyard was on one of the main thoroughfares in the south end of town. It was a heavily traveled street. I parked my car, strolled leisurely across the front lawn, climbed the steps, and entered the front door. My father was with a customer and he waved his hand for me to wait. I looked around resolutely for the telephone. As I did so, the sound of a rending crash rolled in through the front windows. I looked out. There, where I'd left it only seconds before, was my brand-new Chevrolet Six, almost crushed under an express truck. It had only eighteen miles on it and it looked like a total wreck. All I could do was stand there numbly. I wanted to cry. After a long time I stumbled down the front steps and staggered out to the curb.

The accident was simple enough. The driver of the express truck had been forced to swerve to avoid hitting a child who darted out into the street, and in doing so he had run head on into my car. The whole front end of it was folded in like an accordion. The windshield was broken. The motor had been shoved back into the front seat. The two front wheels were lying flat on the pavement. I didn't pay any attention to the driver of the express truck who was climbing shakily out of the wreckage. I had eyes only for my poor car. I walked around and around it, getting angrier and angrier. I think I was almost ready to add to the woe of the expressman by punching him in the nose. Fortunately, my father and some of his truck drivers had arrived on the scene and assessed the situation. One of the drivers put his arms around me and led me away to a safe distance and my father took over the negotiations. I wanted a brand-new car to be delivered immediately, of course, but when the manager of the express company finally arrived, my father agreed that this car would be repaired within the week. If it was not in perfect running order, it would be replaced. I didn't like this outcome, but there was nothing I could do about it. I watched sorrowfully as the wrecker towed the car away.

One whole week! All my plans for taking Molly off and confessing my love for her were in ashes. I had no intention of confessing my love in any secondhand car. My father tried to placate me by offering me the use of his car, but I stuck to my resolution stubbornly although my heart was in an increasingly palpitating condition from love. It was a good thing I did. By abstaining, I assured the success of my suit. Molly had expected me to call, and when the days passed without any word from me, she became anxious. Things were helped along considerably by the local newspaper. At the dance a photographer had taken several pictures and on Sunday morning Monta and I were peering out from the front page of the society section. Monta's beauty was something to see, and it must have appeared to an outsider that I was very popular to have such a gorgeous creature as a date. Molly couldn't possibly have missed that picture. Right next to it on the same page was her picture. It had been taken at the annual horse show the previous day. She was in her riding habit and more adorable looking than ever. It was the riding habit that pushed me irrevocably over the edge. No one at Northern High School had a girl with a riding habit.

On the Monday morning after that picture appeared in the paper I went to work for my father. I had fully expected to have a job driving one of his trucks. To my dismay he handed me a shovel. He had decided to put a concrete floor in his coal yard, and he had bought a cement mixer to that end. My job was to feed the cement mixer. Two other men worked with me, smoothing the cement and building the forms. I had the mixer all to myself and I had to keep the others going. I had to work fast. I would dump a batch of mix, quickly stick a hose in the maw of the mixer, and start shoveling gravel. Every fifteen shovelfuls—or whatever the proportion was— I would stop shoveling and run over to a pile and lift off a one hundred-pound bag of cement, break it open, and hoist it up to shoulder height to dump it in the opening with the water and gravel. All that job required was a good strong back and endurance, but I'd never done any hard labor before. Toward the end of the first afternoon my back began to ache and blisters appeared on my hands. A night's rest didn't help me. My back was sorer in the morning than it had been the night before and new muscles had begun to protest. By noon of the second day all the blisters had broken and my hands were bleeding. I kept on, but I didn't do very well. By Wednesday morning I didn't see how I'd get through the day, but I was still hanging on at the noon whistle. It was during lunch hour that the miracle happened. A man came driving into the lumberyard with my car. I walked around it, trying to find where the dents had been. I got in it and drove it up and down the highway. It seemed as good as ever and my father advised me to accept it. After the man from the express company had gone I hid it in a remote back corner of the lumberyard where nothing more could happen to it and then I rushed to the telephone. I sat in my father's office staring at the instrument for five minutes before I got up enough courage to lift the receiver off the cradle. Molly answered immediately.

"I was wondering if you'd like to go to the movie tonight," I said casually. I could feel a chill running up and down my spine as I waited for the most important answer I'd ever received in my life.

"Why, yes. It would be fun," she said.

"I'll be there at seven thirty," I said. After I'd rung up I just sat there staring. I felt like jumping up and letting out a whoop.

I don't know what happened to all my aches and pains. I shoveled gravel into that mixer like a demon all afternoon. When five o'clock came I streaked for my car. I took every shortcut I knew on the way home and then I took the most thorough bath of my whole life. I tied and retied my necktie until I spoiled it and had to get a new one. I approached Molly's house up a long drive at precisely seven thirty. A maid answered the door, but Molly was right behind her, wearing a white, sleeveless summer dress. I managed to get through the introduction to Louisa Flexner without my usual blunders and then Molly and I were in the car, driving the five miles into town. It was the first time in my life that I'd ever ridden five miles with a girl and remained perfectly at ease. There were no awkward silences or banal talk. The movie was a good one— Richard Dix, I recall. After it was over with, we went to a drive-in and had an ice-cream soda, then started for home.

I had now reached the most delicious moment of my whole life. I was a stripling of seventeen, dressed in a blue jacket and white trousers, in love for the first time and out with the girl I most wanted to be with. It was a soft, warm, June night, bathed in the light of a full moon. Sweet smells were everywhere. I wanted to put my arm around Molly and I hoped she would put her arms around me. I wanted to kiss her. I wanted to tell her I loved her. I wanted perfection, but I was afraid. I didn't know what she would do if I put my arm around her and I didn't want to spoil things before they even got started. I drove along slowly, and we talked. We were halfway home when a farmhouse loomed up on our right. I heaved a sigh and gathered my courage. I told myself I would put my arm around her the next farmhouse we came to. Immediately another farmhouse came into view around a bend. Very cautiously I put my arm along the back of the seat and lowered it around her shoulders. In my wildest dreams I couldn't have anticipated what happened next. She came across the seat close to me and turned up her face to me. I bent down and kissed her, and then her arms were around me and she was kissing me back.

It took me five hours to get Molly the rest of the way home. We'd drive a short distance and then stop and park. Sometimes we'd only move a few feet before we'd have to stop and enfold ourselves in each other's arms. We told each other how wonderful it was that we'd found each other and how much we loved each other. Like all first loves, ours was absolutely pure, uncomplicated by wrestling holds and sensuous fumbling. Sir Walter Scott could have written the whole scene without blushing. It was enough for us just to be with each other. I didn't want to leave her and she didn't want to leave me. After I took her up to the door and said good night, her presence was everywhere about me as I drove home. I couldn't think of anyone else.

There wasn't a cloud on the horizon in that summer of 1929. I divided my time equally between the cement mixer and Molly. For two months I was a man possessed. From the first sputter of the mixer in the morning until I threw in the last shovelful of gravel in the afternoon, I scarcely looked up. I found that by working hard the time would pass more quickly until I saw Molly again. Each night after I dumped the last batch of cement I would streak for my car and rush home to change my clothes. Molly and I did all kinds of things together. We even danced. I had no trouble dancing with her. The awkward, uncertain days at Northern High School were gone forever and I was a different person. When Jim Wiesner came back from Europe he drove by the house several times, but I didn't see him. George French became so concerned about not seeing me that he even volunteered to take me golfing at the country club. Hank Feller came over to see if I was going to room with him at Michigan. I didn't call him back. Suddenly it was the second week of August. One day I flipped the lever of the cement mixer and dumped a batch of cement. One of my helpers straightened up and said, "I guess that does it." To my amazement the floor of the coal yard was finished. As I completed washing out the big rotor, the yard foreman came out and told me my father wanted to see me in his office. I went in, still covered with the gray dust, and stood before him. He told me that he was very proud of the way I'd worked.

"I think you ought to take a little vacation," he said. "Why don't you join Glad and the boys over at Grand Haven for a couple of weeks?"

For a good many years we had rented a cottage for a month on Lake Michigan, and Grand Haven had always been one of my favorite places. Unfortunately, it was 135 miles away from Molly. I stood there and hemmed and hawed, standing first on one foot and then the other, trying to find some way to tell my father.

"You don't have to go if you don't want to," he said, smiling slyly, "but I just had a phone call from Glad. She's invited Lou Flexner and Molly over for a couple of weeks. I thought you might like to drive them over."

The next morning I reported at the farm, bright and early, put my car in the Flexner garage, and got behind the wheel of Mrs. Flexner's big Packard. We rolled up to the cottage late in the afternoon and finished out the day on the beach. Being with Molly in Grand Haven was better than being with Molly in Flint. There was no cement mixer to come between us. We were together from morning until night, boating, swimming, dancing, taking excursions. I didn't think there could ever be an end to our happiness, but there was and it came in a way that left me completely bewildered.

Our cottage sat high on a sand dune in the midst of a thick pine woods. A lane ran up to it from the beach and little footpaths branched off from this lane to run for miles through the woods along the top of the dunes. One beautiful moonlight night Molly and I set out, hand in hand, to explore one of these little footpaths. We walked until we came to a clearing that was covered with pine needles. Through an opening in the trees we could see the bright ribbon of moonlight on the lake far below us. We sat down in the clearing and I took her in my arms and kissed her. She kissed me back and then something happened. I don't know how it happened, but everything was different. Molly's kisses were wet with passion and mine were just as uncontrolled. She was wearing an old sweatshirt and a short, flimsy skirt and I suddenly knew that she didn't have on any underwear. My hands were running up and down her body, and she was responding in a way that I never knew a girl could respond.

I don't know how long this went on, but it couldn't have been very long before one or the other of us, perhaps both, realized what we were doing. We sat up suddenly and looked at each other. It was a terrifying moment. Passion is no joke to a seventeen-year-old boy and a fifteen-year-old girl. We both had a deeply rooted sense of doing something very wrong, and our fear was made worse by the fact that we had had a perfect summer together and that we had experienced an almost perfect love. I think we were both afraid that we would spoil everything good that we had known. Neither one of us knew enough about life to understand this thing that was happening to us. Molly began to cry and I took her in my arms and tried to console her. When she finally stopped crying I pulled her to her feet and led her back to the cottage. When we reached the front steps I kissed her.

"It will never happen again," I said. "I promise."

I was thoroughly shaken as I watched her run up the steps. At that moment I was almost sure I had lost her. In the ambiguity of my thinking about girls, I was convinced that a boy didn't do this to a nice girl. I was afraid that I had degraded her somehow. I certainly didn't know that, although Molly and I had not eaten of the apple, we had seen it and that nothing would ever be the same again.

Molly seemed a little constrained the next morning. We took the trolley into Grand Haven to do some shopping and returned home about noon. After lunch our whole group got into bathing suits and went down to the beach. On most days Molly joined in the sports with great gusto, but on this day she became more and more withdrawn. At about three o'clock she got up from the blanket and said she guessed she'd go up and play tennis if anyone was interested. I said I was game. She held out her hand to me.

We didn't say a word to each other as we climbed the hill, but the closer we got to the cottage the more we hurried. We didn't bother with the preliminaries. There were no kisses and no words. Her room was on the first floor and mine was on the second. She simply dropped my hand at the bottom of stairs and ducked into her room and closed the door behind her. I climbed the steps and quickly stripped off my wet bathing suit. Slowly, I went to the head of the stairs and took a step down. As I did so she came out of her room and started up, then stopped to look up at me. Neither one of us had anything on. We stood there for a moment, feasting our eyes on each other and then we rushed into each other's arms. We stood there in an agony of passion, saying each other's names over and over again, and then I took her hand to lead her up the stairs. Just as I did so I heard loud voices on the path outside.

"Later," Molly whispered. "Later."

She was by me and down the steps and into her room. My stepmother and Mrs. Flexner came noisily up the steps and into the cottage. The arrival of those two grown-ups was no accident. Something of what had happened to Molly and me must have shown plainly on our faces and in our actions. When we left the beach that afternoon, our intentions must have been obvious.

Our love affair ended at that moment. There was no "later." For the rest of that afternoon and evening we were never left alone. Glad accompanied us to the tennis court. After dinner we decided to go to a movie, and just as we were going out the door, Mrs. Flexner remembered that someone had recommended the picture highly. She'd go along if we didn't mind. After the movie when Molly and I had finished the last two dances at the Pavilion and were about to go for a moonlight walk up the beach, both Glad and Mrs. Flexner decided they'd like a moonlight walk, too. It was all done cleverly, and Molly and I had no cause for complaint. We thought we could bide our time and be alone soon.

The telegram arrived at seven o'clock the next morning. It was supposed to be from Mr. Flexner in New York. He was on his way out to Michigan for a few days and he hoped that Molly and Mrs. Flexner could spend the time with him. The women scurried around and packed the bags, and before I could gather my senses, I was standing forlornly in front of the cottage waving good-bye.

I wrote to Molly every day after she left and she wrote to me twice a day. Her father never showed up in Flint, and we soon realized that we had been victimized. When there was no longer any doubt about it, I packed my own bag and announced that I was going to hitchhike home. My stepmother and I had quite a scene over this, but I persisted. When I got back to Flint I called George French and asked him to drive me out to the Flexner farm to get my car. I think I had the idea of whistling under Molly's window and helping her to escape down a ladder, but when George and I drove up to the house we found it dark and lifeless. A caretaker came out with a flashlight to see what I wanted, and I explained about the car. He opened the garage doors and backed it out.

"Mrs. Flexner said you'd be out for it and to let you have it," he said.

"Where's Mrs. Flexner?" I asked.

"Oh, she and the girl went over to Canada to see some relatives this afternoon. Won't be back until Labor Day."

Labor Day was still ten days away, and I had no idea where Molly had gone so I couldn't write to her. She thought I was still in Grand Haven and so all her letters to me went there. I never got them.

I saw Molly once more that summer. She came home on Labor Day and the next afternoon she came down to the railroad station to see me off for school. We only had twenty minutes together and she cried for the whole twenty minutes. The last words she said to me as I boarded the train were "I love you. I'll always love you. Write to me every day."

Part II

I

It was my mother's fondest wish that her sons should have a good education. She talked about it constantly, and whether the family fortunes were up or down, she never let my father forget it. On her deathbed she extracted the promise that at least one of her boys would go to college and get a degree. I was the oldest and much of this educational obsession was focused on me. I don't recall that much was ever said about either of my brothers going to college, but it seemed to be taken for granted that I would go. After my mother's death it was almost a mandate as far as my father was concerned.

Just as it had been preordained that I would go to college, so it had been taken for granted that I would attend the University of Michigan. At some time previous to my graduation from high school I had applied to the university for admittance as a freshman in the prelaw course. In due course I received word that my application was accepted. As the summer of 1929 progressed I thought about it idly, but I was preoccupied with Molly and the whole business seemed rather remote. However, without my knowing it, there had been some discussion in our family after my father's marriage in February. My stepmother had brought a fresh eye to the situation and she was not at all sure that I was ready for college. She thought I was lackadaisical about matters of dress, personal hygiene, and etiquette. She was probably right. My father, who felt guilty at not having given me closer supervision, was more receptive to Glad's protests than he otherwise might have been.

Among the friends that Molly and I attracted during that brief stay in Grand Haven were two boys from St. Louis who impressed my stepmother mightily. They were possessed of impeccable manners, and they always dressed neatly. When Glad learned that they attended Kemper Military School, a combination high school and junior college in Boonville, Missouri, she sat down and wrote off for a catalog. She didn't tell me a thing about it.

I didn't have anything to do after I returned from Grand Haven because Molly was away, so I went back to work at the lumberyard. I was in the midst of unloading a carload of plaster one day when my father sent for me. When I got to his office I found a ramrod-straight man in a military uniform sitting there. Upon receipt of Glad's request for a catalog, the school had dispatched Major Walter MacAaron, the commandant, then on a recruiting tour, to see my father. Major MacAaron was an impressive man, a peculiar combination of bombast, ham actor, and uprightness that could make a person worship the ground he walked on. My father was a superior salesman, but Walter MacAaron could put him to shame any time. Before I'd ever been called to the office he'd already sold my father on Kemper Military School and now he went to work on me. I spent fifteen bewildering minutes in his presence. There I stood, just inside the office door, covered with white plaster. Every few sentences the major would jump to his feet and slap me on the back and tell me to stand up straight. By the time he finished the air was filled with plaster and the major had turned white himself. However, he had somehow painted me a picture of myself in a uniform covered with gold braid, proud and tall and just back from some war or other in which I had distinguished myself. It appealed to my romantic nature, and in the course of that fifteen minutes, my whole educational plan was changed. Before I walked out of the office it had already been settled that I would report to Kemper Military School two days after Labor Day. This left me no time to think about it, or to reconsider my decision. My father sent me home that same afternoon to get ready and less than a week later I was saying good-bye to Molly on the station platform.

My Kemper experience was a disaster from the moment I arrived there on a hot, September afternoon. I was issued a uniform, assigned to a room in barracks, and then along with several other new boys I was shepherded down to the inner courtyard for instruction in facing and marching. There was also a short lecture on the maintenance of equipment and the cadet in charge singled me out of the crowd to suggest that I shine my shoes before supper. I went over to the quartermaster's store, bought a bottle of liquid shoe polish, and took it up to my room. As I was opening this bottle the neck came off in my hand and the black polish spilled all down the front of my uniform. I was still standing there, looking at it in dismay, when the bugles blew for the evening meal formation. I wasn't quite sure what to do. The uniform was the only one I had and there wasn't time to clean it. It didn't seem right for me to go down there in the courtyard with all those people with that shoe polish dripping down my front. I stayed in my room. There was a roll call at the meal formation, of course, and I was among the missing. A missing boy on the first day of school was evidently to be expected and the authorities seem to have quickly jumped to the conclusion that I was just another homesick boy who had flown the coop. Beaters were sent to the bus and railroad stations on the run to head me off, and in the excitement no one thought to look in my room. It wasn't until I sneaked down to the orderly room an hour later to find out what to do about my uniform that I was reported found. I had given everyone quite a fright.

The incident of the shoe polish served to focus the attention of Blake Pitchford on me. Blake was in his last year at Kemper, a cadet officer in my company. He was a tall, thin, hatchet-faced boy with a blotchy complexion and a mean disposition. My first meeting with him came that night after I'd been given a new uniform and sent back to my quarters. He came breezing into my room, called my name, and told me to stand at attention. Then he walked all around me, looking me up and down.

"You're the dumbest son of a bitch I ever saw," he said finally. Then he was gone. I was at war.

At the time I went to school there, Kemper operated under much the same rules as were in effect at West Point and Annapolis. A new boy—or rat—had no privileges. The ordinary discipline was rigid and it was supplemented by a form of hazing. All new boys lived in a silent world for the most part. They had to ask permission before speaking. In the mess hall they sat rigidly at attention on the front edge of their chairs with arms folded across chests until given permission to eat by the table captain. Their rooms were subject to invasion at any time, especially after taps. At the slightest sign of rebellion—or even objection—a new boy would be routed out of bed in the middle of the night and hauled down to a cadet officers' meeting that served as a kangaroo court to administer justice and inflict punishment.

Having drawn attention to myself, I soon became Blake Pitchford's favorite target. He never lost a chance to humiliate me. The more people who heard his epithets, the better he liked it. He was in charge of the hall where I lived and he took great delight in giving me demerits. I came to hate him cordially. The trouble with Blake Pitchford was that I kept getting him mixed up with Kemper. I soon came to detest the school because of him. To be fair, however, it wasn't entirely Pitchford's fault or Kemper's. Molly Flexner was as much to blame as anyone.

I had no sooner arrived in Kemper than the letters from Molly came rolling in. She and her mother had left Flint the day after I had, and on the long trip back to Palm Beach, Molly managed to get off two letters to me each day. They were warm, loving letters. and I was soothed by them. As long as they kept coming I could ignore people like Blake Pitchford.

The letters continued for about a week after Molly got back to Florida. Then they slowed down to one a day. At some time early in October Molly informed me that she was only going to write every other day. She had started back to school and she was very busy. One week went by after the slowdown began, and then the letters began coming every third or fourth day. Finally, at the very end of October, I opened an envelope and read an unbelievable paragraph.

"I'm very sorry to have to tell you this," Molly wrote, "but I have fallen in love with another boy. I told him about you, and he doesn't want me to write you anymore, so this will be the last letter you will receive."

In that one short paragraph Molly cut off my head just as neatly as it was ever done by any ancient queen. I couldn't believe my eyes. After reading it a dozen times, I still couldn't believe it. I was numb with grief. I went to bed that night blaming it all on her mother. She was trying to keep Molly away from me. I tossed and turned all night and got up before reveille to scribble off a hasty letter. I sent it special delivery. I had an answer within five days. Molly said she was not mistaken and no one had turned her against me. She had tried to make it as plain as she could. She was in love with someone else. "I've been as honest as I know how," she said. "You're just a stupid boy. Please don't write me any more letters."

This second letter was deliberately cruel. I don't think Molly was a cruel person. She just didn't know any other way to break things off and keep them broken off. My earlier troubles at Kemper became insignificant now, but I didn't give up easily. I bombarded Molly with letters—pleading letters, reasoning letters, scolding letters, and warm, loving letters. She never answered.

I was still stumbling around in a fog, trying to understand what had happened, when Blake Pitchford came into my room just before taps one night. I was rereading Molly's last letter, and he came over to my desk to stand over me.

"You stupid son of a bitch," he said to me. "Don't you ever stand at attention when an officer enters the room?"

There was that same word—"stupid"—staring up at me out of Molly's letter. Pitchford couldn't have said anything worse to me.

I jumped out of my chair and gave him a shove that sent him reeling across the room.

"Don't you ever call me a stupid son of a bitch again," I said. "Or any of your other pet names, either. If you do I'll throw you right out that window on your God-damned head."

He looked at me in surprise and then, without a word, stalked out of the room. Two nights later I was awakened with a flashlight shining in my eyes. Hands reached out and grabbed me and yanked me out of bed, and I was pushed and shoved down the hall to Pitchford's room. There in the light of a flickering candle stood eight cadet officers. They began pushing me back and forth across the circle, from one to the other, slapping me in the face or punching me in the stomach, all the while chanting obscenities in my ears. After twenty minutes of this, they stood me in the center of the circle and a voice informed me that I was hereby sentenced to twenty strokes with a broom. With my nose bleeding and my pajamas half ripped off I was led across the hall to the big shower room, and there, in the dark, I was told to bend over. Each boy stepped up in turn, grasped the broom by the handle, and swung from the heels. Every time it hit me I thought my lower end was coming right up through my mouth. When the last stroke was administered, Pitchford called me to attention.

"Let me tell you what you are," he said. "You're shit. You smell and no one wants anything to do with you. The time will come when you'll wish an officer would call you a name, any name. In the meantime, we don't want any shit smelling up the places where we are. When you take a shower you make damned sure there's no one else in here, and if somebody comes in while you're in here you leave. When you go to the latrine you go after lights are out. And just one more piece of advice. You'd better not even raise an eyebrow at an officer again. It wouldn't be healthy."

When I went back to my room that night I was frightened and humiliated. I lay awake, trying to make up my mind what to do about Molly and the school. I was close to running away. Indeed, when I got up the next morning I had left Kemper Military School behind me in spirit and I never went back to it. All my life, until that moment, I'd been an easygoing boy who had gotten along fairly well with everyone. Now, for the first time, I had run into a group I didn't like and who didn't like me. I was alone and I stayed alone.

I didn't run away, but I was angry enough to do something. I had to show Pitchford and Molly that I wasn't a stupid son of a bitch. I went to work. The grades of all cadets were posted on the bulletin board outside the commandant's office each week. Two weeks after my session with Pitchford and his cronies, my name appeared at the top of that list. I was at the top of it or second every week for the remainder of the school year. I went after the military end of it, too. During the first nine weeks of school I had four or five demerits each week, enough to keep me restricted some of the time. I went to work on my equipment and on my room. Before each inspection I rolled everything out into the hall and scrubbed the place from baseboard to ceiling. I took my rifle completely apart and scrubbed all its parts each week. My brass sparkled and my leather gleamed. I got five demerits the rest of the school year. I had the highest marks in all military tests. At the end of the school year I had the satisfaction of representing my company in the competition for the best first-year cadet and I was nominated to both the scholastic and military honor societies, the only first-year cadet who made them both.

In the meantime I made no friends at school. The cadets at Kemper were restricted to the town limits of Boonville. At that time the main highway through the town, US 40, crossed the Missouri River on a mile-long, high, iron bridge. The rule was that cadets could go across that bridge but that they couldn't set foot off the other end of it. From about the middle of November on, whenever we had any time off, I would march to the other end of the bridge and settle down there, just as far away from Kemper as I could get. I stood there all alone for six or seven hours, sometimes reading, sometimes just watching the cars go by. When night fell after these long vigils I would walk back across the bridge, go to the village movie, and then go home to bed.

I had four different roommates that year. One dropped out of school at Christmas, two of them asked to be rid of me, and I was finally stuck with a boy that no one wanted, including me. In the beginning I had refused to wait until the shower room was empty to take a bath, but this brought me another visit from Pitchford and his cronies so I decided not to take any bath at all. This determination earned me the nickname of Blind Tom and cost me two of my roommates. Even though I was finally given a broom bath in the presence of all the members of my platoon, I still refused. Eventually Major MacAaron, the commandant, called me in for a little talk. I explained the situation and told him that I was perfectly willing to take a bath but only if I was allowed to do so like everyone else. I won the battle. The commandant put pressure on Pitchford and after three months the restriction was lifted. I could take a bath any time I wanted to.

The war of nerves lasted right down to the last week of school and I gave as good as I got. My greatest single satisfaction came in the spring when I elected to play baseball. All winter long I had fulfilled my athletic requirements by going out for track, not because I was any good at it but because I could jog around the field house by myself without having to talk with anyone. After I reported for baseball I was left absolutely alone. This treatment suited me fine, although it practically precluded my ever making the team. The only mark I'd ever made in athletics at all had been in the spring of my senior year at Northern when I'd forsaken my track manager's spot to go out for the baseball team as a pitcher. The Northern coach had been encouraging and told me that I might even make a success in professional ball. At Kemper, however, I retired to the remotest corner of right field to roam around by myself, shagging an occasional fly ball that came my way. A week or two after practice started I decided that I might just as well practice being a left-handed ballplayer inasmuch as no one seemed to care what I did. I'd always been right-handed, but at various times since I was in the second grade I had experimented with the left-handed business. I wasn't very good at it. I could throw a ball a considerable distance left-handed, but most of the time I didn't know where it would go. Still, I was a lot better fielder as a left-hander, because with the glove on my right hand I could reach further and I was much surer of myself.

The right field at Kemper was not enclosed by a fence. Directly behind it was a little pond known as Kemper Lake. Occasionally a long-hit ball would splash down into this lake. One dreary afternoon while I was standing idly on the extreme edge of the outfield, someone hit a fly ball in my general direction. It was well hit and it was curving to my left. I started to run, and as it gained momentum, I picked up speed, too. At the very last moment I threw my glove hand across my body and over my head and leaped. I just got my finger tips on the ball, but because my right hand was better coordinated, I was able to hold onto it. Unfortunately, my leap had carried me over the bank and the next thing I knew I landed in the lake with a big splash. As it happened, the baseball coach was looking right at me when I made that spectacular catch. Up until that time he had never noticed me, but now he came running out to see if I was all right. He arrived just as I emerged, dripping, from the water with the ball still in my hand. After a few questions he sent me up to the locker room to get out of my wet uniform. The next afternoon when I came onto the field, he was waiting for me. The varsity and the scrubs were going to have a little practice game and I was going to play right field for the scrubs. I had no confidence at all in my fielding as a right hander so I decided to play left-handed. In the first inning someone hit a low line drive at me, and I started in at top speed. At the last moment I bent down and scooped up the ball before it hit the ground. I was running so hard I couldn't stop so I kept right on going for second base and slid into it, thus completing a rather unusual double play. I was rather impressed myself at this little feat, but the coach was popeyed. I'm sure he thought that he was looking at the best right fielder in the history of the game. Of course, he hadn't seen me throw yet.

My success as a right fielder made me pretty bold. I was still try-ing to digest it when it came my turn to bat. I was a pitcher and I'd always felt entitled to strike out on three pitches, but as I grabbed the bat, it occurred to me that I'd been having so much success as a left-handed outfielder that I ought to try batting left-handed, too. Up until then I'd never batted left-handed in my life. On the very first pitch I started swinging when the ball left the pitcher's hand. I may have closed my eyes. To my utter amazement I hit the ball high in the air. It kept going back and back in a long, graceful arch and dropped well out in the lake. When I came back from circling the bases, the coach was waiting for me.

"From now on," he said, "you're my regular right fielder. Go up to the equipment room and draw one of the new uniforms."

I was now a little worried because I didn't honestly think I be-longed out there in the field. No one had seen me throw yet. The day after that practice game I went to the coach and told him that I had originally come out as a pitcher and that I was a lot better pitcher than I was a right fielder. I wanted a chance to pitch.

"I don't care what you think," he said. "You're my regular right fielder and you can forget about the pitching."

Somehow I got through the next few days without any serious blunders and we came down to the opening game. I started in right field, playing left-handed. In the first inning our opponents made five quick runs. In the second inning they made five more runs and the coach was very disgusted. When we came in for our bats in the second inning, he came over and sat down beside me.

"Do you want to pitch?" he asked me.

"Sure," I said.

"You couldn't be any worse than what I've got out there. Go over behind the stands and warm up."

I did as I was told. Of course, I had no intention of trying to pitch left-handed, but I didn't say anything. When I got out on the mound I had made just one warm-up pitch when the coach came trotting out to me.

"What the hell's coming off here?" he said. "If you want to pitch, pitch left-handed."

"I can't. I'm right-handed."

"Don't give me that stuff," he said. "You've been playing left-handed all spring."

"Just wait and see," I said.

There wasn't much else he could do. I got the side out on five pitches. I only gave up two hits all the rest of the game until the ninth inning, but my days as a Kemper pitcher were bound to be numbered. In that last inning I was very tired and I started out by throwing three straight balls to the lead-off batter. The regular shortstop was a cadet lieutenant, one of Pitchford's cronies. After the third ball he came walking over to me.

"Come on, Blind Tom, you stupid son of a bitch," he said. "Get the ball over."

I got it over, all right. I grooved it and it ended up in Kemper Lake. I was seriously considering walking three men and letting every fourth man hit it into the lake, but after I'd put the first man on I thought better of it. I managed to get the next three men out, but I'd had enough. When I went up to the locker room after the game I folded up my uniform and gave it to the equipment man. The next day I was out jogging around the track by myself again. The coach came to see me every day for the next week, but I never went back to the baseball team.

Eight weeks after my debut as a pitcher, my career at Kemper ended. On the last day of school I went over to the quartermaster's store and picked up my uniforms. I'd taken them over there to get the stripes for the various honor societies sewed on. (On that trip, incidentally, I ran into an officer who was graduating. He was trying to raise money and he sold me a pair of boots for four dollars.) On my way back to the barracks with my arms full, I was hailed by Major MacAaron, the commandant. He asked me if I would carry an envelope home to my father. I put it in my pocket and then stood around while the major gave me one of his little talks. He said he hoped he would see me in the fall, that I'd made a fine record and the cadet corps could use a boy like me. He thought I had a good chance to make sergeant in my second year. This was a singular honor for cadets at Kemper and for just a fleeting moment I relished the idea of coming back there to enjoy the honors I had earned. It was the only one of those moments I ever had. Even if there had been another one, it wouldn't have done me any good. The envelope that had been handed me for delivery to my father contained a dunning letter. My father owed the school $1,300. He hadn't paid anything since December.

II

Everyone knows when the Depression began. There is an official date for it—October 29, 1929. I missed the drama of that day completely. It coincided almost exactly with the end of my love affair with Molly Flexner. During the next eight months I was so preoccupied with my own personal troubles that the meaning of events in the outer world never got through to me. This is not as strange as it might seem. I rarely read a newspaper. My family neglected to send me the Flint paper and I never thought to ask for it. Most of the boys in Kemper came from Missouri and the Southwest and I certainly wasn't interested enough in the St. Louis, Kansas City, or Dallas news to read those papers. There was no such thing as a small radio set in those days. I believe there was one radio in the whole school—in the official reception parlor where guests and parents were welcomed. Certainly no cadet had one in his room.

My father had suffered catastrophe in those dark days of 1929. He was heavily involved in the market. He not only lost his holdings. He ended up in debt. He had to place large mortgages on the lumberyard and on our house to pay off the loans that had enabled him to play the market. He did not go bankrupt, but he came out of the debacle with his financial position so badly impaired that he was never to recover. He simply had no assets left unencumbered, and this meant that he had no resources with which to meet the continuing crisis that now faced him. It was a long time before I found out how badly my father had been hurt, however. He felt that he had been very foolish and he was not the kind of a man who talked readily about his own mistakes.

When I came home from Kemper at Christmas time in 1929, the stock-market crash was not yet two months gone into history. In our family the process of cleaning up the wreckage was still going on. The pleasant rather breezy way of life which had marked our existence was gone. Those around me seemed steeped in deep gloom. Still, nothing specific was said to me about what had happened. I certainly wasn't astute enough to realize where the gloom came from and at the moment in my self-centered way I was preoccupied with my own troubles. In view of what had happened to me it seemed natural that the world be a gloomy place right then. There was an interesting parallel between my father and me at the moment which further explains why I was so much in the dark. Almost my first act on arriving home from Kemper was to borrow a car and drive out to the Flexner farm. The house was boarded up and forlorn, almost buried under the deep winter snows. There was no sign of life, and I couldn't bear to look at the place where I had spent such happy times. As I hurried away, I kept telling myself that everything that had happened was part of some awful nightmare. Summer would come again and everything would be all right. In the meantime, the best thing to do was to put it out of my mind and not think about it or talk about it. At Christmas time in 1929, my father, still reeling from the shock, must have been telling himself the same thing about *his* troubles.

That vacation was a joyless two weeks. Jim Wiesner was home from Purdue. George French was home from Michigan State. Hank Feller was home from Michigan. Like my own father, Jim's father had suffered substantial reverses in the market. George's and Hank's fathers were worried because the 1930 cars weren't selling. There was talk of layoffs and cutbacks. In one way or another, therefore, a restraining hand was placed on all of us. Everywhere one turned one saw a difference. All our fathers gave us lectures whenever we asked for spending money, something none of us had ever had before. In our house I noticed that Freda Williams was missing. Of course, my car had disappeared. Freda, I was told, felt she was getting too old to be a housekeeper anymore and had gone back to live with her relatives in Flushing. As to my car, my father explained that it had been taking up too much valuable space in the garage and so he had decided to sell it. He implied that I could have another one when I came home in the summer.

This last little touch, in its own way, was the keynote that was being sounded in December, 1929. Just before I took the train back to school, Grandpa Perry sat down to have a little talk with me. I suppose that he felt that there had been too much soft pedaling of the situation and that someone should explain things a little more fully. Times were hard, he said, and money was scarce. We all had to be careful not to spend it foolishly. And then he added a little phrase that was to become, in its many variations, the watchword of the next few years. Things would be better in the spring when people started building houses again. The situation was only temporary. That was the first time I ever heard that philosophy which was to turn into "Prosperity is just around the corner."

Despite his original intention of issuing a warning to me, Grandpa had not wished to worry me. As a result he had so muted his admonition that I still didn't understand the situation. I went back to Kemper almost as ignorant as I had come home. Kemper itself seemed gloomy when I got back there. All the other cadets must have been exposed to the same sort of thing I had. There were outward signs. My roommate—the only one I liked—didn't come back from Texas. In February the corporal of my squad dropped out of school. Of course, no official reasons were given. Although the fathers of both boys had lost everything in the crash, for all I knew they could have dropped out because of the way I smelled. In the bull sessions along the hall at night there were discussions about money and a good many boys were worried. Unfortunately, I wasn't taking part in the bull sessions so I missed that, too. On the day Major MacAaron handed me the envelope for my father, I still had no firm idea of the situation in the outside world. I think I went home in that June of 1930 expecting to find the same lovely world that I had left ten months before.

When one talks about the early months of the Depression, he soon becomes conscious of a theme that is repeated over and over again—often enough to seem repetitious. It was a dual theme, really, like two threads of counterpoint. One was a profound expression of pessimism, the other a resurging note of optimism. The situation had changed considerably between December, 1929, and June, 1930. The Depression was eight months old when I got off the train in Flint. The panic had subsided and the wreckage had been cleared away. Most people could look about them and see just about where they stood. One big thing had happened. The spring, with all its hopes, had come and gone. It was as though someone had thrown a poorly inflated basketball at the floor. Instead of bouncing back, it had landed with a dull plop. There was an air of puzzlement but the optimism was there, too.

"Things are bad," my father told me as he drove me home from the train, "but there's really nothing to worry about. Sooner or later the cars will wear out, and they'll be buying them again, and when that happens more people will be coming in to work in the factories. We've got to have more houses in Flint. I figure this thing will be all over by fall, but we'll just have to hang on and be careful until then."

There it was again, said in a different way: "Prosperity is just around the corner." It would be repeated and repeated. When the fall had come and gone, people talked about the upturn that would come the next spring. The next spring people would say that the upturn would come in the summer, and so on. The thing is that people really believed this. They had a blind faith in it, and because they did, they set up a pattern of living. It was called "hanging on." If you were in business, you kept the business going any way you could until the upturn came and things got better. If you had a job, you hung onto it any way you could. You took less money and worked longer hours. Sooner or later things would return to normal. If you were laid off from your job, you hung around close by so that you'd be able to go back to work when the call came, as you knew it would. If you were behind on the house payments or the car payments, you gritted your teeth and held on, scraping up enough to prevent foreclosure or repossession until things got better. This was where the optimism came in. No one that I knew ever thought that things would stay bad forever. The silver lining was there somewhere, and it was bound to turn up.

One of the big troubles in 1930 was that people got tired of looking ahead into the murkiness for the ray of light. Now and then they would look back at 1929. That's when they got pessimistic. Actually, things weren't so bad in 1930. It was only when you compared it with 1929 that it looked bad. In that bonanza summer of the year before, my father had furnished lumber for fifty houses. In the summer of 1930 he furnished lumber for ten houses. That was enough to net him a modest profit but a modest profit wasn't quite enough. My father was still thinking in terms of that million dollars he was supposed to have had. In order to recoup to the position to which he thought he was entitled, he had to sell more houses than ten. He couldn't do it. Therefore he was pessimistic at the same time he was optimistic.

On the day that I came home from Kemper and was met at the train by my father, he informed me that I could have a summer job driving a truck. He would pay me ten dollars a week. (He'd paid me twenty-five a week for shoveling gravel in 1929.) When I eventually got to work at the lumberyard, I found that all the truck drivers and office help were grousing about how hard times were. Yet, in looking back at it from this distance, I am amazed. In the summer of 1929, we had twelve trucks operating out of the yard. In the summer of 1930 we still had twelve trucks going. No one was laid off so that I could have a job. There was enough business to keep us all going. In looking around at the people who worked at the yard, I found that the labor force was still pretty much intact. Out of the twenty-five people who had worked with me in 1929, twenty-one were still there. The four people who had disappeared had left for other reasons than poor business conditions. One of the truck drivers had joined the Navy. One of the stenographers in the office had left to get married. One of the men who had helped me put the floor in the coal yard had died during the winter. One of the draftsmen in the office had been fired for getting drunk on the job. None of the four had been replaced. It was people like the alcoholic, I think, who first felt the full bite of the Depression. Lacking stability even in good times, they were the ones, in the end, who ended up in the breadlines or selling apples. There weren't so many of them as dealers in Depression nostalgia would have one believe.

That summer of 1930 was the perfect example of the philosophy of "hanging on." All over the country people were living off the fat they had accumulated in good times. Savings were slowly used up. Investments were liquidated. In Flint the summer was a reasonably good one because the factories made an early change to the new 1931 model cars, a device which kept most of the working force employed through the summer months. Even my father, for all the financial disaster he had encountered, had a little fat left. He had good stocks of lumber and coal and he could sell them off for enough cash to keep a dribble of money coming in. Moreover, his credit was still good enough so that he could replenish these stocks. He had a sizable file of accounts receivable and money trickled in from this source. It never seems to have entered his mind to cut down his expenses during this period. The important thing was to keep his organization intact and busy until they were needed again in the coming era of prosperity. The reason we had twelve trucks operating was that my father had decided the way to keep his men busy was to institute a hard campaign to get people to buy their next winter's coal at summer prices. The campaign was successful because most of the coal was sold on credit and it didn't make any difference to most people when their fuel was put in as long as they didn't have to pay for it at the time. So eight of those twelve trucks scurried about busily filling coal bins. As they did so, all of the modest little profit was used up. So were the stocks of lumber and coal and the line of credit that constituted the last vestige of my father's resources.

There were two disquieting undertones to the summer of 1930 which, more than anything else, make me remember it as the gloomiest of all Depression summers. The Depression produced all kinds of casualties. People went crazy. They committed suicide. They had heart attacks and strokes. They went bankrupt. They were sent to prison for embezzlement. The first real casualty of the Depression in my family was my stepmother. I suppose that she was the one person who knew the full extent of the disaster which had befallen my father and the knowledge nearly killed her. In that summer of 1929 she had been a youngish looking woman who always dressed in the height of fashion, a charming gracious person who was given to playing bridge and going to teas and other social functions. In one short winter she changed so completely that I hardly knew her. I came home to find a woman whose hair had turned gray, who was thoroughly frightened. Each morning she would put on an old housedress and go down to the basement to spend long hours over the washing machine and ironing board. In the afternoons one would find her on her hands and knees in the kitchen scrubbing the floor. In a way, all this was an act. I suppose she was trying to shame the rest of us into being careful. For Glad had become penurious almost to the point of insanity. Each evening she would sit in the living room with the daily paper going over the advertisements. At some time during the next day, with one of my brothers driving the car, she would run all over town, buying a bargain here and a bargain there. At dinner each evening she would proudly announce that she had saved so much during the day—twenty cents on groceries, thirty cents by ironing my father's shirts. I soon came to realize that she was trying to keep track of every penny that came in or went out of our house. She even argued with my brothers over how they were to spend their allowances.

We were not the type of family who would take kindly to this sort of thing. We had been used to an openhanded way of life for too long. My father did everything he could think of to argue my stepmother out of the frame of mind she had gotten into. He patiently pointed out that she might have saved twenty cents on her grocery shopping, but that she'd used up fifty cents worth of gasoline to accomplish her saving. At least five times a week he argued that he didn't want her to iron his shirts. She wasn't very good at it and he wanted it done by the laundry as it always had been. When the disputes over my brothers' allowances reached a crescendo, he bluntly told her to let the matter lie. It did no good. She kept right on pinching pennies and interfering in everyone else's affairs, throwing tantrums if any of us so much as talked about going to the movies. If we hadn't been aware of the Depression and worried about it, we soon would have had it drummed into our consciousness with this constant nagging. It was a real gloom producer.

As it turned out I became a prime target. On the afternoon I came home, Glad came into my room while I was unpacking my suitcases. She stood silently by the door for several minutes and then grimly informed me that she expected me to get out the first thing in the morning and look for a job. I told her I was going to work at the lumberyard for ten dollars a week. My father and I had already agreed on it. That was too much for her. Her voice became shrill and she launched into a tirade about parasites. Working at the lumberyard wouldn't be working at all. I would be sponging off my father. I was to go out and get a job some place else. That way I would be bringing money into the family. I was embarrassed. Nothing like this had ever happened to me before. I tried to tell her that the job had been my father's idea, not mine, and that it was up to him what I'd do. I got nowhere. That evening at the dinner table she resumed her attack on the summer plans. My father put down his silverware and pointed a finger at her.

"I'll run my business and you run yours," he said. "If you say one more word about this, just one more damned word, I'll pay him fifty dollars a week."

My stepmother's antipathy toward me had deeper roots than a ten-dollar-a-week job. I represented a *real* menace to the family finances. There was that matter of a college education. She well knew that it had been my mother's fondest wish that I go to college and she was also aware that my father looked upon this wish as a mandate. It was taken for granted that I was going to school again in the fall. This prospect must have hovered over our house like a dark cloud all summer. Every day or two Glad would drop hints that if I had any regard for my father I wouldn't insist on going back to school. These were only hints, however. It wasn't until the middle of September that she told me, point-blank, that she was not going to allow my father to take any money out of his business to pay my college expenses.

Things were a good deal different in September from what they had been when I came home in June. Around Labor Day we moved out of the first—1930—phase of the Depression and began edging into the real depths. My father was just beginning to feel the pinch. His creditors were beginning to dun him. Money wasn't coming in the way it should. People had stopped making payments on those year-old accounts. None of the money for all that coal he'd been putting in people's basements had come in yet. Most of the building activity was over for the summer and he could no longer count on selling truckloads of lumber out of his stock and getting cash out of it. I was working at the lumberyard every day and I had been able to see how difficult things were becoming. I was worried about it, and long before Glad put the matter to me bluntly, I had begun to have doubts about going back to school. It is possible that I would have been willing to forgo the whole business. Unfortunately, my stepmother didn't know when to let well enough alone. Having spoken her mind to me, she chose to speak her mind to my father at dinner one evening. She simply forbade him to send me to college. My father didn't react well when anyone forbade him to do anything. The next morning he called me into his office and gave me a $100 bill.

"If you're going to school," he said, "you'll need some new clothes. Go down and buy some."

It was his gesture of defiance. The very fact that I went to school at all was a gesture of defiance on his part. Glad might have done better to keep her mouth shut.

All through this summer, as the Depression became more and more a matter of overriding importance to me, I had another source of gloom—Molly. I had come home firmly convinced that I would be able to talk her into resuming our love affair. The Flexners took their good time in coming north. They didn't arrive until after the Fourth of July. When they got in, I called Molly on the telephone.

"I don't want a date with you," she said. "Do I have to hit you over the head to make you understand?"

That should have ended it, but I couldn't get away from her. Her picture kept cropping up in the society section of the paper every few days and there was much news about her activities. One of the big song hits of 1930 was "Dancing with Tears in My Eyes." I spent the whole summer moaning the words over and over. It was terrible for me. I shudder to think what it was like for people around me.

It was the end of July before I actually saw Molly. My father had given me the job of light delivery man. Twice a day I would start out with fifteen or twenty orders on my truck and I would deliver a few two-by-fours here and a bag of cement there. On the morning of July 29, 1930, I had delivered the last order of my morning stint and was heading back across town to the lumberyard. I had to cross a complex of railroad tracks in the center of the city, about four blocks west of the business district. As I came to these tracks, a switch engine was working on the crossing, shunting cars back and forth into various sidings. Because this switch engine was on and off the crossing, a long line of automobile traffic had formed. Every time the switch engine backed out of the way, several autos would skedaddle across the tracks. In five or six advances I had finally gotten to the point where I could make my own move the next time the crossing was clear. Just ahead of me, between me and the switch engine, was an old sedan. Two women sat in the front seat of this car. In the back seat were six small children crawling back and forth over each other and wrestling and playing as children do. The two women were engaged in a deep conversation and seemed to pay no attention to the children or anything else. I observed this in an idle way until the switch engine backed off the crossing, and then I put my truck in gear and moved slowly ahead. The woman driver had been even quicker to move. She had put her car in low gear and stepped heavily on the accelerator so that her car lurched forward onto the crossing. I became aware of a frantic shouting and I looked up to see that the crossing lights were still blinking. Off to one side a brakeman was whistling shrilly and shaking his head. In the tower at the middle of the complex the crossing watchman had his head out the window and was waving his arms for the woman to stop. She didn't notice any of this, but I had automatically reacted by jamming on my brake. I craned my neck to see what was causing this commotion and to my utter horror I saw a passenger train bearing down on one of the other tracks. It was slowing down for the Pere Marquette station about a block away, but it was still moving quite fast. Even as I opened my mouth to shout, the cowcatcher of this passenger train caught the sedan squarely in the middle and began rolling it over and over down the tracks. It took seventy-five yards to get that train stopped. I was out of my truck and running before the train stopped moving and I arrived at the wreckage before anyone else. Even before the enginemen had climbed down from their cab, I had pulled a bleeding child out of the mass of twisted and shattered steel and was standing there holding her in my arms. In the next twenty minutes I helped pull six more people out of that car. After the ambulances came and took the injured away, I had to give an account of the accident to the police. It was two in the afternoon before I got back to the lumberyard. When I walked into the office my father's secretary screamed and fainted. I hadn't realized that the front of my overalls was covered with blood. After we revived the secretary, my father told me to go home and change my clothes and take the rest of the afternoon off.

After I'd cleaned up that afternoon, for some reason or other I put on my old Kemper uniform, along with the boots I'd bought that last day. The breeches were tightly cut and the boots shone like a mirror. Those boots made a dashing figure out of me, incidentally —a lot more dashing than I'd ever been at Kemper where I always wore leather puttees. When I came downstairs in this outfit, I heard voices in the living room. Molly and her mother were there.

This was the first time I'd seen Molly since that afternoon at the railroad station. There had been a big change in her. There had been an innocence and a freshness about her the year before. Now she looked drawn and hard-boiled. To add to this illusion, she was smoking a cigarette. I think Molly must have seen a change in me, too. I wasn't a dewy-cheeked boy anymore. That awful year at Kemper had had its effect. Not only had I matured, but I stood straighter. I must have seemed taller. Molly actually seemed interested. When I asked her if she'd like to walk up to the drugstore and get an ice-cream soda, she came along.

I soon discovered that Molly had turned into a silly girl. From the very beginning she concentrated on trying to belittle me. When she asked me if I smoked and I said no, she informed me that she liked men who smoked. They were more mature. Then she went on to drinking. It was fun to get pie-eyed, she said. From there her conversation moved on to dreamy boys with curly hair who owned shiny automobiles. By the time we walked up to the drugstore and back, I was faintly disgusted with this girl I'd been so much in love with. Unfortunately, I wasn't free of her. As she and her mother drove off she waved her hand and told me to call her. This was what I'd been hoping for all summer and I forgot how disgusted I was. I called her for a date the next day, and she accepted. I was overjoyed.

I prepared for that date with great care. I really expected to get back to the place where we'd been the last summer. As we drove away from the farm she nonchalantly lit up a cigarette and offered it to me. I declined politely.

"What the hell's the matter with you?" she said. "You'd better start growing up."

I took the cigarette lamely and smoked it. That was the beginning of a lifetime habit, and the evening got worse. As I began to park the car at the theater, she grabbed my arm.

"Movies are kid stuff," she said. "I want a drink."

That set me back on my heels. I not only had never taken a drink, I didn't have the faintest idea where to buy one. Prohibition was still in effect and the thought of going to a speakeasy was frightening. Molly berated me. I was a prude and she didn't like prudes. She told me to drive on. She knew where there was a place to get a drink. After we had circled several city blocks she admitted she was lost so I suggested going back to the movie. That did it. I was the all-American boy scout and I could take her home. I took her home. It was still daylight when we drove up to the farm. She hardly waited for the car to stop before she was out and running for the front door. I scrambled after her, but I arrived at the door just in time to have it slammed in my face. I went back to dancing with tears in my eyes, but they were less salty now.

Molly was heading for trouble. Three nights after my aborted date with her, she became involved in a very serious auto accident in which her date was killed. There had been heavy drinking before the accident. The scandal from this had scarcely died down when she began dating Arnold Garber, an uncontrollable wastrel of sixteen. She was still dating him when he got drunk one night and went home and bludgeoned his mother to death in an argument over money. Although Molly had nothing to do with the murder, she was known as Arnold's girl and the resultant notoriety frightened her mother to death. Long before Labor Day Mrs. Flexner packed the family up and took them back to Florida. I didn't hear from Molly for a whole year. By the time I did see her again, I had gotten over her.

III

During that gloomy summer of 1930, my father had been able to scrape together the money to pay off the debt to Kemper, but long before he had done so we had agreed that I wouldn't go back for a second year. I sent off another application to Ann Arbor and was accepted again. My credits for the year at Kemper were also accepted and in September I enrolled in the University of Michigan as a sophomore. My roommate was Hank Feller, also entering his sophomore year.

From the very beginning I was much more at home in the relaxed atmosphere of Ann Arbor than I ever had been in the spit-and-polish rigidity of Kemper. There was one significant thing that should be remarked about Michigan in that first fall I was there. School started just before the real pinch of the Depression set in, so that the general tenor of college life that fall was more carefree than it might otherwise have been. It was closer in spirit to the twenties than it was to the thirties. The centers of campus social life were still the fraternities and sororities, and much emphasis was put upon good manners, good taste, and good living.

As an accepted member of the athletic establishment, Hank Feller had chosen a room for us from a list given to him by the Michigan track coach. Although I expected Hank to be my guide and mentor, he was not present when I had to make my first big decision. I had to report to the campus a week early for Orientation Week and I had no sooner checked into my rooming house than I received a telephone call from a boy at Phi Kappa Sigma fraternity, who invited me to dinner that same evening. Because my cousins had all belonged to this house, I was considered a legacy. They made sure I didn't get away. After the first look at me, they booked me solid for lunch and dinner every day during that first week, and on the last day before classes began they offered me a pledge pin. I took it. As far as Hank Feller was concerned, I had made a bad mistake. He had been rushed by several houses in his freshman year, but Hank simply was not good fraternity material, having no sense of humor, and being rather narrow and unrelenting in his views of dancing, drinking, and other things that he considered the essence of fraternity life. He'd never been offered a pledge pin and he now was militantly antifraternity. It was the beginning of the end of our long friendship.

Actually, I was a long time warming up to the fraternity myself. I was required to eat one meal a day at the house, but I usually took lunch and dinner there. I also gave one afternoon of work each week—washing windows, raking leaves, or shoveling snow—but for one semester I preferred to spend most of my time at Mrs. Schoneman's rooming house on South Division Street, where I lived. As it turned out, my best friends were there. Two of them were to be my lifelong friends.

All the occupants of Mrs. Schoneman's rooming house were athletes, the house having long been at the head of the list given out each year by the athletic department. That fall of 1930 all of them came from Bay City, Michigan, and all of them were members of the varsity football team. They were a ribald, good-natured bunch of ruffians who had been close friends for a long time. The ringleader of this little band was one of the most unusual men I ever knew. His name was Bill Hewitt. Bill was built like a child's top, rounded and burly in the upper reaches and tapering to a point at the bottom. He was unquestionably the toughest physical specimen I ever saw. After his college career was over, he went on to play end for the Chicago Bears. For fourteen years—his whole professional career—he never wore a football helmet.

Bill Hewitt was as good a student as he was a football player. Most of the time he was at Ann Arbor he got straight A's. The only thing that kept him from making Phi Beta Kappa was "an occasional lazy spell," as he put it. Bill and his roommate, Fred Clohset, and I became the best of friends from the very beginning for we had three classes together. Consequently, almost every evening we studied together and this led to our chumming around together outside. Fred had joined a fraternity at the same time I had, and we both tried to get Bill to join. In an effort to get my fraternity brothers interested in him I gave him a bid to one of our dances. He showed up with a gorgeous-looking girl and he was quite presentable in a blue suit and a stiffly starched shirt, but his dancing killed any chances of my getting him into our house. In the fall of 1930 most fraternity men danced in place, swaying gently to the music in a darkened room with their eyes closed, singing softly in the ear of the girl whose cheek was generally right up against theirs. In the course of a whole dance set a couple might move twenty feet. This was sophistication carried to its ultimate and sophistication was the watchword of the moment. Bill didn't like to stand still. He was light on his feet and he liked to whirl around. Five minutes after he got on a dance floor he would clean it off completely, sending other couples flying in all directions. He was apologetic about it and spent most of the evening saying, "I'm sorry," but he was just too big for a fraternity dance floor. Neither my brothers, nor Fred's, dared to offer him a pledge button.

Several events, in all of which Bill Hewitt and Fred Clohset were involved, made that first fall memorable. One had to do with a girl named Virginia Van Buren who entered Michigan that fall as a freshman. She was tall and blonde and exquisite, and she held herself erect and proud, but she had a warm, wistful smile that could do things to a man. Indeed, it did.

Those of us who lived in Mrs. Schoneman's rooming house had one big advantage because Virginia lived next door in the Rock House, a girl's rooming house that was separated from us by a narrow driveway. I was in a particularly advantageous position because I could sit at my desk and look directly into the window of Virginia's room. In spite of the fact that she was always careful to pull her curtains at the crucial moments, I was able to keep track of everything she did with a minimum of effort. I was the first person in our house to discover this gorgeous creature and the first one to talk to her, because when she came to sit in her window on warm September afternoons, she wasn't more than fifteen feet away from me. There was something of an invitation in our first conversations and during the first week after classes started I decided to see if she meant it. I asked her to go dancing at the Michigan Union and she accepted.

That date with Virginia was something to remember. When I went to pick her up, she appeared in a long, low-cut, blue velvet gown. She was absolutely stunning. I proudly escorted her over to the Union and up to the ballroom. It only took me five minutes to discover a lot of friends I'd never had before. Most of my nodding acquaintances came over to slap me on the back and ask me how everything was going. I fumbled for names in the back of my head and in the first half hour I think I introduced thirty fellows to Virginia. She was very attentive to everyone and made sure she was getting all the names right. She responded to each introduction with an adorable little wink. Suddenly, after quite a while, she informed me that she had come to dance with me, that she was my date, and that she thought we ought to stop being the center of the social whirl. She wanted no more introductions. From that moment on she was perfect. She was an excellent dancer and she made me feel as if I was one. She was attentive and witty. My evening passed rapturously. When the dance ended I walked her home, and we went up on the porch and sat on the swing. I put my arm around her and she put her arms around me. I kissed her and she kissed me back, warmly. My torch for Molly Flexner sputtered and went out. When the chimes rang for her to go in, I led her over to the door, and we stood there nuzzling one another until the chaperone spoke sharply to us.

"When can we go out again?" I asked her.

"Call me," she said.

I called her. I called her a dozen times. Every time I called her she informed me that she was sorry but she had another date. I was completely exasperated. I couldn't understand what had gone wrong. I went back over that date I'd had with her, trying to pick out the thing I had done to offend her. It didn't make sense, because the last thing we had shared were those warm affectionate kisses. I could only reach the conclusion that what had happened had happened *after* I left her. Yet this was strange, too. I could still look over at her window and each time I did she would give me a wave of the hand and one of those wonderful smiles.

Of course, before I had that date, the other fellows in our house had noticed Virginia, too. They joined me in talking back and forth across the driveway with her. A week after my date, Fred Clohset announced that he had a date with her. Two weeks later, Bill Hewitt had one. I must confess that I began to be suspicious of both of them and I was just about to invade their room and ask what was coming off. Before that happened, however, Fred came into my room one night and gave me a peculiar look.

"Did you say anything to Virginia about me?" he asked.

"Nope. Why?"

"Because I can't get another date with her. I don't understand it. I thought she liked me."

When Bill Hewitt had the same trouble we began comparing notes. I discovered that Virginia had followed exactly the same script with each of them, even to the kisses on the porch swing.

"We're some kind of suckers," Bill said.

We had been. Toward the end of October we stumbled on the truth. Virginia came from Muskegon and one of the boys on the football team had a letter from his cousin over there with a word of warning. Before leaving home Virginia had made a boast. She was going to have a date every single night of her college career and she was going to have a date with a different man every night. In a normal four-year university course this would mean that she would have dates with 1,200 different men. Virginia was admirably equipped to accomplish this but she wasn't leaving anything to chance. All that warmth was a come-on. She knew the word about how good a date she was would get around.

One would think that when this news got out Virginia would be ruined. She wasn't. If anything she was more popular than ever. It was a challenge. For a fellow like Bill Hewitt, I suppose, it was a game he could play and win. He intended to get that second date and be the champion. I was a little more romantic. I hoped the second date would be the signal that I had won this girl for my very own against great odds. It didn't make any difference whether it was a game or not, Bill Hewit and Fred Clohset and I were rivals. In the meantime the field was increasing. From our windows we could watch a steady stream of first dates going up on that porch. I saw three of my fraternity brothers arrive and Bill Hewitt saw ten members of the football team come and go.

Because I could keep such close watch on Virginia I was bound to pick up a lot of information about her. One of her major interests, besides dating, was horseback riding. Every afternoon she would appear on the front porch of the Rock House in a chic little riding habit. A station wagon marked "Washtenaw Stables" would come sliding up to the curb and whisk her away. The same car would bring her back about three thirty. The importance of this information never registered on me because I had never ridden a horse in my life and had no interest in doing so.

Along toward the end of November I was called over to my fraternity house to rake leaves. I put on my old clothes for the chore and in the fall of 1930 old clothes meant my old Kemper uniforms. On that particular day, because I would be wearing the old clothes to class, I put on the breeches and those boots I had bought. I raked the leaves, cutting my usual fine figure, and then came back across the campus to Mrs. Schoneman's. Just as I was walking up the driveway the station wagon arrived and Virginia got out. I waved my hand at her and she waved back in her cheery fashion but I noticed she cocked her head at me in an interested sort of way. It raised my hopes. I walked over to her.

"I didn't know you were a horseman," she said. "If I had known I'd have asked you to go riding with me."

I was puzzled until I saw that she was running her eyes over me, then I knew it was the boots. I was just about to blurt out the truth when Mrs. Schoneman's front door slammed, and Bill Hewitt and Fred Clohset came down the steps on their way to football practice. They waved as they turned toward the field house and a thought took shape in my mind. A date was a date. It didn't make any difference whether it was a date to go dancing or go horseback riding. I was going to win the campus sweepstakes. The opportunity had been placed squarely before me.

"Of course, I go horseback riding," I said "I'm ready any time. How about tomorrow?"

"You be over here in front of the house at one o'clock sharp," she said.

I was inclined to just go ahead and have that date and inform people about it afterward, but after dinner that evening Bill and Fred started kidding me about my playing up to Virginia.

"You haven't got a chance," they said.

"Maybe I'd better tell you two clowns," I said. "The contest is over. I've got another date with Virginia."

Bill was sitting with his feet on his desk, a book on his lap. He looked up at me with a skeptical grin and then he slammed the book shut, took down his feet, and sat up.

"You don't think I'm going to believe that, do you?"

"It's true. Tomorrow afternoon at one o'clock we're going horseback riding. You just sit here in your window at one o'clock and you'll see us go."

He pointed his finger at me. "Of all the dirty low-down tricks I ever heard of, this is the worst. Horseback riding? What kind of a date is that?"

"It's too bad you didn't think of it first," I said.

He reached over and took down the blue letter sweater from its hook and slipped it over his head.

"I'll bet you can't even ride a horse," he said. and turned to Fred. "Come on, Freddie. We've got work to do."

The two of them slammed down the stairs and out the front door leaving me standing there.

The next day I was standing in front of the Rock House at one o'clock. It was a sunny day, very warm for November. Virginia came tripping down the steps behind me, slapping herself with a riding crop. She was adorable. As she flashed her lovely sad smile at me the station wagon came around a corner and pulled up in front of us. I bent over and opened the door for Virginia. As I did so, the whole street came alive. Fellows came out from behind trees and around the corners of houses. They advanced toward us, a magnificent collection of ragamuffins. One fellow had on an old sweat suit. Another had donned greasy overalls. Still another wore plus fours. Bill Hewitt, who led this motley crowd, was decked out in a pair of football pants topped by his letter sweater. I counted forty of these fellows and I knew that they included members of the Virginia Van Buren Dating Society, some of them members of the varsity football team.

"We want to go horseback riding," Bill said.

"I can't take all of you," the station wagon driver said.

"You got twelve horses?" Bill asked.

The man nodded.

"Let's go then." Bill ticked off the twelve fellows with his finger, motioning them to get in the car. He, himself, climbed up onto the top and sat down cross-legged like a Buddha. Virginia and I watched all this in surprise. I finally motioned for her to get in. She glared at me.

"You needn't come," she said. "You've had your fun."

"I didn't have anything to do with this," I sputtered. "I don't like it any better than you do. This is Bill Hewitt's idea. He thinks he's keeping me from having a second date."

Her eyes were smoldering, but she got in and let me in beside her. We started out driving through the streets of Ann Arbor, so heavily loaded that we crunched every time we hit a bump. Bill and his friends on the outside were whistling and catcalling at people on the sidewalks. Virginia was looking straight ahead and biting her lip.

"I hate them," she said once. "I hate them."

When we came to the stable she turned to me. "I've just decided. You'll have your second date. I promise. Leave it to me."

Virginia took the stable man off to one side and talked earnestly to him. He went away and began leading out horses. I noticed that he led two very sleek-looking rather nervous animals off to one side. All the others were quiet and well-behaved.

"I don't suppose any of you fellows have ever ridden a horse before?" the stableman asked Bill.

"Nope," Bill said.

"Well, I've given you the twelve gentlest horses I have. You shouldn't have any trouble."

Virginia went over to one of the nervous horses and swung up into the saddle in one easy motion. All of the other fellows began grunting and groaning, trying to heave themselves up onto the horses' backs. I reached for the first horse at hand, but the stable owner grabbed me by the arm and pointed toward Virginia.

"That's your horse over there," he said.

I strode over and looked up at Virginia and started to mount. I was lucky. Just by chance I picked the correct side of the horse and I managed to get up in the saddle on the third try while Virginia was laughing at the others. Watching Tom Mix get up there was one thing. Getting up there myself was something else and the minute I settled down I wished I was back on the ground again. It was an awfully long way down from where I was, it was narrow up there, it was slippery, and there wasn't anything to hang onto. The horse was prancing up and down with little mincing steps and I knew I was in mortal danger. I hardly dared look around and when I did look the horse started moving forward. I gritted my teeth and devoted my whole being to staying up there in that saddle.

Virignia led the way. She wheeled her mount and cantered out to the road where she turned and looked back at us. I wasn't having any of that cantering business. It seemed to me like my horse was just jumping straight up and down, and in the nick of time the others came up to me and I found myself inching forward in the middle of the saddest cavalry troop ever assembled. All around me I could hear cooing noises and voices saying "Steady, boy. Steady, now." I joined in the chorus. It must have seemed like a long time to Virginia before we finally made it out to the road and caught up with her. As we all sighed in relief she gave us a contemptuous look, wheeled, and cantered off for another fifty yards, then stopped to wait for us again. We just let her stand there and wait while we nursed our horses forward.

We'd gone about a mile in this fashion when Virginia made the move she had planned. Her horse began acting up. It reared up on its hind legs a time or two and made a loud whinnying sound, then turned and romped off down the road as fast as it could go. Faintly, as she disappeared over a hill, I heard Virginia cry, "Help!"

The other horses didn't seem to pay any attention to this, but mine did. It began to prance up and down again. I think it even ran a few steps. Fortunately for me someone in the crowd knew enough to reach out and grab the straps at my horse's head, and after a few soothing words, the animal calmed down. I was well aware that Virginia expected me to ride out after her and save her. I have always thought that, had I been able to do so, we would have ridden off into the sunset together and all kinds of delicious things might have happened. As it was I inched forward to the rescue as part of that great inert posse, huddled in the middle of the group, talking my own version of horse language.

We came upon Virginia a half hour later. She was sitting under a tree, holding the reins of her horse and smoking a cigarette. She was scornful, but she seemed more beautiful and desirable than ever. She got to her feet and came walking toward us, shaking her head.

"What a sight!" she said, and sighed. "Well, I guess the only thing for me to do is to teach you something about riding. If you're going to make a habit of this, you might just as well learn to do it the right way."

She taught us, all right. She led us up hill and down dale for two hours or more. She spent time with each of us, showing us how to sit a horse properly, giving us confidence. It wasn't a bad afternoon and it might have gone on until dark if Bill Hewitt hadn't remembered that he and the others were due back at the field house at five o'clock for signal drill. We even cantered a bit as we all headed home to the stable.

That evening while I was finishing my dinner I began to notice sore spots developing on my anatomy. By the time I got to bed I was so sore and stiff that I couldn't get comfortable and I slept only fitfully. The next afternoon when I went out to the stadium to see the last football game of the season against the University of Chicago I found myself unable to sit on the hard seats and I had to stand at the back of the stadium for the entire game.

The University of Michigan had one of its better teams that year, winning the Big Ten championship. Unfortunately, six of the starting players that last afternoon felt the same way I did. It had been reliably predicted that the final score against an inept Chicago team would be 50-0, but at half time the score was 0-0. It was not until the last quarter that a substitute guard—a nonhorseback rider—broke through to block a punt and fall on it in the end zone. Michigan hung on to win, 6-0.

That evening I went to a dance at the Union and as I moved around the floor in the dim light I suddenly came upon Bill Hewitt. He was dancing in place, swaying to the music cheek to cheek, just like any good fraternity man. He saw me and gritted his teeth.

"You son of a bitch," he said to me as I danced by, "if I could move I'd break you in two."

I never had a second date with Virginia. As far as I know no one else on the Michigan campus did, either. She went right on having a date with a new and different fellow every night and flunked out of school at the end of the first semester. A long time later someone told me she had married a Michigan State man.

It was a strange thing, especially after the record I'd made at Kemper, but I almost flunked out of school myself that first semester. It may have been a letdown, but I didn't study too hard. I carried five courses and I came to the final exams with a C in four of them. Because I was in my first year, however, I was on probation and if I flunked one course I was in trouble. That I didn't flunk was due entirely to Bill Hewitt and Fred Clohset. All three of us were taking a course in geology and all three of us had flunked the mid-semester exam. There was a reason for it. The course was taught by Professor William Halliwell Hobbs, a venerable, distinguished old gentleman who was one of the world's foremost geologists. He gave two lectures a week, supplemented by reading, principally from a ponderous volume called *Earth Features and Their Meaning* written by himself. Our big problem was the lectures. Every Monday and Friday at eleven o'clock Professor Hobbs would step up on the platform of the room where three hundred students had assembled. At his signal an assistant would turn out the lights and a slide would be projected on the screen over the professor's head. Dr. Hobbs would use a long stick to point out the features he wanted to talk about. I don't know whether it was the hour of the day or his mellifluous voice, but five minutes after the lecture began everyone in the room would be sound asleep. Just before Christmas vacation there was an embarrassing moment when something went wrong with the projector. The assistant quickly turned on the lights, and Professor Hobbs found himself looking down on a whole roomful of sleepers.

Bill and Fred and I were desperate as final exams approached. We all decided that the only way we were going to pass geology was to memorize Professor Hobbs' book from cover to cover and we set aside a twenty-four-hour period just before the exam to do that. We started at eight in the morning, asking each other questions as we went along, but by nine in the evening we were only halfway through the book. At about that time Fred slammed his book shut and announced that he had taken as much as he could take. There was a widely held theory that once a man started a cramming session he should never go to sleep or he would forget everything that he had jammed in his head and Bill Hewitt called attention to this. Consequently, we all went out and got a jug of coffee. It didn't do any good. We were still sleepy. We struggled valiantly and Fred even got out the daily paper and read the comics aloud to us.

"Professor Hobbs's book is funnier than those funny papers," Bill said. "I can prove it."

He pointed at a page in his book and took up a pencil and scribbled in the margin, erasing something every now and then. I read what he wrote and laughed.

> Consider the volcano Krakatoa
> Made the God Pele very soa
> With one powerful blast
> It burned Pele's ass
> Now Krakatoa is no moa.

He turned to the next picture and began working on another limerick. Fred and I started composing them, too. We managed to get a few chuckles out of Bill, but we weren't anywhere near as good as he was. He had a genius for this kind of thing and he had us laughing our heads off. By morning, between us, we'd composed four or five hundred of those things, but the only other one I can remember is one of Bill's.

> Don't pee in the sea
> It might freeze, you see
> And then you'll end up
> With another Maumee.
> God damn it to hell!

We had done what we intended to do. We had stayed awake. At eight o'clock in the morning we stumbled blindly across the campus and took our seats for the examination. Professor Hobbs, his white beard flowing, stepped into the middle of the amphitheater and pointed majestically upward.

"Ladies and gentlemen," he said, "I shall cause to be projected on the ceiling a selection of the various slides on which I've been lecturing this semester. You will please identify each slide briefly, in one sentence, if possible. You will have about two minutes for each slide."

I was worried but I needn't have been. The very first slide showed the area covered by the great glacial lake, Maumee. From the seat next to me I heard Bill Hewitt snicker. At the next slide he laughed aloud. By the end of that examination he was laughing so hard the tears were running down his cheeks. Every one of those slides shown that morning were from Professor Hobbs' book and we had made up something about every single one of them. I got

100 and passed the course with an A. Fred got 98. Poor Bill! He only got 94. He forgot and wrote down the limericks on several occasions. A good many years later I had a fellow in my company in the Army who played tackle next to Bill on the Chicago Bears.

"He was the damnedest guy I ever saw," this fellow told me. "He used to memorize some of our plays by writing limericks about them. Once he had a sure touchdown and dropped a pass because he was laughing about one of those limericks."

IV

My participation in the affairs of my fraternity had been spotty during the first semester at Ann Arbor, but at the beginning of the second semester I began to take an active interest in what went on at the house. This all came about, strangely enough, because of a run-in with Prohibition law-enforcement agencies.

I suppose it might be well to say a word about Prohibition here and about my attitude toward it. It is almost forty years since the Eighteenth Amendment was repealed, and I have a feeling that certain misconceptions have grown up about it. My generation was seven years old when national prohibition went into effect, but parts of the Middle West had been dry long before that. This included Genesee County where I was born and brought up. In a subtle way this long dry spell was having an effect. My father was a "wet." He liked a drink himself and he liked to serve a drink to his friends when they visited our house. I can never remember a time when there wasn't a bottle of some kind in the kitchen cupboard. Whiskey was hard to come by, however, and there was none of this ritual of having a daily drink before dinner. Drinking was done only on special occasions and there might be weeks between drinks. This was the situation that existed in the homes of most of my friends. As far as the younger generation was concerned, there was no drinking at all to speak of. In my high-school class of 146 members I think it is safe to say that only two or three members had the reputation of being flask toters and the vast majority of my classmates disapproved of them. And this was during what was known as the Flapper Age! As far as I was concerned personally, there had been no rules laid down by my father. The subject of personal habits was only raised once that I can remember.

"I don't care if you drink or smoke," my father told me. "I'd rather you didn't, but I suppose you will. Just don't sneak around about it."

At various times as I was growing up my father had offered me a taste of something he was drinking. I hadn't cared for it, and because I didn't care for it, I saw no use in going to a lot of trouble to get liquor. Getting it was trouble and it was dangerous. Almost every day the Flint paper would record the fact that someone had been sentenced to Leavenworth penitentiary or Jackson State prison for six months. Fines were uniformly heavy. It wasn't just a case of selling liquor, either. If a person was in possession of liquor or if he was just sitting on the premises where there was liquor, he was in danger of being arrested. To the younger people like myself there was a great stigma in being arrested even if it was for violating an unpopular law. I had reached the age of eighteen feeling that it was wrong to drink, not morally wrong but legally wrong. The various prohibition laws were somewhat of a deterrent for me, as for almost everyone. Whatever else they did they kept the volume of consumption down.

When I enrolled in school at the University of Michigan I found a different attitude from what I was used to at home. Ann Arbor, being a college town, was much more cosmopolitan about things like liquor. I soon discovered that a seedy-looking character arrived at the back door of the fraternity house every Friday afternoon and dragged two or three gunny sacks into the landing at the bottom of the fire escape. Then, cupping his hands, he would yell up the stairs, "Bootlegger!" The boys would come running. This little episode amused me a great deal. The fact that it did probably tells more about my attitude than anything else. Anyone who wanted a drink could have one. I didn't approve or disapprove. Nevertheless, I still hadn't taken a drink myself. I didn't intend to. One of the basic reasons for the cooling of my relationship with Hank Feller was the very fact that he still maintained his narrow prohibitionist attitudes that he'd brought from home while I, quite without realizing it, was discarding mine. Every time he made some snide remark about "booze-guzzling, rah-rah fraternity boys," it rubbed me the wrong way. I came to look upon him as an anachronism. The thing I didn't realize was that Ann Arbor was a wet island in the midst of a dry sea. I found out soon enough.

Final semester examinations were spread over a two-week period at Michigan. It was possible for a student to take all his examinations in three days and then enjoy an extended vacation. While this didn't happen very often, it usually worked out that students had four or five days between their last examination and the beginning of the second semester. Most of them used this free time to go home or visit friends. I was unlucky at the end of the first semester because I didn't finish my last exam until late on the last Thursday afternoon of the examination period. It was too late in the day to hitchhike home. I found myself stuck in an Ann Arbor that was largely deserted. The fellows at my rooming house had gone off and I was quite alone. Of the more than seventy active members and pledges at the fraternity all but seven had left the campus. Even the dining room was closed down. Still, seven fellows were better than none so I wandered over to the house, hoping to find someone to go to the movie with. I found the place all dark except for some lights in the cardroom at one end of the building. I discovered that the small group in residence had started a poker game and I sat down to play. I was still there at midnight when the telephone rang. Because I was the only pledge in the house, it was my job to answer it. I ran across the darkened living room, ducked into the booth by the front door, and lifted the receiver. I heard a distraught voice.

"For God's sake," it gasped out, "if you've got any liquor in the house, get rid of it. The Federals are in town, and they're raiding the fraternities."

We certainly had liquor in the house and I knew it. Beginning the next day was the biggest social weekend of the whole year in Ann Arbor. The annual J-Hop was held on the Friday night between semesters and it was traditionally the most elegant ball of the winter. Five or six thousand students attended this dance. It was an occasion when most fellows invited their best girls from out of town. After the Friday night affair most fraternities rounded out the weekend by having their own formal dances on Saturday night. Faced with a social whirl such as this, anyone who took a drink was bound to lay in a supply of liquor. Most fellows bought their bottles early and had hidden them away somewhere before going off to celebrate the end of examinations. Everyone would come trooping back into town the next afternoon to start the weekend festivities.

The various Prohibition authorities knew there would be plenty of liquor in Ann Arbor and they had timed their move to catch the largest number of culprits. A huge raiding party had arrived on the eastern outskirts of town about eleven o'clock and had invaded the first fraternities it came to. One of these happened to be the local chapter of Delta Kappa Epsilon—the Dekes. The Dekes were the same as we were. Most of the members had stored their liquor and had gone off some place, leaving a few boys on the premises. The raiders had rounded up the boys and searched the house. They had found plenty of liquor and had confiscated it. Then they had shipped the boys off to the Washtenaw County jail before moving on to the next house. By chance just before the raiders arrived at the Deke house, one of the Deke freshmen had been sent down to the kitchen for something and he was still there when the commotion began upstairs. He had realized what was happening and had jumped into the dirty laundry hamper, burying himself under the sheets and tablecloths until the raiders left. Then he crawled out into the darkened and padlocked house and began calling the other fraternities to give the alarm.

None of us in our house hesitated for a moment. It never seems to have occurred to any of us to get out of there and save ourselves. The only thing on our mind was to find the liquor and get rid of it. We rushed up to the second floor like a herd of stampeding horses. In our house all the brothers slept in a dormitory on the third floor. Below on the second floor, a series of small rooms furnished with desks and casual furniture opened off a long central hall. It was in these rooms that the brothers studied and kept their belongings. Most of the occupants of the more than twenty rooms had locked their doors before going off. Getting in wasn't easy; we found skeleton keys that opened some of the doors and we had to break the locks on others. We had to chop two of the doors down with a fire ax. Once we got inside the rooms we split up into teams. One team went through the closets looking for flasks and bottles that might have been hidden away in pockets. Another team went through desks and bureau drawers. We didn't have time for niceties. We just threw things around. Clothes and books and furniture were tossed into big piles in the center of the room. Attila the Hun couldn't have done a better job.

We found thirty-seven quarts of whiskey or gin, five bottles of champagne, two cases of beer, four quarts of wine, and one jug of hard cider. As fast as we found anything we dumped it down the drain in the bathroom. I was given the job of disposing of the empty bottles. I was a little puzzled as to what to do with them. I couldn't bury them in the snow because there wasn't any snow. The ground was frozen too hard to dig a hole for them. On my first trip with a load of empties I stood out in our back driveway for several minutes, trying to decide what to do. In the middle of it I happened to look across our backyard at the Gamma Phi Beta sorority house. Outside the Gamma Phi's kitchen windows was a long line of garbage cans, and I headed for them. On the third trip, as I was putting bottles in the garbage cans, I was joined by a pledge from another fraternity with the same idea. By the time of my last trip there were three different pledges from three different fraternities putting bottles in nearby sorority garbage cans. When daylight came the next morning I could see bottles sticking out of cans all over the neighborhood. It was a good thing we were still living in the age of chivalry. If the Federals had ever raided sororities there would have been quite a scandal.

In our house we worked steadily until just before six in the morning. When we dumped the last bottle down the drain we were so tired we could hardly keep our eyes open. At a little after seven our front doorbell rang and six grim men pushed their way into the house. They made us stand in a line in the living room while the party clomped up the stairs. We could hear them up there banging closet doors and opening bureau drawers. When they came back down stairs they were quite angry because they hadn't found a thing. They stood around for some little time trying to find out who had tipped us off, but we didn't know, of course, so we couldn't tell them. As they left the leader pointed his finger at us and told us we were lucky. If they had found just one small bottle they would have run us in.

Those agents hadn't been gone from our house for more than five minutes when we heard a peculiar snoring noise from our guest room on the first floor, not twenty feet from where they had been standing. One of the brothers went over and opened the door. There stretched out on a bed was our porter. Clutched to his chest was a bottle half full of whiskey. At some time during the night while we were up dumping liquor, he had wandered in drunk to flop down on the bed in the guest room. None of us had been aware of it.

The results of that raid were awesome. Seven fraternities were suspended for a year. Some of them never reopened. The boys caught on the premises were expelled from school and most of them given jail sentences or fines. The whole business disgusted me and when Hank Feller began gloating over it our friendship ended for good.

The experience during Raid Night—as we called it—established a bond between me and my fraternity brothers. My falling out with Hank Feller turned me more toward the house, and my integration was completed two weeks later by Hell Week. Hell Week, I'm given to understand, is a thing of the past nowadays. It might surprise a lot of people that it was beginning to disappear as early as 1931. My pledge class was the last one to undergo a full-scale, old-fashioned Hell Week. We considered ourselves enlightened. The very next year we cut the time of trial from the traditional eight days to one weekend.

In Ann Arbor during my time Hell Week activities were already largely confined to the premises of the fraternities. We were not required to make idiots of ourselves by performing stunts in front of bored spectators. About the only time we emerged into the town was when we went to classes or when we debouched into the streets late at night in search of some hidden treasure. Nonetheless it was easy to tell that we were undergoing Hell Week during the second week of the new semester. Each fraternity's pledges wore some little badge that told who they were and what was going on. In our case we wore white canvas gloves wherever we went. One house had decked its pledges out in yellow slickers and another required its men to wear sneakers—quite a feat for Ann Arbor in February.

The two basic ingredients of any Hell Week were sleeplessness and paddling. From the Friday afternoon when it began at five o'clock, until eight days later when it ended with a formal dinner and initiation, no pledge was supposed to sleep. For twenty-four hours each day he followed an intricate ritual that allowed no time even for a nap. He was supposed to be ingenious enough to get around these rituals and steal forty winks now and then. The time that such respite could best be achieved was at night. At eleven o'clock each evening, we would be sent out on some fool's errand. One couldn't ignore these errands for failure to perform them resulted in wholesale paddling. The trick was to accomplish them as quickly as possible and then curl up in some secluded spot and sleep for the two or three hours that remained before one was supposed to report back to the house at seven in the morning. One had to be careful about this, however. The logical place to sleep was in one's own rooming house, but spot checks were often made on them and it was a sad and sore pledge who was caught in his own bed. (I got around this by trading rooms with Bill Hewitt. I slept in his bed and he slept in mine. On the one night some of my brothers flashed a light in Bill's face, he dumped a pail of water over their heads and threw them bodily out of the house. He was no man to monkey with.)

I soon discovered one of the many ways to beat Hell Week. Because there were many pledges from other houses in my classes who were undergoing the same tortures, we did a considerable amount of comparing notes. I knew what they had done the night before, and they knew what I had done. If on a certain night I was sent to find a tombstone with the name Hezekiah on it, I would usually know which house's pledges had been out looking for tombstones the previous nights. I would find some of those fellows and question them. I might not find where Hezekiah was, but I could usually narrow it down to the most likely section of the most likely cemetery. It was because of this interchange of information that I made a financial killing.

On the third night of Hell Week, my twenty-eight pledge brothers and I were put out into the street with instructions to report back at seven o'clock with black cats—one per man. I hadn't gone more than a block from the house when I ran into two Sigma Nu pledges who were looking for black cats, too. I wasn't sure what the black-cat population of Ann Arbor was, but if there were very many fraternities out looking for them, it stood to reason that there weren't going to be enough to go around. Consequently I decided to go someplace else. I walked down to the nearest traffic light and thumbed a ride to Ypsilanti seven miles away. I debarked in front of the Greyhound bus station and walked in the front door. There was my cat curled up in front of a stove. I captured it with no difficulty at all and put it in the gunnysack that had been provided me. It wasn't midnight yet and I looked forward to six full hours of sleep. On the way back to Ann Arbor I was picked up by the driver of a bread truck who told me that he had to stop and make a delivery at an all-night restaurant on the way. There was another black cat in the restaurant, and while the owner was somewhere in the back of the place, I sneaked in and grabbed it and put it in the gunnysack with the first one. The driver of the bread truck pulled down the road a mile and stopped for gas. There was a black cat sitting outside the men's room of the station so I added it to my collection. When I got back to Ann Arbor the bread-truck driver let me out in front of the Union and I walked through the backyard on my way to Mrs. Schoneman's house. As I suspected there were ten fellows prowling around near the Union kitchen looking for black cats. Two of them were my pledge brothers so I called them over and showed them what I had in my bag. They immediately offered me a dollar apiece for my two extras and I made the sale.

The next morning, on my way back to the fraternity house I stopped in at a diner for a cup of coffee before checking in. There were two Theta Xi pledges, both of whom I knew, sitting on stools. They'd been out looking for cornerstones all night. I asked them if they had been out looking for cats yet. They hadn't, but they expected to do that soon. I showed them the cat I had in my bag and told them I didn't know what would become of it, but that I would try to keep track of where it went. If they would meet me on the corner of South University and Washtenaw as soon as they were let out that night, I'd see if I could give it to them.

Seventeen of our fellows had managed to find black cats. While the unsuccessful hunters were being lined up for their paddling, the active chapter members told me and the other pledges to take our seventeen cats over to the Gamma Phi Beta house and dump them in the kitchen window. It seemed like an awful waste of black cats to me, especially when they'd all be needed by someone again that night. On the way across the backyard I told my pledge brothers to hold off dumping the cats for a few minutes. I took two empty gunnysacks and scurried around to the front door of the Gamma Phi house, which couldn't be seen from our windows. When I banged on the door, my knock was answered by a girl in a housecoat. I told her that some bad boys were about to dump some black cats in the kitchen window. If she'd like me to I'd catch them before they ran all through the house. Evidently the Gamma Phis had been through this black-cat business before. They understood immediately that they were about to have their annual deluge and they let me right in. As a matter of fact they accompanied me to the kitchen, and when the windows inched up and the cats came tumbling in, they helped me catch them. They also helped me a lot by screaming and carrying on. Two of them ran out the back door and around to the front of the house as though they were in a panic. Everyone was satisfied— my pledge brothers who were outside listening to the screams and the members of our active chapter who were watching from the back windows. I was satisfied. I had all seventeen of those black cats tucked away in gunnysacks. They were doing quite a lot of growling and fighting in those two sacks, so I had to send one of the girls out to pick up more bags. I eventually got compatible cats in the right bags.

In order that my brothers wouldn't see me, I had to detour around two blocks and approach our house through the bushes by the kitchen. I put the cats in the coal bin in the subbasement and gave the porter a dollar to keep quiet about it. That night I met the Theta Xis on the corner. They were looking for cats all right, and I took them over to the coal bin and sold them the whole lot for a dollar apiece. I was now eighteen dollars ahead.

As I wandered around on my errand that night I got to thinking about those cats and that eighteen dollars. I knew I was in a seller's market. I tried to put myself in the position of a Theta Xi. It seemed to me that if I was a Theta Xi and that if I was going to dump seventeen cats in the kitchen of a sorority house, I'd dump them in the Kappa Alpha Theta house right across the street. After I'd checked in at our house the next morning and was dismissed, I rushed for the Theta house and knocked on the door. I told the girl in the housecoat that I thought some bad boys were going to dump some black cats in the kitchen windows. I knew my business by this time. When the first cat popped through the opening I had my team ready. Some girls squealed, some helped catch cats, and some stood ready with brooms to rush out and chase the boys away. The whole operation took ten minutes and the Thetas let me out through the screen porch on the side away from the Theta Xis. I took the cats and put them back in the coal bin and paid the porter another dollar. There was one thing I hadn't counted on; there were twenty-two cats instead of seventeen.

I sold the twenty-two cats to the Phi Psis and I was thirty-nine dollars ahead. It would be nice to report that I went through the whole thing the next morning but I didn't. I made a slight miscalculation. I was sure the Phi Psis would dump the cats in the Chi Omega house, but some influential member was dating a Kappa and so the cats were dumped there, two blocks down Hill Street. Before I realized what had happened my collection had been dispersed to chase mice up and down sorority row or find their way back to wherever they came from. (Two of them showed up at our back door and hung around for a long time. I suppose they thought the coal bin was home.)

Hell Week ended soon after the cat episode. At the end of it I was given my pin and made a full member of Phi Kappa Sigma. I never did have a chance to make any more money out of cats. Long before I ever took part in another fraternity initiation, Hell Week had become a thing of the distant past. No one needed cats anymore.

V

I needed the thirty-nine dollars I got from those cats. There wasn't a day in that whole school year when I was not financially strapped. As I have mentioned, there was a significant change in the Depression in the early fall of 1930. The fat on which people had been living all summer was gone. Once again the expected upturn did not come and there was nothing to do but jam on the brakes. The auto factories had kept a substantial part of their work force employed by making an early change to the 1931 models, but the new models weren't selling. The factories shut down. In Flint, for the first time, there was mass unemployment. Instead of spending money grudgingly, no one was spending any money at all. Prices began to drop. Gasoline sold at six gallons for a dollar. Then it was seven gallons for a dollar. Then eight. Cigarettes dropped to fourteen cents a pack, then twelve, then ten. One could get a complete luncheon in a restaurant for nineteen cents. Coal, the staple on which my father had come to depend, declined. In the summer of 1930, soft coal retailed at seven dollars and a half a ton. In the fall it dropped to six-fifty, then to six, and finally to five-fifty. There was no comparable decline in what it cost my father. A fifty-ton car of coal came to about $225, of which $150 went to the railroad for freight —an item that didn't go down. At the 1930 summer prices, this car retailed at $375, a profit of $150 before delivery costs. By the middle of the winter my father was realizing only thirty-five dollars before delivery. He estimated, then, that he was netting about fifteen dollars per car of coal. If three tons of coal went out of the yard without his getting paid for it, he lost money, and that was exactly what was happening. As the people in the auto factories were laid off the whole credit structure collapsed. At the first sign of cold weather people began calling for fuel. They wanted it on credit. After it had been delivered they would use it up. A day or two before it was gone they would rush in and pay for it, and the very next day they would call for another ton on credit. It all amounted to a cash business except for that first ton for which they always owed. Sooner or later a cold spell would come along and they wouldn't quite get the first ton paid for before they needed a second ton. It was then a question of deciding whether to extend extra credit. It was never an easy decision to make and it caused my father hours of anguish. He knew that these people were not dishonest. They were just trying to keep body and soul together. They were sitting up nights, wracking their brains, seeking some way to get through until more money came in. No matter how carefully they figured, things wouldn't work out right. In that winter of 1930–31 destitution was a new experience for everyone. My father didn't turn many people down. For almost everyone in a business where necessities were being sold, this was the pattern. In businesses that sold things which weren't needed desperately it was worse. Days would go by without a customer coming into a store. If the businessman was lucky enough to have a reserve left he could keep the store open, usually sitting there all by himself. He let his help go and hung on until there was nothing left. Business places began to disappear. The clothing store where we'd always traded closed its doors. The furniture store down the street from the lumberyard went bankrupt. And every time a store closed there were more people out of work. Even my father, who was relatively busy hauling coal, began letting his help go. The office force went first, then the mill men. By the end of the winter he was down to six truck drivers, a yard man, and one woman in the office. His credit was gone, too. With people losing their jobs all over the place they weren't paying their bills, and so he couldn't pay his bills. No one would sell him a car of coal on credit. The railroad demanded cash for its freight charges. He had to have coal or go out of business and in order to get the coal he had to have cash. Every third or fourth day a carload of coal would be shoved into the yard, and he knew that if he didn't have the money on hand to pay for it, it would be taken away. From Monday morning until Saturday night he lived with one eye on the railroad and the other on payday. Every five-dollar bill that he took out of the cash drawer might be the five-dollar bill that would keep him from paying the freight on one of those cars of coal or from paying the help on Saturday night. It was a grim and desperate time.

Under these conditions my attendance at the University of Michigan was ridiculous. Unfortunately, my father had scraped together the $300 to send me off just before the pinch set in, and once enrolled in the university, the only logical thing I could do was keep going until the end of the first semester. That $300, incidentally, was the last money I got from my father. It is surprising how far it went. The tuition at Ann Arbor was forty-nine dollars a semester for residents of the State of Michigan. I paid it and I paid my room rent for the whole semester, a total of eighty dollars. I spent twenty dollars for books and ten dollars for various fees. All of this expense was incurred in the first few days so that $159 of my money was gone before I ever attended a class. When I joined the fraternity and agreed to eat two meals a day at the house, I paid the first six weeks' board bill in advance—sixty dollars. I had eighty-one dollars left and four months to go. Despite little escapades such as going horseback riding and dancing with Virginia Van Buren, I didn't spend my money foolishly. I ate my breakfasts at a diner near the rooming house, an item of expense that came to a little more than a dollar a week. My laundry was done at home and was carried back and forth by whoever happened to be hitchhiking up to Flint for a weekend. When the first of November came I still had enough money to pay the month's board bill in advance, but it only left me fifteen dollars. This dwindled away as the month passed and when

I went home for Thanksgiving Grandpa Perry gave me ten dollars out of his jury money. My father wasn't able to give me a thing. For the next month I had a hard time. For the last two weeks before Christmas vacation I had to walk all the way across the campus to the fraternity house for breakfast because I didn't have enough money to eat in the diner. I went home still owing my December board bill.

When I went to Flint for Christmas I wasn't sure what was going to happen to me when school resumed in January. There would be a new board bill waiting for me. I would owe eighty dollars. I wasn't sure whether the fraternity would cut off my meals or not, but it seemed to me that I simply had to get through one more month until the end of the semester, even if it meant that I didn't eat anything. I didn't dare think beyond that. When I sat down and added up what I would need to get through to June it came to a total of about five hundred dollars, a truly astronomical sum. I couldn't talk to my father about it. I knew that he winced every time Glad asked him for five dollars for household expenses. All I could do was hope for a miracle of some kind. It came on the last Saturday night of my vacation.

There had been a cold spell while I was home and I had gone over to the yard and got out one of the old trucks to help fill orders for coal. My father gave me ten dollars and a half for the week's work—the half was intended for movie money, a bonus. That ten dollars would get me through a few days if the fraternity cut me off.

On that Saturday night after dinner everyone in the family had gone out somewhere while I was still in the bathroom washing off the coal dust. I was alone in the house and I had just finished dressing when the front doorbell rang. I found a stranger standing on the front porch. He asked me my name and when I gave it to him he shoved a piece of paper in my hand. It was a summons. I was to appear in court on Monday morning, January 19, 1931. I protested. I said I couldn't be there because I would be in Ann Arbor attending classes. The man was pleasant and he apologized for serving the paper. He wondered if I could take the time to talk with him. Perhaps I wouldn't be needed. I ushered him to a chair in the living room. He began by telling me that he was the attorney for the Pere Marquette railroad. I had witnessed an accident on July 29 in which several persons had been injured. These people were now suing the railroad for $50,000. He had found my statement among the witnesses' accounts. I had said that the warning lights were blinking and that several people had tried to warn the woman not to drive onto the tracks. He wondered if I could go through the whole thing again. I did. Every now and then he would stop me to ask a question. When I was all through he nodded his head judiciously. My testimony was crucial to his case, he said, and under the circumstances he could not excuse me from testifying. He understood my position, however, and he would try to call me as his first witness so that I would not lose more than a day of school. There was nothing I could do about it and I showed him to the door and shook hands with him. Just as I reached for the door knob he held up his hand and took a wallet from his pocket and removed three bills from it and gave them to me. I looked down to see thirty dollars.

"That ought to take care of your round-trip bus fare between here and Ann Arbor, and it will provide you with meals and lodging while you are here," he said.

After he'd gone I stood there and looked down at that money in some disbelief. Since I would hitchhike both ways and eat and sleep at home, the thirty dollars was pure profit. With it and the ten dollars I had for shoveling coal I was assured of getting through the first semester. I hummed a little tune as I went to the closet to get my hat and coat. I had just turned out the lights when the doorbell rang again. I had a sinking feeling. I was afraid the lawyer had come to get his thirty dollars back, but there was another stranger standing on the front porch. *He* asked me my name and then *he* handed me a summons. It was for the same date in January. I told him someone must have their wires crossed because I'd just received a summons. He asked me whom I got it from and I said the railroad. He laughed.

"Well, I represent the plaintiff in this case," he said.

I ushered him to the same chair in the living room. It must have still been warm. When he began to ask me questions he wasn't interested in blinker lights or warning shouts. He wanted to know how fast the train was going. I fenced around a bit, trying to think, and then said I thought it must have been going twenty miles an hour.

"You stick to that," he said. "I can win my case on it."

We went through the same business about missing school and my being *his* first witness. When we went to the door he pulled out his wallet and handed me twenty-five dollars with the same statement about expenses. This was a little too much for my sense of ethics. I pushed the money back at him, explaining that I couldn't take it because I'd just taken thirty dollars from the railroad. He promptly pulled out his wallet and gave me another five dollar bill.

"I wouldn't want you to be prejudiced against the plaintiff," he said. "If the railroad can give you thirty dollars, so can we."

The next day before I left for Ann Arbor Grandpa Perry gave me twenty more dollars so I was able to pay my January board bill, too. The first semester was assured.

The time arrived for the trial and I hitchhiked up to Flint and put in my appearance. That was when I learned about the law and lawyers. The jury wasn't picked until Tuesday and then neither lawyer kept his promise about calling me as his first witness. The lawyer for the plaintiff never did call me. He was waiting to sandbag me when I got up to testify for the railroad. By the time I went on the stand on Friday morning, I'd missed a whole week of school. Needless to say I badgered both lawyers all week. I testified for six hours. It was plain to see that the railroad considered me its star witness. The lawyer deftly made his points about flashing lights and shouted warnings and the driver's negligence. When he turned me over to the plaintiff for cross-examination there was no attempt made to shake my testimony. The lawyer took up the matter of the train's speed. The minute I said that the train was going twenty miles an hour, there was a flurry of objections. The railroad attorney said I didn't have any way of knowing exactly how fast the train was going and the judge accepted his point. That didn't stop the other lawyer. He had diagrams and maps showing how far the train had traveled before stopping and how far I had run. By intricate and long-drawn-out questioning, he very carefully established that I was close to being right about the speed. Finally, at the very end, he triumphantly read from a Flint city ordinance. No train could travel at a speed of more than eight miles an hour within the city limits. There was now no question but that the train had been going faster than that.

When I came down off the witness stand at four o'clock that afternoon, the court took a recess. I went to the back of the room to pick up my coat and hat, and the railroad attorney came up to me and patted me on the shoulder. He told me that I had been an excellent witness and that I had established that there had been contributory negligence on the part of the woman driver. He didn't think that the speed of the train was important at all. After this brief discussion he quietly beckoned for me to follow him down to a small office nearby. There he took out his wallet. He apologized for having kept me away from classes all week but said that he couldn't help it. He realized that my time was very important and wondered if I'd care to put a price on it. I looked at him in bewilderment. I didn't have the slightest idea what my time was worth. I was about to blurt out that Grandpa Perry got three dollars a day for serving on juries and that I would settle for that when he removed three bills from the wallet and slipped them in my hand. Then he walked quickly away. I watched him go and then looked down at the bills. I expected to see ten dollar bills. What I saw almost made me sit down and catch my breath. The bills were fifties!

I didn't go back to Ann Arbor until Sunday afternoon. I spent most of the intervening time in my room with a pad and pencil, trying to figure out some way to stretch that money so that I could get through to June. I needn't have worried. While I was figuring, the case went to the jury. On Saturday afternoon the plaintiff was awarded a judgment for $25,000. On Sunday morning, while I was reading the papers, the front doorbell rang again. I found the attorney for the plaintiff standing on the porch. He came in out of the cold, but politely declined the chair I offered him. He stood in the hall and told me that he wanted to thank me for my testimony. It was my frankness and patience on the witness stand that had won his case for him. Then, just as the other lawyer had done, he apologized for having kept me away from classes for a whole week. It was really his fault. He could have called me as his first witness on Tuesday but he knew I would be the star witness for the railroad and he thought that my testimony would be more effective on his side if it came during cross-examination. He wanted to compensate me for my time and trouble and my additional expense. He pulled an envelope from his pocket and handed it to me. I opened it after he was gone. It contained a $100 bill, two twenties, and a ten!

In three short weeks my situation had changed completely. I had enough to finish the school year. The thirty-nine dollars for selling cats helped. When I left Ann Arbor in June I still owed my last board bill of thirty-two dollars. I was able to pay that off during the summer.

VI

By the summer of 1931 we were deep into the Depression. Another spring had come and gone without an upturn. All over town in Flint a big "71" appeared on the store windows. It was a reminder that each car sold meant seventy-one days of work for one man or one day of work for seventy-one men. A day or two after I came home from Ann Arbor a headline in the local paper announced that the Post Office Department had bought 185 new mail trucks from Chevrolet. It was almost a cause for a community celebration.

My own immediate world was my father's lumberyard. It was almost deserted. My father ran the office by himself. He had one man working in the mill. He had two truck drivers hauling coal. My brother and I went to work on trucks. We both got five dollars a week. It was no longer a case of needing us to take care of added summer business. We were there because we were good cheap labor and that was all my father could afford. Those big piles of lumber in the yard had dwindled to a few pitiable stacks. The concrete coal yard that I had helped build in 1929 had two very small piles of coal on it. In our family the whole effort was concentrated on keeping the yard going until the coal business started in the fall. We knew there'd be no one building houses that summer. The one house job we did sell was a surprise to us all. It was bought by a bootlegger.

The Depression kept people at home. I always think of the early 1930s as the jigsaw-puzzle years. The main means of recreation were listening to the radio and working jigsaws. In almost every house there would be a jigsaw puzzle on the table. Family and visitors would sit around and talk and put pieces in the puzzle. Whole circulating libraries of jigsaws sprang up in every neighborhood. Now that summer had come, people looked for some new means of recreation. There was a passion for gardening in 1931. Whole families would be out with trowels and hoes. There would be a vegetable garden in the backyard and a flower garden in the front yard. It struck my father that with all this beautification going on there might be a market for trellises and lawn furniture. He had lumber in his yard that he wasn't going to sell anyway and his mill was all but closed down. He had a whole showroom full of paint that wasn't moving. Late in May he and his truck drivers landscaped the front lawn of the lumberyard. They put in a rock garden and fountain and flowers and installed two big floodlights. Scattered around this miniature Eden were trellises and lawn furniture and flower boxes that had been built in the mill. Every evening from the first of June until Labor Day my father sat out there on that lawn in one of the chairs until after midnight. When it got dark a lot of Flint people, tired of working around the house and tired of being confined to it, would take the only vacation they could afford—a short ride in the family car. The lumberyard happened to be located on the main road to the only sizable lake in the vicinity and a good part of the population of the city drove by it at one time or another that summer. All of them were captivated by the lovely floodlighted garden with its flowers and the water playing on the rocks. Most of them stopped to wander around and look at it and my father was sitting there waiting for them. He sold trellises and lawn chairs and flower boxes as fast as he could write the orders. He sold them painted or unpainted. He sold them any way people wanted them. Above all else, he sold them dirt cheap. Every single morning when I started out in my truck I would have at least ten of these items on the back. They sold at anywhere from fifty cents for a simple, unpainted trellis up to fifteen dollars for a two-seater lawn chair. Every sale was cash. All of them were made in our mill; my father, brother, and the truck drivers helped build them. These sales brought in about fifty dollars a day. Beginning on Monday morning my father would put aside enough money for Saturday night's payroll. After that he would try to accumulate the $225 for a car of coal. As soon as he had enough money he would order one. The cars began coming in about the fourth of July at the rate of one a week. By fall we had enough to get a good start on the winter's business.

I have referred to 1930 as the gloomy summer. I always think of 1931 as the bleak one. Flint seemed deserted. The factories were closed down. The downtown streets were almost deserted. There were empty stores and boarded-up gas stations. The casualties were mounting. One of our neighbors was arrested for embezzlement in June. He was sent away to prison and the family were evicted from their house. It sat there, vacant and forlorn with legal notices posted all over the front of it. In July the casualties came closer to home. Jim Wiesner's father had lost a lot of money in the stock market. He didn't have any coal business to fall back on as my father did and no one wanted any plumbing done. At sometime after the crash he started drinking. By the spring of 1931 he was getting drunk every day. In the week after the Fourth of July he began to turn yellow. He had cirrhosis of the liver. He kept right on drinking and within five weeks he died of hemorrhages. My father seemed to think he had committed suicide in his own way. Whatever the case, it ended Jim's education for all time. He'd finished his sophomore year at Purdue where he was studying mechanical engineering. He took over the remainder of the family plumbing business and moved his mother and sister away from Welch Boulevard to a small one-room garage-type house in the south end. There were times in the next five years when he didn't have enough to eat.

George French had his troubles that summer, too. It was the policy in most of the auto plants to keep supervisory people busy one way or another and after the 1931 model run closed down

George's father was put to work as part of a gang that was putting new tar on the factory roofs. One day in August George's father slipped and fell three stories to the ground. He was never able to walk again. George took this very hard. He'd always had a small chip on his shoulder, and now it became a big one. I suppose that it was only natural that he would resent the circumstances that put his father up on a roof doing manual labor, but George resented everybody and everything. For two whole months he wouldn't even answer my telephone calls. And while he was in this funk he threw over the one big chance of his life. In his sophomore year at Michigan State he had been a star of the football team and Jimmy Crowley, who was then the coach at State, thought that he was almost bound to be an All-American with a great future after his graduation. After the accident Crowley came over to Flint and talked to George. Some kind of provision was made for him to stay in school, but it was typical of George that he took it as a sign that he was being made an object of charity. He told Crowley to go to hell and withdrew from school entirely. It was several months before he did anything but sit around and sulk. Finally, when it became apparent to him that he was the only adult male in his family capable of earning any money, he condescendingly took a job in a General Motors plant. By then several months had gone by and he'd lost most of his friends and opportunities.

I missed George and Jim Wiesner, but I had very little time to brood about their absence that summer. I had a lot of new interests. One of them was baseball. I hadn't been home a week before I received a phone call from Bernie O'Brien who had been my catcher on the university freshman baseball team that spring. He was going to catch for a team sponsored by Bromley's Paint Store in one of the sandlot leagues and they needed a pitcher. I joined the ranks. We played two games a week, late in the afternoon on Wednesdays and Saturdays. I pitched on Saturday and played the outfield (right-handed) on Wednesdays. I personally won eleven games and lost only three. Although we were supposed to be amateurs, old Ted Bromley would slip me five dollars every time I won a game and with the five dollars a week I was making at the lumberyard, I felt I was quite well off. After we won the championship incidentally, Ted Bromley gave me a twenty-dollar bill. That helped me pay off my bill at the fraternity.

Out of the other five evenings available to me each week, I spent two helping my father sell trellises at the lumberyard. On the three free evenings I devoted myself to girls. I'd been slow getting around to girls, but I began to pick up a little steam with Virginia Van

Buren. However, none of the girls I met at Ann Arbor was memorable. I hadn't wholeheartedly kissed a kirl since Molly Flexner, and it stands to reason that if I hadn't kissed one, I hadn't done anything else. This situation almost corrected itself that summer.

One of my pledge brothers at Ann Arbor was Bugs Huntley. Bugs came from Durand where his father was an engineer on the Grand Trunk Railway. When school was out in June, Bugs piled most of my belongings into his family car and hauled them home to Durand. I was supposed to go over there and get them, but before I ever had a chance to do so Bugs came driving up to our house one night to deliver them. Two girls were in the car with him. One was his fiancée and the other was his sister Sarah. Bugs had never mentioned the fact that he had a sister, but the minute I laid eyes on her, I approved of the idea. The best way to describe her, I think, would be as curvy. There wasn't very much of her that ran in a straight line. She had a boyish bob and a peaches-and-cream complexion. Her manner was a throwback to the flapper days. She was coy. She loved to snap her fingers, and she jiggled her clothes around in a provocative way when she walked. Sarah had just graduated from Kalamazoo State Teacher's College that June as a music major and she was about to take a job as a teacher in the Upper Peninsula.

On the night I first saw Sarah Bugs suggested that we go dancing over at Lake Fenton, seventeen miles away, so I crawled in the back seat and away we went. We hadn't covered one of those seventeen miles before I discovered that Sarah was a great girl in a back seat. We began rolling around like a couple of gymnasts. From the moment I first touched her, I had the feeling that I was always on the verge of seducing Sarah. My hands wandered up and down and she let them wander. As they wandered she purred in my ear, whispering sweet "oooohs" and "aaaahs." She bestowed warm, lipstick-laden kisses on me and ruffled my hair with her hands.

Our dancing took up very little of our time that first evening— about ten minutes out of every hour I would say. I didn't get home until four o'clock in the morning and I was thoroughly aroused and thoroughly pleased. Unfortunately, there had been one drawback to the whole business. Every time we left the dance floor and sneaked out to the car to resume our necking, we found that Bugs and his girl had beaten us to the back seat. That in essence was the story of my whole summer with Sarah. It is simply impossible to seduce a girl whose brother is always in the front or back seat. The Depression played a part in my frustration, too. Our family was now down to one car and in 1931 that car was two and a half years old. The tires were going bad and there had been some engine trouble. My father was reluctant to let me drive it the eighteen miles over to Durand and back. There was the further fact that my brother Walter had graduated from high school that summer and he was now old enough to compete with me for the car's use. As it turned out, I only managed to get to Durand three times all summer and when I did get there I always had to take Bugs and his girl with us. There wasn't any way I could refuse him. After all, he'd driven Sarah over to Flint to see me a dozen times. I liked Sarah immensely. She was a warm, witty, and pleasant person. Her main contribution to my life was a subtle thing. I stopped thinking of girls ambiguously. For the first time in my whole life I realized that the angels and the devils were one and the same person, and that there was a little of each in every girl. That's what made them so wonderful. I only saw Sarah that one summer—for a few brief weeks. She soon got married and disappeared from view, but I always remember her fondly for what she was and for the awakening she brought me.

There were other girls that summer. I had a date here and a date there. I even had a few dates with Molly Flexner, but that love affair was gone forever. It was along in August that I first met Gretchen Hoeffner. She was tall and lovely and blonde, and she had been a member of my brother's graduating class at Northern High School. She'd started coming around our house a lot and I took it for granted that she was there as part of my brother's crowd. It took me a long time to realize that she was there to see me. This may sound egotistical, but it is the truth. When I finally woke up, stupid dolt that I was, I asked her for a date.

From the very beginning I was conscious of all the good things about Gretchen. She was the most truly beautiful girl that I had ever known, inside and out. Her accomplishments were many. She was the best dancer I ever danced with in my life. She was utterly charming and considerate. Because she was Austrian, she spoke with a captivating Viennese accent. She had a delicious sense of humor. Many years later, in *Guys and Dolls*, Frank Loesser described what happens between two people as "a matter of chemistry." I can well believe it. In that early fall of 1931 I was practically presented with one of the real prizes it has ever been my pleasure to know, and nothing happened. For the next three years, when I was in Flint, I had two dates with this wonderful girl every week. Sometimes I had more. And I regret to say that in that whole three years I never kissed her once. She was probably the nearest thing to a sister that I ever had.

VII

There was no chance that I would go back to Ann Arbor in the fall of 1931. When it came time for school to open, my father called me into his office and said he wouldn't be able to get the money together. I had accepted that state of affairs for a long time and I wished that he hadn't felt it necessary to call me in and break the news. I think that his admission that he couldn't fulfill my mother's wish was one of the worst defeats he suffered.

It was a peculiar thing about my father and everyone else. No one had any perspective on things. We were living in a world where all the people were broke, where everyone was struggling for survival, where forces beyond our understanding and remedy were operating on us, and still we were embarrassed to death at our predicament. While part of my father's predicament stemmed from his foolishness in the days of the bull market, those original roots of his trouble no longer had any meaning. By the fall of 1931 while tiptoeing along on the verge of bankruptcy, he seemed unable to realize his true situation. All of his failures caused him shame and anguish.

The thing that most Americans forget about the Depression after all these years is that even as late as 1931 nearly everyone still thought in old-fashioned terms. A man's troubles were his own troubles and it was expected that he would face them and surmount them by himself. There had been some discussion during that summer about a dole, but hardly anyone favored it. Even those who did favor it talked about it as though it applied to someone else not themselves. People like Jim Wiesner, who was going hungry that fall, would never have gone on the welfare. It was unthinkable in a society which still talked of the inhabitants of the country poorhouse as ne'er-do-wells. And in 1931 the county poorhouse was still about the only center for public assistance.

In our family we had a good example of the way most people

were thinking and acting. We lived on the corner of Welch Boulevard and Euclid Avenue. In the house behind us lived an old couple by the name of Berry who had owned and operated a small grocery store in the neighborhood for many years. In the spring of 1930 while I was still in Kemper, their car had been struck by an interurban during an evening drive. Mr. Berry was killed and Mrs. Berry was paralyzed from the waist down. The old lady had spent more than a year in the hospital and had finally been brought home in that summer of 1931. She was helpless and needed the services of a full-time nurse, but in the months since the accident the interurban company had gone bankrupt and there had been no financial settlement.

Grandpa Perry was our family ambassador to the neighborhood and old ladies were his field of special interest. During the warm weather he would go over and sit on Mrs. Berry's front porch in the evening. It didn't take him very long to discover that she was in desperate straits. There was literally no place for her to go except the poorhouse, but this was impossible because she wasn't a pauper. She still owned a store and that house even if she didn't have a penny. Grandpa Perry didn't think she belonged in the poorhouse anyway. As he put it, she had never done anything in her whole life to deserve a disgrace like that. In August Grandpa undertook to liquidate the grocery store which had been closed since the accident. It was the wrong time to try to liquidate anything, and only enough money came in to pay off the old lady's accumulated medical expenses. It was at this point that Grandpa dismissed the nurse and moved right into Mrs. Berry's house. He did everything for her. He cooked and cleaned the house; he carried her up and down the stairs; he dressed and undressed her and lifted her in and out of bed; he bathed her; he even lifted her on and off the toilet. Every day he took her for long walks in her wheelchair and he organized the other neighbors to come in and stay with her so that he could go down and sit on his juries. He used what money he made to buy her food and medicine.

Grandpa was then a man of eighty and my father thought he was trying to do too much. My stepmother was scandalized. After all, Grandpa was a man and Mrs. Berry was a woman, and it wasn't right for Grandpa to be living over there. Grandpa stuck to his guns and went right on with what he was doing. Somebody had to take care of the old lady and he seemed to be the only one to do it. After his experience in liquidating the store, he wasn't going to put the house on the market where it would bring nothing. All that fall Grandpa lived over there at Mrs. Berry's. She finally died in her sleep just before Christmas and Grandpa came back home. Early in 1932 it developed that Mrs. Berry had made out a will. The only thing she had to leave to anyone was her house and furniture, and she left them to Grandpa, her "great and good friend."

The house that Grandpa inherited was not very pretentious. It was a square box of a place with three bedrooms and a bath upstairs and an old gas hot-water heater next to the coal stove in the kitchen. There was even a hand pump on the sink. It was probably the first house built in our part of town. There was considerable argument in our family about what Grandpa should do with the house. The consensus seemed to be that he should sell it but Grandpa wouldn't do it. All through the winter after Mrs. Berry died, he puttered around over there, painting the place and papering it himself. He used what jury money he made to modernize the plumbing, install a new gas range, and put in a new furnace. In the spring he planted a big vegetable garden in the backyard. Eventually in the summer of 1932 he rented it out for thirty dollars a month. That house eventually played a big part in our family history.

The decision that I would not go back to school in the fall of 1931 was made in the midst of the scandal that surrounded Grandpa's moving in with Mrs. Berry. I think that my stepmother would have prevented his moving, except that his removal next door made one less mouth to feed in our house. Glad was still watching every penny and still nagging at us day and night. Of course, my decision to stay home removed one major worry from her agenda, but this was partly offset when my father decided to let my brother Walter enroll in Flint Junior College, a move which cost thirty-five dollars. The truth of the matter is that we were learning to live with Glad's constant preoccupation with money. As time passed it became a standing joke. My father no longer snapped back at her, and my brothers and I had found that the best way to handle her was to agree with everything she said and then go and do what we wanted to. Now and then my father would give one of us an extra half dollar with the warning, "Now don't tell Glad about this." I have long since come to the view that Glad was good for all of us, because we never spent a dime without thinking what she would say when she found out. We needed some restraint. The one important thing to remember about our family and most other families of the time was that the Depression welded us into tight-knit little groups. In spite of the bickering, it would never have occurred to any of us to act outside the interests of the family. I was nineteen years old in the fall of 1931 and the thought of leaving home and going out on my own had never occurred to me. It wasn't simply a question of having no ambitions. I knew that my father needed my help and at the moment all our interests were centered in the need to keep the lumberyard going for our livelihood was there. When the decision was made that I wouldn't go back to school it was a foregone conclusion that I would work for my father. There was no discussion of it at all. About a week after my brother entered junior college there was a change in the weather. The coal season was at hand. I took over one of the coal trucks.

Driving a lumber truck is one thing. Driving a coal truck is something else again. Delivering coal is the hardest work I know. On an ordinary day I delivered eight tons of it. It had to be shoveled on the truck and it had to be shoveled off the truck. Sometimes I stood at the back of the truck and threw each shovelful through a window into the coal bin. Sometimes I shoveled it into a chute. Quite often I had to shovel it into baskets and then carry the baskets down a flight of stairs into the basement. It didn't make any difference. I was forever bending over and lifting. Like all other coal-truck drivers I worked with a huge scoop shovel that held about fifty pounds of soft coal or coke. At some time during that winter I figured it out that it took me forty scoops to load one ton and forty to unload it. This meant that I lifted fifty pounds 640 times a day.

There is one trouble in using the word "ordinary" in this occupation. Only a few days were ordinary. The coal business was a peculiar one during the Depression. In Michigan everyone had to have fuel. It was as much a necessity as food. In an era when practically everyone was broke, it had become a habit with most people to put off buying anything until it could not be put off any longer. Householders would eye their coal bins, expertly estimating whether they could get by for one more day or over a weekend without having to replenish the supply. Quite often people would wait until they had thrown the last shovelful into the furnace before they spent their precious dollars for another ton. In a period of ordinary weather we would go along for several days delivering our eight tons a day, but at the first sign of a dropping temperature the phone in my father's office would start to ring in earnest. That dropping temperature meant that a hotter fire would be needed and that more coal would be used. Those carefully nursed last shovelfuls in the bin wouldn't go as far as had been expected. The colder the weather got the more the phone would ring. During any one of the four or five bitter cold spells we could expect in the normal Michigan winter the phone would be busy from early in the morning until late at night. Saturdays were always busy days as homeowners reluctantly decided that they couldn't take the chance of getting over the weekend. On Saturdays, and for as long as a cold spell lasted, a coal-truck driver knew he would deliver more than eight tons a day. On an eight-ton day it wasn't hard to get the work done in eight hours. On a moderately cold day when we would deliver ten tons, we could still finish in eight hours by stepping up the pace. But when a blizzard or a long, bitter cold spell came along we would move up to twelve, fourteen, or sixteen tons a day and our hours of work would extend in proportion, depending on how hard it was to get around in traffic. On a sixteen-ton day we could expect to work from seven in the morning until ten at night. If one of the cold spells coincided with a Saturday, which was busy anyway, we could expect to haul twenty tons. On one bitter, cold Saturday in February, 1932, I hauled twenty-two tons. I went to work that day at six in the morning and I weighed out with my last load at eleven thirty that night. I got back to the office at twelve forty-five in the morning after eighteen and three quarter hours of back-breaking work. In Michigan most of the cold spells would last for several days so that I often put together a whole week of sixteen-ton, twelve-hour days, one right after another. During that bitter blizzard in February, 1932, when I had my twenty-two-ton day, I went to bed six nights in a row at midnight or after and I was back on the road again at six in the morning.

Driving a coal truck was dirty work and it was performed under the worst possible conditions. Toward the end of the winter I could never get clean. The coal dust was deeply imbedded in my pores. Whenever I washed or took a bath the water would run down the drain like ink. Once on a Sunday I took three baths in one day, and after the third bath the water was as black as after the first one. The worst part of all was the weather. Driving a coal truck is outdoor work and there is no way to get out of the cold. On that day when I delivered twenty-two tons I was outdoors for the whole eighteen and three quarters hours in temperatures that ran as low as thirty below zero and which never got above fifteen below. Of course, the colder it was the harder I worked. It was the best way to keep warm. The worst days were the wet ones when I was out in a driving rain or sleet storm. I came home more than once to wring the icy water out of my underwear.

I don't recall that any of my father's truck drivers complained. To begin with they were thankful to have a job. In the second place there was a definite responsibility to driving a coal truck. When that phone started ringing there was no way to avoid it. It was absolutely unthinkable to leave a family without heat in the house on a cold night. Until the last customer was served no one thought of going home. I took pride in holding up my share of the load. The hard work certainly didn't harm me. Those seven months on the coal truck were the healthiest I ever knew. My appetite was amazing. On one of those cold days I remember eating seven pork chops and a whole loaf of bread for lunch. God knows what I ate for dinner, my main meal.

Beginning in that fall of 1931 my father's truck drivers were paid on a tonnage basis. During one of those nonexistent ordinary weeks they would make about twenty-five dollars, but during one of the cold spells a man could and often did make sixty dollars. That was good money for those times. When I took over the coal truck, however, my father agreed to pay *me* ten dollars a week. Alas, it was a myth. From the time we opened the yard on Monday morning, at which time we usually had nothing in the till, until we closed on Saturday night, we were in a perpetual financial squeeze. As the money came in my father would put the fifty cents a ton for the drivers in a tin box under the counter. All over and above that he would put in the safe for more coal. Whenever it reached the sum of $225, he would send off a postcard ordering another carload. As the winter of 1932 progressed more and more people began to burn coke instead of the traditional soft coal and the coke came from the local gas company. Usually on my first trip of the morning I would take enough money out of the coal-reserve fund in the safe to pay for the coke we had on order for the day and deposit it at the gas-company scales. No one trusted us for a dime, but we were still in the position of having to extend credit ourselves. It was always a question whether we were going to make it or not. On Saturday nights I was always the last one to be paid and by then there was hardly enough left to pay me. Quite early in that winter my father and I adopted a ritual. After everyone else had gone home and we were alone in the office he would bring the cash drawer in and put it on his desk. Then we would split whatever was in it. Now and then I got my full ten dollars, but it wasn't often. I usually got three or four dollars. The low point in that whole winter came on that cold February night after I had delivered twenty-two tons of coal. On that occasion my father and I each took home the magnificent sum of $1.08! Nights like that were hard on me but they were harder on my father. He almost cried that night. A few weeks later I discovered he was keeping a sheet in his ledger on which he faithfully kept track of all the money he owed me—the amount he was short of the stipulated ten dollars. I never collected any of it; I didn't want to. Late in the summer I tore that sheet out. It seemed useless for him to have to see it every time he thumbed through the book.

The time passed quickly that winter. It was bound to with all that hard work. Yet in spite of all the frustrations, in spite of those nights at home working jigsaw puzzles, and in spite of Glad's constant chanting about pennies, I had a good time. The most enjoyable thing about that winter was the dancing. The nearest thing to a community center in Flint was the Industrial Mutual Association Auditorium, commonly called the IMA. It was huge and could accommodate four thousand people for dancing. In the early fall of 1931 the IMA inaugurated a big-name-band policy. This was the heyday of the big-name bands and I think I danced to every one of them. It didn't make any difference how much coal I had shoveled during the day or how long I had worked, I always went dancing with Gretchen on Wednesday and Saturday nights when the bands were there. That dancing was the one wonderful thing about the Depression. It was primarily for the young and the young all came, but a lot of older people came too. It was an inspiring sight to go up in the balcony and look down at the crowd moving to the music. The lights were low, and every now and then a spotlight would roam over the dancers. It was always a cheerful crowd. There was something about the singable music and having a lovely girl in your arms that made you forget your troubles. It was even possible to dream a little.

Dancing at the IMA was not expensive. It cost a dollar a couple to get in. If one wanted refreshment a Coca-Cola cost a nickel. After the dance a fellow could take his girl to a hamburger stand and buy a bag of six sandwiches for a quarter. Even at those prices I wasn't always able to scrape the money together. It made no difference. If I was up against it, Gretchen would say, "Let's go dutch." Girls often did that in the 1930s.

Paradoxically the Depression was a period of great elegance, not only in Flint but all over the country. Girls had taken to wearing long dresses that swept the floor and most of them did their hair up in elaborate coiffures. This elegance was in reaction to the everyday drabness about us, I suppose. Whatever the case, most people jumped at the chance to get away from the jigsaw puzzles and Eddie Cantor warbling his incessant "Potatoes Are Cheaper" on the radio. Every few weeks, whenever the IMA could think up a reason for it, a formal night would be decreed. Tuxedos and formal gowns weren't required, but people were encouraged to wear them if they had them. I always wore mine. (I had trouble with my tux because the coal dust used to rub off on my shirt.) The longer the Depression went, the more elegant people got. By 1937 most of the fellows I knew had stopped wearing tuxes. They were wearing white tie and tails. And it wasn't only the young who went in for this kind of thing or what had once been the middle class. Factory workers would dig out the best they had to go out and celebrate anything and everything they could find to celebrate if they could scrape up the pennies to do it. One night I went to an IMA formal and ran into Buddy Grandy and his wife. Buddy was nearing forty at the time, the father of six children who always looked hungry. Somewhere Buddy had borrowed a tux and his wife had borrowed a black formal, and they were dancing around cheek to cheek. I asked Buddy about it the next time I delivered his coal.

"I couldn't stand it any longer," he told me. "I just had to do *something*."

VIII

The long cold winter of 1932 came to an end and with the spring came the newest disasters. Most of the factory workers in Flint had averaged about four months of work on the new 1932 models and now they were all unemployed again. The 1932 cars had been the most tremendous failures in the history of automaking. In an effort to sell them the manufacturers had put all kinds of new gadgets on them—things like free wheeling and wizard control. Some of these devices had never been adequately tested and when people began to complain there was an uproar. Of course, the cars wouldn't have sold anyway. Very few people had money enough to buy new cars. It made no difference. There was a wholesale firing of the engineering staffs at the various plants. Herman Weckler, the chief engineer at Buick, was our next-door neighbor and he received the bad news. Within four blocks of our house I could count ten men who lost their jobs in this purge. A man with the genius of Herman Weckler didn't suffer, of course. He soon moved down to Detroit as chief engineer at Dodge, but among the others I knew it wasn't that easy. Three of these men committed suicide in the ensuing months. Some of them suffered physical breakdowns. Most of them lost their houses.

Once again my friends were involved in tragedy. If cars weren't selling they certainly didn't have to be transported. About a month after the spring layoff, Hank Feller's father went bankrupt. Three days later he had a stroke. He lingered on in his house for three years, unable to move or talk, while the battle over his crumbled assets was waged by a horde of lawyers. Item by item, the family treasures were sold off until Mr. and Mrs. Feller were living in a bare house with three straight-backed chairs and two cots. Hank was just finishing his junior year at Ann Arbor when this happened. In spite of his athletic scholarship, things became hard for him. He not only had to get through school but he had to help his parents. He was a dogged, determined boy, and because he had put so much store in that degree, he elected to try the impossible. He took all kinds of jobs. He mowed lawns and swept out university buildings. He also worked a full ten-hour day as a dishwasher in an all-night restaurant. He made only two brief visits home to see his father all summer long. When school started in the fall he did the board job furnished him by the athletic department. He also acted as the janitor in an apartment house. Now and then he clerked in a down-town Ann Arbor store. He became gaunt and uncommunicative. He survived and he got his degree, but I still don't know how he did it. It left a permanent mark on him.

One of my father's best friends was a man named Ed Ellington, a wholesale lumber dealer. One night in the early summer of 1932 he came to our house and sat on the swing with my father. He was in obvious distress. The mortgage had just been foreclosed on his house and he didn't know what to do. He had no place to move to. He'd sold just three carloads of lumber in three years. His car had 250,000 miles on it and he didn't have enough money to buy new tires for it. Without that car he couldn't travel and sell any more lumber. My father gave him a drink and tried to encourage him, but it was like the blind leading the blind. My father had about thirty cents in his pocket at the moment and that was his complete fortune. Mr. Ellington disappeared. No one knew what had happened to him for a long time. Mrs. Ellington was taken in by neighbors. About three years later a man came to see her. He was a lawyer who represented the Chicago and North Western railroad. Mr. Ellington had been killed in a train wreck up in Minnesota. He was a hobo riding in the reefer of a refrigerator car when the wreck occurred. He had been well over sixty when he left home.

Things didn't look very promising for my family that summer either. We had limped through another winter and had come to the end of another coal season. We still had no money and we could look forward to absolutely nothing. It was obvious that no one was going to buy any lumber in that summer of 1932, but even if anyone had wanted to buy any, we had precious little to sell. The trellises and lawn furniture we had built the previous summer had used up most of what we had and there was hardly a respectable board left in the place. We didn't even have enough to make any more trellises and lawn furniture. It was going to take some kind of a miracle to get us through that summer. Fortunately, there were a few assorted miracles left around and one of them came walking into my father's office early in May.

I've often wondered how much money my father had on his books that people never paid him. It must have been a considerable amount. By 1932 we had been through three Depression winters. In each one of them a lot of people had ended the season owing him for one or two tons of coal. When one has five hundred people, each one owing ten dollars, it represents a tidy sum. Beyond that, there was all that coal that had been put in under summer contract in 1930. We had only received about half the money for that. Every day someone would come into the office and pay fifty cents or a dollar on one of those old bills, and my father would put the money in the safe, trying to accumulate coal for the coming winter, but in that whole summer of 1932 he was only able to buy three cars. In the meantime, he and my brother and I took care of everything that had to be done in the lumberyard. The last truck driver had disappeared with the coal business in April.

There was one substantial group who owed my father money whom I have not mentioned. Back in 1929 there had been twenty or thirty contractors buying lumber in the yard. Most of these contractors had been caught in one way or another when the crash came. We hadn't heard from them or seen them in three years. Some of them were dead. Most of them were bankrupt. I would have to say that, as a group, these men must have owed my father in the neighborhood of half a million dollars. My father took the same view of them as he did of his coal customers. They were all honest. If they could pay him what they owed him, they would pay. There was no use dunning them for what they didn't have. To dun a man who was broke did nothing but add to his misery.

The man who came walking into the office on that May day was David Kringold. David had built a hundred houses before the Depression and he had ended up owing my father $50,000. Among the houses he had built was a whole block of modest workingmen's homes on the street directly behind the lumberyard. At the time he had built them they had sold for $3,000. Now they had all come back to him one by one. He had twenty empty houses on his hands. He came to see us with a proposal. He wanted to settle his debt to my father for twenty-five cents on the dollar. Twelve thousand five hundred dollars would have solved all my father's immediate problems. Unfortunately, Mr. Kringold was offering a paper twenty-five cents on the dollar. He offered three of those empty $3,000 houses on the next street and an empty lot in another part of town for which he had paid $3,500 in 1928. Even if those houses could have been sold, and they couldn't have been, they weren't worth more than $800 apiece. It didn't make any difference. It was either take the deal or nothing at all. My father took it.

It was that empty $3,500 lot that provided the miracle. It was in what was known as the East Court Street subdivision. The East Court Street section had been laid out in the late 1920s as the most exclusive residential area of the city, but the development had gone slowly and not more than twenty-five houses had been built before the crash. All of them were fine big homes on large lots. Some of them were mansions. Since 1929, however, not one new house had been built in the whole subdivision. George French and I had driven out through that area at different times in one of his old cars and it was a pretty forlorn area. Street signs stuck up out of the weeds and we thought it a great joke to drive out across the fields and stick out a hand for a left turn at one of the nonexistent street intersections that had been planned so hopefully in good times.

The day after my father became the owner of a lot in this subdivision, he went out to have a look at it. He found that it was a choice lot indeed. It was a wooded corner lot on a small hill about two of those nonexistent blocks from an imposing house that had been built by the city's leading surgeon in better days. It had water, sewer, and gas.

After his visit to the lot, my father did a strange thing. He came back to the lumberyard and walked all around it. It was almost as forlorn as the East Court Street subdivision. The biggest pile of lumber in it was at the back of the yard. It was a pile of cull lumber that had accumulated over the seven years my father had been in business. Every warped and twisted two-by-four, every splintered sheathing board, and every other stick of unsalable wood had been thrown on that pile. Some of the two-by-fours looked like corkscrews. Some of the boards were so full of holes they looked like soup strainers. No one had ever known what to do with this pile of scrap lumber. For a time it had been cut up for kindling and a bundle had been sent along with each ton of coal, but the Depression had long since stopped that practice, for we couldn't afford to pay anyone to cut it up. By 1932 the pile had grown to be three stories high.

From this old pile my father pulled two crooked sixteen-foot two-by-fours. He carried them back to the mill and turned on the saws. He cut a piece off here and another piece there, studying each cut carefully before he made it. He ended up with two fairly straight eight-foot two-by-fours. The next thing I knew he had called in three of his truck drivers who had been out of work for nearly a month. He offered them a deal. He would deed over to each of them one of the three houses he had been given by David Kringold. They would own the houses free and clear. In addition he would advance them grocery money when they needed it. In return for this he wanted them to work through the summer for nothing. None of them had any prospects and all agreed. The first job he gave them to do was to tear down that old pile of lumber, carry it up to the mill, and cut it up. He didn't care how long the two-by-fours, two-by-sixes, and two-by-eights were as long as they were straight. He didn't care how rotten and splintered a board was. He wanted it ripped down and the usable portion saved.

While this work went forward, my father and I made a complete inventory of every scrap of material we could find in the lumber-yard, good, bad, and indifferent. In some places where there had once been piles of planks, we found only a few. In other places there might be ten bundles of siding. We found twenty bundles of select oak flooring, for instance, and eight bundles of #1 Common. There was a fairly substantial pile of maple flooring and about five hundred square feet of tongued-and-grooved yellow pine. In the finish warehouse we found a small assortment of paneled interior doors, all different sizes. There were odds and ends of window sashes in different styles. There was some special sap gum interior trim that had been ordered by someone and then forgotten. There was a metal medicine cabinet with a mirrored door and there was one without a mirror. It was amazing the number of different kinds of odds and ends of things we found around that lumberyard, the relics of better days.

When our inventory was completed my father studied it for several days and then got down the books of house plans that had been accumulating dust for three years. He went through them carefully, picked out a plan, took it to the drafting board and went to work. A week after he'd begun he began calling contractors who owed him money and found one who still had a little equipment and got him to dig a basement on the lot. In the meantime, I brought George French over to the lumberyard and we wheeled out the old cement mixer into which I'd shoveled all that gravel in 1929. George overhauled the motor and got it to run, and I towed it over to the basement. It took a lot of cement to build a foundation and put in a basement floor and my father didn't want to touch any of the treasure he was hoarding for the winter's coal so he gave my brother Walter a list of his accounts receivable on which nothing had been paid for a year or more. Walter went out knocking on doors, collecting a quarter here, fifty cents there. Each morning I would take whatever he had brought in and drive the twenty miles over to the cement plant at Silver Lake and buy all the cement I could. By nine o'clock I would be back at the basement with the mixer running, pouring concrete into the forms that the truck drivers had built. Each afternoon when I shut the mixer off I would drive out to a gravel pit and load up what I needed for the next day. When the foundations were finally in and we began to lay the floor joists we found we were short by twenty two-by-eight twelves of having enough, and Walter had to go out and collect more money to buy them from another lumberyard. From time to time that summer we had to buy other things but not much. We used every scrap and all the odds and ends we had. Some of those sawed-up two-by-fours ended up three or four feet long, but the truck drivers nailed them together to make eight-food studs. When the house was finally closed in, before the siding went on, it was a most peculiar-looking place. It looked more like a shack than a shack did. There were narrow boards and wide boards, dirty boards and clean boards. It was a rare room which had two window holes the same size. One room had steel sash and another had wooden sash. During our inventory we had found a huge piece of plate glass in a crate so we used it. It may have been one of the first picture windows ever put in a living room. As the men began the task of finishing they put one kind of siding in the back and another kind in front. Two rooms had oak floors, three rooms had maple floors, and two had knotty-pine floors. I found myself reciting "There Was a Crooked Man Who Lived in a Crooked House." It seemed to me as though that place was the biggest mishmash ever constructed and I wasn't far wrong, but I had badly underestimated my father's powers of imagination. As white paint was applied, the house turned out to be absolutely beautiful. It was completed in January, 1933, at the very bottom of the Depression. As bad as things were at that time, my father sold it for $9,300 cash the same day it was put on sale. The man who bought it was a General Motors executive who had just been transferred to Flint. The house still stands on its wooded lot, surrounded by a sweeping lawn. The East Court Street subdivision eventually became what it had been intended to be and the homes surrounding the crooked house are all substantial pleasant ones, but it holds its own in this fine neighborhood. I often wonder, however, if the people who now live in it are ever puzzled by the fact that no two doors are the same size.

On the June day that I finished mixing the cement for the basement of the crooked house, I hitched the old mixer to the back of my truck to haul it back to the lumberyard. It was quite late in the afternoon so I decided to stop by home and eat dinner before putting it away. I parked on the side street beside our house, and the truck and mixer were still there when Grandpa Perry came out after dinner to smoke his evening cigar. At that time he had just rented out Mrs. Berry's house. During the winter months while he was puttering around over there, I'd put some coal in the basement so he'd have a warm house to work in. I had made the delivery on a cold rainy day during a thaw. Mrs. Berry's driveway consisted of two narrow concrete strips that ran across the lawn to the garage. When I started to back out, my wheels slipped off the strips and sank into the soft ground. Before I got back out to the street I'd torn up a lot of the lawn. It was not an unusual experience because these impractical driveways existed all over Flint and our trucks were always slipping off them. Each spring after the coal-delivering season our drivers usually spent a whole week going around to smooth out the lawns we had ruined during the winter.

I found Grandpa looking at the mixer when I came out of the house. He pointed his cigar at it and suggested that it might be a good time to put in a new driveway for him. He would pay me the first three-months' rent for it. I went back and talked to my father and he figured we could make a profit, so I agreed. The next day one of the men came over from the crooked house and helped me tear up the concrete strips and build forms for a wide solid-type drive. It took me a week to pour the concrete, and when I was done we found we'd made a twenty-dollar profit. My brother watched all this with interest and finally went around to all our truck drivers and compiled a list of those bad driveways that we'd been having trouble with over the years. It didn't seem like a good time to sell new driveways, with everyone broke, but Walter concentrated on people like policemen and school teachers and postal workers, people who had worked steadily through most of the Depression and had a little money. By the time I finished Mrs. Berry's driveway, he'd sold two more. Altogether that summer, we put in thirty-one driveways. I ended up doing nothing but hauling cement and running the mixer. We made about twenty-dollars profit out of each job. It kept us going all summer and the money helped pay for a few of the things we needed for the crooked house like plumbing supplies, wire, electrical fixtures, and hardware. We had survived. That was about all we could ask.

IX

One rainy August morning when it was too wet to pour cement, I received a telephone call from another chum of mine who wanted to know if I could ride down to Detroit with him. Lou Norris was the son of a foreman at Buick. He'd been a year behind me at Northern High School and after his graduation he had spent two years at Flint Junior College. Now he was about to transfer to Ann Arbor where he intended to complete his premedical studies. He wanted some advice about rooms and fraternities and campus life. Although Lou warned me that he would be busy talking to doctors at Ford Hospital all afternoon, I accepted the chance to go with him. It was the first time in fifteen months that I'd had an opportunity to get away from Flint.

We arrived in Detroit about one in the afternoon. Because it had stopped raining by then I went over to Navin Field, hoping to see the Detroit Tigers play the Boston Red Sox. Alas, the game had been called because of wet grounds. I tried to find a movie to while away the afternoon, but I couldn't find one that interested me. After wandering aimlessly for half an hour, I decided to take a ferry ride across the river to Windsor, Ontario. The minute I got on the ferry I realized something unusual was going on. The boat was jammed with people. They were going to the horse races at Kenilworth Park, I soon found out. I'd never been to a horse race in my life and I knew nothing about them, but this seemed like a good time to find out what it was all about. I followed the crowd and soon found myself sitting in a grandstand. I sat through the first race without quite knowing what was going on. The man next to me was jumping up and down and waving his fists in the air and shouting at the top of his voice. When the race was over he sat down looking just as exhausted as though he'd been running instead of the horses. I'd found the whole thing pretty boring and I finally asked my neighbor what all the excitement was about.

"What horse did *you* bet on?" he asked, a strange expression on his face. I told him I hadn't bet on any. "Well, you just put a little bet down," he told me. "You'll find out why I was excited."

I had seven dollars. That was all the money I had in the world. After some soul searching, I decided I would risk a quarter, but when I asked my neighbor how to go about making a bet, I was shocked to learn that the smallest amount I could bet was two dollars. A quarter was one thing. Two dollars was a great fortune. I asked a lot of questions, trying to make up my mind whether to take this momentous step. My neighbor answered somewhat impatiently and it wasn't until I found out that I could bet a horse to take third and still collect if he won that I got up the courage to bet. The last question I asked my neighbor was which horse would be a good bet. He was peevish by this time and he snapped as he moved away that maybe I ought to try Sun Worship. I went down and bet two dollars on Sun Worship to show. The man had given me the red-hot favorite, of course, but it wouldn't have made any difference if he was 100–1. I cheered for him every foot of the way and after he'd won I sat down with a big sigh of relief. To my utter delight I soon found that Sun Worship had paid $2.60 to show. I was sixty cents ahead! This was the easiest way to make money in the world.

I sat there savoring my discovery for several minutes. Among the other things I noticed was that Sun Worship had paid $3.40 to place. I could have made eighty cents more if I'd been smart. I decided that the next time I bet I would bet a horse to place. Unfortunately, my next-door neighbor had moved to another part of the grandstand and I had no one to tell me whom to bet on. In a newspaper on a nearby seat I found that some reporter had predicted that Sun Worship would win. It was right there in black and white. The same reporter predicted that Grasshopper would win the next race. That was good enough for me. I went down and bought a ticket on Grasshopper to place.

I soon discovered that Grasshopper wasn't anywhere near as good a horse as Sun Worship. He seemed to stagger as he ran and he never did get into first place. I lost track of him right at the end and I was a little surprised when I learned that he had taken second and that I would get $4.40 back. Only the fact that I was now three full dollars ahead gave me the courage to go on. It eventually struck me that I could lose a race and still be ahead. I decided to plunge. I would bet a horse to win. I picked up the newspaper and read what the prophet had to say. He said that a horse named Midshipman was a sure thing to win the fourth race. Others agreed with him. I put the paper down and wended my way down to the betting ring. On the way I stopped and bought a hot dog. As I ate it I gawked at the crowd around me and eventually got around to joining the line in front of the betting windows. I'd been so far off in the clouds that I wasn't paying attention to business. When I put my two dollars down I couldn't remember which horse I was supposed to bet on. I started to open the newspaper to look for the name and when I did so the people in line behind me began yammering at me to hurry up. The ticket seller told me to bet or get out of the way. I stammered and finally blurted out that I couldn't remember the name of the horse, but that it had something to do with the Navy. He looked at his program, took a ticket from his rack, and shoved it at me. I slipped it in my pocket and hurried away. I didn't look at it until I got back to my seat and then I almost had heart failure. The ticket was on a horse named Commander. I looked in the paper to see what was said about this horse. It was horrible. One writer said he hadn't won a race in two years and there was no reason to believe he was going to change his habits at this late date. I ran back down the stairs and got in line again, intending to make the ticket seller change my ticket. I never got close. A bugle blew and the horses were on the track. I went gloomily back to my seat and tried to pick Commander out of the crowd. His jockey had on a bright green shirt. That was all I could see.

I watched the race half-heartedly. The first time the horses went by the grandstand Commander was dead last. He was still last all the way down the back stretch. At the far turn I lost sight of him. He seemed to have buried himself in the middle of the pack for shame. I agreed with him that this was probably a wise course of action. As the horses entered the home stretch, however, I saw a flash of green and sat up. That green shirt was leading the way, out in the middle of the track. The further those horses came toward the finish line, the further Commander got out in front. I sat there stunned as he won. Being a true neophyte, I had no idea what the figures meant on the odds board. I certainly wasn't prepared for what came next. A man came out and posted some numbers. Commander had paid $89.40 to win! I sat there for several minutes and then comprehension overtook me. I let out a wild whoop, jumped from my seat, and ran down the steps three at a time. I watched excitedly while a man counted out the money and shoved it out at me. I just wadded it up and shoved it in my pants pocket, then turned and ran for the exit. Twenty minutes later I was on a ferry headed back for Detroit. At the foot of Woodward Avenue I jumped on a streetcar and rode all the way out to Royal Oak. Then I rode all the way back again.

I don't suppose anyone could imagine what that experience meant to me. I hadn't seen that much money at once in years. On the way back home to Flint that evening, as Lou Norris asked me questions about Ann Arbor, I began to think about school. When I got home I went straight up to my room and took the money out of my pocket and spread it out on the bed and counted it. I had ninety-seven dollars. (It was Canadian money, incidentally, and I had to have it changed the next day.) It would cost me forty-nine dollars for tuition. Books would come to another fifteen dollars. I could surely get a room for sixty dollars a semester. It totaled $124. Even if I could get a board job, I was going to be twenty-seven dollars short of what I needed. I don't know where I got the idea that I could get along without any pocket money, but I wasn't much of a realist.

About ten o'clock that evening, after staring at the money for two hours, I went down and confronted my father. He gave me no argument. He wanted me to go back to school as much as I wanted to go back. He was overly optimistic in his turn. He would find the twenty-seven dollars I needed. He'd do better than that. He'd take the first five dollars out of the till every Monday morning and send it to me. And if he could finish the crooked house and sell it before February, he would give me $500 from the proceeds of the sale so that I could finish out the school year. And so, in one short day, my life had changed again. From a grubby laborer on the business end of a shovel I was about to turn into a college boy.

I had to find a board job. When Lou Norris went down to Ann Arbor a day or two later to find a room, I rode along with him. The minute he let me out of his car I streaked for the office of the dean of students and asked if there were any jobs. The clerk scribbled an address for me and told me that I might find a scullery job. To my surprise, the address belonged to the Gamma Phi Beta sorority house.

Our fraternity cook was named Lucretia. Her sister Lottie cooked at the Gamma Phi house. Lucretia and I had always gotten along well in that year I was a pledge. On the nights I did pledge duty and had to go out for sandwiches, I always stopped to ask Lucretia if there was anything she wanted and she had always appreciated this courtesy. Now, when I knocked at the Gamma Phi back door, my knock was answered by Lucretia who happened to be visiting her sister. She threw her arms around me and gave me a big kiss and led me inside to meet Lottie. Ten minutes later I had my board job. It wasn't a job washing pots and pans, either. Because of Lucretia, I was going to be a table waiter.

I spent too much time laughing and joking in the kitchen with Lottie and Lucretia afterward, however. I didn't leave myself enough time to find the room I wanted and I had to go back to Flint without one. Several days later I received a phone call from Bugs Huntley in Durand. Bugs had been elected the steward of our house for that year and he'd just received a note from Lucretia telling him that I would be back in school. Bugs wanted me to live in the fraternity. Phi Kappa Sigma had been hard hit by the Depression and we needed every boy we could get. The best price he could make me for a room was twenty-four dollars a month, which was almost double what I wanted to pay, but I remembered back to that other year when I had been carried after my board bill was overdue. If my father's optimistic promises didn't work out, it seemed like a good idea to keep a line of credit open. A week before school started, therefore, I called Bugs back and told him I would live in the fraternity house.

I'd had one big surprise that summer—the change from coal-truck driver to college boy. I was about to have another. Late on the Friday evening before I went back to school I had a telephone call from Molly Flexner. She wanted me to come out to the farm the next afternoon. She was getting married. I wasn't very keen about going to Molly's wedding, but she sounded so forlorn that I couldn't refuse. I was shocked when I got out there. The house was more or less boarded up from the last winter. Only three of the windows had the shutters removed. The whole place had been allowed to go to seed. The once-beautiful grounds were unmowed and uncared for. Inside the house, most of the furniture was still covered with white sheets. There were only five people present. One of them was a diffident, pleasant young man by the name of Sam Hendricks. He was to be the groom. Five minutes after I got there I discovered that I was to be the best man. There was a good reason. The Flexners were having a hard time. Mr. Flexner had lost control of his auto-parts business. His personal financial position was precarious and he had come back to Flint to see if he could make a living out of that farm he had bought for a plaything in 1929. Under the circumstances he had not felt up to going down to Palm Beach for a big wedding. So the wedding had come to him. Sam and Molly and Mrs. Flexner had jumped into Sam's old car and had driven four days to get to Flint. Sam hadn't felt like asking any of his friends to make the long trip for the affair. He didn't know anyone in Flint, but Molly thought he ought to have a best man and I was the only person she could think of. And so my first experience as a best man was at the wedding of the only girl I'd loved until that moment.

X

The Ann Arbor that I went back to was like a ghost town. The Depression had taken an alarming toll. The enrollment of the university had dropped to seven thousand students. Of the twenty-eight pledges who had been initiated with me, only six were still in school, and our previous year's pledge class consisted of only nine members of whom four had now dropped out. Seventy fellows had eaten in our dining room during my first year. Now there were only thirty-two. All the campus gathering places had closed.

No matter how broke I was, however, I spent that fall in a very posh atmosphere. Our house had been constructed in 1924 at a cost of $125,000. It sat on a huge plot of land on Washtenaw Avenue, Michigan's fraternity row, and it had sweeping lawns, front and rear, with a stand of great trees surrounding it. The house itself had four floors, luxuriously furnished. At the ground level were the dining room, kitchen, and servants' quarters. The dining room was the scene of all our social functions, including dances and chapter meetings. It could accommodate a hundred people at meals. The first floor included a spacious living room, cardrooms, and guest suites. The second floor was given over to study rooms, while the third floor contained the dormitory. Enough double-decker bunks to sleep a hundred boys were ranged along the wall of a narrow hall-like room whose windows were always open. In the winter time it was like sleeping outdoors and the brothers piled bearskin rugs, blankets, and fur coats on their beds to the depth of several inches. Separated from this dormitory by a heavily insulated wall was a short, carpeted hallway from which three more of those study-living cubicles opened. These third-floor rooms were cozy and quiet and were the most desirable in the house. They were usually occupied by seniors. (They had the additional virtue of never being visited by chaperones during parties.) All of the floors were joined by a wide, sweeping staircase at the extreme eastern end of the building, but there was a concrete-enclosed, spiral fire escape that ran straight up from the ground floor to the top floor in the middle of the house. At the bottom this debouched onto the long driveway that looped around the backyard. At the top it opened into the short hallway within a few feet of the dormitory and the three senior study rooms.

When I arrived in Ann Arbor that fall there was a state of confusion in the fraternity for no one knew who was coming back. Assignment of rooms and roommates had not been made, and in the last-minute rush I ended up with Marty Williams, a senior, whose roommate had dropped out. Because of this lucky chance I got to live in one of those choice third-floor rooms. For a good many reasons Marty and I were isolated from the ordinary things that took place in the house. Not the least of these reasons was that fire escape. Both Marty and I used it, Marty because he preferred it and I because I was waiting table at the Gamma Phi house just across our backyard. I always entered and left by the back door, and it was the natural thing to do to run straight up the fire escape to my room rather than detour out through the main body of the house. Some days I never saw any of the brothers at all.

Marty Williams was an all-A student in the School of Engineering. He affected a big handlebar moustache and a Gay Nineties wardrobe complete with derby hat and turtleneck sweaters. He was madly in love with some girl in his hometown and he went home to see her every weekend. In consequence, he worked hard while in residence, rarely taking part in the usual bull sessions and other social amenities of fraternity life. The unusual thing about this was that Marty's hometown happened to be White Plains, New York. It was no mean trick to get from Ann Arbor to White Plains and back in one weekend at a time when flying was not yet commonplace. Marty had arranged it so that he had no Saturday classes—in itself a remarkable feat for an engineering senior. Every Friday evening he would rush down to the Michigan Central depot and get aboard the Wolverine Limited for the trip to New York. This would give him Saturday and Sunday with his girl. On Sunday evening he would be aboard the Wolverine Limited for the return trip and would arrive just in time to attend his first class on Monday morning. It was no wonder that none of the brothers saw much of him. He was able to accomplish this without going into bankruptcy because his father was a high official of the railroad and Marty had a free pass. About a week before Christmas, ironically, Marty had a fight with the girl at home and almost immediately fell in love with a graduate nurse at the University Hospital. He spent most of his Christmas vacation riding the Wolverine Limited from White Plains to Ann Arbor to see his new girl.

I had my own heavy schedule. I was still on a prelaw course and I had elected one extra class so that I had very little time for socializing, but the main reason why I didn't see much of my brothers was that job at the Gamma Phi Beta house. Not only did I not eat my meals with the others but I was busy on weekends. I had five straight eleven o'clock classes which meant that I never left the campus until noon each day. We were supposed to serve lunch at 12:20, but I never got to the Gamma Phi house until 12:15 so that the other waiters had to set up the meal for my table—put out the water and perishables. In return for this favor I took over the breakfast servings on Saturday and Sunday mornings for the other boys. This kept me over at the Gamma Phi house during most of those forenoons. As time passed, moreover, Lottie, the Gamma Phi cook, came to depend on me to help her with extra chores like shredding lettuce and peeling potatoes. I was convenient, living right across the backyard. All Lottie had to do was come over to our back door and yell up the fire escape to me in my room. I didn't mind. I reaped a good many dividends—extra pieces of pie and so forth. If I was in a hurry to get out for a date or something in the evening, Lottie would set up my table for the next meal.

I had never waited table before in my life but I learned fast. The Gamma Phis wanted no trays in the dining room. Each waiter was responsible for a table of ten girls. Soon after I went to work I had learned to serve the entire table with one trip from the kitchen. I simply lined four plates along my left arm, carried four more in my left hand, and two in my right hand. This is quite a trick when accomplished with soup or aspic salads, but I never spilled anything and I never broke a dish during the entire semester.

The Gamma Phis were a good bunch of girls. Very early in the fall I discovered that one of them, Irene Young, had several classes with me. She was a pert, freckled-faced little thing who seemed to like me so I asked her for a date. All through October and November we saw each other regularly, and then I made the mistake of introducing her to Allan Higgins, one of the brothers. That was the end of Irene for me. She fell in love with Allan.

I wasn't in position to fly very high. As I had feared, I was in financial straits from the beginning. After paying tuition, buying books, and paying two-months' room rent in advance I had twenty-five dollars left. This dwindled steadily. I knew I was going to have to get some more money, but I had no idea where. I couldn't go home to Flint for weekends because of the job so that even Grandpa Perry was cut off from me. My stepmother's letters were ominous and I knew I couldn't expect anything from my father. He hadn't even been able to get thirty-five dollars together to send my brother back to Junior College. All I could do was hang on and hope.

Homecoming weekend was traditionally the first weekend in November. It meant nothing to me. For some reason I hadn't gone near the fraternity house during Homecoming in the fall of 1930 so that I had missed all the festivities surrounding the return of the alumni. Because I wasn't much a part of things in the house, I was only vaguely aware that decorations were going to be put up. I knew that two kegs of beer had been ordered from the house bootlegger but I didn't think of it as a gala occasion. I even made a date with Irene Young to go dancing at the Union.

The whole business of Homecoming began on a Friday afternoon. About four o'clock I heard Lottie's voice calling me from the bottom of the fire escape. I slipped on a sweater and ducked down to the back door and walked across to the Gamma Phi house. I never left there until I finished setting up my table about seven thirty in the evening. I was quite surprised, therefore, to find our backyard full of cars when I started home. I could see that all the lights in our house were turned on. I had originally intended to go up the fire escape to my room as I always did, but when I opened the back door the sounds of gaiety that assailed my ears were enough to make me curious. I detoured out into the main part of the house to see what was going on. I walked into the midst of a happy, milling crowd in the dining room. Men I'd never seen before, most of them with glasses in their hands, were engaged in a variety of activities. There was a group standing around a piano singing songs. There was another group gathered around a keg of beer, reminiscing. Others were taking food from a buffet table in a corner. Over at the back of the room two of the dining-room tables had been pushed together and covered with green cloth. Surrounding these tables were fifteen or twenty fellows shooting crap.

I was almost twenty-one years old and I'd never seen a crap game before. The only pair of dice that had ever entered my life belonged to the Parcheesi set at home. It didn't take me very long to understand about sevens, elevens, snake eyes, boxcars, and points, but I was rather amazed at the amount of profanity which accompanies an operation such as this. All around the table were fellows with fists full of bills, exhorting and insulting the dice. Most of these crapshooters were alumni. Only a few of the active chapter mingled with the crowd, and most of them were jiggling silver in their hands. Every now and then one of the brothers would timidly shove out a quarter or half dollar and say, "A quarter he comes," or, "A half he doesn't make it." I asked for an explanation of this phenomenon, then reached in my pocket and pulled out my money. I had the sum total of five dollars in bills and fifty cents in silver, and it had to last me until some angel gave me some more. One dollar of that sum, incidentally, was already earmarked to take Irene Young dancing at the Union that same evening. I jiggled the silver thoughtfully, and finally, when one of the brothers shoved out a quarter on the come, I plopped down two dimes and a nickel with the words, "I've got it." Almost at once the man with the dice rolled snake eyes. That had been so easy that on the next roll I put the quarter down and said, "A quarter he comes." I was covered, and a seven came out at once.

The dice moved steadily around the table, and I won several of those quarter bets in a row. I eventually had two dollar bills in my hand along with several coins. Someone nudged me and said, "Your dice." It didn't seem proper to refuse so I threw one of the dollar bills on the table and picked up the dice. I'll always remember that first roll. I threw boxcars and it almost ended my career as a crapshooter for all time. I watched forlornly as someone scooped up my money, and then, very reluctantly, I threw out the other dollar bill. I rolled a seven at once. I had noticed, among other things, that most of the dice shooters were going for "triples." This meant leaving one's winnings on the table through three rolls. I decided to go for a triple, too. I left my two dollars in the center, saw it covered, and promptly rolled an eleven. I had to win one more roll and my one dollar would turn into eight. I quickly rolled a six and came right back with another six. I picked up seven of the eight dollars, leaving one out there, and prepared to roll again. After that I lost track of everything—time, the people around me, money. Everything I did was lucky, whether it was rolling the dice myself or covering someone else's bets. I must have had one of the hottest streaks since crapshooting was invented. The word got around and some of the brothers gathered to watch me. I have no idea how long it was before someone tapped me on the shoulder, but I turned around, a fist full of bills in hand, to look into the face of Nick Woods. Nick was the best friend I had in the fraternity at the moment. We'd been pledged together and we did a good deal of chumming around. On that evening he was just getting ready to go out on a date and he was all dressed up. He had, among other things, a derby hat.

"I hear you've been lucky," he said.

"I guess so." I had no idea just how lucky. I was vaguely aware that I'd been wadding up bills and stuffing them in my pockets as I went along, and they were now sticking out everywhere. I even had a few rolled up like a cigar and stuck behind my ear.

"How about letting me count it?" Nick said, and held out his derby. I began pulling the wadded money out and trying to straighten it. "Never mind that," Nick said. "Just dump it in the hat. I'll take care of it." I went on turning my pockets inside out and letting the money fall into the derby while Nick reached up and took the bills from behind my ear. For some reason I didn't give him the bills I was holding in my fist. He took the hat and retired to a corner to count while I turned back to the game. I continued to roll the dice and cover bets, as feverishly as before. After some time I discovered, suddenly, that I had no money left in my hand. I felt in all my pockets and there was no money there, either. I had no intention of quitting, of course. I turned and looked around the dining room for Nick Woods. He was nowhere in sight. Someone said he'd gone upstairs. I bounded up the steps and looked around the first floor. He wasn't there, nor was he on the second or third floor. Nick had disappeared with my money!

I was furious. I sputtered and fussed as I wandered around looking behind shower curtains and in closets, still thinking it was some kind of a joke he was pulling. I was in the midst of this when I was called to the phone. It was Irene Young and she wanted to know why I was half an hour late for my date. I made a lame excuse, rushed up and took a shower and changed clothes. It wasn't until I got all the way down to the Union that I discovered I didn't have enough money to get Irene into the dance. Fortunately, she was a good sport and lent me enough to get in, but I was embarrassed. And I was good and angry at Nick.

I didn't see Nick the next morning. By the time I got back from serving the Gamma Phis breakfast, he'd gone off to his Saturday morning classes. I had to leave to serve lunch before he returned and I missed him again. By the time I got back to the house he'd gone off to the stadium for the football game. The Gamma Phis had a big Homecoming crowd, too, and after the game I had to go over and set up extra tables. With all that extra work it was after eight in the evening before I came across the backyard. The crap game was in full swing, but I had no money to get in it and Nick Woods had gone to take his girl to a movie. By this time I was a little numb.

After breakfast on Sunday morning Nick came up to my room and stood before me, a big grin on his face.

"I heard you were looking for me," he said.

"Of all the stinking tricks to play on a guy," I said. "I didn't even have enough money to get in the dance. I had to borrow from Reenie."

He reached in his pocket and pulled out a roll of bills and held it up for me to see.

"I think there's enough here to pay her back," he said, and tossed it to me. "If I hadn't taken it, you'd have put every cent of it back in the game." I took the rubber band off it after he'd left. There was $167 in the roll. I didn't have to worry about getting through the semester. I might add that I've never ever won another dollar shooting dice in my whole life.

XI

My education was progressing, and times were changing. I still hadn't taken a drink by the fall of 1932, but there had been a big shift in attitudes about drinking. Franklin D. Roosevelt, an out-and-out wet, had just been elected President of the United States. Even before he took office, legislation had been introduced into Congress to effect the repeal of the Eighteenth Amendment. Although students at Ann Arbor still had to deal through bootleggers, there would be no more raids on fraternity houses and we had been able to buy two kegs of beer for Homecoming without fear of any recrimination.

I'm not sure what my fraternity brothers thought of my non-drinking. I was of the opinion that I'd never made a big thing out of this virginal aspect of my life, but no person ever knows what he looks like to others and I may have made more of it than I thought. Shortly after Christmas vacation our fraternity scheduled a dance. Marty Williams had invited his new girl—Jeannie, the nurse. He suggested that I might like a date with Jeannie's room-mate, whom he kept describing as a walking dream. I had no one else in view and I agreed. The arrangements were made. About a week before the dance, Marty informed me that he was ordering a pint of whiskey from the bootlegger. He said that Kate liked a drink and that maybe it would be a good idea for me to order a pint, too. I was blatantly broad-minded about it.

"Hell, Marty," I said, "you know I don't drink so there's no use of my getting a bottle, but if Kate wants a drink, I don't mind.

I'll give you five bucks and you get a quart instead of a pint. You and the girls can all drink out of it."

Marty ordered the quart. I think he also talked to the brothers. On the evening of the dance I trudged across our backyard from the Gamma Phi house and let myself in at the bottom of the fire escape. I heard Marty yell down from the third floor as the door slammed.

"Roomie!" he shouted. "Go out in the kitchen and get us some glasses and ice before you come up."

I detoured out into the house to get the glasses and ice from the kitchen and then wandered up the main stairs instead of taking the fire escape. When I came up to the head of the stairs on the second floor, I found Nick Woods standing in the doorway of his room in shirttails, putting in some cuff links. He waved to me and pointed to a glass sitting on his dresser.

"Johnny and I are getting the party started right," he said. "How about a drink?"

"Naw," I said. "You know I don't drink."

"Well, a little ginger ale won't hurt you any."

I shrugged and went in and sat on his sofa, and he pushed a glass into my hand. We talked and I drank, eventually putting the glass down empty. I sauntered down the hall and turned into the door that led to the fire escape. As I did, Allan Higgins stuck his head out of his door. He asked me if Reenie had given me any messages for him. She hadn't.

"Damn it!" he said. "That means she couldn't get anyone to go down to the library for her. Now she'll be half an hour late." He threw up his hands in disgust. "Come on in and help me wait. I'll buy you a drink."

"Naw," I said. "I don't drink."

"A little ginger ale won't hurt you." He thrust a glass into my hand.

It was when I finished that glass that I noticed I felt differently. I went up the fire escape three steps at a time. I think I burst into song. Marty was standing in front of the mirror working on his tie.

"Hey, Roomie," he said, "how about a glass of ginger ale to get things started?"

"Damned good idea!" I banged my fist on the dresser as I took the glass he offered me. I gulped it down and then started to undress. I was singing at the top of my voice. I was also having trouble getting my pants off. Finally, I was standing there naked, looking at my clothes strewn around the floor, when I noticed an unearthly silence in the room. I looked up and there, in the doorway, were the grinning faces of half my fraternity brothers. Several of them advanced purposefully toward me, grabbed me, and lifted me horizontally over their heads to carry me down the stairs to the bathroom. There they lowered me gently into the bathtub. The tub was full of ice water. It was literally full of ice water. There were big cakes of ice floating around in it. One by one, the brothers stepped forward and pushed my head under. By the time I'd been submerged a few times I was sober—cold sober, as Nick Woods said. He extended a hand to help me out and escorted me to a hot shower.

"Let that be a lesson to you," he said. "Just be damned careful who you take a drink with."

As I dressed for my date, I had a horrible headache and there was a bad taste in my mouth. I shivered now and then. In the meantime, Marty Williams had gone off to get our dates. He and the girls arrived just as I was getting into my tuxedo jacket. He waved at me grandiloquently.

"There he is, girls. Look him over. I think he's nursing a hangover so let's all have a drink."

I turned around and immediately felt better. Kate *was* a dream. Her hair was piled high on top of her head and she had misty brown eyes and a warm smile. She was wearing a black evening dress that left her shoulders completely bare. This was at the very beginning of the strapless gown era and Kate's was the first one I'd ever seen up close. She was admirably equipped for wearing a dress like that. Without any protest I let Marty pour me a drink and after I took a few sips of it I felt better, but I was cautious. I sipped it. I didn't drink it down. By the time I finished my first one Kate was well into her second. Jeannie and Marty had long since departed for the dance floor, and Kate and I were sitting on the sofa, feinting like two Japanese wrestlers. I'd already made an exploratory run or two on that strapless gown. Whenever I managed to get Kate to sit still for a moment or two, she could be surprisingly friendly. She finally threw her arms around me and gave me a long kiss that I was sure would lead to something interesting, but right in the middle of it she jumped to her feet and pulled me to mine.

"I love you," she said. "Let's go down and dance,"

I led her down the fire escape and out the door at the bottom into the dining room. She settled down in my arms with her head on my shoulder and her arm around my neck. She closed her eyes, and we danced. She was soft and warm and danced beautifully. When the dance set ended she raised her head and blinked her eyes, then reached up and kissed me.

"That was scrumptious," she said. "Come, my love. I want to cuddle and have another drink."

We climbed all the way to the third floor, using the front stairway this time. This meant we had to go through the dormitory to get to my room. As the door opened and the long row of beds was revealed, she gave a little start.

"Oh, sir, I can't resist beds," she said. "Please protect me from myself. Please, sir."

I thought this was pretty funny. I pulled her through the dormitory and into my room, fixed us each a drink, and settled down beside her on the sofa. We had reached the very heart of the business of a 1933 fraternity party. It was almost a ritual. As I started to work on that strapless evening gown, Kate devised little interruptions. Sometimes she'd straighten up and ask me a question that didn't seem to have very much to do with anything. A good deal of the time she'd just reach over and take a sip of her drink. Whatever the case, these interruptions had the effect of making me go back and start all over again so that I wasn't really getting any place at all. I just thought I was. Of course, there was one obvious result. Her drink was going down pretty fast and all I had to do was be patient. She finished the glass long before I finished mine. The minute it was empty, she got slowly to her feet.

"I think we'd better go down and dance some more, lover," she said, and led the way out into the hall.

Back down the fire escape we went and out onto the dance floor. This time we danced cheek to cheek and she closed her eyes and sang the songs to me. However, I noticed that she got a little mixed up on the words sometimes. I also noticed that little strands were beginning to stray from that elegant hairdo, and toward the end of the dance she was a little heavier in my arms than she had been. The music stopped, and she looked up at me with misty eyes.

"I love you," she said, "and I need another little drink, but I have a wonderful idea. I'll race you. You go up that winding stairs we just came down and I'll go up the stairs we used last time. I'll bet you a nice warm, loving kiss I can beat you."

We solemnly shook hands and I led her over to the main stairs and watched her start up, then I ducked for the fire escape. I came pounding up at full speed and flung myself down on the sofa. After I got my breath I went over and poured two drinks and settled down to sip mine. I was a little hazy myself, and it was several minutes before I realized it was taking Kate an awful long time to get up those stairs. I resolutely pulled myself to my feet and set out to find her. I got all the way down to the dance floor without running into her and then I retraced my steps, looking carefully in all the places she might have got sidetracked. When I got back to the second floor, I looked in every study room along the hall. I found her way down at the end, sitting on the lap of one of my fraternity brothers, wrapped in a passionate embrace. My fraternity brother saw me out of the tops of his eyes as I popped in and he waved frantically for me to get back out of there, but I wasn't having any of that. He obviously didn't know whose girl he was kissing. I said, "Hi!" Kate disengaged herself and turned her head.

"Where've you been?" she said. "I've been waitin' for you an awful long time. You're not a very fast stair man."

"There's nothing the matter with my stair climbing," I said. "I got up to the room a half hour ago. Where were you?"

"Isn't this your room?"

"No. And that's not my lap you're sitting on, either."

She looked at my fraternity brother and frowned.

"*I beg your pardon,*" she said haughtily and held out her hand to me. I helped her to stand up and led her to the door. She was quite disheveled and decidedly unsteady on her feet. She made me stop in the hall while she shifted things around under the gown, then I guided her to the stairs.

"Show me where I made the wrong turn," she said.

"You just stopped climbing too soon. You have to keep climbing until you see the beds. Remember?"

I started up the steps but she hung back. She said she wanted to dance, so we turned and went down the stairs. When we reached the first floor we came to the guest room that had been converted into a powder room for the party. She promptly informed me that she wanted to go to the little girls' room. She'd meet me down on the dance floor. After losing her once I was reluctant to let her go again but I couldn't go in there with her and I didn't want to stand there ogling all the girls as they came in and went out, so I went on downstairs. On the bottom step I met Irene Young and Allan Higgins. Irene said she wanted to dance with me, so I danced with her. After Allan reclaimed her, I danced with another girl, then another. I was dancing with about the tenth girl when the orchestra played "Good Night, Sweetheart." It wasn't until then that I realized I hadn't seen Kate since she went into the powder room. I looked all around the dance floor, but she wasn't there. I went all the way to the top of the house and back again but I couldn't find her anywhere. All the fellows had gone to take their dates home and the house was almost deserted. I climbed forlornly back up to my room and took off my tux jacket. Suddenly there was a crash as someone burst out of the dormitory. A wild-eyed fraternity brother was standing in the door of my room.

"For God's sake," he gasped, "there's a girl in my bed and I don't think she's got anything on."

I rushed out into the dormitory. There was Kate, sleeping blissfully under a pile of blankets. On the floor beside the bed, where she'd stepped out of it, was the black evening gown. There was also a pair of shoes, silk stockings, and some interesting-looking lingerie. We were in trouble. A fraternity could get kicked off the campus for having an unclothed girl in the dormitory in 1933. All we needed was a postparty inspection by some dean. My fraternity brothers were already drifting back from taking their dates home, and as they got the news, panic gripped them. It didn't take them very long to discover whose date it was, and I was finally given ten minutes to get her out of there.

I wasn't very well prepared for getting a naked girl up and dressed. I was quite frightened by the prospect. I shooed everyone down to the second floor, but when I advanced on the dormitory, it struck me that maybe I ought to have a witness so I wasted time going down and talking two not very reluctant brothers into coming up and watching. I was just at the point of throwing the covers back when I heard the welcome feminine voice of Jeannie, Kate's roommate. She and Marty had discovered that Kate hadn't gotten home and they'd come looking for her. She got Kate up and into my room and put some clothes on her. Then, after the whole active chapter went out to look for university policemen in the vicinity, I helped carry Kate down and put her in a taxi. It wasn't until we saw the red taillight disappear up a nearby street that any of us felt safe.

I thought a good deal about Kate in the ensuing days. Unfortunately, I never did see her again after that one night. The Depression was about to overtake me again. One thing is certain. Never again was I to say, "Naw, I don't drink."

XII

Three days before the end of the semester my father called me to tell me that he had sold the crooked house. With the $9,300 he got for it, he had bought five cars of lumber and ten cars of coal, and he had put aside $500 for me. I could finish out the school year.

My final examinations that first semester were squeezed into the first five days of the two-week examination period. Because the Gamma Phi dining room closed down the second week, I decided to go home. I hitchhiked up to Flint on Friday afternoon, February 3, 1933. I found my father cheerful and busy. I got out my overalls and went over to the lumberyard. All the next week I helped unload lumber from boxcars and ran the conveyor that dumped coal on the concrete floor at the back of the yard. On Saturday night when I finished, the lumberyard looked like a lumberyard again. There were five carloads in it, plus six carloads of coal.

On that Saturday night when I collected my pay for the week's work, my father handed me the check for $500. He had forgotten one thing: Sunday was Lincoln's Birthday, and it would be celebrated on Monday. I would have to wait until Tuesday to cash the check. It didn't make any difference. I called Lottie and arranged for a substitute waiter. It wouldn't hurt if I was a day late registering for the second semester.

That weekend was the happiest my family had experienced in over three years. It was as though a cloud had been lifted. On my extra day at home, Monday, Gretchen and I went down to the IMA where Isham Jones was playing at a special Valentine's Day dance. The next morning, my twenty-first birthday—February 14, 1933—I came down to breakfast at six o'clock. I found my family sitting around the table. I believe they intended to sing "Happy Birthday" to me, but before I arrived something puzzling had happened. Someone had brought in the morning paper from the front porch. My father looked up from it and frowned.

"Who do you think you are?" he asked me. "Abe Lincoln?".

I shook my head, not understanding.

"Well, they've closed the banks on your birthday," he said, and held up the paper for me to see. All across the front of it, in letters half a page high, were the words "Bank Holiday!"

We had finally arrived at the very bottom of the Depression! In the State of Michigan we had arrived at this point two weeks before the rest of the country. Michigan was the first state in the Union to close its banks. One by one, in the succeeding days and weeks, the other states followed and then, on March 4—his inauguration day— Franklin D. Roosevelt closed all the rest.

No one was prepared for anything like this and very few people had any understanding of what it meant. There had been no warning—in Flint, at least—that there was anything the matter with the banks. Just as there had been in those early days after the crash, there was now a peculiar reaction, half optimism and half pessimism. The optimism arose from the fact that everyone was sure our banks were sound and this was only temporary. The pessimism was slow in getting hold of people and gradually built into panic as succeeding extra editions of the papers and radio commentators speculated on the meaning of it. One thing was certain. It was the only time in my whole life when cash money was important—the only acceptable form of wealth. The truck driver with fifty dollars in his pocket was better off than a corporation president who was caught with only five.

The initial reaction in our house was optimistic. I was the one on whom attention centered at first. The new semester had opened and it was important that I get back to the Gamma Phi house and my job. The $500 check in my pocket was worthless until the banks opened, but my father asked me how much I would need on that first day. I only had to pay my tuition of forty-nine dollars. I could buy my books and pay my room rent later in the week when the banks reopened. My father took all the cash out of his pocket and counted it. He had four dollars. Grandpa counted his. He had sixteen dollars. My brother Walter had three. My brother John had one. I had thirteen. After some urging, even Glad counted her money. She had two dollars. The total was thirty-nine dollars. We were ten dollars short. My father collected all the money and gave it to me. He said that the other ten dollars was bound to come in during the forenoon from the sale of coal. Inasmuch as the lumber-yard was right on the road to Ann Arbor, he suggested I ride over to the office and hang around until the money came in. I went up and got my suitcase and climbed into the old Buick. I had the entire family treasury in my pocket.

When we got out of the car in front of the lumberyard that morning, it was just seven o'clock. We walked across the lawn and my father unlocked the door and opened it. As he did so, the telephone was ringing. My brother ran across to the front desk and answered it. He had no sooner taken the receiver off the hook than the second phone rang. My father answered that one, and as he did so, the third phone started, so I answered that. The ringing of those telephones signaled the beginning of the wildest day I ever spent in my life. I never got up from the chair in which I sat down that morning until ten o'clock at night. My father couldn't get away from his phone, either. My brother did sneak off to man his truck.

We were hearing the sound of mounting panic. Because we were dealing in coal, we were the custodians of a vital service. Food and fuel were the primary concerns of everyone in the State of Michigan that morning. In our climate, in the middle of February, we could still expect six or seven weeks of cold weather. An unheated house would be a disaster. When the news of the bank holiday hit, people began to worry about being cold and hungry. The scene in our house must have been repeated everywhere. There were family councils at which the money was brought forth and carefully counted. Plans were made to ration every penny. Nothing would be spent unless it was absolutely necessary. I would imagine that inventories were made of what was in each house. The head of every household in the city of Flint must have gone down to his basement to look over the fuel supply. Then he called to make certain he was going to get through the crisis. By seven forty-five, three quarters of an hour after we had pushed through the front door, we had enough orders to keep all of our trucks going until midnight. At that time my father shouted out to me not to take any more orders for that day. He told me, incidentally, to make it quite plain that it was a question of our inability to deliver any more coal, not a question of a customer's ability or inability to pay cash. By ten o'clock we had booked enough deliveries to keep us busy for the whole week, and the orders were still coming in as fast as we could write them down. At a little before eleven my father scribbled out a little speech for me to make. We couldn't take any more orders at all unless the people were right down to the last shovelful of coal. That didn't help any. Everyone insisted that he was right down to his last shovelful. At around noon we began telling people that we wouldn't deliver a ton or even a half ton. We'd deliver five hundred pounds, enough to keep people going until the crisis was over. The orders kept coming.

From the start we had trouble over the cash-and-credit situation. Half the people assured us that they had cash in hand. The other half wanted credit, and when we told *them* we couldn't deliver because we were swamped, they jumped to the conclusion that we were holding out for cash. We had bitter arguments. We had abject pleas for mercy. People actually offered to pay us for coal with jewelry, furniture, or anything else they thought we might want. Slowly, as patiently as we could, we tried to talk people out of their panic. In most cases we succeeded. A good 75 percent of the callers were our faithful customers who had dealt with us right through the Depression. We knew that if they wanted credit we had to grant it. One of our big troubles was that we were getting calls from people who had left us two or three years before and many of them still owed us old bills. We also got calls from complete strangers. A lot of people in Flint must have called fifteen coal yards that day. We sorted them out as best we could, the old customers from the new customers, the cash customers from the credit ones, the truly desperate ones from the selfish ones. In the meantime, our trucks were loading out three tons to the load separated into compartments of five hundred pounds each. We tried to send these loads out to addresses reasonably close together. At various times during the day our drivers delivered coal to twelve houses right in a row. Some money came dribbling in but not nearly enough. We had six fresh carloads of coal out in the yard, but the bank holiday came at a time when most people were in the process of switching from soft coal to coke, and for each truckload of coke we had to pay the local gas company in cash. As fast as we got in the money for a load of coke, we would send a truck scurrying across town to the gas company, the driver carrying a fistful of pennies, nickels, dimes, quarters, and half dollars with which to pay for it. We tried to switch customers from coke to coal, but it was hard work. All kinds of fantastic things happened that day. Several times our drivers got coal in a basement where cash had been promised, and then the householder wouldn't pay. We finally told the men that, when "C.O.D." was written on the order, they should collect the cash before they took the first shovelful off the truck. One of our drivers was promptly forced to shovel his whole load into a basement at gunpoint. We had to pay cash for everything—gasoline, food, newspapers. One nearby druggist was breaking open his packs of cigarettes and selling them for one cent apiece to accommodate his customers who were caught short. He wouldn't trust anyone for a pack. Interspersed with the calls ordering coal were calls from my father's creditors. They all wanted him to settle his bills immediately—for cash. Some of them were willing to settle their accounts for five cents on the dollar. It didn't do a bit of good. There just wasn't any money. The whole world was grubbing for nickels and dimes, it seemed to me.

As luck would have it, a bitter cold spell hit Flint a day or two after the bank holiday. The cold weather made really desperate people out of those who had been crying wolf in the beginning. We had to continue rationing deliveries for two full weeks. In that short space of time the whole six cars of coal that my father had accumulated as the result of his summer's struggle to build and sell the crooked house were used up. Three weeks after the bank holiday there wasn't a pound of coal in the yard. As we should have known, a lot of the coal and coke we delivered in those hectic days was never paid for. We were back struggling for survival again.

The bank holiday was the beginning of the end for the lumberyard. It came about as the result of the most ludicrous happening of all. At the time of the stock-market crash my father had put fairly large mortgages on the lumberyard and family home. Our bank held these mortgages. In the three and a half years since the crash, it had been impossible to reduce the principal amounts, but my father had kept up the interest payments by delivering coal to the two big office buildings that the bank owned. About one out of every ten of those cars of coal that my father had scrimped and saved to buy over the years was a car of what we called nut, pea, and slack, intended for the bank. Every third or fourth week one of these cars would be shoved on our siding, and our biggest dump truck would work all night hauling it downtown and dropping it in the big bunkers under the buildings. The effort involved in buying and delivering this coal had been a tremendous strain, but it kept the mortgages from being foreclosed. Four of those ten cars of coal which my father bought with the money from the crooked house were meant for the bank. Unfortunately, there had been some delay in delivery. Everything else he had bought and paid for was already in the yard at the time of the bank holiday, but the four cars of nut, pea, and slack were not yet there.

That Tuesday morning, in the midst of all the panic, a Grand Trunk switch engine came chugging out to the lumberyard with the four cars in tow. They were pushed onto the siding and a few moments later the conductor of the switching crew came stomping into the office waving the freight bills in the air. He wanted $1,346.52

in cash money or he wouldn't leave the cars. Of all the absurd things that happened that morning, this was the worst. We didn't have fifty-two cents in the cash drawer. Even the money collected around the breakfast table—including Glad's two dollars—was gone by then. If we'd gone through the pockets of every man, woman, and child in Flint, I don't think we would have found $1,346.52 at that moment. The railroad was doing what everyone else was doing, of course, demanding cash on the barrelhead.

The money was reposing in the bank. While the conductor stood by, my father tried to get through to someone to get the money released. He finally reached a harassed and ill-tempered bank official who made the mistake of calling my father a stupid ass. The bank wasn't paying out any money at all, and the official couldn't see any reason why my father should be an exception. When my father asked when the money would be released, the official gleefully told him, "Never." Whatever money was on deposit would be applied to the mortgage that had been owed so long. It sounded as though the bank man was blaming my father for the whole bank holiday. My father didn't take very kindly to ill-tempered people and he hung up the phone and told the switchman there was nothing he could do. The engine pulled the four cars out of the siding and took them back to the switching yards. There was one significant thing about all this. My father had carefully refrained from telling the bank official that the money was for the bank's own coal.

Toward the end of the week, when the weather turned cold, the same bank officer called my father. He wanted to know where the coal was. Both of the office buildings were low on fuel, and the heat had been cut back so much that the tenants were complaining. My father let fly.

"That money in my account, which you applied to the mortgage, was set aside to pay the freight on *your* coal," he said. "What do you think I'm running out here, the Bureau of Engraving and Printing?" He went on to say that if the bank wanted its coal it would have to raise the money for the freight. Not only that, the bank could raise an extra $900. For three year my father had been furnishing the fuel at cost. Now he was going to sell it at the regular retail price, which was five-fifty a ton. "And like everyone else these days," he concluded, "I want cash money. None of *this* will be applied on any damned loan. As for you, I hope the tenants cut your damned head off."

The bank tried to get the coal somewhere else, but no one else had it in stock and no one else was in the mood to be kind to bankers at that moment in history. In the end the bank officers had to go out among the tenants and take up a collection. The money was raised slowly and painfully over the next few days and the coal was delivered one carload at a time. The $900 profit enabled us to get in three more cars of coal, enough to get through the rest of the winter, but the episode ended the long truce with the bank. A little later in the year the mortgages were foreclosed. We had eighteen months to raise the principal sum or face eviction.

My father was philosophical about it. As he pointed out later, the bank never did reopen its doors. The liquidators would have gotten around to foreclosing sooner or later. As for me, my $500 was in the bank, too. I could forget about going back to school. On the second morning I put on my overalls and went back to driving a truck. I don't think my father and I even discussed the matter. I went to Ann Arbor and picked up my clothes the next Sunday.

XIII

About eleven thirty on the first night of the bank holiday, my father and I were sitting in his office wearily discussing the events. As he talked, he happened to reach in the pocket of his jacket. He pulled out a package, looked at it, and tossed it to me.

"I meant to give you this this morning," he said, "but I forgot it in all the excitement. Anyway, it's yours. Happy Birthday!"

I opened it and found a shiny new fountain pen with my name engraved on the side. I thanked him for it.

"Just remember one thing," he said. "Every time you use that pen, it counts. You're twenty-one years old. I guess that makes you a man."

I was a man—almost. In the days following the bank holiday I settled down to the routine I knew so well. My battered old truck was my companion by day. I was always short of money. On Wednesday and Saturday nights I went to the dances with Gretchen. The summer loomed ahead and I worried about getting through it.

One morning in the last week of March, just after the first heavy rain of the spring, a chubby little man in farmer's overalls came stalking into the office. His name was Dan Dawes. He lived on a farm out near Flushing. Twenty years before, in 1913, his house had been struck by lightning and had burned to the ground. On the morning after the fire, my grandfather Love—then in the lumber business in Flushing—had loaded his wagons with lumber and hauled it out to the farm so Dan could get started rebuilding. It was an openhanded gesture made to a man who had no visible resources at the time, and Dan Dawes had become my grandfather's warmest friend as a result of it. There's an old saying that lightning never strikes twice in the same place, but it didn't work with Dan Dawes. On a stormy night in 1933 the lightning had come again and it burned down both the house and the barn. This time Dan was fully covered by insurance, and when he walked into my father's office, he plopped a house plan onto the desk.

"You can start hauling as soon as you get a truck loaded," he said. "After we get the house rebuilt, we'll start on the barn."

The lightning that struck Dan Dawes's farm provided the miracle that got us through the summer of 1933. My father gave me the job of hauling all the lumber. For the next three months I made two trips out to that farm every day. I hauled every piece of material that went into the house and barn.

In about the middle of April, the carpenters had begun to put the roof boards on the house, and one unseasonably warm morning I loaded out the asphalt shingles. It had been raining hard during the night, and the Dawes driveway was a quagmire. I got only a few feet off the country road when my rear wheels sank up to the axles. I was stuck good and proper, and there was nothing to do but unload where I was. The shingles had to be put under cover inside the house and I had to carry each one of those heavy bundles about one hundred yards. Each bundle weighed ninety pounds and was of an awkward shape which made it hard to handle. I had only carried a few when the sun came out and I perspired freely. I took off my blue shirt and after a few trips I took off my undershirt.

I had those shingles half unloaded when, as I came up to the house, a girl came walking around the corner. She had on a light, shapeless gingham dress that whipped about whenever the breeze caught it. She had an unusual but pleasant look. Her hair was jet black and her eyes were green and narrow and she had high cheekbones which gave her an oriental look. She was barefooted, but even with that and the old gingham dress, she was obviously a sensuous woman. She moved with the grace of a predatory animal. She stood off to one side and watched as I carried the bundles of shingles into the house. When I came out she cocked her head.

"Are those bundles heavy?" she asked.

"Ninety pounds," I said.

"May I carry one? I want to see if I can carry ninety pounds."

I thought she was fooling, but she followed me right out to the truck and stood there while I wrestled another bundle into position to get hold of it.

"Oh, come on!" she said in some exasperation. "I'm a farmer's daughter. I'm used to hard work. Let me try."

"Who are you?" I asked.

"I'm Tracy Dawes. You ought to know. I know who you are. My mother told me. I go to Michigan State. I'm home on spring vacation."

"Look, Tracy," I said. "These things are too heavy for you."

"I want to try." She flexed an admirable muscle. I shrugged my shoulders and pointed at the bundle of shingles I had ready. She stepped over to it and grabbed hold of it. It wasn't the weight that conquered her. It was the awkward shape. She stood there for a full second trying to control it, and then it began to slip from her grasp. I dove at it to help her, but I wasn't quick enough. It fell toward the ground and landed squarely on her instep. She didn't cry out, but I knew she'd been hurt. She reached over and leaned on the back of the truck and buried her face in the crook of her arm. I bent down and looked at her foot.

"I don't think anything is broken," I said.

"It really hurts," she said, shaking her head. "Can you help me back up to the house?"

I told her to put her arm around my shoulder, and I put my arm around her waist. We hopped along for a few steps, but it was awkward and I finally stopped.

"Put your arms around my neck and I'll carry you," I told her.

I bent down and picked her up. She was light enough and I had no trouble carrying her. The trouble with Tracy was that she moved around. She pressed against me and in some way she managed to shift her legs so that my hand ended up more than halfway up her bare thigh. When I put her down at the end of that hundred yards, I had the feeling that I knew quite a lot about how she was put together. Moreover, I was almost certain that she intended it to be that way. She perched herself on the railing of the half-finished porch and cocked her head at me as I went back to retrieve the bundle of shingles. Every time I walked by her with a bundle after that, she would toss her head and give me a long, slow, provocative wink. I was giving the matter a lot of thought.

When I finished unloading and dug my truck out of the mud, I went back to stand before her.

"How's your foot?" I asked.

She wiggled the toes and held it out to look at it, displaying a fine expanse of bare thigh in the process.

"I'll have a bruise but I'll be all right tonight."

"Are you going out tonight?"

She shook her head.

"I'll be here at eight o'clock," I said. "All right?"

She turned and pointed down the road at a house.

"That's where we're living these days." Then she gave me another of those long, slow winks.

I borrowed my father's car and arrived at her house on the dot of eight. She was sitting on the front steps waiting for me and she got up and half-limped out to the car, opened the door, and slid into the seat beside me. I hadn't even had a chance to get out and let her in. I'd had only a cursory glimpse of her in the twilight but I thought she looked extremely attractive. She had on a very simple, very chic, black jersey dress and somehow or other she had managed to get that sore foot into a high-heeled shoe. In high heels her legs were something to see. I backed out of the driveway and started down the road. After we'd gone about two city blocks I put my arm around her. Four hours later we were still sitting on that country road less than half a mile from where I'd picked her up. Tracy Dawes didn't care about movies or dancing or ice-cream sodas. She was interested only in what could happen in an automobile. Her first kiss was all passion, and within minutes I had learned how sensuous is the feel of a black jersey dress. Soon after that I discovered that she didn't have anything on under that dress but a pair of panties. Her body was the perfect female body, and I explored it with my hands. She didn't draw back and she didn't try to stop me. She just seemed to tense herself and purr with pleasure.

For almost four hours that first night we indulged ourselves in an ecstacy of sensuality. I felt as though I'd been unloading shingles all night. I ached all over and I was groggy with weariness. Yet we had stopped short of consummation. I've never been quite sure why it was that way, but always at the crucial moment Tracy pulled herself together and found the strength to push me away. Then she would withdraw to the opposite corner of the seat and ask me for a cigarette. After it was lit she would sit there, staring off across the dark fields, while she smoked. The minute the cigarette was out she would come back to my arms, and we would resume our fumbling.

For the next five days I made three trips out to Dan Dawes's farm every day. On two of those trips I hauled lumber. On the third I picked up Tracy. We would drive down the road out of sight of the house and begin our love making. Each night we went through the same performance. Our sessions became stormier and stormier as I became more frustrated. On the last night we had no more than started when I called her a damned tease. That ended the evening then and there. She made me take her home but then she seemed to try to patch it up with one more torrid session as we sat in the driveway. I think that Tracy *was* a tease in her own way but I had no way of knowing just what kind of an inner struggle she was going through that prompted her resistance. I was to blame, too. I didn't know enough about girls or love making to understand what was expected of me. I think that I was waiting for her to make the final move. She didn't do it, and nothing happened.

That last session was on a Saturday night. The Daweses had no telephone in their temporary home, and on other nights I'd just gone out there and Tracy would be waiting on the porch. She wasn't waiting for me on Sunday, and when I went to the front door, Mrs. Dawes informed me that Tracy had gone back to school. There had been no good-byes. I didn't hear a word from her for two months, but I couldn't very well forget her because I was delivering lumber out at the farm each day and every time I looked up at the house I remembered what she looked like on that day she first walked around the corner. The last load of lumber was hauled late in June, and I thought I was probably through with Tracy. I wasn't. One afternoon Dan Dawes and his wife came driving up to the lumber-yard while I was mowing the front lawn. While Dan went into the office, Mrs. Dawes wandered around the lawn. She eventually picked out three trellises and brought them over to me.

"I'll have Dan pay for these," she said. "You can deliver them to the house but you don't have to make a special trip. Tracy is coming home this afternoon, and I imagine you'll be coming out to see her tonight. Just bring the trellises along when you come."

I didn't go out to see Tracy that night and I didn't go out to see her the next night, either. I was tired of being frustrated and I suspected there would be more of the same old arguments. But sensuality is a powerful stimulant and it always prevails in the end. On the third night I put the trellises on the car and bumped over the country road to the Daweses' new house. Tracy was lying in a hammock on the front porch when I got there.

"It certainly took you long enough to get out here," she said sarcastically.

"Your mother wasn't sure when you'd be home."

"Don't lie to me. I told her to tell you exactly when I'd be home. You've been having a snit, and now we've wasted two valuable days. I have to go away tomorrow. I have a job as a counselor in a summer camp until August."

"I'm sorry," I said.

"If you aren't, you soon will be." She held out her hand to me. "You'd better come in and take a look at this place. Mother said you hauled all the lumber for it."

"Every stick of it," I said.

She pulled me through the door and began pointing out all the features. We did the living room and the kitchen and came to a long hall with several doors opening off it. One led into her father's room, another into her mother's. When she led me through the third one she did a little pirouette.

"This is my room," she said. "I like it best of all. So will you."

I looked around at all the lace curtains and frills, and as I did so, she threw her arms around me and reached up her mouth to kiss me. I put my arms around her and kissed her back. It was a kiss I shall always remember. It was all sensual movement and passion. We stood there for a long time, swaying back and forth, our bodies pressed together, and then as always she pushed me away and took several steps backward. She stood there for several moments, her eyes shining, and then suddenly she reached down and took the hem of her dress and pulled it up over her head and let it drop on the floor. There she stood, on tiptoe, her head held high, letting me look at that wonderful body.

"Hurry up!" she whispered at last. "Hurry up!"

I hurried. I have always remembered that summer night in every detail, from its beginning in the soft twilight until its ending in the bright morning sunshine. Tracy was a gifted woman in matters of sex. She knew how to arouse a man with touch and sound. She would whisper to me in her husky voice one moment and shriek with delight the next. She was the teacher and I was the pupil. I'd never known anything could be quite like that.

It must have been four in the morning when I wondered about her parents.

"You don't have to worry about them," she said. "They went to Canada day before yesterday and they won't be home. If you'd only come out here when Mother told you to, we could have been doing this for three nights instead of one."

"Couldn't you stay over for an extra day?"

"The job's too important. Most of my clothes burned up in the fire and I've got to get some more for school this fall, but don't worry. I'll be back before Labor Day and I'll fix a nice little place for us so we can spend a whole week out in Daddy's haymow."

I stumbled out of the house at six o'clock that morning. There was one nice little touch to our farewell. Tracy came tripping out to see me off without a stitch on.

"You can do this on a farm," she said. "The nearest neighbor is half a mile away."

I was a man at last. Alas! I never saw Tracy again. She never came back to the farm. At the time she was supposed to be fixing up a place for us in the haymow, she was fixing up another kind of a love nest for her new husband.

Part III

I

There were two Depressions. There was the Depression of Herbert Hoover and there was the Depression of Franklin D. Roosevelt. In one sense, I suppose, a person could say it was the same old Depression, but there was a difference.

Franklin D. Roosevelt was *the* man for my generation. For those of us standing on the threshold of adult life, Herbert Hoover had seemed a stodgy, fumbling, tired old man. The new President said, "The only thing we have to fear is fear itself." He said it every time he spoke, if not in words then in the tone of his voice, in his bearing, in his personal courage, and in his rapport with the people. From the time I first heard him speak in the 1932 campaign, he was my man and I was his. That first summer of his Presidency, more than any other summer, was the summer of Franklin D. Roosevelt. As the new laws came flinging at us out of Washington, it was a little like watching St. George slay dragon after dragon. At last we had a man who was *doing* something. When one looks back from a distance of forty years, it is easy to see that the New Deal did not accomplish very much in good hard terms. The period is euphemistically called the era of Recovery, but the same old disasters were overtaking us and the casualties continued. We were still as uncertain in 1936 as we were in 1932. The big difference was that we felt better.

I always think of the summer of 1933 as the cheerful summer. There were two main sources for my good feeling, and though neither one stemmed from Franklin D. Roosevelt, I always have a tendency to give him the credit. It is perhaps as good an example as any of how his personality reached out and touched everything. In our family the feeling of well-being came from our improved situation. The Dan Dawes job had been another bonanza of about the same proportions as the crooked house. The barn on his farm was especially good for us. Barns are made almost entirely from lumber, and there was still some profit to be made from lumber, even in 1933. After Dan Dawes's insurance company settled with my father, there was enough money to replenish the lumber stocks again and to get in the ten cars of coal we needed for the winter. There weren't very many sales, and my brother and I spent most of July and August puttering around the yard unloading the new lumber and coal that came in. Toward the end of August my father sold a substantial bill of lumber to remodel a building for the new regional offices of the NRA. (It was finished, incidentally, about the time the NRA was declared unconstitutional.) Late in September, when we received payment for this, my father proudly showed us a bank book with a $1,500 balance, enough to get us comfortably through the winter. (The money came in too late for me to think about using any of it to go back to school.)

In the meantime, there had been another event in my life which added to my buoyant spirits. About the middle of August, George French came driving up to our house one evening. He had just finished rebuilding another of those old cars of his. On other occasions George had been content to take his masterpieces out for trial runs in the immediate countryside, but he wanted to give this one more extensive tests. He had in mind a trip to the Chicago World's Fair. It had been a long time since I'd just gone off anywhere for the fun of it and the idea appealed to me. I'd been getting my usual five dollars a week and I'd managed to save twenty-five dollars of it. I asked my father for a week off. He not only gave it to me but he added ten dollars to my fund. Five of us made that trip to Chicago. We left Flint about three o'clock on a sunny afternoon and got to Chicago around three in the morning. We hadn't made any hotel reservations and after we got into the city we vainly drove about trying to find accommodations. About five thirty in the morning, as we drove up Michigan Boulevard, we came up behind a supremely intoxicated young man wandering around in the middle of the street. He was carrying a lighted kerosene lantern that he'd stolen from some construction site. It seemed pretty dangerous for a drunk to be walking up Michigan Boulevard, so we stopped and led him over to the curb. He wanted to know if we could tell him where the Stevens Hotel was. We knew exactly where it was because we'd just been there, so we put him in our car and drove him there. He was in such bad shape, however, that Lou Norris and I decided we'd better help him up to his room. We half-carried him across the lobby and into the elevator and got him to the sixth floor. When we led him in the door, he thanked us and told us to make ourselves at home. Then he tumbled onto the bed and passed out. We made ourselves at home, all right. Lou Norris ran down and got the others. After parking the car they all trooped upstairs and I let them in. One of them slept on the bed with our host, two curled up on the carpet, and Lou Norris and I shared the sofa. Around noon our unknown friend woke us up and told us he was sorry but he had to check out and go back to Iowa. We talked to him quite a long time. In the end he finally agreed not to check out. He'd let us have the room. He gave us the money to pay for the time he'd been there and picked up his battered old suitcase and lantern and left. The five of us stayed in that room for six days, three sleeping on the bed and two on the sofa. At the end of it, it cost us six dollars apiece—a total of thirty dollars.

The Chicago World's Fair was wonderful. We wandered about the fairgrounds and each evening we met at the Pabst Blue Ribbon Casino to have a beer and listen to Ben Bernie and compare notes. That was the big thing that summer, to meet at the Pabst Blue Ribbon Casino, and it seemed like the whole world was doing it. There were many wonders to see at the fair, including the first streamlined, diesel-powered passenger train, but the important thing about going there was that it furnished us with a vacation from the Depression. With its gay flags and its fountains it was a bright spot in a drab world. A person could forget, for a time, that everyone was broke, that the banks had been closed, and that there were long lines of unemployed everywhere. I'll never know where all the people got enough money to go to Chicago that summer, but they scraped it together, and like me, they walked about blithely. It was truly a place to lift the spirits.

For me, personally, the affair with Tracy Dawes and the visit to Chicago served as a kind of transition between one world and another. From the beginning of the Depression until the fall of 1933, my private universe was more or less centered in my father's lumberyard. My association with that enterprise was about to end.

It was the practice in Michigan for the taxes on mortgaged property to be paid by the holder of the mortgage. It was simply a method of protection for the mortgage holder, and it did not mean that the money came out of his own pocket. In my father's case, for example, only about 65 percent of the cost of those cars of coal he had been delivering to the bank was applied to the interest. The rest went for taxes. Up until the time of the bank holiday, there had never been a hitch in this arrangement, but at the time the banks closed, the 1932 taxes had not yet been paid over to the city. In the turmoil that followed the closings, conservators were appointed to protect the assets of the insolvent institutions, and these conservators were expressly restrained from paying out any money except to depositors. This meant that a lot of Flint property had delinquent taxes owing the city in the summer of 1933. Unfortunately, a large number of property holders were not aware that they were delinquent, the banks never having notified them.

It was in this situation that a man named Dexter G. Conklin began what he called a campaign to get money into the city treasury. He happened to be the city treasurer. His tactics were high-handed to say the least. He took the attitude that there was no use in talking things over. The one sure way to get money was to padlock the premises and keep them padlocked until the back taxes were handed over. Dexter Conklin did exactly that. In many cases he gave no warning at all. My father certainly had no inkling of what was about to happen. One afternoon, early in October, 1933, just as the coal business was getting under way, Dexter Conklin drove up to the lumberyard, and without saying a word to anyone, he swung the big gates shut and hitched a padlock to them. Then he walked across the front lawn, closed the office door, and padlocked that. He then tacked a big sign on the door which announced that the property had been seized for taxes. Having done all these things, he got back in his car and drove off. He hadn't said a word to anyone. My father had been sitting at his desk when all this happened. When he realized what was going on he rushed to the door and tried to open it to call to Conklin, but the door wouldn't open with the padlock on it. By the time he managed to get one of the front windows open, Conklin had driven off.

It was a fearful moment in my father's life and in mine, too. At the time it happened, I was out in the backyard loading my truck with coal and when I drove up to the scales I found I couldn't get out of the yard. There were two customers loading boards on their cars and they couldn't get out, either. There was no question about the fact that Dexter Conklin had acted hastily and arbitrarily, but that didn't help the situation any. For three hectic hours my father was on the phone to various individuals, including lawyers and peace officers. As the result of his phone calls, a county judge issued an order, and Conklin had to come out to the yard before closing time and let the customers out. He was quite dilatory about this and didn't arrive until after six o'clock, with the result that the customers both knocked him down and gave him a bloody nose. He later tried to have them arrested, but when the judge heard how tardy he'd been in carrying out the court order, he fined Conklin for contempt of court. While this served as something of a personal triumph, it didn't solve the matter of the taxes. There, at least, Conklin was on firm ground. There wasn't any way out of it except to pay them, and so my father took the $1,500 he had put aside from the Dan Dawes deal and paid. In the meantime, the yard had been closed for twenty-four hours.

This blow hurt my father worse than anything that had happened to him so far. Part of it was the defeat. The disgrace of having his yard padlocked and posted was almost too much for him to bear. Added to this was the knowledge that once more he was back to the same old day-to-day struggle for survival. All the things he had done—the trellises, the crooked house, the Dan Dawes deal—had come to nothing. It was one blow too many. He was just fifty years old that fall. He'd always been a vigorous, young-appearing man. Now he became dull and listless and he seemed to age in a matter of a few days. He seemed to quit fighting. For as long as I'd known him he'd always gotten up early and opened his office at seven o'clock. Now, on some days he would sit around the house until ten or eleven in the morning. He didn't want to answer the telephone for fear that it would be more trouble.

It was fortunate for our family that my younger brother Walter was as doughty a fighter as my father had ever been. During the two months that my father was in the doldrums, so to speak, and for four months thereafter, the fate of the lumberyard was in Walter's hands. He ran the business and he kept it going. Conditions were no better than they'd ever been. There was the same constant financial pinch brought on by the slim margin of profit and the necessity of extending credit, but Walter wasn't of the same temper as my father. Each morning he would take a list of delinquent accounts and go out collecting money. He banged on doors and hounded people until they paid fifty cents or a dollar on those long-overdue bills. It was the money he brought in that bought the first loads of coke to start each day. The lumberyard teetered along, surviving one day at a time.

My father perked up a little when Dexter Conklin was arrested for embezzlement. It developed that a sizable amount of the money he'd been collecting through his brutal tactics was going into his own pocket. The news served the purpose of turning my father from a culprit who didn't pay his taxes into the innocent victim of a sadistic crook and thus removed much of the disgrace that he felt. (Conklin eventually received a heavy prison sentence.)

Unfortunately, the news about Dexter Conklin came too late to make any difference to me. The lumberyard had become important in my life through accident. In the early days when I was in high school it had never been intended that I would go into the business. I was the one who was going away to school to learn a profession. From the very first the thought had nagged at me that I didn't want to spend the rest of my life in the lumber business. I was perfectly happy when I was driving a truck, but on the rare occasions when my father had called on me to work in the office, I felt uncomfortable and out of place. On the other hand, my brother Walter loved the give-and-take of the business world and he was good at it. By 1933, it had begun to dawn on me that it was his world and not mine, that there would never be enough business to support the two of us, and that I ought to get out and let him have a chance to see what he could do.

These vague thoughts were never voiced to anyone because I still had no firm idea of just exactly what I did want to do. While it was easy to come to a decision that I didn't want a career in business, I hadn't been able to focus on any way of making a living that would be a substitute. (By this time I'd definitely decided I didn't want to be a lawyer, either.)

For all the years I could remember I had been an avid reader. Through the Depression, when I wasn't in school, I must have averaged a book a day. I must have thought, somewhat idly, of being a writer during these early years but I have no firm recollection of it. Then, in the early summer of 1933, something rather silly happened which focused my attention on it. Flint had produced one author. His name was Arthur Pound. Although he had moved away from the city some years before, he got a lot of publicity in the Flint *Journal*. In June he and his family visited Flint, and one Sunday morning the whole front page of the society section displayed a picture of him and his four beautiful daughters. I sat there and looked at those girls in their long afternoon dresses and floppy hats. They were gorgeous. They came from a world I'd never known, that vague romantic place where princesses dwelt, the place that Sir Walter Scott and Jeffery Farnol wrote about. Although I'd never bothered to read anything that Arthur Pound had ever written, he was an author and I assumed that he was out of the same mold. I began to build my own fantasy. Although I didn't know what kind of a writer I wanted to be, and although I still didn't know whether I had any talent for it, the idea was always in the back of my mind. It has always amused me, when I read about my contemporaries who were having stirrings in such fields as the proletarian novel about this time, that this was the way I got started.

This rather vague and unsound fantasy of mine had no importance whatsoever except that it gave me a sense of direction that led straight away from the lumberyard. I had become almost certain that my future lay somewhere else. This feeling was accentuated in the anguish that followed Dexter Conklin's descent upon us. I had to ask myself why I went through so much for something that didn't mean much to me in the first place. I knew the answer, of course. Most of what I'd done so far in my life had been done because my father's life was all wrapped up in the lumberyard and because I loved him and wanted to help him. Until he released me, I had to stand by him.

My father had sensed my restlessness and my lack of direction. About a week after the Conklin incident when his spirits were at their lowest ebb, he asked me into the sun parlor after breakfast one morning. He looked glumly out over the backyard and asked me if I had thought about going back to school. When I said I hadn't he said he wished I would think about it. In view of what had happened, he was afraid that there wasn't much future in the lumberyard for any of us. In my case he thought that I had a good start on an education and that it might be a good idea if I completed it. There wasn't a chance in the world that he'd ever be able to help me get back to Ann Arbor, but if I could get a job somewhere, I might be able to earn and save enough to go back on my own.

My father had given me the opening I wanted. I thought about it for twenty-four hours and while I was thinking about it I talked to a few friends. They informed me that the factories were calling back men. The 1934 model runs would begin the next week. There were always a few new jobs opening up at such a time and if I was serious about looking for something, this was the time to do it. I made my decision and I told my father about it that same night. He nodded and shook hands with me and wished me luck. On the next Saturday night when I walked out the front door of the lumberyard, it was for the last time. One phase of my life was over.

II

My venture into the outer world began on a cold November morning in 1933. I got up at two o'clock in the morning and walked the two miles over to the Buick factory employment office on Industrial Avenue. Although it was not yet four o'clock when I got there, I found a line stretching back along the street for three blocks. I got at the end of it. By the time the employment office opened at seven, the line stretched out behind me for another six blocks. I shuffled along all that forenoon and it was three in the afternoon before I had my job interview. It was the shortest job interview I ever had. I filled out a card with my name, age, and address. That was all the information they wanted. No questions were asked about how much education I had or what kind of experience I had. The man on the other side of the table from me simply pulled a card at random from a file and looked at it. He told me he had a job that would pay forty-six cents an hour. He didn't tell me what it was. He just asked me if I wanted it. I said I did. He filled out a paper and time card, gave me a badge, and called a guard. Ten minutes later I was being led out through the plant.

My job, it developed, was in the press room of the die-stamping department. About half the 1934 models carried their spare tires in fender wells on the front fenders. All of the front fenders were stamped out of metal sheets on the big presses in the shop. On the completed cars they were supposed to be attached to the frame by a series of metal bolts, and holes had been placed in the flanges of the fenders through which these bolts would fit. Somehow or other, in stamping out the fenders with tire wells, there had been metal distortion. The holes for the frame bolts turned out to be narrow slits through which the bolts would not fit. It was too expensive to change the dies to correct this and Buick had decided to solve the problem by having men hand-file the holes into the proper shape. I was one of the hand-filers. Each fender was a huge thing, measuring three feet wide and seven feet long, and weighing about one hundred pounds. As they came off the presses they were piled in stacks. I would take a fender off a stack, wrestle it over to a nearby bench, clamp it in place with a vise, climb upon it as though I were mounting a horse, and from a position astraddle it, insert the file in the slit and run it up and down until the hole was round. There were four holes on each fender, and all had to be reamed out. When I was done, I would climb down from my perch, unclamp the fender, and carry it over to another pile. It was monotonous work and it seemed endless. It was noisy and it was lonely. We were surrounded by the din of the great presses and, closer at hand, the constant rasp of metal files. I worked on the job for eight weeks and I never did find out the names of the men who were working with me. It was too noisy to talk with them.

The filing job paid well. My average paycheck was eighteen dollars a week. After three years of working for five dollars a week, that seemed munificent. I paid my mother four dollars a week for room and board. The only other thing for which I spent money was to take Gretchen to the IMA dancing. At New Year's I had managed to save $100. I used that to buy a car.

I didn't intend to buy a car, but about a week after I went to work at Buick, I went downtown on a Saturday morning to get my paycheck cashed and I ran into Bugs Huntley, my fraternity brother from Durand. Bugs had graduated in Business Administration the previous June and he had a job with a finance company as a collector. This included repossessing cars. On that morning I ran into him he was on his way out to the country to repossess one and he wanted me to go with him and drive it back into town. He was having trouble getting anyone to do it. The repossession of an automobile seemed like pretty ghoulish business. Bugs offered me a dollar and gave me quite an argument. In the end I went with him because I felt sorrier for him than I did for the man whose car was being repossessed. Furthermore, he had convinced me there would be no trouble. The whole thing had been arranged in advance. It was about like Bugs said it would be. He parked his car a quarter of a mile up the road from a farmhouse and left me sitting in it. He walked up on the front porch and knocked on the door. After talking with someone for several minutes, he went around to the back. A moment later he drove the car out of the driveway and up the road to where I was. It had all been very impersonal, so when Bugs called me the next Saturday, I went again. I went for the next eight Saturdays in a row. Not all the repossessions were as simple as that first one. Once or twice the owners wouldn't give Bugs the keys, and we had to tow the car into the garage. Once a man chased Bugs off the front steps with a shotgun, and he had to go and get a deputy sheriff. That was the case that made me decide not to go anymore, but by then I already had my car. Just before New Year's we had to go all the way out to Holly, twenty miles south of Flint. Some young fellow had bought a car three years before and hadn't made a payment on it in more than a year. Bugs had looked for him all over southern Michigan and had finally tracked him down in Holly. When we got the car that snowy morning, it turned out to be a beautiful, red, 1931 Chevrolet coupé. It had wire wheels and fender wells and had been kept in top-notch condition. It had less than ten thousand miles on it. Best of all, it had a little radio attached to the steering column. This was the first auto radio I'd ever seen. During the twenty-mile drive back to Flint I fell in love with that little car, and after we got into the garage I asked Bugs if it would be for sale. He went right over to the dealer and inquired about it. The dealer wasn't very happy about having one of his three-year-old cars come back to him and he jumped at the chance to get rid of it. He made me a price of $181 for it. I paid $100 down and agreed to pay six monthly installments of $15 each.

I had no sooner bought that car than my fender-filing job ended abruptly. It ended during the first week after New Year's, 1934, when one of the vises that held the fenders in place broke off and let the fender I was sitting on crash to the floor. My foot was caught under it, and I suffered a cut that required twenty-three stitches to close. I was confined to our house for almost a week, and just as I began to be able to hobble around on crutches, my father had a heart attack. The Dexter Conklin business had taken a greater physical toll than any of us had known.

The new crisis was on the order of a catastrophe in our family, but it was just one more in that long series of catastrophes that marked the course of the Depression. That same month of January seemed to bring the world crashing down all around us. Within two weeks after my father was taken to the hospital, there were three more deaths in our immediate circle of friends, all directly attributable to the pressure under which we were all living. The most frightening of these deaths, to me, occurred one blizzardy January morning while my father was still convalescing. Molly Flexner's father had been living alone in that forlorn, boarded-up house on the farm that had been so lovely and gay in those days when I'd been going out there. He just gave up and went out to the garage, closed the doors, and started the motor on his car. He died virtually destitute.

During those days when my father lay sick in the hospital and when I was trying to get around on crutches, my brother Walter and I talked back and forth about what to do. I was only twenty-two years old and Walter was twenty, and we were woefully inexperienced, we were broke, and it was obvious that we were going to have added expenses. The doctors told us that my father would have to have a long period of rest, away from the business cares that had brought on the attack. We took up our problem one step at a time. My grandfather Love had died the previous summer. Many years before he'd built himself a small cottage in Clearwater, Florida, and our first step was to get enough money together to buy my father and Glad railroad tickets to Florida. They were to stay there until late in May. After we'd seen them off, Walter and I talked about the next step. I volunteered to come back to the lumberyard and drive a truck, but before I had a chance to do so, George French dropped around at the house one evening. The year before he'd been given a football scholarship at General Motors

Institute of Technology, a cooperative engineering school in Flint whose students worked a month in one of the plants and then went to school for a month. George was sponsored by the AC Spark Plug Company and he worked in various parts of the plant so that he knew everything that was going on. He informed me that the AC was reorganizing its shipping department and that there would be some good jobs available. If I could get over to the factory the next morning, I might get one of them. After George had gone, my brother Walter told me that he thought it would be more help if I had a job on the outside and could bring in money than it would be if I drove a truck at the lumberyard. Still hobbling on a crutch, I went over to the AC the next morning and I got a job. It would pay me sixty-four cents an hour or about twenty-six dollars a week. It was a good thing I had that job, for the lumberyard was no different from what it always had been. I sent my father and Glad fifteen dollars a week the rest of that winter. It was all we had to send. Even with that, and with making the payments on my car, I still managed to save another $100 by the last week in May.

The AC Spark Plug Company made a great many things besides spark plugs. The company manufactured more than three thousand parts, which it sold throughout the auto and electrical-appliance industry. During the first two weeks at AC, I served an apprenticeship, learning all these different parts. When I finished the apprenticeship, I was put in charge of the daily hot list. The daily hot list was a compendium of about forty items which were on order by other companies. It varied from day to day. The items on that list *had* to be shipped to the customers before the plant closed for the day. Most of them were sent out by the night shift of the shipping department, which worked from four in the afternoon until midnight—as did the night shift in the various production departments. I came to work at eight in the evening and worked until five in the morning. When I came in to work each evening, I had to check the status of every item on the hot list. I usually found that half of them had already been shipped and that five more items would be on the shipping-room floor, ready to go out. When I had ascertained which items were missing, I would go over to the factory and check with the various foremen on the production lines to determine exactly when the missing items would be ready. On an average night I would end up with ten to fifteen items coming off the production line just as the night shift went off duty. I had to load them on hand trucks, wheel them over to the shipping department myself, pack them, make out manifests, deliver them to a special truck that was waiting at the loading platform. It was lonely work, because my last five hours were spent in a deserted factory, but I enjoyed it because it was varied and because many times it tested my ingenuity. Except for the weather, that was an extremely happy period in my life. The months of January and February in 1934 were especially stormy and cold months. Two or three mornings a week I would go out to the parking lot in the winter morning darkness and have to dig my car out of the drifts before I could go home.

With the departure of my father and stepmother for Florida, my two brothers and I kept a bachelor household, supervised by Grandpa Perry. Grandpa kept house, sweeping out now and then, making the beds, and emptying the ashtrays. He also did what cooking had to be done. I ate most of my meals at a diner near the plant and my brother Walter was eating out, too. My brother John, who was eighteen and a senior in high school that winter, ate one big meal a day in the school cafeteria. The rest of the time he ate hot dogs from a supply we kept in the refrigerator. I'm not sure what Grandpa ate, but I have always supposed he ate hot dogs *all* the time.

During the first week in February our numbers were augmented. One Saturday morning I answered the doorbell to find my fraternity brother Nick Woods standing on the front porch. It will be recalled that it was he who saved my winnings in the crap game and supervised my first drink. Nick had a sad story to tell. He had just flunked out of the University of Michigan at the end of the first semester of his senior year and he didn't dare go home and tell his parents. Nick's trouble, ostensibly, was that he hadn't been able to get out of bed to attend Saturday morning classes. He flunked one physics course three times running and that was too much for the School of Engineering. Nick's real trouble, however, was love, and I was partly to blame for that. The year I waited table at the Gamma Phi house, I had introduced him to Flo Sorenson, a Flint girl, and poor Nick had become completely discombobulated. I never saw two people so completely in love as those two were. The trouble with it was that they stayed out late every night, especially on Friday nights, and poor Nick just didn't make it on Saturday mornings. Nick and Flo were going to be married in the fall, and inasmuch as Flo was a Flint girl and it was likely that they would live in Flint after the wedding, Nick had come up there when he flunked out. He had a letter to an official of the AC Spark Plug Company that might get him a job, but what he needed was a place to stay. He had come to the right place at the right moment. I took his suitcase and led him upstairs to my father's vacant bedroom, and there he stayed until May, even though he got a job on his first try at AC. He was a naturally gregarious fellow and he fitted perfectly into our way of life.

Our way of life that winter consisted of a poker game. It was *some* poker game. It began one blizzardy day toward the end of January and it lasted right through until the last week in May. It started by accident. At the time of his death, Molly Flexner's father had been struggling to get a dairy started. He had all those cows he had bought in 1929 and he had to do something with the milk. He left five brand-new milk trucks and his milking, bottling, and pasteurizing machinery—all heavily mortgaged. The only way the Flexner family was going to salvage anything from the wreckage was to get that dairy in operation before things were repossessed. So Molly's husband, Sam Hendricks, came up from Florida to get things started. He brought along three of his out-of-work friends— the Riley brothers—to help him. These four admirable young men thus undertook a very difficult enterprise, complicated by the fact that they were working among strangers in a strange city in the midst of a particularly bitter winter. Molly was pregnant and decided to stay in Florida until after the baby came, so Sam and the three Rileys were living a bachelor existence out at the farm.

I was the only person Sam Hendricks knew in Flint. I had met him briefly when I was best man at his wedding. He needed all kinds of information about the layout of the city and the people he was dealing with. From the first day he arrived in Flint, he got into the habit of dropping around to the house to ask me questions. He would park his milk truck beside the house and come in and unfold a city map and we'd talk. The Rileys soon began joining him there after they finished their own milk routes. One very blizzardy day after the business meeting, Tom Riley—the fun-loving one—picked up a deck of cards that had been left sitting on a table in our sun-room. He asked the rest of us if we'd like to play a little poker. We all sat around the dining-room table. A few minutes after we started, Grandpa Perry joined us. At around four in the afternoon, my brother John came home from school with a friend and they sat in the game. At six o'clock, when I left the house to go to dinner and work, they were still playing. Sam Hendricks and the Rileys went home to bed about eight o'clock, but by then my brother Walter and two of his friends had arrived. The game broke up about one in the morning. When I came home from work at six that morning, the cards and chips were still on the dining-room table. I went to bed and woke up around noon. When I came downstairs Sam Hendricks and the Rileys were playing with

Grandpa. I sat in the game and the same thing happened as the day before. When the weekend came, George French dropped around to see me and he sat in the game. During the next week he dropped by every evening with one or two of his friends. When Nick Woods moved in, he joined the game and eventually he was bringing fellows home to play.

All told, there were about thirty-five fellows involved in that game. By the time two weeks had passed, it was a twenty-four-hour-a-day proposition. It wasn't an expensive game because none of us had much money. There was a nickel limit and it is still my impression that very little changed hands. There wasn't any drinking —only an occasional bottle of beer on a weekend. The only person who played with *all* the various groups was Grandpa Perry. He'd start when he got up in the morning and play straight through until midnight. Although he was eighty-three years old, he was younger in spirit than any of us and he dearly loved to play poker. He didn't go down to the courthouse for jury duty once in that whole winter. He didn't have to. He was the only day-to-day winner. He must have taken three dollars a day away from us, which was about what he'd have made if he'd gone downtown.

The only other development which came out of that winter had to do with Nick Woods. Nick was an Easterner. He was the first fellow I knew who didn't know how to drive a car. I'd been able to drive since I'd been able to reach the floor pedals and I had my first license when I was fourteen. My friends were the same. In Flint one almost needed a car, and I undertook to teach Nick to drive. It was difficult for him. He had trouble coordinating. I got him through the road test and he received his license, but I was never sure of him and he was never sure of himself.

Shortly after he got his license, Nick began driving my car to work. It was a good arrangement, for we were on different shifts. I would get home at six in the morning just as Nick was ready to go to work, and he would get home in the evening as I was ready to start out. Unfortunately, he never improved as a driver. He had several minor accidents. Early in the winter he broke off a wheel against a curb on an icy day. Another time he jammed a fender in the parking lot. Once he backed into a pole and broke the taillight. When the weather got good in the spring, he borrowed the car on weekends to go down to Ann Arbor to see Flo. On one of those trips he broke off another wheel when he failed to make a corner. Nick always offered to pay for the damage, of course, but I put him off for one reason or another, telling him we'd settle up when he moved out.

Late in May there were some far-reaching changes. My father and stepmother came back from Florida. Glad made short work of the poker game and Nick Woods. She swept the whole conglomeration out the front door in one easy motion. At almost the same time my job came to an end with the seasonal layoff. Poor Nick! He needed a car, but he didn't have enough money to buy one. I knew this, and when he tried to settle up with me for the damages, I told him to keep the money a ,d apply it toward the purchase of a good used car. I'd had two spare wheels in the fender wells, anyway, and I didn't need them for the time being. A week after he'd left the house he still hadn't found a car, and he borrowed mine to go down and see Flo. While he was gone, I got to thinking about it. I was out of work and I wasn't sure whether I could afford to maintain an automobile. Besides that, if I really needed transportation, I could always borrow my father's old Buick. Consequently, when Nick got back from Ann Arbor, I told him to take the car. He could pay me for it when he got the money. We argued about it for several hours and he finally agreed to do it only if I would take exactly what I paid for it.

III

The Depression was four and a half years old. The average factory worker in Flint had worked about four and a half months on the 1934 models. From about the middle of April on there had been a steady reduction of force at AC Spark Plug. I'd been lucky. Because of the nature of my job and because my boss liked me, I was one of the last to get my pink slip. I'd worked seven months. I had about one hundred dollars in cash, but I was told that I probably wouldn't be called back to work until November.

I didn't have any plans except that I intended to go out and get another job. I started on that immediately and I soon found out that the Depression was still on, even if Franklin D. Roosevelt did call this the era of Recovery. I began by pulling strings. For almost three weeks I visited friends who owned small businesses, I talked with people I thought were in key positions, or I just plain snooped, trying to ferret out some news of openings. This line of attack got me exactly nowhere. My friends had long since laid off all their help and they had no intention of hiring any more. The people in key positions were helpless. All the factories were closed down.

They couldn't help me if they would. And there was no news. It was along about the end of June when I turned to the want ads in the Flint *Journal*. Every morning I would put the classified advertising section under my arm and start out. At first I took the streetcar or a bus, but as the summer progressed and I saw my hundred dollars dwindle to seventy and then sixty, I decided to walk and save money. By the end of July, I was walking six or seven miles a day. I never came close to getting a job. Everywhere I went I found a line waiting ahead of me. All of these people, usually fifteen or twenty of them, were answering the same ad I was answering. It was always the same. After we'd waited for an hour or two someone would come out and tell us that the job had been filled, and then we'd all trudge off and wait in line somewhere else. A few times—a very few—I was actually interviewed after one of these waits, and my name and phone number were taken down, but no one ever called me back. Once or twice I was offered a job as a door-to-door salesman, but each job required a cash investment for samples and it was on a straight commission basis. I knew the products were largely unsalable and I knew that I was a poor salesman, even in good times. I declined the opportunity.

I was increasingly discouraged and I tried all kinds of things. I decided that I was finding out about jobs too late so I resolved to go to the Flint *Journal* and get the first paper off the press when it came out in the afternoon. Every unemployed person in Flint must have had the same idea. When I arrived at the newspaper office at two o'clock—publication time—I found a double line clear around the block waiting for that first paper. The next day I went at one o'clock. I was fiftieth in line. The third day I went at noon. I was tenth in line. That afternoon there was an ad placed by the streetcar company. They wanted five car cleaners. I ran down the block and jumped on the trolley, hoping to be the first man to reach the carbarns. I almost made it. I found five people ahead of me. I was sixth in line for an ad that promised five jobs. The employment man hired the first five and slammed the door in my face. I continued to go to the *Journal* at noon every day for some little time, but I never got anywhere. Eventually I decided that two hours a day was too much time to waste. I gave it up. In desperation I tried to get a job with the CWA (Civil Works Administration) or the PWA (Public Works Administration), or whatever it was that summer. I was told that I had to be married in order to qualify. The only thing available for single men was the CCC (Civilian Conservation Corps). When I investigated that, I found that I would have to enlist for at least six months. I couldn't do it because the term of enlistment would run past November when I expected to be called back to AC Spark Plug. I finally gave up altogether early in August. There was no unemployment insurance at that time, of course, and my little nest egg was dwindling.

I had one good reason for giving up on my job hunt. I was still reading as much as ever, and early that summer I had discovered Francis Parkman. As I waded through his works, I came to the volume on the Pontiac conspiracy. Pontiac stirred my imagination. I thought of him as a great patriot, and it seemed to me that more people ought to know about him. This was a period when historical novels were quite popular, and not long before I had read Kenneth Roberts' *Rabble in Arms*. It was a whole year since I'd seen Arthur Pound's picture in the paper and I still hadn't done anything to launch my writing career. Very slowly I began to put a few ideas together. If I wanted to tell people about Pontiac, the way to do it was to write about him. The best way to get the greatest attention was to write a historical novel. I began to try to block one out. To my surprise I came up with what I thought was a good plot. It was in this situation that I decided I'd have to find out more about Pontiac. One day I stopped in to see Bill Webb, the director of the public library, and asked him if he knew what else was available besides Parkman. He informed me that there was a rich reservoir of original material about the period of the French-Indian War in the Burton Collection at the Detroit Public Library and in the Clements Library in Ann Arbor, but in order to use it, I had to have special permission. He could get that permission for me, but he had to know why I wanted it. Somewhat sheepishly, I told him I was thinking of writing a historical novel. This news fired Bill Webb to fever heat. I think he'd always hoped to incubate a writer in Flint and here one had walked in right off the street. He got me my permission, all right, and I went down to Detroit five times to go through the Burton Collection, but Bill Webb did more than that. He called me at least twice a week to give me pep talks. By the middle of July I was sitting down in my room each evening to write a few pages. By the first of August I had fifty pages done and I was beginning to catch fire. A week later I pulled myself together and decided to go all-out in the writing game. If I was going to be a writer, there wasn't much sense in looking for jobs as a streetcar cleaner or a soda jerk. I gave up the job hunt, and each morning after breakfast, I would retire to my room and peck away at the typewriter.

A person couldn't get away with this kind of thing in our house. Glad was still there, and a person who wasn't bringing in money was a parasite to her. When he didn't even make any effort to go out and find a job, he was beneath contempt. The nagging set in at once. It went on morning, noon, and night. I stood it for two weeks, by which time I'd got up to page one hundred in my epic. Then I had to get out and run. Fortunately, I had a place to run to.

My grandfather Love had died early in the fall of 1933. When his will was read, we discovered that he had left my brothers and me a legacy of a section of land which was vaguely described as being in the southwest quadrant of Luce County, Michigan. No one in our family, including Grandmother Love, had the faintest idea what this was, where it was, or what it was worth. Grandmother seemed to think that it was some logged-over land that Grandfather might have bought in the 1880s when he'd been a lumberjack in the Upper Peninsula. We located it, all right, but we never went much beyond that. In the excitement of the Dexter Conklin business, which came along about that time, we more or less forgot about it.

When my father came back from Florida in May, 1934, there was a big stack of mail waiting for him, and he slowly began reading through it. Toward the bottom was a letter written in pencil on cheap tablet paper, postmarked Germfask. It was from a man who signed himself David MacKenzie. He identified himself as an old friend of Grandfather's from the logging days. He'd just heard of Grandfather's death, and he wondered what disposition had been made of "the property on Manistique Lake." If it was available, he was willing to make us a small offer for it.

None of us had any idea what a "small offer" was. For some reason or other, the figure of fifty dollars kept sticking in my mind, and I think a somewhat similar figure must have lodged in my father's mind, also. He answered David MacKenzie's letter asking for a figure, but we never received an answer. From time to time, as the summer progressed, my father would say that he thought someone ought to go up to Germfask and take a look at the property. My brother Walter was busy in the lumberyard, and my brother John was peddling milk for Sam Hendricks. (He got the job the week before I was laid off and started on my futile search.) Since I was the only unemployed member of the family, the hints about going to the Upper Peninsula seemed to be aimed at me, but I wasn't interested.

At about the time my stepmother's nagging reached a crescendo, George French came over with another one of his rebuilt cars— this one a 1916 Buick—and suggested going for a road test. I don't think he had anything in mind but a run around the local countryside, but I was exasperated enough by the situation at home to propose something more extensive. I suggested a real test. He could drive me up to Germfask. We could look over the property. We could even do a little fishing. It would be a nice vacation. George loved to fish and he jumped at the chance. Almost without thinking twice, we piled into that old car on an August Sunday morning and headed for Germfask, some four hundred miles away.

It was one of the most horrendous trips I ever took. For once, George hadn't done a good job on a car. We were beset by blowouts and breakdowns, and it took us a whole week to get across the Straits of Mackinac. We finally arrived at Germfask in the middle of the night, and while wandering around lost, we ended up in a fishing camp run by a man named Charlie Fuller. There, in a kind of last gasp, the old 1916 Buick expired of a broken rear axle. It was two weeks to Labor Day, and we never did do any fishing. George hitchhiked all over the Upper Peninsula in a futile search for parts for his eighteen-year-old car. While he was doing this, I tried to explore Big Manistique Lake on foot in a search for Grandpa's property. I found the property, all right. It consisted of the whole north shore of the lake, but it was a tangled wilderness of swamps and scrub growth and it was inaccessible by car. In my exploration I walked through poison ivy without knowing it, and for four miserable days I had to hitchhike to the nearest town, Newberry, each morning for medical treatment. Newberry was forty miles away. I'd just gotten over the poison ivy when I made the mistake of getting too friendly with a porcupine. One night George suffered the greatest indignity of all when he crawled into our tent to find it already occupied by a skunk. Through it all we were camped on Charlie Fuller's property, and Charlie charged us two dollars a day rent. What had started out to be an innocent little camping trip soon became a total disaster. As far as I was concerned, Grandfather's property was worthless, living in the Upper Peninsula was impossible, and I was rapidly going broke. George felt much the same way. The day after Labor Day we packed our belongings into bundles and began the long retreat home. On September 10, 1934, I wearily dragged myself up the stairs of our house. I had one dollar left to my name. There were still two months to go before I'd get back to work. In the ups and downs of the Depression, I'd reached another low point.

IV

Just before George French and I left for the Upper Peninsula, Nick Woods dropped by the house one evening to tell me that he was going to be married on Saturday evening, September 15. He wanted me to be his best man. I'd gotten home just in time for this event, but it presented some financial problems. It was to be a formal wedding, and there was a wedding present to buy. I went to my old reliable source, Grandpa Perry, and borrowed ten dollars. With that money I got my tux cleaned and pressed, then set out to find Nick some kind of a wedding present. I found what I thought was an appropriate one. For a dollar apiece, in a junkyard, I bought two wire wheels for a 1931 Chevrolet and painted them red. My mother wrapped them all up in colored paper and put big bows on them, and I delivered them to the bride's house. I don't know whether Nick appreciated them or not, but he certainly got a laugh out of them.

On the night before the wedding, I used my last money to pay for my share of the refreshments to be served at Nick's stag party. I went to that party without a cent in my pocket. I didn't come away broke. About halfway through the evening, Nick took me off to one side and pulled out his wallet. From it he counted out eighteen new ten-dollar bills to pay me for the car he had bought in June. I was a little reluctant to take that money from a fellow who was on the eve of marriage, but Nick insisted. As a matter of fact, Nick had done extremely well since his arrival in Flint. The first job he'd gotten with the AC Spark Plug was measuring spark-plug porcelains with a micrometer. During the days of the poker game he'd regaled us with funny stories about that work. He claimed to be measuring five or six thousand of them a day and he had a ready wit that could turn the monotony of it into a very comic routine. Of course, Nick had a good mind and all the time he was performing this relatively simple task, he was giving it some thought and in May he'd invented a new way of doing it that saved the AC Spark Plug Company thousands of dollars. As his reward he was given a bonus and a nice salaried job at the rate of $140 a month. In 1934, that was a good job indeed, for it was a year-around thing, not subject to layoff.

Among the invited guests at Nick's wedding were several of our fraternity brothers. There was much singing of Michigan songs, especially one that ran, "I want to go back to Michigan, to dear Ann Arbor town." It made me lonesome for Ann Arbor, but the wedding had a more profound effect on me than that. All the fellows who came to Flint for the occasion had been in my pledge class, or a year ahead of me in school. All of them had graduated in the past two years and every one of them had a job. The jobs weren't necessarily good ones, but they were jobs and at that particular moment in my life any job was worth having. I would gladly have repossessed cars as Bugs Huntley was doing. I came away from the wedding convinced that the only way I was ever going to get anywhere was to get a college degree. As my father had said, that was the key.

On the Monday after Nick's wedding, while I still had Nick's $180 in my pocket, my father called from his office and asked me to come over to the lumberyard. When I walked in, I found a ferocious-looking little rooster of a man sitting there. He was introduced to me as David MacKenzie, from Germfask, the little town near Big Manistique Lake. None of us was aware of the fact that my grandfather Love's property on that lake had been the subject of a thirty-year feud between Mr. MacKenzie and Charlie Fuller, the owner of the fishing camp where George French and I had stayed. The three men had bought it in 1884, as Grandmother surmised, after it had been logged off. They'd bought the land all around the lake. At some time around 1900 they'd had a falling out and had split the property amongst them. David MacKenzie had taken the south shore. Grandfather had taken the north shore. Charlie Fuller had taken both ends. The only access road into the property had been the old logging road and this ran through Charlie Fuller's land. He immediately blocked it off, and for fifteen years neither Grandfather nor David MacKenzie could set foot on his own land. It wasn't until Governor Sleeper, a Democrat, was elected in 1913 that David MacKenzie, a power in Upper Peninsula Democratic politics, was able to do anything about it. Then, through his influence, he had a road built through the wilderness. In subsequent years, both MacKenzie and Fuller developed substantial hunting and fishing camps on the lake—very lucrative enterprises. As the automobile became more dependable, tourists began coming into the Upper Peninsula in great numbers, and Big Manistique Lake became a center for wandering fishermen and hunters in all seasons. That property of Grandfather's began to loom as important, and that is why Grandfather had kept up the taxes on it through the years. (They couldn't have amounted to much.) Both Charlie Fuller and David MacKenzie had tried to buy that land. Grandfather detested Fuller and it was a foregone conclusion that he was going to sell to MacKenzie, if he sold at all, but David MacKenzie was as tightfisted a man as ever lived. In all the years, knowing that he was going to get the property one way or another, he never offered Grandfather more than a hundred dollars for it, and Grandfather simply held out.

With the arrival of another Democratic administration in Michigan in 1933 and with the organization of the Civilian Conservation Corps, David MacKenzie knew he could get a road built down to the north shore of the lake and he decided to raise his offer. He evidently wrote Grandfather a letter that arrived after Grandfather's death and was told by the lawyers that my brothers and I now owned it. I'm almost certain, now, that he did intend to offer us some insignificant figure for the property—such as fifty dollars— taking advantage of our ignorance of the situation.

It was at this juncture that George French and I made our trip, and as luck would have it, we blundered into the camp of the enemy, Charlie Fuller. I never once went near David MacKenzie all the time I was in the Upper Peninsula. And because I was preoccupied with poison ivy, porcupine quills, broken rear axles, and skunk troubles, I never got around to discussing the property with Charlie Fuller. In looking back on it, I think it may even be possible that Charlie never knew I was the owner. Nevertheless, shortly after George and I headed for home, David MacKenzie discovered that I'd been up there and, worse yet, that I'd spent two weeks or more in Charlie Fuller's camp. I think he jumped to the conclusion that I was conniving with the devil. It had never entered his mind that anyone named Love would sell that land to Charlie Fuller. He wasted no time. There he was in Flint, sitting in my father's office. Even before I got there he had pulled out five one-hundred dollar bills and plunked them down on my father's desk.

I was still ignorant of the true situation at Big Manistique Lake. All I knew about that property was that it was swampy, that it was covered with poison ivy, and that there was no way to get into it except by boat. My father asked me if I thought $500 was a fair price. I didn't hesitate a moment.

"We'll take it," I said.

If I'd really known about things, I think I could have gotten three or four times $500 for that property, but there can be no mistake about it. At that moment in my life, $500 seemed like an enormous amount of money, and I was glad to have it. Of that amount, $165 was mine. With the money from Nick Woods, I now had a total of $345. I never had the slightest doubt about what I was going to do with it.

I had to work fast. School started the next Monday, and I had a lot to do, most important of which was finding a board job and a room. Lou Norris was now a senior and was president of his fraternity—the Sig house. When I called him on the phone he informed me that he was driving down to Ann Arbor the next morning to help get his fraternity's rushing under way, it being Orientation Week. I packed everything I owned—it all went in one suitcase—and jumped in Lou's car when he arrived at seven o'clock. I hardly took the time to say good-bye to my family. I had done a minimum of planning, incidentally. I'd made a few optimistic scribblings on a tablet, arriving at a figure of what I could spend for a room and other essentials. I had no idea of whether I could get through a whole year or not. I just made up my mind to go as long as I could.

It was now Lou Norris' turn to fill me in on Ann Arbor. Things had changed a lot in the two years since I last went down there. The enrollment was still down, and most of the frills of college life had disappeared in the general belt tightening of the Depression. It was a good thing I rode with Lou Norris that day, for he told me the one most important thing I had to know. Board jobs were almost impossible to get. All fraternities and sororities were now saving these jobs for their own members. All seven of the dining-room and kitchen jobs in the Sig house, for instance, had been allotted to his brothers before school let out the previous June. (Ordinarily, when a boy got a job, he would trade it to some boy who had the same job in another house. In that way he wouldn't be waiting on his own brothers.) Lou suggested that I go to my own fraternity before I did anything else and see if all the jobs were taken.

I hadn't intended to go near the fraternity because I knew it would be expensive to live there. On top of that, I was now something of an outsider there. Most of the brothers I had known well had graduated. The senior class, the class of 1935, had been sophomores the fall I'd worked for the Gamma Phis. I'd never really gotten to know them. I scarcely knew the names of the men we had pledged that fall, the men who were now juniors. Nevertheless, what Lou said made sense, and so when he let me out of his car that morning, I made a beeline for the house.

As in most fraternities at that time of year, my brothers were just gathering. The big job immediately ahead was rushing, and when I came through the front door, I found half a dozen of the boys sitting around the living room sifting through long lists of prospects. I was greeted cordially enough, but when I got around to broaching the subject of a board job, I sensed a general cooling off. Fortunately, I knew one boy well. He was Jack Benjamin, who had been initiated a year ahead of me and who was now back as a graduate student in the School of Engineering. Not long after I'd mentioned that I needed a job, and while there was still a good deal of hemming and hawing going on without any definite answer, Jack found an opportunity to change the subject, and then he took me by the arm and led me up to his room to see some memento or other from bygone days. Once we were alone, he told me what I was up against. There was a board job open, all right, because there had been a dropout, but the boys were inclined to hang onto it in case one of their own classmates needed it. There might be a real scramble for it, in which case I would lose out. It might be a good idea to do a little horse-trading. For instance, did I know any freshmen who were coming down from Flint? More important, could we pledge them?

"I have a feeling that if the fellows thought you were bringing five or six prospective pledges into the house with you, you could get the job," he said.

I did know some boys who were coming down from Flint as freshmen, and I knew them well. My brother John had brought most of them into that long-running poker game the previous winter. Strangely enough, most of these boys were good prospects, for they were the sons of factory foremen or superintendents and professional men, people who hadn't been hurt badly in the Depression. Moreover, at least three of them were bound to make the Michigan football team. I didn't leave anything to chance. I left Jack sitting in his room and went to the telephone and called my brother John long-distance. He gave me the names, Ann Arbor addresses, and telephone numbers of fourteen boys, all of whom were already in town for Orientation Week. I sat in that telephone booth for three hours calling those boys. When I finished I had every one of them sewed up for rushing dates so solidly that no one else could get at them for more than a week. I went over the list with Jack.

"I can almost guarantee you six pledges out of this bunch," I told him. "Maybe more."

Jack took it out to the brothers, and he was back in ten minutes. "The job is yours," he said, "but you'll have to live in the house."

It wasn't much of a job. I was the scullery drudge, but the house got its money's worth out of me. Besides clean pots and pans and freshly mopped floors, we got pledges. Eleven of those fourteen boys became members of Phi Kappa Sigma. Three of them became regulars on the Michigan football team in the days of Tom Harmon. Two of them were all-Americans. One of them was president of the house.

In looking back over the years, however, it is strange, I suppose, that I don't think of securing that job as the most important thing that happened to me on that first day of school. About four o'clock that afternoon a little man, about five feet six in height, came struggling up the front walk of the fraternity burdened down by three large suitcases. When he reached the sanctuary of the front hall, he threw the suitcases halfway up the stairs and let out a rebel yell that could have been heard all the way down to the campus. No one of us had ever seen this imp with the sardonic gleam in his eye before he burst in on us that day. He was Fred Squires and he came from Owensboro, Kentucky, but I don't think anyone used his proper name in all that school year. He was known as the Squirrel. If he wasn't actually engaged in some kind of devilry, he was thinking up some. He was twenty-five years old and he had been initiated into our fraternity way back in the fall of 1927. Those were the days of raccoon coats, flappers, and the Varsity Drag, and the Squirrel was firmly convinced that college was a place to have fun. He'd finished three years of premedical course before the Depression came and forced him to drop out of school. Now he'd come back to take up where he'd left off. Because the Squirrel was by far the most senior member of the fraternity, he got his choice of rooms and he picked the same room on the third floor where Marty Williams and I had lived in the fall of 1932. At some time just before dinner that day Jack Benjamin came out into the kitchen where I was mashing my first potatoes and asked me if I would mind rooming with the newcomer. I wearily carried my suitcase up the winding fire escape and settled in. It was the last weary moment I had all year. I have often described the next ten months as the only normal college year I ever had. It was also the most enjoyable one and it was made enjoyable by the Squirrel.

V

In the fall of 1932 I had taken a course on the French Revolution and Napoleon which was taught by a professor named Howard Ehrmann. Ehrmann was a precise, crisp sort of man who was undoubtedly one of the best teachers I ever knew. When I went back to school that fall, I had to choose a new faculty adviser and I picked him. And because he was offering a course in European history that covered the period between the Congress of Vienna and the Congress of Berlin, I elected to take it.

Howard Ehrmann had a lot of little idiosyncrasies as a teacher. Having taken one course from him, I was well acquainted with most of them. I knew that he took great pride in his ability to remember names and faces and I also knew there was a trick to it. He allowed people to sit anywhere they wanted to in his classes as long as they sat in the same place every day. At the end of his second class, he would always stop his lecture and clear his throat and say, "Ladies and gentlemen, would you please be kind enough to make a note of the seat in which you are now sitting, and will you please be good enough to occupy it for the rest of the semester? I have caused my secretary to make up a seating chart and this will facilitate the taking of the roll." He would memorize that seating chart, picking out two or three students each day and concentrating on learning everything he could about them. I don't think most people knew this and they used to marvel at his ability to meet them on campus and call them by name.

As it turned out, this little morsel of information was to prove exceedingly important to me. That fall my class with Ehrmann met on Mondays, Wednesdays, and Fridays at eleven o'clock. It was held in Haven Hall, a large, old-fashioned building that sat on the extreme northwest corner of the campus. Because of its location, students had to rush to get to classes on time. The room in which the course met was an amphitheater equipped with wooden tables, two students sitting side by side at each table. The entrance was on the left side of the room, and a student could turn either down or up to one of the semicircular rows of tables.

On the first day that Ehrmann's class met, I arrived in the lecture room early. It was a warm, sunny, Indian summer day and the windows had been thrown open. I climbed to the very back row of the amphitheater so that I could look out on the campus diagonal and watch the students scurrying to their classes. At precisely six minutes after eleven o'clock, the door behind the lectern opened and Professor Ehrmann entered. As usual, he was putting his watch away in his vest pocket. He stood quietly on the dais, looking out over the room, waiting for silence. When all was quiet he took the rubber band off the registration cards, flipped one over, and read off the name. As he did so, the door at the side swung open and a girl entered. She took two quick steps across the aisle and settled into the chair at the table nearest the door. Although she was quiet and accomplished her entry quickly, it upset the well-oiled precision that Ehrmann liked to affect. He paused and looked squarely at the girl and frowned. It was enough to focus the attention of everyone in the room on her. I turned my head and in that moment I forgot Ehrmann and history and everything else. I knew I was looking at the girl I wanted to marry.

I'd been in love just once in my life and it had been a long time since 1929 and Molly Flexner. It was this girl's physical beauty that struck me first, of course. She was exquisite. Her hair was jet black and her eyes were dark and flashing. Her face was expressive. A smile or a frown always lurked just beneath the surface. Above everything, there was a pride in her bearing that lent a certain jauntiness and verve to her whole character. As the professor called the roll, stopping at each name to make sure to whom it belonged, I watched her to see if she answered. When her name did come out —Jill Ryan—I felt like heaving a sigh of relief.

I knew that Jill was a different kind of girl from any I'd ever met before. At the very beginning, I knew that I'd have to work hard if I was going to get anywhere with her. Yet I also sensed that I couldn't push her into anything. If there was to be a love affair at all, it would have to have the appearance of happening casually. I had to make it come out that way. In some ways, it was going to be like a military campaign. I would have to maneuver things without her ever realizing that she was the object of any maneuvering.

I began my campaign for Jill Ryan on the afternoon after I first saw her. I tried to find someone who knew her, someone who might pave the way for me, but no one in my little group of acquaintances had ever heard of her. We were in the first week of school, so there was as yet no student directory out, but it suddenly struck me that she couldn't possibly have elected Ehrmann's course if she was a freshman. I found her in the previous year's directory. She was a member of a sorority that I shall call the Mu Alpha Gamma—familiarly known on campus as the Maggies. She came from Youngstown, Ohio. With that to go on, I hurried down to the library and got out the old year book and looked up her sorority group picture. There she was, standing in the front row. She was a senior. She was president of the Maggie house. She'd been quite active in campus politics throughout her career and served as a vice-president of the Pan-Hellenic Council and a cochairman of the J-Hop committee. There was one piece of discouraging news that I dug up somewhere. She was supposed to be the best girl of George Glass, the regular first-string tackle on the football team. It all added up to a pretty formidable undertaking for a fellow who didn't have much money and who, as a matter of fact, had only one good suit and that now four years old. I wasn't in the least bit daunted. I was a little like the cat who gazed at the queen, but this was exactly the situation I'd been reading about in all those romantic novels. I knew it was all going to work out to the happy ending. And I did have one big advantage: I knew all about Howard Ehrmann.

I planned the early part of my campaign around that knowledge of Ehrmann's class. When I went to the second meeting, I sat down in the seat next to the end of the row nearest the door. I figured that if Jill had been late the first day there was a good possibility she'd be late again. If she was late she would probably try to slip unobtrusively into the seat nearest to the door—next to me. Ehrmann emerged from his door behind the lectern right on time—at six minutes after the hour. Thirty seconds later the door on my left swung open and a slightly breathless Jill Ryan popped in. She took two quick steps across the aisle and slipped into the chair beside me. The class went on for fifty-three minutes, and then Ehrmann cleared his throat and made his little announcement about occupying present seats for the rest of the semester. Without even knowing that it had happened, Jill was frozen into the seat next to me for four months. I hadn't won the war yet, but I'd won the first skirmish.

I won the next ones, too. On most days before classes began, an assistant would write several reading assignments on the board. Ehrmann never mentioned these assignments and never called attention to them, but it was impossible to pass his course without doing the reading. He simply took the attitude that his students were adults and that they would have enough sense to do the things they should do without being led around by the hand. He expected that the assignments would be noted and copied down before the lecture began. Unfortunately, he had an annoying habit. He liked to dramatize his teaching with graphic demonstration at the blackboard and quite often, with a grandiloquent sweep of his eraser, he would inadvertently erase the whole reading assignment. A person had to be on the alert. I suspected that Jill would be careless about copying these assignments in the beginning, as most people were. So, at the end of class on the second day, as she slammed her notebook shut and prepared to pull her sweater over her shoulders, I shoved a piece of paper at her. She looked at it and then looked at me with a puzzled frown.

"Those are the reading assignments," I said. "I'm afraid Ehrmann erased them before anyone had a chance to copy them. I made an extra copy. It's a good idea not to miss them."

She smiled at me.

"Thank you," she said.

That was the total extent of our first conversation. It was enough. I had accomplished my first objective. From time to time during the next week, I did the same thing, and she always smiled and thanked me. I was waiting for the next move that I knew was coming. Ehrmann believed in surprise examinations. Ordinarily, he would stop halfway through a lecture and put a single question on the board, such as "What was the guiding principle during the Congress of Vienna?" Students were supposed to write everything they knew on the subject. From long experience with Ehrmann, I knew that he telegraphed these examinations in a peculiar way. As he lectured he would whirl to the blackboard from time to time and scrawl a phrase or a name or a date. He did this for emphasis, but when he underlined one of these little tidbits, it was always the subject for his next examination, usually given the next class meeting. At about the sixth meeting of our class, he turned and scrawled the words "Holy Alliance" and then, with a magnificent sweep of his arm that broke the chalk, he drew a heavy line under it. I promptly drew three heavy lines under the phrase in my notebook. When the class was over with I jumped out of my chair and headed for the door, then I pretended to have a second thought. I came back to Jill and opened my lecture notes and pointed at the three heavy lines. She looked up at me with a question on her face.

"When he puts anything like that on the board and draws a line under it, make sure you underline it in your notes, and make sure you study what he has to say about it and what the reading assignments have to say about it. The next time we come in here, we'll have an exam and you'll have to write on that question."

She opened her notebook, underlined the phrase, and then walked beside me to the door.

"How do you know this?" she said.

"I've had courses from Ehrmann before. I know his habits."

"I certainly do thank you," she said. We walked down the stairs together and out onto the campus and I waved my hand at her and started off toward my own house. I didn't pay attention as she went off in a different direction.

I was right. Ehrmann put his question on the board. I finished my paper in twenty minutes, handed it in, and coolly walked out without so much as a nod at Jill. When we next came to class, I had my reward. Our papers were waiting for us. We both had big, fat A's. Jill's smile was a wonderful thing to see. When the class ended she looked over at me.

"I sure had that one cold," she said. "You're a big help, you know. The Maggie house is on pro. With a few more marks like that, I'll pull them up all by myself."

We walked down the stairs together. This time I didn't walk toward my own house. I walked right along with her. She didn't seem to notice or mind. Our conversation wasn't exactly scintillating. I restricted it to the only thing we had in common at the moment—Ehrmann's class. We came to the Maggie house and I waved my hand as she turned in. I don't suppose that it seemed very important to her that I had walked home from class with her. I didn't think she was even conscious of it. It was a milestone to me, however. I was busy establishing a routine, a habit that I hoped she would accept without question.

That first walk home had been part of my little plan from the beginning, and I knew it would work out the way it had. Long before I took it, I was already looking for some way to make the next move. That was to get the conversation out of the trenches, so to speak. Ehrmann and his class would furnish enough fodder for about one more walk, and I had to find something I could drift to without being obvious. I was lucky. The Squirrel provided the situation without being aware of it.

From the time he'd let out his first rebel yell in the downstairs hall, the Squirrel had been agitating for a house dance, but every time he brought up the subject in chapter meeting, he met evasion. It was some little time before the brothers told him the truth. The

Phi Kaps were also on social probation. At first this dismayed him, and then he decided to try to find a loophole in the regulations. For two or three evenings, each time I came in the room, I'd find him studying them, scratching his head, and muttering to himself. He didn't have any success, of course. One night I had to pick up something off his desk and I saw the sheet lying there and I read the clause that was vital to us: "Each fraternity and sorority in good standing shall be permitted to entertain at three evening dances and one open house afternoon tea during the course of each semester." The key part of that phrase was "in good standing," which we weren't, but I was surprised about that tea and I took it up with the Squirrel when I next saw him.

"I've been coming to this university for five years, off and on," I told him. "I don't recall going to a tea in the whole time."

"Aw, Christ," he said, "that's for the God-damned sororities. They have those prissy little things during rushing season. You wouldn't be caught dead at one."

"I know a girl whose sorority is on probation," I said. "I'm almost sure she said something yesterday about rushing and I'm almost sure she said they were going to have a tea this week. What do you suppose they do at those teas?"

"How the hell should I know? I never been to one." He grabbed the regulations back from me and looked at them. "I suppose they all sit around and impress the hell out of each other."

"Read a book once and there was a tea party in it. You know what they did? They danced. That ought to be all right. A tea dance."

I was sitting at my desk and I went back to my work, whatever it was. After ten minutes or so, something made me turn around. The Squirrel was sitting there staring at me, a sardonic look in his eye.

"You know what? I'm living with a God-damned genius. That's what."

"Nuts," I said. "What makes you say that?"

"When you put together all those things you just said, you've got the whole thing licked." He came over to me and threw the copy of the regulations in front of me. "A tea dance is just about perfect. I've read those things a hundred times, and it doesn't say a thing in there about what you can or cannot do at a tea. It just says you can have one open-house tea a semester if you're in good standing. You can stand on your head and pour it in your ass if you want to."

"I never cared much for tea myself," I said.

"Hell, we can fill the teapots full of Haig and Haig if we have to. No one would know the difference."

"I know, Squirrel, but you can't have a tea anyway. You still have to be in good standing and we're not. We're on social pro."

"I think somebody has slipped up here someplace. These open-house teas are supposed to be some kind of reception, I guess. I suppose everybody from President Ruthven right on down through the faculty are invited. The thing they forget is that there isn't any difference between one of those big formal affairs and a rushing tea. A tea is a tea no matter what you do at it or what you call it. And if they let a sorority have a rushing tea while the sorority is on social pro, they've broken their own regulations. Look, we're going to start calling some sororities. First we'll find out which houses are on pro. Then we'll find out how many of them have had teas. We need some statistics here. You go call that girl you know and find out if you heard right. Make sure you get the facts."

That gave me a good reason to call Jill and talk to her about something besides class. I was properly mysterious about the whole thing. When she wanted to know why I was asking about her rushing tea, I simply told her I'd tell her later. I was saving up things to talk about on the walks. But even talking to Jill wasn't as interesting as watching the Squirrel once he got to work. He called every sorority on the Michigan campus that night. The next morning he told me he'd made an appointment to see the dean. He wanted me to come along with him for moral support.

The dean of the university at that time was Joseph Bursley, affectionately known as Uncle Joe. He was a short, wiry man with steel-gray hair and a large hawklike nose. He had a reputation for being hard-boiled but fair. I've always suspected he had a good sense of humor, too. When we were ushered into chairs in his office, the Squirrel was wearing his best Machiavellian manner. He started out with a very simple little question. Did the fact that our house was on social pro prevent us from having a tea? The dean rocked back in his chair and looked from one to the other of us as though he suspected something wasn't quite right.

"What do you fellows want to have a tea for?"

"Well, sir," the Squirrel said, "I guess I'd better confess. I'm not sure we want to have one. I guess you'd call that an academic question."

"Then I'll give you an academic answer," the dean said. "It would be against the rules for you to have a tea when you're on social probation."

"Then I want to register a protest." The Squirrel took a piece of paper out of his pocket and gave it to the dean. "There are the names of four sororities. All of them are on probation and all of them have had teas."

"I know, but those are rushing teas not receptions."

"A tea is a tea," the Squirrel said. "I don't care how you describe them. When you throw open your doors and invite people to come in, I don't see any difference between the president of the university and a freshman girl from Kalamazoo. You're still entertaining them."

I'm certain that Dean Bursley realized, too late, that he'd been led into deep water. A struggle of epic proportions loomed before him. Student-administration confrontations could be embarrassing, even in 1934, and the dean wasn't about to get involved.

"All right," he said simply. "I'll let you have your tea. When do you want to have it?"

"Saturday afternoon, October twentieth."

The dean reached over and scribbled something on the master calendar he had, then wrote out our permission on a little pad he kept. It was like the issuance of a license, and the Squirrel waited until he had the valuable document safely tucked away in his pocket before he threw his next curve ball.

"Does it make any difference what we do at this tea? As long as we serve tea, I mean?"

"Just what do you have in mind?" the dean said, rubbing his chin. He smelled another rat.

"Quite a few things," the Squirrel said, "but dancing, mostly."

The dean studied the Squirrel over the tops of his glasses for some little time.

"Supposing I was to say you couldn't dance?"

"Then I'd have to register another protest. I've read those regulations over and over, and it doesn't say one word about what you can or cannot do at a tea."

The dean looked back and forth from one to the other of us.

"Well, boys," he said, "I've read those regulations, too. In fact, I wrote them. Although it doesn't say what you can or cannot do, I think I have the discretion of saying yes or no to this. I'm inclined to say no, but there's something interesting about this case. In all the years I've been dean of this university, no one's ever asked to hold a tea dance before. You've seen fit to think of something new and different. I know this is a trick to get around your social pro, but I'm going to say yes, because I want to see what you're going to do. You can depend on it, I'll be there. Every time someone finds a loophole in these regulations, there's a good possibility we'll have to plug it up. What time does your party start?"

"Two o'clock, sir."

The dean pointed a finger at him. "I'm going to put one crimp in your sails, young man, seeing as how you're making a big thing out of reading regulations. These teas are supposed to be open houses. See that this one is. You're not going to get away with a closed party while you're on probation."

Holding a party wasn't very important to me. I certainly wasn't as excited about this one as the Squirrel was. Consequently, I took almost no part in planning it after that visit to the dean, but I did have a kind of interest in it for I recognized immediately that this was going to furnish me with a conversational gambit that I could use to cement that small embryonic friendship I had going with Jill Ryan. After the next class, as was now my habit, I walked along with her as she hurried back to the Maggie house for lunch. As I suspected she would, Jill asked me about that phone call I'd made.

"Don't look now," I said, "but I think you're in the company of a man who has found a way to beat social pro."

"Really? How?"

I told her what we were planning and how we'd worked it.

"A tea dance?" She stopped in her tracks and looked at me. "That's a marvelous idea. I've never been to one on this campus."

Of course, after that, *what* we talked about wasn't really important. What *was* important was the thing that happened in that one walk. On the previous occasions that I'd walked home with Jill, we'd plodded along at a brisk, businesslike pace. Now we strolled. She cocked her head at me when she asked a question. She was thoughtful. Sometimes she chortled at something I said. We'd come into full and complete life for each other. We were no longer two people who just happened to sit next to each other in a history class.

I was a long way from winning Jill Ryan yet. The next move, obviously, was getting a date with her. In that first love affair of mine with Molly, things had been completely different. Then Molly had fallen in love with me at almost the same time I'd fallen in love with her. Now, while I was falling more deeply in love with Jill every minute, there was no reciprocal feeling. It was going to be a case of being patient until something happened to strike a spark. In the meantime, I had to keep things light and gay, and never let her know how much I wanted her and how hard I was working. I sensed that if I made one premature move I'd never see her again. That first date, when it came, would have to be like the conversation, something that seemed to happen naturally and easily. I struggled to bring it about in exactly that way. Once again, I was lucky.

After our session with the dean, the Squirrel had devoted all his energies to making the tea dance a success. He was a master. In order to get around the danger of having the whole campus descend on our house when they heard the news, the Squirrel hit upon the idea of making the party a neighborhood affair. He invited the members of the three sororities and two fraternities nearest us to come, not only as guests but as participants. The party was to be held on the afternoon of the Michigan-Illinois football game (played at Urbana). The Phi Delts from next door found a small section of bleachers and set them up in our living room facing a mock-up of a football field. As the game progressed, people could sit in the bleachers and listen to the radio and follow the action on the mock-up. The Gamma Phi Betas were to provide other entertainment. They went all over collecting card tables and set them up in the big entrance hall so that anyone who wished to could play bridge. The Collegiate Sorosis took charge of the tea and coffee and the serving of it. The Thetas, from across the street, made cookies and cakes and sandwiches. The SAEs set up a soft-drink bar in our cardroom. Our chapter, of course, furnished the music for dancing which took place downstairs. The whole thing was ingeniously set up, and as the plans unfolded, Jill expressed a lively interest. At some time or other she informed me that the girls at the Maggie house were so intrigued by the idea that they were thinking of trying the same thing. This gave me the opening I wanted.

"Why don't you and your boy friend come over and see how it works?" I said.

"Oh, George will be busy in Urbana that afternoon."

"You don't need a boy friend anyway. You can probably pick one up on the premises. Bring along a couple of your sisters."

"I might do that little thing," she said.

Of course, I was well aware of where George Glass would be on that Saturday afternoon and I was hoping she'd come unescorted. I was pretty certain who the boy friend would be that she would pick up on the premises. Actually, I was kind of backing into a date, but that's the way I figured it had to be. I didn't know for sure that she was coming until the day before.

"What time does this shindig of yours start tomorrow?" she asked as we strolled toward the Maggie house.

"Two o'clock. Would you like me to come and get you and show you the way?"

"Nope. I'll find my own way. You'll be busy enough without worrying about me. By the way, are you the president of your house?"

"I'm the Delta," I said.

"What in heaven's name is a Delta?"

"Delta stands for dog. I'm in charge of the freshmen who comb the dog."

She threw back her head and laughed. When we came to the Maggie's front walk, she reached out and patted me on the arm.

"Brother Delta, old boy," she said, "I'll see you tomorrow afternoon."

Everything turned out beautifully. People began wandering up our front walk about one thirty. All the Gamma Phis walked across our backyard in a group. We'd hired an orchestra to play in the dining room from two to five, but when five o'clock came no one wanted to go home so we took up a collection, and the music played for another hour. The radio blared forth the progress of the game. Everyone walked around carrying tea cups or soft drinks. There were at least a dozen tables of bridge going. Dean Bursley and several other faculty members dropped by in the course of the afternoon, and every one of them stayed to the end. At around six in the evening, as I was walking through the living room, the dean stopped me. He was standing there munching happily on a sandwich.

"Young man," he said, "you and your friend the Squirrel are to be congratulated. I've never attended a social function on this campus quite like this one, and it's the kind of thing we could use more of. I think you've started something and I want you to know that I have enjoyed myself thoroughly."

That compliment was a very important one for me because Jill Ryan was standing next to me when it was delivered. She had come strolling up the walk with two of her sorority sisters at a little after two. I knew exactly when she had arrived, of course, because I'd been watching for her but I let her wander around for a while and let her get separated from her sisters, before I pretended to run into her. After that we were together all afternoon. We listened to the game. We danced several times. We even played a rubber of bridge. Only one small cloud crossed the horizon, but even that had a silver lining. All fall I had carefully ignored the rumor that Jill was George Glass's girl. It wouldn't be important anyway unless I started to get some place, and now I'd reached that moment. While Jill and I were dancing, a tall young man came up to us. He addressed himself to her, ignoring me.

"While the cat's away, the mice will play, eh?"

"Oh, Alfred," she said. "This is a wonderful party. Why do you want to spoil it?"

"Don't worry. I won't report you."

"Brother Delta," Jill said, angrily, after he'd gone away. "That was one of George Glass's watchdogs. I hate them."

When the party began to break up, Jill seemed reluctant to go.

"I'm stuffed. I don't really feel like eating, but if I don't go home, I'll miss dinner, and there's nothing more to eat until morning."

"I'll stake you to a hamburger and a glass of beer if you feel like walking down to the Pretzel Bell."

She pursed her lips and then nodded.

"I think I'd like that. You're on."

We strolled leisurely across the campus and down to the Pretzel Bell, the big beer garden beyond Division Street. It was full and we couldn't get in, so we strolled on across Main Street into the old part of town until we found a little German place. It was well after eight when Jill finished her beer and looked at her watch.

"I'm going to be late," she said. "I'm supposed to have a date with one of the watchdogs at nine o'clock. George thinks that with them around no one is going to beat his time while he's out giving his all for Michigan."

"I'll take you home in a cab," I said.

"Want to get rid of me, eh?"

"Nope. If I had the nerve, I'd kidnap you."

"Brother Delta," she said, "I don't like watchdogs anyway. I think I'll consider myself kidnapped. I won't even make you tie me up. You just sit right there while I call my roommate. I've just come down with a frightful headache."

She was back in five minutes. "We have four hours. What will we talk about? Louis Philippe?"

"To hell with Louis Philippe," I said. "We'll plan the house we're going to live in when we get married."

"I didn't know we were getting married. What brought this on?"

"I've compromised you. You don't go around kidnapping girls willy-nilly, you know."

We decided on a castle. It started out with two dungeons for the children and ended up with seven stories underground to take care of the nineteen children we added after the first two. Every time we thought we'd settled on the number of children we'd have, Jill would think of another name she wanted to use, and we'd add another child and another dungeon. It was the pleasantest kind of foolishness and we did a lot of laughing and the time passed quickly.

When we came strolling along the street to the Maggie house, there were several couples standing around near the front door. Jill put her hand on my arm and steered me up the street for half a block.

"You're kind of a mystery man, you know. Some of the sisters have noticed this little business of your walking me home every noon. There's been some curiosity."

"I didn't even know *you* had noticed I was walking you home every day."

She threw back her head and laughed. "Brother Delta, I was onto you the first day. You didn't think you were fooling me with all that reading-assignment business, did you?"

"I sure did."

"I've had that pulled before, but you've done pretty well. You're clever, you know." She stopped smiling, and a soft, warm look came into her eyes. "There's just one thing, Brother Delta. Please don't fall in love with me."

"Why not? George Glass?"

"No. I don't love George. He's really quite a nice fellow, but he's much too possessive. I'm not ready to be possessed yet and I don't think I'm ready to fall in love myself. The kind of a relationship I want with a boy right now is exactly the kind I'm having with you. I don't want to get all tied up in knots. I want to enjoy your company and I want you to enjoy mine. Let's keep it that way."

"I guess that's plain enough."

"I hope so. Brother Delta, I'm not any great prize, but I've had trouble in the love business before and I always have to end up by sending a boy packing. I don't want that to happen to you. You're fun, and I like you."

"Do you think you could find time to give me a date now and then?"

"You mean, am I going to be true to George Glass?"

"I guess that's what I mean."

"No. I'm not very afraid of George. He's not very aggressive. If he was, we'd have a better football team." She suddenly reached up and kissed me on the cheek. "How about next Friday night, Brother Delta? George will be out at the Barton Hills country club with the team, meditating on Minnesota."

I had to share Jill with George Glass, but for seven weeks or until early in December, I had one date every weekend. If the football team happened to be playing out of town, I managed two dates in a week. Of course, there were all those walks across the campus—three a week. On the surface, our relationship was easy and unusually pleasant. Our place was the little German one we'd found that first night. It was patronized mostly by townspeople not students. We would drink beer and talk and sing along with the Schnitzelbank. If we had a date on Saturday night, we would get the Sunday papers and spread them out on the table. This wasn't easy on me, however. I was falling more deeply in love with her every day. I wanted to tell her but I had to wait. I hoped that she would come to me with her own love one day. There was evidence that this might happen.

A few days before Thanksgiving, Jill surprised me by announcing that she was going to Flint for the holiday. It developed that one of her sorority sisters was from Flint, a girl that I'd never met. Her name was Helen Tarkington and she was the daughter of Flint's most prominent lawyer, Judge Tarkington. The reason I'd never met Helen, I suppose, was because she'd been away to school in the East. I met her and liked her at once. She was a round-faced girl, short and rather full of figure. When she asked me if I'd like to have Thanksgiving dinner at her house with her family and Jill, I accepted. It was a gesture that told me a great deal. Helen had guessed how I felt about Jill. I hoped she had spotted something in Jill that indicated there was a fondness for me. At any rate, it was obvious that Helen had arranged the whole business for the two of us. When I found out that Helen had no boy friend in Flint—she was supposedly engaged to a West Point cadet—I asked her if she'd like a blind date and then arranged for George French to be her escort. As it turned out, that was a historic blind date. I don't think George had ever been in love up to that point in his life, but he certainly went head over heels for Helen—and she for him.

It was a very enjoyable holiday, and once more I was lucky. On the first night at home we went dancing at the IMA to the music of George Olsen and his orchestra. George just happened to be the most illustrious graduate of my fraternity house, and I'd met him a few weeks before at Homecoming. I took Jill backstage to meet him, and he invited us to his dressing room for a drink during intermission. Then he dedicated a song to Jill. It was "The Object of My Affections," and forever more it became Jill's song in my mind. All this impressed Jill very much, and things progressed rapidly.

On Thanksgiving day, after the dinner, George and Helen and Jill and I retired to the Tarkington recreation room, and put some records on the Victrola and lit a fire in the fireplace. It was a luxurious room that looked out on a terraced garden. In the early winter twilight it had begun to snow, and big fluffy flakes floated down outside. Jill had on a soft green dress of wool that had a full skirt. At some time in the evening, when we finished a dance, she put her hands in the pockets and pirouetted around the room, the skirt flaring out from her beautiful legs. She came to a stop near a window seat and stood looking out at the big snowflakes. I went to stand beside her.

"What a beautiful sight," she said.

"Maybe we'd better give up the idea of all those dungeons and build a house with a room and a garden like this one has."

"I don't want a castle, either," she said.

"I've been thinking. Maybe I ought to settle for a house on a hillside that overlooks a river with a big lawn and trees. I guess I've got a pretty good idea of what it will look like."

"When you're having your little fantasy, what else do you see?" she said almost in a whisper.

"You," I said.

She stood there looking up at me with eyes that were soft and misty, and when I put my arms around her, she put hers around me. She'd given me little pecks on the cheek now and then, but now she gave me a warm, loving kiss on the mouth. I had never been as much in love as I was at that moment, and I wanted to pour it out to her, but when I opened my mouth to say it, she put her finger up to my lips and shook her head. The moment ended then, and she led me over to where George and Helen were sitting before the fire. On the way back to Ann Arbor that night, Jill and I sat in the back seat. I didn't kiss her again, but she held my hand and put her head on my shoulder and went to sleep.

The next two weeks were the happiest I had in Ann Arbor. When Jill and I walked home from class now, we walked hand in hand. Unfortunately, I'd forgotten all about George Glass, and sad to say, he was there lurking in the background all the time. About ten days before Christmas vacation, on a chilly gray day, I'd hung my mackinaw at the back of Ehrmann's classroom. When the class ended, I went back to get it, expecting to find Jill waiting for me at the door when I came back. She wasn't there. I rushed over to the stairs to catch up with her and I was just in time to see her below me, going out the door of the building with a big man in a dark blue sweater with a big yellow *M* on it. George Glass had no more football obligations, and he had obviously decided to reclaim what he thought rightfully belonged to him. The main threat to his plans had developed in that stretch of campus between Ehrmann's class and the Maggie house. Now that he could give his full attention to the matter, he intended to eliminate it.

I was quite amused by the whole business on that first day George Glass appeared. There was every evidence that Jill felt the same way. When she came to class the next time, she winked at me as she settled into her chair. But George was there again at the end of the class, and now it wasn't quite as amusing. Not being able to talk with her on the walk home, I was forced to call her on the telephone. Her roommate told me she'd gone off to Detroit for the weekend. I don't suppose I could have expected anything else. The Detroit Alumni always gave an annual football banquet and gala weekend to members of the team and their best girls. They were treated royally. I'll never know what happened to Jill on that weekend, but when she came back from it she was different. There were no more smiles and she seemed annoyed when I pushed the reading assignments at her. After class George Glass was waiting for her. I tried to call her three different times that week and she was always out. I couldn't even wish her a Merry Christmas.

When Jill came back after the holidays she was coldly formal. Then, to my horror, on the third meeting of the class, she didn't sit down beside me when she came in. She had gone to Ehrmann and asked for a seat change, claiming it was too drafty near the door. I didn't do anything about it. I just let her go. She'd told me not to press her and I didn't. The semester ended, and she didn't enroll in Ehrmann's course for the second half. Now and then, in the bleak days of February, I walked by the Maggie house, trying to get a glimpse of her. I never did.

VI

Falling in love with Jill Ryan was the worst thing I could have done from a financial standpoint. Compared to my usual living standards, I spent money like a drunken sailor. At Christmas time I was almost broke. When I took stock of my situation, I knew I'd never make it beyond the end of the first semester. One of the things I did while, I was home was to go over to the AC Spark Plug Company and ask if there was any chance of getting my old job back. My former boss told me to come back and see him when I dropped out of school in February. He might have something for me.

It was under these circumstances that I returned to Ann Arbor in January. I needed cheering up, and the Squirrel was just the fellow to do it. Unfortunately, the Squirrel didn't show up, and the whole first day passed without any word from him. That night, as I settled down to my studies, I was glum indeed.

It was almost eleven in the evening when I heard feet pounding up the steps of the fire escape. There was a bang as the door burst open and another bang as it slammed shut. The Squirrel was standing there with his back to the door, wild-eyed and gasping for breath from his climb.

"Quick," he said, holding out his hand. "Give me two bucks!"

I expected a taxi driver to come pounding on the door any minute. I reached in my pocket, fished around, and pulled out two crumpled old bills and gave them to him. He relaxed and grinned with satisfaction.

"Son," he said, "that was the best investment you ever made in your life. You're going to make a fortune." He came away from the door, put his suitcase down, and reached into an inner pocket, fishing out a folded piece of paper. He handed it to me with a flourish.

"What's this?"

"You just bought it," he said.

I opened it and read the first lines, then looked up at him. I felt like throwing him right out the window. I was holding a chain letter in my hand. I'd seen chain letters before. They claimed to have some connection with the mysterious East. If you dutifully sent off your letter some luck would come to you within a specified number of days. If you broke the chain you were sentenced to everlasting damnation. Only recently I'd seen a letter that involved sending a dime through the mail. I thought chain letters were silly and I couldn't see much difference between them and the one I was holding except that this one involved dollar bills.

"God damn it, Squirrel," I told him, "give me my two dollars back."

"I'll be damned if I will. You've got to hit some guys over the head to make them see the light of day."

It turned out that he'd been standing in the Louisville station, waiting for a train to bring him back to school, when an old friend of his walked up and talked him into buying this letter. He'd been as unenthusiastic about it as I was, but on the train he'd read it over a couple of times and had the beginnings of an idea. He had relatives in Dayton, Ohio, and when he reached there, he got off the train. He went to an uncle's office and mimeographed four hundred copies of the letter. He was supposed to sell two copies, but he'd only sold one in Dayton. By selling the second one to me, he had now recouped his investment. He promised me that I would get my two dollars back almost as quickly, but I had to promise to do exactly what he said. I promised, somewhat wearily. He opened his suitcase and pulled out a bundle of stamped envelopes.

"There's almost a hundred of these here," he said. "I'll furnish what we need tonight, but you'll have to go to the post office tomorrow and get your own supply. These are the most important part of the whole scheme. Now watch exactly what I do."

He looked carefully at the name and address at the top of the list on the letter and carefully copied it on the envelope. Then he took one of the dollar bills I had given him, put it in the envelope, and sealed it. After that he scratched the name off the top of the list and added my name and address on the bottom. When he'd finished this he told me to put on my hat and coat. I followed him down the stairs and out the front door and down to the mailbox, where he ceremoniously deposited the letter. When he was done, he turned to me and brushed his hands together.

"There, God damn it, my part of this transaction is officially over. I invested two dollars and now I have it back. You are a witness to the fact that I have mailed one dollar to the guy at the top of the list, just as it says in the instructions. So help me, I never heard of him before in my life. Now, everything I take in is velvet, and I'll get you started. This is another important part of this business. Just because you've done what you're supposed to do doesn't mean that you wash your hands of it."

Getting me started was fairly simple. We walked back to the fraternity house and into Jack Benjamin's room. The Squirrel closed the door and leaned up against it, to keep Jack from getting out, I suppose.

"Quick," the Squirrel told Jack. "Give us two bucks." When Jack dazedly handed them over, the Squirrel handed them to me. "One of those is yours," he said. "Now aren't you sorry for all the nasty things you said to me?" He didn't wait for an answer. He just grabbed the folded copy of the chain letter out of my hand and whisked it over to Jack. Jack read it and bristled.

"God damn it, Squirrel," he said. "Give me my money back."

"I'll be damned if I will. You got to hit some guys over the head to make them see the light of day."

The Squirrel not only repeated the same words, he went through exactly the same series of actions. We ended up by trooping down to the mailbox together and depositing the envelope. Then the three of us went back to the house and invaded Harold Anderson's room. At about two in the morning, ten of us trudged down to the mailbox together and watched as the envelope was deposited. This last one was addressed to the Squirrel. He led us solemnly back to the house and told us all to sit down in the living room.

"Now I want to explain to you fellows what I've been doing," he said. "I've been cultivating proper habits in you. You'll notice that last letter was addressed to me. I spent the whole day taking fellows to mailboxes in Dayton, Ohio. I saw fifteen letters sent off to me with dollar bills in them. I reckon there've been quite a few more sent off to me since this afternoon." He told me that my name was now at the top of the list. The next letter that was mailed would come to me. That would be before he went to bed. "And from now on, remember, *every* letter that's mailed to you represents a clear profit. What I've been trying to impress on you fellows is that you can't take anyone's word for things in this business. You yourself have got to see to it that a letter is put in the mailbox after every transaction. It does two things: it shows people that everything is on the up and up, and it keeps this chain from being broken. There will be breaks in this chain and every break in it means just that much less money you take in, so you don't want to let it break anywhere if you can help it. I've spent a lot of time establishing you in the right habits and I want you to spend as much time, or more, impressing others to have the same habits. Each one of you has one more letter to sell. Whoever you sell it to, you be damned sure that the dollar bill gets in the envelope and that the envelope gets in the mailbox. Then you go with the guy you sold it to and help him sell it to someone else and then you see that *that* letter gets in the mail, and so on. You ought to keep going with these guys, just like I have, until you actually see a letter put in a mailbox with your name on it. Then you ought to go back with your original guy and help him sell his second letter and do the same things over again. As fast as you get those letters in the mail to yourself, go back down to the lowest link in the chain and start over again. Drill, drill, drill! Keep harping to these guys that there can't be any breaks and that they shouldn't allow any breaks until letters get in the box to themselves."

"That's a lot of work, Squirrel," Jack Benjamin said.

"Sure it's a lot of work, but if you just see fifteen bucks put in the mail to yourself, that's fifteen bucks clear profit. Where else can you make fifteen bucks a day in these times? And if you get fifteen, you'll get more, I'll guarantee you, just from the momentum."

Jack Benjamin shook his head wearily. "I think you've got something, but we'd better get together and decide who's going to work which part of the campus. It isn't going to take very long to saturate the town."

"Aaaaaah," the Squirrel said, that impish look coming into his eyes. "You're not going to sell your other letter in Ann Arbor. You're going to sell it in Saginaw."

"Saginaw?"

"That's where you live isn't it?"

"You want me to go all the way back up to Saginaw and sell this thing? Christ, I just came back from Saginaw this morning."

"If you want to make any money, you'll get your ass right back up there as fast as you can. Nobody in Saginaw has heard about this thing yet, but by a week from now they will have. You get there first, while it still looks like a fresh idea. You get your name to the top of as many lists as you can in one day and then you get out before anybody has a chance to get skeptical or get tired of it. It will run down eventually, but not before you've made a nice little thing out of it." He turned to the last man on the list. "I'll take one of your letters off your hands. I'll take care of Ann Arbor in the morning."

I was on the road hitchhiking to Flint at daylight. I took my letter straight to Bugs Huntley at his finance company, and by five minutes after nine I had the first dollar bill in the mail and Bugs was running off copies of the letter on his mimeograph machine. Without even getting out of Bugs's office, I'd seen my name reach the top of two lists by ten thirty. By noon I'd seen seven letters mailed to myself, all from right there in that one office building, and letter salesmen were walking all over the corridors. At lunch hour I took two of Bugs's chain holders out to the AC Spark Plug Company and got it nicely under way there. At three thirty I collared George French when he got out of work, and he and I got it going in our own neighborhood. At five o'clock, on my way back to Ann Arbor, I stopped off at my father's lumberyard and got it going there. I'd sure been a busy boy, and I wasn't the only one. My fraternity brothers had spread out all over Michigan. One of them even carried the letter home to Buffalo.

The Squirrel didn't start the chain-letter craze of 1935, but he must have got in on it very close to the beginning. All of my fraternity brothers were in on it early, too. I think that the Squirrel's understanding of how to make it work had a lot to do with the success of it, for wherever his methods were used, it flourished. Within six weeks of that January night the chain letters were sweeping the country. The Depression saw a lot of crackpot schemes, but the 1935 chain-letter craze was the zaniest of them all. Before it was over, the President had to step in and put a stop to it before the post office broke down.

In our fraternity, the Squirrel had started things on a Monday. A few scattered letters, mostly for the Squirrel, dribbled in on Wednesday. I got my first letters, four of them, on Thursday. On Friday I got ten. On Saturday there was a flood. Early in the next week the mailman was carrying three or four big mailbags into our house every day. It was like Christmas. The biggest single day I had was on the second Thursday, when I took in $153. The potential take for the scheme was $1,056 dollars. As the Squirrel had predicted, there were breaks in the chain, but I didn't care. I took in the magnificent sum of $586, all in one-dollar bills. My money continued to come in for weeks and months. The last dollar bill I received came in June and it was postmarked Honolulu. The Squirrel was the biggest winner because he had bought into the chain twice. He took in more than $1300.

I didn't have to worry about getting through to the end of school. I even had enough to buy a new suit.

VII

When I first went back to school in the fall of 1934, I was concerned enough about my finances to ask my faculty adviser if there was any kind of a loan fund for students. He gave me a pamphlet which listed all the various scholarships, university awards, and student-aid societies. While looking down the long list to see if I could qualify for anything, I discovered the Hopwood Awards. These were prizes given each year for proficiency in creative writing and they were good prizes, too. There were four of $1,500 each to be given for the best works of fiction, drama, poetry, and exposition produced by university students during the academic year. There were also a number of lesser plums. In order to be eligible for them, a student had to enroll for at least one semester in any one of several English or journalism courses and submit manuscripts to a committee of judges toward the end of the school year.

This was of great interest to me. I considered myself a writer. I'd even done some writing and it seemed to me that I had a big jump on all these callow youths I saw around me on the campus.

I was sure I would be able to walk off with one of the prizes with no trouble at all.

The courses required for entry in the contest were all courses in advanced English composition, and most of them were open only with special permission from instructors. Despite the fact that I hadn't taken any courses in English composition since I had completed freshman rhetoric, I brashly chose something called English 153—creative writing—and went to see the instructor, Erich Walter, who was then the assistant dean of the Literary College. My footsteps must have been guided by some fond angel, for Erich Walter was the kindest, gentlest man who ever entered my life. He had a delicious sense of humor. I can't account for what happened on any other basis. I had no record of achievement, and I had nothing to show Dean Walter, but after talking to me for ten minutes, he let me enroll in his course.

I was an outsider in English 153 from the very beginning. There seemed to be three major cliques, about evenly divided among would-be novelists, poets, and playwrights. They ran around together, had obviously known each other for a long time, and liked to compare themselves favorably with James Joyce and Henrik Ibsen. Before the first meeting of the class, they had already divided the Hopwoods up among themselves. I came to regard them as arty-arty. I didn't aspire to anything more significant than *The Saturday Evening Post* myself, and a good deal of what went on in that class went right over my head. There was one pretty good writer there, however. His name was Arthur Miller. I remember that he impressed me favorably at the time, not because of what he wrote, but because he seemed to be the only sane member of the group.

For one semester—and beyond—I plugged away at my novel on the Pontiac conspiracy. I had it sent down from Flint and I started right in from the point where I'd been run out of the house by my stepmother—in midsentence, I believe. From the very beginning, Dean Walter suggested that I might do better to concentrate on something a little less ambitious, but I wasn't capable of listening to suggestions. The rules of the Hopwood contest stated that the first prize would be awarded to "a major work of fiction." I intended to collect that $1,500.

I wasn't a good writer, of course. I was a terrible writer and my novel was a terrible novel. Dean Walter knew how awful it was, but being a kindly man, he never found the words to disillusion me. I missed his hints completely. I became a man obsessed. I was working for my board. I was deeply in love. I was putting up with the didoes of an eccentric roommate. I had serious financial worries.

These things bothered me not at all in my writing. Quite early in the year I established a routine that I followed for ten months. I would finish all my studying by eleven, or a little after. Then, for three hours I would pound away at the old typewriter my father had given me. I rarely got more than four hours of sleep in that whole school year.

There wasn't room for English on my schedule during the second semester, but I'd fulfilled the requirements for entering the Hopwoods. Shortly after I completed English 153 with an A, I went around to see Dean Walter to ask him if he'd keep on reading my novel even though I wasn't in his class anymore. He was willing but not very encouraging.

"I suppose your heart is still set on entering that novel in the contest," he said.

"Yes, sir. Why not?"

"I don't think it's good enough," he said.

"But you gave me an A," I protested.

"That A was for effort. Of course, it wasn't all for effort. You improved. I've never had a student who learned to write as fast as you have. I think you'll keep on learning and improving, but you had a long way to go when you started out, and in spite of your improvement, you have a long way to go yet. I'd prefer you to wait awhile before you enter the Hopwoods."

"Maybe I'll improve enough between now and April to win it," I said.

I plunged ahead. The contest deadline was at four o'clock in the afternoon of April 22, the day after spring vacation. I didn't go home. I stayed up in that room at the house, all alone, doing one more draft. When I was hungry I traipsed down to the nearest diner for a sandwich. When I was tired I flopped down on the sofa for two or three hours. At one in the afternoon of the 22nd, I wrote "The End," gathered the manuscript together, and carried it down to a bindery. At five minutes to four I plunked it down on the desk in Dean Walter's office. My momentum carried me on for ten more days. In quick succession I dashed off a term paper and a short story. One morning I came down to breakfast and looked out the window to find that everything was green and flowering. It was just as though I had emerged from a deep sleep. It was the first of May, and school had only another month to run. When I went back upstairs that morning, I put the cover back on the typewriter. I didn't take it off again for months.

On the last Friday in May I went up to the ballroom of the Michigan Union on a hot, steamy afternoon. I listened while the names of the arty-arty students were called out. They went forward, one by one, to receive their checks. Arthur Miller got one that day. My name wasn't mentioned—even for one of the small prizes. I wanted to go somewhere and hide my head, but as the people filed out of the room, Dean Walter came up and touched me on the elbow and asked me if I'd take a little walk with him. He steered me along the corridors of Angell Hall to his office and got out my manuscript.

"The judges didn't care much for this," he said. "Mr. Sinclair Lewis said it was one of the worst novels he ever read." A look of compassion came into his eyes. "I suppose it's cruel of me to tell you this at this particular moment. I'm well aware of how much you wanted to win one of those prizes. I have a reason. You're going to have to learn to shrug off adverse criticism. I had more than fifty students in my classes this year. Some of them got prizes, but I doubt that any of them will be writers—except for Arthur Miller. I could have brought Arthur back here, but he doesn't need encouragement. You do, because you are going to be a writer, my friend. No matter what black moments the future brings, don't you ever forget it, and don't ever give up."

That was the big moment in my life. I was twenty-three years old, and for the first time in my life, I knew what I wanted to be —was going to be.

VIII

Toward the end of the first week in May, shortly after I put the cover on my typewriter, I came up to the room one evening to find the Squirrel muttering to himself. He was obviously wrought up over a letter he had just received. As a true son of the old Blue Grass, he had been making plans for a pilgrimage to the Kentucky Derby for some days past. He had been touting a horse named Omaha and he had collected a considerable sum of money from the brothers to put on Omaha's nose. Now, less than twenty hours before his departure for Mecca, he was in receipt of a letter from his mother. He tossed it to me.

"Dear Frederick," this letter said. "On this coming weekend your third cousin, Arbonna Higgins, will be in Ann Arbor. I don't believe you have ever met her or that I have discussed her with you. She is the daughter of my second cousin Jennifer who married a man from Port Huron, Michigan, when you were still a baby. Jennifer has written me a very nice letter. She is quite anxious that Arbonna has a good time in Ann Arbor. She doesn't know any boys there, but Jennifer knows you are attending the university and wonders whether you can see that Arbonna has a good time. According to her mother, Arbonna loves to dance.

"Now, Frederick, I don't ask you to do very many things for me, but this time I'm going to. Arbonna's mother has always been one of my dearest friends, and I think I owe it to her as a person and I think our family owes it to her as a blood relative to see to it that Arbonna has a good time. I want you to be nice to her. While I realize that Arbonna may not be the most beautiful girl in the world, I'm going to place the responsibility squarely on your shoulders. She will arrive in Ann Arbor from Detroit by bus at four o'clock on Friday afternoon and she will be staying at the Michigan Union. I will expect to hear from you that you have done as I ask."

After I handed the letter back to the Squirrel, he threw it high in the air and began pacing the floor. "God damn it!" he said. "God damn it! I've got my bags all packed and I'm ready to go and my mother pulls a trick like this on me. Roomie, you've got to help me and take care of this dame."

"Why should I get stuck with your horse-faced cousin for a whole weekend?"

"What makes you think she's horse-faced?"

"When your own mother says she's not the most beautiful girl in the world, you know she's got to be awful."

"It doesn't look good, does it?"

"The next guy you ask to do this, just don't show him that letter."

The Squirrel spent the best part of the evening buttonholing the brothers. About ten o'clock he came into the room with a long face and a long list. He handed me the list.

"That's a schedule," he said. "It's the best I could do. I have to depend on you to see that it's carried out. You start things off by meeting her at the bus and seeing that she gets registered at the Union. Bill Wooten will take her out to dinner the first night. Afterward, Mike Gilpatrick is going to take her to a movie. On Saturday morning Joe Siegel will show her around the campus and take her to lunch. MacDougall will probably take her to a matinee, but I told him it would be all right if he played tennis with her or took her for a hike—you know him and his God-damned physical fitness. Downey will take her out to supper on Saturday night and Andy will take her to a movie afterward. Darden will take her to church on Sunday morning. I'll be back to take over on Sunday afternoon."

"How come no dancing? She likes to dance."

"I couldn't ask these guys to push some frump around a dance floor. She'll have to live with it. It's the best I could do."

The Squirrel got away to Louisville the next morning. He wasn't out of sight before a crisis arose. I had to cross MacDougall off the list because he had a handball match. At lunch that day, the cook asked me to come in early, at four o'clock, to peel potatoes for dinner. I tried to find someone to trade places with me. If Mike Gilpatrick would meet the bus at four o'clock, I'd take Arbonna to the movies.

"Nuts to you," Mike said. "You're not going to stick me with anything like that. I know you. The guy who meets her at the bus is liable to be stuck with her all weekend. Go find another sucker."

The reaction from Joe Siegel was worse. "What makes you think I'm going to show up in the morning?" he asked me. "I might decide to sleep in."

By the time I'd canvassed the whole gang, I realized that Arbonna stood a good chance of spending a lonely weekend. I began feeling sorry for the poor girl and I couldn't let a thing like that happen to her no matter how she looked. I went down and peeled my potatoes early so I could meet her.

No woman could enter the Union by the front door in 1935. She had to go around to the back and come in by a stairway that led up through the main lounge. When I arrived at the Union that afternoon, I was a little early and I decided to go in and buy a pack of cigarettes before going down to the Greyhound bus stop, a block away. As I went through the front door I was hailed by someone from one of my classes and I stopped to talk with him inside the front door. From where I stood, I could look up into the lobby. There, hiding behind a pillar, with his eyes glued on the entrance from the ladies' stairway, was Joe Siegel. I tiptoed up the front steps until I could view the whole lobby and lounge. Bill Wooten was sitting on a sofa with a newspaper in front of his face. Every now and then he would peek around it at the entranceway. Off in a corner, Tom Darden was hiding behind a potted palm. In the main lobby, Larry Downey was pretending to study the arrangement of some chess pieces on a table. I knew the rest of the brothers were there some place. I knew, also, that if Arbonna Higgins was what we all expected her to be, I was about to see the biggest disappearing act in the history of the University of Michigan. It made me angry, not only for Arbonna's sake, but for my own. As I walked over to the bus stop, I made up my mind that I'd have to do something to get even, even if it meant hiding her from them until I could tell them all that she was a dream.

It was the Friday afternoon of a spring weekend, and a lot of fellows were standing around the bus stop, waiting for the usual bevy of girls that descended on Ann Arbor for the dances. As the girls got off the bus, each one carrying her little overnight bag, a fellow would step forward, bestow a kiss, and lead her away. The very last girl stopped on the bottom step and looked around expectantly. No one moved forward to meet her, and she descended to the curb. It was several moments before I realized she was the girl I was supposed to meet. I was stunned. She was absolutely gorgeous. She was tall and had auburn hair. Even though she was wearing a severely cut, modish suit, it was obvious that she had a lovely figure. I stumbled forward, holding out my hand for her suitcase.

"Are you Arbonna Higgins?" I asked her.

"I'm Bonnie Higgins," she said, cocking her head and smiling adorably. "I haven't been called Arbonna since my christening. It's a good password, isn't it? You must be my cousin Fred."

"Nope," I said, giving her my name. "I'm Fred's roommate. He's playing golf. He's on the university golf team, and they're playing a match over in Madison this weekend. There wasn't any way he could get out of it, but don't you worry. You're in good hands."

"I haven't any doubt of it. I have perfect confidence in you. Do you have a program?"

"I'm supposed to do anything you want to do. Your wish is my command."

"I'm fresh out of wishes. What kind of ideas do you have? Do you know what an idea is, son?"

"I have a few. After we get you registered in the Union, we'll stroll down to the Pretzel Bell—that's our local beer garden—and I'll get you oiled up a bit. That's the best way to get acquainted. After that, I'll feed you. Then we'll go dancing. That will take us until early tomorrow morning and finishes off Day Number One. Now, as for Day Number Two—"

"Wait a minute!" she said, holding up her hand. We'd been strolling toward the Union and she stopped. "You just hold it right there. Let me say that I adore your program for Day Number One, especially that part about getting me oiled up and dancing the legs off me. We'll do every bit of it, but I'm afraid Day Number Two is out. I'm a working girl and I came out here to Ann

Arbor to work. I start early in the morning and I'll be busy until late in the afternoon."

"What kind of work do you do?"

"I adorn things." She smiled mischievously as we resumed strolling. "Look, son, I guess I'd better tell you, right now, you're out with a celebrity. I just happen to be a past Miss Blue Water Carnival. I'm in the beauty-queen business."

"No kidding? What is the Blue Water Carnival?"

"That's a little shenanigans they have up in Port Huron every summer. It's hard to describe. All kinds of water gets splashed around by girls in bathing suits."

"What do I call you? Your highness?"

"You can call me Queenie if you want to, but I prefer just plain old Bonnie." She took my arm as we crossed the street to the Union and started up the walk to the ladies' entrance. (I'd given up my idea of hiding her. I was going to flaunt her.)

"How does a girl get to be Miss Blue Water Carnival?"

She took her hand from my arm, stepped away several paces, and hitched her skirt above the knee.

"Take a good look," she said. "It's mostly legs." She came back and took my arm. "With legs you can do anything. Last year I was almost Miss Michigan. Just a month ago I turned down a chance to be Miss Indianapolis Speedway."

"You didn't want to ride in those racing cars?"

"Don't kid yourself. All you get to do is kiss those guys with greasy faces. Anyway, I'm not mechanically inclined. I'm just a country girl at heart."

"I like country girls," I said. "I've heard some great stories about farmers' daughters."

"Son," she said, scowling, "I know all those stories about farmers' daughters and I don't like them. I, sir, am the marrying kind."

"All right," I said. "Will you marry me?"

"Of course, I'll marry you. I wouldn't think of marrying anyone else."

I stopped and put the suitcase down and took off my fraternity pin. I was thinking brilliantly at the moment. I knew how to fix those brothers waiting in the lobby.

"If you're going to marry me," I said, "you'd better wear this. It's an old custom here." I pinned it in a prominent place on her suit. She heaved a big sigh.

"How divine!" she said. "How absolutely divine! And you haven't even got me oiled up yet." She sighed again. "I'm yours forever—or at least until Sunday night. Let's get on with the program." She turned into the ladies' entrance and tripped up the steps. I wasn't quite done yet. I waited until she reached the archway that led into the lounge, then called her name. She stopped and waited for me, a question on her lovely face.

"We forgot something," I said.

"What did we forget, son?"

"We didn't seal our engagement with a kiss."

"How stupid of us." She took a step toward me and threw her arms around me, reached up and gave me a warm, loving kiss. As she turned to walk across the lobby, I looked at Bill Wooten, peeking around his paper, and thumbed my nose.

It didn't take long for the reaction to Bonnie to set in. My fraternity brothers emerged from everywhere and gathered in a circle around the registration desk. When she turned around from signing the card, she raised her eyebrows.

"Are you Arbonna Higgins?" Joe Siegel asked.

"I'm Queen Higgins," she said. "Who are you?"

"Your cousin Fred sent me," Joe said. "He's sick in bed."

"Poor Fred," Bonnie said, glaring at me, "I hope it's nothing trivial."

"He'll be all right," Joe said. "He asked me to entertain you for the weekend."

"The hell he did," Bill Wooten said, giving Joe a shove. "He asked *all* of us to entertain you for the weekend. I'm supposed to be first."

"He might have *asked* all of you guys to entertain her for the weekend," Larry Downey said, "but you were all fixing to back out. You've been hiding around here to see what she looked like, and if she was a frump, you were all going to run."

"What were you doing?" Tom Darden asked.

"I was sitting over there waiting for her, studying some chess problems. I was in plain sight."

"You never played a game of chess in your life, you faker," Joe Siegel said.

Bonnie held up her hand. "Now wait a minute, boys." She pointed her finger at me. "How does it happen you didn't stand around waiting to get a look at me first?"

"Fred told me to meet the bus. I met it."

"How does it happen none of the rest of you met the bus?" She looked all around the circle.

"We weren't supposed to," Bill Wooten said. "None of us knew you were coming by bus or when you were coming."

"I'm sorry but I don't believe you," Bonnie said. "You all knew I was going to be here at four o'clock, or you wouldn't be here. The courteous thing for a man to do is meet a girl and help her with her bag. All of you were being curious when you should have been courteous and now you've all lost out. Things have a strange way of happening. On the way over here from the bus I fell in love with a wonderful man and got myself engaged." She pointed at the fraternity pin. "Now, all of you can just scram out of here." She stamped her foot and then turned to follow a bellhop to the elevator.

After she disappeared there was a short fraternity meeting in the lobby. I was branded a stinker but I pointed out that I'd given every one of them a chance to meet the bus. None had taken it. Moreover, they'd all been so indefinite about keeping the schedule the Squirrel had left that I'd torn it up. I would take over. They all drifted off and I called the cook and arranged for a substitute to handle my scullery duties. By the time Bonnie emerged from the elevator, I was free to devote all my time to her.

"I don't really know whether you're any better than they are or not," she said, "but I'll give you a try. By the way, just what did happen to old Fred, anyway?"

I told her the truth, making it quite plain that the Squirrel had received his mother's letter at the last minute and it was too late to change his plans.

"Omaha better win and you'd better be good," she said, "or Fred better not show up at the next family reunion."

While we were drinking our first beer at the Pretzel Bell, Bonnie asked a few questions about Ann Arbor.

"Tell me," she asked, "are all Michigan men fast workers like you? I mean, do you all propose to girls five minutes after you meet them?"

"Nope," I said, "I usually take the time to find out whether a girl has my qualifications before I propose. I didn't think it was necessary in your case. You're perfect."

"I'm flattered but I'd like to know what kind of qualifications you have."

"I don't think it's necessary."

"Out with it, son. What are they?"

"There are only three. To begin with, I expect any girl I marry to have a blue velvet, strapless evening gown."

She looked at me skeptically for several moments and then looked up at the ceiling.

"Are you psychic? Or did you look in my suitcase? I just happen to have a velvet, strapless evening gown. It's green, though, not blue. Do I have to run out and trade it in?"

"Green's all right."

"Tell me, what's this all about?"

"I just figure anybody who could wear anything like that would be equipped the way I like them."

"Hmmmmmmmmmm," she said. "You're more subtle than I thought you were. Well, let me tell you, I'm equipped. I'm really equipped. About a size thirty-six, I'd say. What's the second qualification?"

"Have you got a nightgown with fur around the bottom of it?"

"What kind of fur?"

"I hadn't thought about that. Do you have one?"

"No, but I'm willing to get one." She pointed a finger at me. "As long as it's my neck that fur is going to keep warm, I'm going to demand mink. And as long as you're going to be the beneficiary of it, I'll let you buy it." She reached across the table and patted my hand. "You know, you're looking better to me all the time. I didn't know I was going to get a mink nightgown out of it when I accepted you. What's the last qualification?"

"You have to be able to play cribbage."

"Cribbage? What on earth for?"

"To keep me entertained when you're not wearing the evening gown or the nightgown."

She sat there and stared at me for a good thirty seconds, and then she threw back her head and started to laugh. That was the thing that broke the ice between us. From that moment we had a most wonderful time together. She was witty and warm and accomplished. That evening when we went dancing, she sparkled like champagne, and she was utterly beautiful to look at. On the dance floor she was as light as a feather and she had that knack of making me feel like the best dancer in the world. When we finally said good night she pointed down at the fraternity pin.

"I'll keep this another day. You certainly did a great job on Day Number One. Tomorrow night we'll do the same thing. By the way, you'll be picking me up at another place." She rummaged around in her purse and pulled out a slip of paper. "Here's the address. My photographer friends are lending me their apartment on Huron Street for the night. Even beauty queens have to save money."

"I don't suppose you'd want me to go around with you while you're being photographed, would you?"

"Do you know how to get up at seven in the morning?"

"Sure."

"It will be boring. There aren't to be any pictures of me in a bathing suit."

"I don't care about that."

"You would, son. I'm pretty good in a bathing suit. I'm not Miss Blue Water Carnival for nothing."

The next day was delightful from beginning to end. It developed that the State of Michigan was preparing a tourist brochure, and scenes of the university were to be included. Bonnie was right. She was an adornment who sat on the steps of the library, strolled through the Engineer's Arch, and stood in the middle of the stadium. She was more than an adornment, however. The photographers were a young married couple and they whisked us about in their car. As the day passed we picked up a regular little retinue. There were reporters and photographers from the daily papers, a representative from the university, and three or four innocent by-standers. At a little after four in the afternoon, Bonnie threw up her hands.

"That's all folks. The rest of the day belongs to my true love, over there, and I'm dying for a glass of beer."

By that time it would have been impossible to separate her from the group. She'd been absolutely captivating. As a result ten of us trooped down to the Pretzel Bell. We sat there drinking beer until almost seven o'clock. Through it all, I was the one to whom Bonnie paid attention. I'd never been known as a wit but I certainly seemed to be that day. After the others had gone we had dinner, and I took her home to change clothes. That evening we went to the annual spring formal at the Michigan League. Bonnie was stunning in her green velvet gown. Everyone noticed her and I was immensely proud of her.

We came back to the apartment about one in the morning, arm in arm, laughing and talking a mile a minute. Inside, she went out to the kitchen and returned to hold up a bottle.

"I think I could do with a drink," she said. "If you'll solemnly promise that there'll be no hanky-panky, I'll fix you one."

"I solemnly promise," I said. "No hanky-panky."

She sat on one end of the sofa with her legs curled up under her and I sat on the other end, and we talked. At first we talked about the "beauty-queen business" as she called it.

"I'll soon be superannuated," she said. "I'm wild to get married. Just be careful of me."

"I thought that was all settled. You've already accepted me. Be careful or I'll sue you for breach of promise."

She looked down at my fraternity pin for quite a long time, very thoughtfully. When she looked up there was something different about her. She was softer and quieter somehow.

"I wonder what you'd be like when you're not scintillating," she said. "Tell me, what are you going to be when you grow up?"

"I don't know. A writer, I guess."

"And travel to Bangkok and all those places."

"I guess so."

"Tell me about all the places you're going to take me."

"I'm not very good at geography," I said, "but I have some ideas. I think I'd start with California. You could pick grapes and support me until I make my fortune."

She looked at her glass.

"Speaking of grapes," she said. "I think I'd like another drink. Will you fix me one?"

"Maybe I ought to go home."

"I'm not anywhere near talked out yet. It's a funny thing about you. I haven't had one dull moment since I met you. You may end up talking all night if you're not careful."

I got up and took her glass and mine and went out to the kitchen. At first she stayed on the sofa, waiting for me, but then she came out to the kitchen and stood in the doorway watching me. When I turned around and handed her the drink, she didn't move. We stood there looking at each other for a moment and then I took the drink out of her hand and put it down on the table. After that I went back. She didn't move. I put my arms around her and kissed her. She finally pushed me away and looked up at me.

"So much for promises," she said. "A girl should never make a man promise her anything." She took my hand and led me into the living room and quietly turned out the lights. When it was dark, she kissed me again. "I hope you'll forgive me if I don't have a nightgown with fur around the bottom, dear. Of course, I don't think I'm going to need a nightgown at all."

And so Bonnie Higgins became the second woman I had known in my life. In a way, she was the first, for being with her was like being with one of those princesses I'd always dreamed about. With Tracy Dawes the whole thing had been a little wild and abandoned. Bonnie taught me the quieter side of love. We lay there, close together, all the night long, warm and comfortable, completely one. I think Bonnie said it best.

"This is the most wonderful thing that can happen to two people. It's one of the few times when you know you're not alone in the world. It's a small bit of perfection in a big, cold universe. You know, there's an old joke about this being the most comfortable way for a man and woman to talk to each other, but it's not really a joke at all. I don't think any man or woman can be friends until they've experienced this. For a little while I love you and you love me, and nothing else matters. That's the way it should be."

It was one o'clock on Sunday afternoon when Bonnie sat up in bed, stretched her lovely arms, and yawned.

"I hate to break this up," she said, "but the time has come for us to find out how Cousin Fred made out at the races."

As we were going out the door, she took my pin off and gave it to me.

"I'm pleased you gave me the chance to wear this."

"Will I see you again?" I asked.

"Some day, maybe. The beauty-queen business keeps me on the move. You never know where I'm liable to turn up. But if I don't see you before, I'll invite you to my wedding. I think you'd make a peachy wedding guest."

IX

When I came home from Ann Arbor in June, 1935, I had only one thing on my mind—to finish school and get my degree. I had one semester left, and it seemed to me that I ought to have no trouble in accomplishing this simple chore. The Depression was now almost six years old. In the relative security and isolation of a university town, I had been out of touch, as usual. I'd been home for week-ends twice during the year, in addition to the trip at Thanksgiving and Christmas vacation. I knew that things were as hopeless at the lumberyard as they had always been, but I had no idea that the rest of the population was as bad off as ever. The factory workers had their usual four months of work. The downtown district was as drab and deserted as ever. Perhaps the big difference, in Flint at least, was the fact that people had learned to live with hard times by now. They didn't stand around muttering about it as they used to. In most cases they had learned to pinch a penny like an expert.

Before I left Ann Arbor, I had the promise of a board job from the house. I'd still be washing pots and pans, mopping the kitchen, and cleaning the stove, but I was used to all that now. What I had to have was money for tuition, books and room. The first thing I did was to sit down and figure what I'd need. I came up with what

I thought was a bare minimum of $150. I knew I was overly optimistic, but I thought that if worst came to worst the house could carry me for my room bill until I got out and got a job after graduation.

I set out at once to collect that $150. My first target was Grandpa Perry. I was thinking of that thirty dollars a month he was getting from Mrs. Berry's house. I met my first frustration and shock almost at once. Our own house had been foreclosed. Less than two weeks after I got home, our whole family moved next door so there was no thirty dollars a month anymore. In spite of that, Grandpa promised me what he could from his jury duty. He must have figured it down to the penny because he came up with the odd figure of $27.40. I didn't give up. I went out to see my Aunt Esther in Flushing. She was a schoolteacher. I thought she'd have some resources. She did, but they were very meager. She thought that she could lend me $75.00. I was $47.60 away from my goal, and I had two months to earn it. I was pretty sure I was home free.

I tried the same things I'd always tried. I asked everyone I knew if they had anything for me to do. They didn't, although I did get ten jobs at mowing lawns for one dollar apiece—they were big lawns. In desperation, I asked my father if he could afford to pay me five dollars at the lumberyard. He couldn't. He and my brother were running the place all alone, and they had so little to do that they were closing the place three afternoons a week. The same old line was strung around the Flint *Journal* waiting for the first paper with the want ads. Every place I went in answer to one, I found twenty people ahead of me. It wasn't until after the middle of July that I got something. One of my brother's friends had started a delivery service and he needed a man. I learned to ride a motorcycle and went to work. I got ten cents a package for each one I delivered. By August 15 I'd taken in the magnificent sum of $7.70.

I was desperate. I was frustrated. I was never as low in spirits as I was as Labor Day approached. It was about then that Nick Woods and Flo invited me over to dinner to help celebrate their first wedding anniversary. Nick had done very well indeed since he came to join our poker game. He was an imaginative and personable young man with the ability to get his ideas across to his superiors and he had just been transferred by General Motors to the Fisher Body Corporation, where he now held a good job in the south-end plant. Nick was wise and understanding, and when he heard my lament, he put his arm around my shoulder and asked me why I was knocking myself out. He didn't think it would hurt me to stay out of school one more semester. The new model runs would be starting in the plants within two weeks. He would get me a job and I could earn enough money to go back to Ann Arbor in February. When he called me to see if I wanted to do it that way a week later, I jumped at the chance. He told me to go and see a man named Al Moriarty in the wood mill. I found Mr. Moriarty to be a big red-faced, tough-talking man who had worked his way up from the machines to be superintendent of the wood mill. He was pleasant enough to me, but I knew he'd be a hard man to work for. Things were black or white with him. There was no in-between. He gave me a job at a salary of thirty dollars a week.

I came to work at Fisher Body at what might be called a revolutionary moment—in more ways than one. The new 1936 model cars were a radical departure from all those that had gone before. Except for a few small insulation blocks for wiring and glass, practically all the wood had been eliminated from standard body models. There were five basic cars in the General Motors line at that time, and each auto-manufacturing division had its own body factory nearby. The plant in which I worked supplied bodies for Buick. It was known in Flint as Fisher No. 1. The corresponding plant for Chevrolet across town was known as Fisher No. 2. Fisher No. 1 was a relatively new plant and its equipment was modern and up-to-date. Although wood was eliminated from standard body models, station wagons and convertibles still had large wood components, as did the interiors of luxury models which had arm rests and other accessories. It was decided that all these wood parts would be made in one plant and shipped to other plants for assembly. Because Fisher No. 1 had the most modern mill, it was kept open. All the others were closed. There were 115 machine operators in the Fisher No. 1 mill, but there must have been five hundred other skilled wood-mill men around the state who were now out of work.

My official title was payroll coordinator, a high-sounding designation that only partly described my duties. All the machine operators were paid on a combined hourly and piecework basis. Each man might make a straight hourly wage of fifty cents an hour. In addition, he was expected to turn out enough items of work each hour, at so much an item, to bring his compensation up to the level deemed commensurate for him. The piecework system was not new in American manufacturing, nor was it confined to the auto industry, but in the Fisher Wood Mill it was a tremendously complicated process, because no machine operator ever worked on the same job for two hours in a row. If he was a sander, for instance, he might spend forty-five minutes working on dome-light insulation blocks at three cents apiece and then switch to convertible struts for an hour and a half at eighteen cents apiece. Altogether, there were four thousand different jobs that might be performed in the course of a week, and each job had its own price. Each machine had a little black book attached to it that gave the price of each job performed on it. The price for each item of work had been determined long before, but it was always subject to change. Under the rules of employment at Fisher, each operator was bound to accept the prices in the black book and he was also bound to accept any changes made by management.

Throughout the history of the piecework system, management and labor were always at war over the prices. Each price was set, theoretically, so that a man would have to turn out a certain amount of work each hour to get his wage level up where it should be. An expert lathe operator, for instance, was expected to turn out forty dowels each hour at five cents each, which would bring his pay up to two fifty an hour. The trouble was that most expert lathe operators, after a time, could turn out fifty dowels an hour without overexerting themselves, thus bringing their pay up to three dollars an hour—more than they'd been hired in for. If lathe operators consistently turned in those ten extra dowels an hour, the factory management would reduce the price to four cents a dowel. The lathe operator, and all other lathe operators forever more, were then committed to turning out fifty dowels an hour. This process was known by all the operators as the "speedup," and they were committed to fight it. And, of course, management was under the eternal compulsion to cut costs wherever and whenever it could.

The tactics in the long-drawn-out war between piecework operators and management were as old and time-honored as work itself. The most common stratagem used by management was the time-and-motion study, but this rarely worked. The minute a stranger appeared in the plant with a clipboard and stopwatch, one could almost feel the tempo of the plant slow down. Management tried to disguise the study men as janitors, push-cart vendors, repairmen, and even helpers, but the men in the wood mill had been around a long time. In the time I worked at the mill every stranger who entered the gates was scrutinized carefully. A person who was well acquainted with the plant could catch the danger signals as they ran down the line of machines. A man would bang on the floor with a stick. A man behind him would raise his hands over his head as though stretching. The next man would pull out a red bandanna handkerchief and blow his nose. The whole place would slow down.

Because the time-and-motion study was so ineffective, management sought a solution for its problems in another way. It was a well-known fact that most operators were carefully turning in coupons for just enough work to maintain their accepted pay level. The lathe operator would turn in his forty dowels and hold back ten. These ten pieces were known as his "bank." As long as he held a bank, it was impossible to tell whether a job was overpriced or not. Management had tried to stop the holding of banks by stipulating it as grounds for immediate dismissal. This rule did not deter the men at all. One of the men I knew very well was Dave Rock, a veteran joiner operator whose rate was supposed to work out at three dollars an hour, which made his weekly pay check about $120. In an average week, however, Dave was able to complete enough work to bring his pay up to $140. Every Wednesday night, if I had dropped around to the neighborhood beer garden, I would have found Dave sitting at a table with his coupons spread out before him, figuring out their value. He would take out $120 worth of them to turn in to me on Thursday morning. The rest would go back in his bank. This practice would go on for most of the model run, which ran for twenty weeks on the 1936 cars. In about the sixteenth week, Dave would have accumulated $320 in his bank. That's when he would start getting rid of it. In the seventeenth week he might turn in $180. In the eighteenth week he might turn in $200. In the nineteenth week he might go as high as $250. In the last week he would turn in what he had left. In between times, in those last four weeks, he might take a day off now and then, having someone else punch his card in and out. Once in a while he and some of the boys would go behind a lumber pile and play poker for three or four hours, thus getting in some overtime. This was the practice all over the mill. In the last four weeks of a model run, payrolls would double or triple. Production would slow down so badly that sometimes an extra week would be added to complete the year's schedule. While it was obvious to management as this pattern unfolded that the men had been keeping banks and were therefore subject to dismissal, it was very hard to catch any one man in the act, for the more efficient workers would unload some of their banks by selling them to less efficient workers. In addition, most of the foremen had worked on the machines themselves and were long-standing friends of the culprit. They covered up. Last, but not least, there was always the ultimate goat—the payroll clerk. By claiming delays and mistakes, enough confusion could be created so that no one knew exactly whom to blame for any one thing. Every payroll clerk in the Fisher Mill labored in the sure knowledge that, when the end of the model run came, he would be fired. I was the eighth payroll clerk in as many years and I knew right where I stood. On the morning I took the job, Al Moriarity told me, in no uncertain terms, what I could expect.

"You have one main job. You are to determine who keeps banks and you are to turn the information in to me, and I will do the firing. If you do not find the banks, and if they crop up at the end of the model run, you're through, and I mean through. I'll personally see to it that you never get another job in this plant and I will endeavor to see to it that you don't work in any other General Motors plants. I don't care how you do it, but you find those banks."

I found them. I had been put on a straight salary for a good reason. My job required sixteen or seventeen hours of overtime each week. If I'd been working at an hourly rate, I would have been able to draw checks of almost fifty dollars each and every week, but being on salary, I couldn't collect overtime. I was expected to do my job no matter how much time it took. From the time I went to work at Fisher in September until the time I left, I worked until after seven o'clock each evening, and on Saturdays I would come into the deserted plant and work all morning by myself.

The key to finding the banks lay in the piecework coupons— which we called travelers. As payroll clerk I had complete control of the travelers since I issued them all. Each Friday morning a copy of the next week's production schedule would be brought into my little cubbyhole. If that production schedule called for 125 Pontiac convertibles, for instance, I would go to my safe and get out a traveler for Pontiac convertibles, carefully mark it so that each coupon called for 125 pieces of work. I would then carry this traveler out to the superintendent of the lumberyard. He and his crew would load the necessary lumber for 125 Pontiac convertibles on hand trucks, tie the travelers to the loads, and shove them into the mill, where a router would take over. The router would know which machine that load had to go to first and he would push it there. When the machine operator finished whatever it was he had to do, he would tear off the bottom coupon of the traveler and have it signed by his foreman. The foreman would then call in the router and have the load moved to another machine for the next operation, where the process would be repeated. When the load of lumber came out the other end of the mill several days later, it would be bundled up and shipped to wherever Pontiac convertibles were assembled. The shipping department would send me back the stub of the traveler. None of these loads of lumber would ever follow the same route through the mill. Some of the travelers would be six feet long and consist of forty separate coupons, because that many operations would be required to shape the lumber. Other travelers might be six inches long and have only three coupons. Each of these coupons had an operation number printed on it and, of course, a serial number. To this, at the time of issue, I added a coded date as well as the number of pieces on the load.

I contrived an extremely complicated system in order to track down and determine the amount of the banks. I kept several dozen logbooks in which each traveler had its own full page. At the top of that page I would list the date of issue. Each evening at the end of the day's work, after everyone else had gone home, I would take my logbooks out into the mill and visit every single load of lumber on the floor, usually about five hundred of them. I would put in the logbook how many coupons had been removed during the day, who had removed them, and where the load was physically located. I could find the identity of the operators who had removed the coupons simply by consulting the router's logbook. I always knew who had the coupons and on what date they had been removed. By the simple process of going back each Saturday morning and checking the turned-in coupons against my logbook I knew exactly who was holding back which coupons. By keeping still another set of logbooks with each man's name and the number of coupons he was holding, I knew exactly how big a bank a man had and how much it was worth. By the middle of November I had enough data on every man in that plant to have him fired, and because I made my inspections at night and on Saturdays when no one was around, I was quite sure that no one knew what I was up to. It was a simple matter to catch a man with his bank. All Al Moriarity had to do was post a list of traveler-coupon numbers, and announce that they were missing and would not be paid. That would make a man's bank worthless. He would either have to keep his mouth shut and lose all that money, or he could come forward and admit that he was holding the missing coupons.

I had the information, all right, but I wasn't sure what to do with it. On the surface of the matter, it seemed as if I had no alternative except to turn in my information to Al Moriarity, but I had to consider another factor. Out of the 115 machine operators in that plant, I had known about twenty before I ever came to work there. Most of those whom I knew lived in the south end of town and they had been customers of my father. Back in those cold, nasty days of 1931 and 1932 I had delivered coal to their houses. On more than one bitter cold day I had been invited into their homes for a cup of coffee or just to get warm. This handful of men was the nucleus of a wide friendship that I had gradually established in the mill. I was among them all day long, checking travelers, straightening out payroll figures, getting pay vouchers signed, and giving out checks. I had come to have great respect for most of them. Practically all of them were approaching middle age. They were buying homes, raising families, and endeavoring to improve what they had. I knew that these men were the backbone of any community and I trusted them and thought of them as honest and reasonable, despite the evidence I was accumulating against them. For the first time in my life, I had come to the point of view that a system was wrong and that a man who fought it was not necessarily a crook.

I didn't know what to do. I knew I would be fired if I didn't turn my information in to Al Moriarity. I didn't really care about that because I planned to quit anyway, but I thought I saw something that the men didn't see and I had to tell someone about it. I decided to be straightforward about it with one person and see what his reaction was. I chose Dave Rock, a joiner operator whose son Bill had worked for my father as a truck driver and whose daughter Frances had dated Lou Norris for a long time. Quite often, during lunch hour, Dave would bring his pail over and sit beside me and give me news of Bill or Frances.

One Sunday morning I called Dave on the telephone and asked him if I could come over to his house. As I walked in the kitchen door, Mrs. Rock gave me a kiss and a hug. Frances came out in her housecoat and put a pot of coffee on the stove. We all sat around the kitchen table drinking coffee and eating pie and talking, then Dave led me down to the basement recreation room he'd built for himself, and we sat down facing each other across a card table. I had brought along some of my logbooks with the figures I'd been keeping on Dave. I put them all on the table and explained all the figures. I told him exactly what traveler stubs he was holding in his bank and how much they were worth. I was right, almost to the penny. He got up and paced the floor and came back to stand over me.

"What did you show me all this for?" he asked me. "Are you going to turn me in?"

"No. I'm not a heel. I just wanted to show you the predicament I'm in."

"What kind of a predicament are you in?"

"If I don't turn this information in to Al Moriarity, I'll be fired when your banks turn up at the end of the run."

He shook his head. "Do you have this much information on every man in the mill?"

"Yes."

"You could sure raise hell with us. What do you want me to do?"

"I think there's only one thing to do. Get rid of your banks. Spread it out over the next three months and don't keep any more. I'll be off the hook and so will you."

He shook his head. "I have a hundred and seven dollars here. By the end of the model run I'll have about three hundred. If I spread that three hundred over fifteen weeks, I'll be getting about twenty a week more than I am now. If I did that, and if all the guys in the shop did that, every single price would be reduced. Nobody would agree to that. Son, there's only one question here."

"What is that?"

"How important is your job to you?"

"Not very. I'll probably quit anyway and go back to school when I save enough money."

"Well, my job's pretty valuable to me. I have a family to support. I guess that's your answer, isn't it?"

"Not quite, and that's the reason I came to see you," I said. "Look, Dave, I'm the eighth guy to hold down that payroll job in eight years. Next year there'll be another one. I don't know whether I'm the first guy to figure all this out or not, but I promise you, sooner or late somebody else is going to do it again, and that someone's going to turn you all in. I think you ought to do something about it while you've got somebody like me around to help out."

"I appreciate it," he said. "I'll talk to the boys about it. You'll hear from me."

Two or three days later at lunchtime, a man named Fred LaBeau plopped down beside me and began taking things out of his lunch pail. I didn't know Fred very well, but I did know that most of the men in the mill looked up to him as some kind of a leader.

"I understand you've got the goods on us," he said, between bites. "What are you going to do with it?"

"Didn't Dave tell you?"

"He told me what he thought."

"Do you believe him?"

"I guess I do. I just think you ought to know that we kicked this thing around in our shop committee. We're not going to turn in our banks—definitely. Will that change your mind?"

"No, but I don't see why some guy like me has to be sacrificed every year. There ought to be a better solution."

"There's a solution all right. Join our union."

"What union is that?"

"The United Auto Workers of America. It ain't going to be long, boy, before we strike this place and put an end to all this piecework and blacklisting and other crap."

"I don't think you'll ever get away with it, Fred."

"You wait and see. Anyway, don't you do anything about our banks."

"I won't."

"Will you shake on that?"

We shook. Of course, I'd opened Pandora's box. There was a gang-saw operator in the mill named Big Alex, a brute of a man. Alex was a drinker. Every morning he carried a bottle of whiskey in to work in his lunch pail. From time to time during the day he would take a nip, and by quitting time every afternoon he was drunk. The gang saws were dangerous machines, and as the year progressed, he couldn't keep helpers. There was a lot of grumbling about Big Alex around the shop. One afternoon, just before Christmas, Fred LaBeau came into my little office.

"If Big Alex keeps on the way he's going," he said, "he's going to kill somebody. We want you to get him fired."

"Why don't you see the foreman or Al Moriarity? It's not my job to fire him."

"The foreman is Alex's brother-in-law, and Al Moriarity is a stubborn son of a bitch. He knows we're organizing a union out here. He calls us a bunch of God-damned Communists, and every time we ask him to do anything, he does just the opposite. You're the only guy that can get Alex fired."

"How?"

"Turn him in for keeping a bank."

"Jesus, Fred, if I can't use the banks against the rest of you fellows, it isn't fair to use it against Alex."

"You'd better do it, boy."

The next day I had to walk by Alex's machine. He saw me coming and stepped out into the aisle to confront me. He was drunk and mean.

"I understand you're going to turn me in for keeping a bank," he said, towering over me.

"You heard wrong," I said.

"I think I heard right." He reached out with his big hand and grabbed my sweater. With hardly any effort at all, he ripped it right off me. I was angry. I doubled up my fist and hit him in the stomach. It didn't hurt him at all but it drove him blind. "I'll kill you," he said, and grabbed my shirt and started to pull me toward the saws. Before he pulled me more than a step, the other men in the mill swarmed around and grabbed him and knocked him to the floor. Not more than ten minutes later, Fred LaBeau showed up in my office.

"Are you ready to turn him in yet?"

"You told him I was turning him in."

"Somebody told him. It's either you or him, now. I don't think you're any match for him."

I didn't give in. I didn't like the idea of getting a man fired just before Christmas and I was still arguing with myself over the scruples of the thing. I stayed away from Alex for a week, but on the day before New Year's, he came after me with a club in his hand. Someone saved me, but I'd had enough. I picked up my sheets on him and headed for Al Moriarity's office.

"I'll fire him tonight," Al Moriarity said.

That was the end of Big Alex. It was also the end of me. Two days after New Year's I was called up front.

"I've been going over these sheets you gave me on Big Alex," Al Moriarity said. "You had him pegged right to the penny. When are you going to give me the figures on the rest of the men? I know you must have them."

I didn't say a word. Al Moriarity's face reddened.

"I want the figures on the rest of the men," he said. "You know why I hired you."

"Are you going to fire *all* of them?"

"It's time I cleaned out this mill and now's a good time to do it. They're dabbling with a union, and for every man on one of those machines, there are four better ones walking the street."

"I know, but you can't fire the whole mill."

"It's none of your God-damned business what I do. If I want anybody's advice on how to run this mill, I'll ask for it. First it's the God-damned union trying to tell me what I can and cannot do, and now it's a lousy payroll clerk." He pointed his cigar at me. "You've got until five o'clock this afternoon to turn in those figures, or you're fired."

And so my job at Fisher Body ended at five o'clock in the afternoon of January 3, 1936.

X

My firing from Fisher Body came at a most embarrassing time. Although I was already planning to quit and go back to school in February, I badly needed the six extra weeks of work that I had now lost.

I had taken in a little less than $500 in the four months I'd worked. As late as the second week in December, I still had most of it. I'd led an ascetic life. Gretchen had been married the previous summer, and I didn't even go to the IMA dances. The event that upset all my plans was the marriage of my brother Walter. He had come home early in December to announce that he was to be married on the first Saturday night in January. The girl he was marrying was a member of one of Flint's most prominent families, and the wedding was to be a sumptuous, white-tie affair. I was to be the best man. As I have already mentioned, the longer the Depression lasted, the more elegant people got. By 1936, we had gone beyond the tuxedo stage; white tie and tails were now *de rigueur*. All of Flint's social season was traditionally geared to the Christmas holidays, and most of the white-tie-and-tail outfits had been rented far ahead. When I went down to get one, they were all gone. I finally had to go and *buy* a suit of tails and all the accessories, a wildly ironic situation when one considers the fact that I'd only been able to buy one suit of clothes in five years.

The tails cost me sixty dollars, but that was only the beginning. I wanted to buy my brother a good wedding present, and I finally settled on an electric refrigerator. It cost me $130, but it was worth it. My future sister-in-law had a fine sense of humor. When I bought the refrigerator, I got a card from the dealer which said that the happy couple could claim it whenever they set up housekeeping. That wasn't good enough for Helen. She sent right down and had the refrigerator delivered to her house, and there it sat in her living room, the centerpiece in a lavish display of presents. She kept it filled with champagne, and the guests who filed in and out during the prenuptial festivities always got a glass or two. There were a few casualties from this champagne drinking. One was Grandpa Perry who got tipsy and lost his way between his bedroom and the bathroom. We found him sleeping peacefully on the hall floor. I was another casualty. I didn't get tipsy. I just got a happy glow. When I floated out of Helen's house a day or two before Christmas, I found a light snow falling, and I decided to get into the holiday spirit. The next thing I knew I'd bought tickets to the three biggest holiday formals at ten dollars apiece. I had decided that I might just as well get some use out of those tails I'd just bought, and while I was in this finger-snapping mood, I called Bonnie Higgins in Detroit and invited her up for all three parties. Fortunately for me she was only able to make one of them. That was expensive enough for I had to get her a room at the Durant Hotel for the night.

Bonnie was her usual captivating self. She set my friends on their respective ears. She brought a milk-white formal in the Empire style with a train that she carried by means of a loop that slipped over her wrist. From the time that we showed up at our first cocktail party until I took her back to the hotel at five in the morning, she was surrounded by men. Yet, she still managed to make me feel as though I was the center of her universe. There was no hanky-panky after the dance, incidentally. When I took her back to her hotel room, she flashed a mischievous smile at me.

"We have now come to the most crucial point in the whole evening," she said. "I suppose you've been considering the proper approach?"

"I guess I have," I said.

"Well, I've been considering the proper countermeasures. If you won't try any approaches, I won't try any countermeasures."

"If that's the way you want it," I said.

"For now. It's been a long, long day."

She did give me a lovely kiss, and I came away feeling just as pleased as though it had been the other way.

In a sense, the other two dances were more important to me than the one to which I took Bonnie. I took a Flint girl, and the two of us double-dated with another couple, the male half of which happened to be a teacher in one of our junior high schools. At some time during one of the dances, I mentioned the fact that I was expecting to go back to Ann Arbor in February and get my degree. He asked me what I was going to do *after* I got my degree. Up until that moment, I don't think the thought had ever occurred to me. He suggested that I look into the possibilities of teaching. Whatever else the teaching profession offered, it offered security. A degree by itself was no guarantee of security at all. I could still find myself walking the streets looking for jobs, but a degree with a teacher's certificate was like an insurance policy. I was still thinking about this conversation when I got fired from my job at Fisher Body, and I decided to look into it.

The assistant superintendent of schools in Flint was Leroy Pratt, one of my former teachers who had always taken an interest in me. I went to see him, and he immediately called my attention to the fact that the University of Michigan was offering a new concentrated course for people who wanted a teacher's certificate in the State of Michigan. People who had degrees, or who were about to get degrees, could elect the nineteen credit hours of education needed for the certificate in one semester. This course was undoubtedly Depression-born. In the six years since the stock market crash, a great many people had lost their jobs—a great many women had lost their husbands. A lot of these people had college degrees but no teaching credentials, and many of them wanted to turn to teaching to make a living. Under the old rules a person would have had to spend a year in Ann Arbor to take the education courses he needed. It was almost a financial impossibility for a man or woman who was already in trouble to take a year away from families and responsibilities. Not long before I went to see Leroy Pratt, the hardships in this reeducation process had been called to the attention of Raleigh Schorling, the dean of education at Michigan, and he had responded by thinking up the concentrated course. Not only could the degree holder get his requirements out of the way in one semester, he could do it quite inexpensively, for arrangements could be made for him to do six weeks of practice teaching in his own hometown. This meant he would spend the first six weeks at Ann Arbor going to classes, the next six weeks at home, and the last four weeks back in Ann Arbor. As Leroy Pratt unfolded this plan to me, I decided to take the course, and before I left his office, I had a letter authorizing me to take my practice teaching in the Flint schools.

I had one more near disappointment. I hitchhiked down to Ann Arbor to see my faculty adviser for permission to enroll in the course. To my great dismay I discovered that only ten of those nineteen hours of education would apply toward my degree. The only way I could teach was to get a degree, and the only way I could get a degree was to attend summer school that year. That would involve finding another three hundred dollars. I wasn't at all sure I could find any such sum. I'd about exhausted all horse races, crap games, chain letters, and other assorted miracles. It was a gamble, and I had no alternative. On the sixteenth of February, 1936, two days after my twenty-fourth birthday, I left for Ann Arbor again, hoping to get my degree this time. It had been almost seven years since I had graduated from high school.

In the meantime, my brother Walter was married. His wedding was close to being the biggest social event of that winter in Flint. It came the day after I'd been fired from my job at Fisher Body. It took place in St. Paul's church in downtown Flint on a Saturday night. The church was crowded with guests. The women were in beautiful gowns and fur wraps, and the men wore starched shirts and white ties and tailcoats. I stood there beside my brother in my own new tailcoat. When the ceremony was concluded, I offered my arm to the maid of honor, and we began the long walk up the aisle past that glittering assemblage. Everything seemed normal until I arrived at the back three rows of pews. There, packed in like sardines, were more than fifty, blue-shirted, mackinaw-clad men, some of them with their wives, some of them burdened down with bags of groceries. As we passed them they all began to wave at me and several of them shouted good wishes. I winked at Fred LaBeau and managed a little wave to the others. A week or two later I ran into Fred on the street.

"What the hell were you guys doing at that wedding?" I asked him.

"We were having a union meeting at the Dresden Hotel across the street," he said. "I guess we had you mixed up with your brother. Anyway, some of us thought you were the one that was getting married. We just wanted to give you some moral support after the way you did by us." He beamed. "Say, that was some fancy affair, wasn't it? I'd never been to a wedding like that before and I sure enjoyed it. I was telling my old lady we ought to throw one like it for our daughter when she gets hitched this spring."

In the thirty-five years since her wedding, my sister-in-law has often remarked about all those gate crashers at her wedding. She has always thought that they were Saturday night shoppers who just dropped in out of curiosity.

During my last semester at Ann Arbor, I didn't work for my board and I didn't go near my fraternity house. There was no time for any of this. The concentrated course was aptly named. It met every morning at eight o'clock and it stayed in session in the same room until six in the evening. Each professor would come in and teach his specialty for two hours. There was very little interruption between teachers and subjects. When one professor left and another arrived, we were given five minutes for a cigarette or a stretch. Most of us ate our lunch right there at the long conference table where we sat all day. When the class was dismissed at six o'clock, we would run out to the nearest lunchroom, get a bite to eat, and then come back to the library to study until ten o'clock. After that we'd go home and study for another two or three hours. We saw no other students from the School of Education or from the other schools and colleges of the university. There were twenty-six of us enrolled in the course, Ten were widows, five were businessmen who had gone broke during the Depression. I was the youngest student by four years. We hardly had time to get acquainted with each other, but even if we'd had the time, it is doubtful whether I would have been inclined to socialize. The grind continued until the first of April, at which time we all went off to our separate hometowns to do our practice teaching. The grind continued at home. I did my practice teaching at Central High School in Flint. I taught five classes in five different subjects, and this meant that I had to prepare five different sets of lesson plans in quadruplicate each day. When we came back to Ann Arbor in May, evening seminars were added to the day-long sessions of the class. I went through four months of such unremitting labor that I can't remember any part of it, but there was one bright and shining moment.

After my last class, after I finished my practice teaching, I was asked to report to the assistant superintendent of schools. When I walked into the office, Leroy Pratt got up from his desk and came around to shake my hand.

"I've followed your practice teaching with great interest," he said. "I think you're going to be a fine teacher, and for that reason, it is my privilege to offer you a contract to teach in our system next fall."

He pulled a paper across his desk and handed it to me. I didn't even bother to read it. I just signed it. That evening I ran into Bugs Huntley somewhere and I told him that I had a contract to teach, but I wasn't sure it would do me any good because I didn't know how I was going to get the money to go to summer school and get my degree.

"Hell, that ought not be any problem," he said. "Ernest Potter is the president of the bank, and he's also president of the school board. Why don't you go see him in the morning and ask him if he'll lend you the money?"

I went and I walked out of the bank with three hundred dollars. I was home free.

The summer session was anticlimactic after the grind of the concentrated course. I elected four easy courses and sailed through them with no trouble at all. A strange thing had happened to me in those months after my brother's wedding, however. The hard work and the lack of companionship had made a real loner out of me. I rather enjoyed being alone, or I thought I did. I'd always been an occasional golfer, averaging about 110, never breaking 100. Soon after I enrolled in summer school, a daily visit to the golf course became a ritual. I would attend classes in the morning, and right after lunch I would strip down to a pair of shorts and golf shoes and take a bus out to the university golf course—a fine one by any standards. The summer of 1936 was one of the hottest on record, and I usually had the course all to myself in the midday heat, a fact which heightened my conviction that I preferred to be alone. By the end of August I was burned as brown as a piece of old leather, and I was in as good physical condition as I'd ever been. With eighteen holes of golf a day (thirty-six on Saturday and Sunday), my game improved steadily, and I finished up shooting consistently in the 90s.

The trouble was that I was never a natural loner, no matter what I told myself. I thought I was enjoying my solitude, but I was pretty lonely. On an especially hot day late in August, I took my golf clubs up to the Michigan Union to wait for the bus to the golf course. I was sitting on the wall, staring absentmindedly at the sidewalk when a lovely pair of feminine legs planted themselves squarely in front of me. I looked up to find Jill Ryan standing there, smiling down at me. I'd forgotten how beautiful she was.

"What are you doing here?" she asked me.

"I'm still plugging away," I said. "This time I think I'm going to make it. What are you doing here? You're an old grad, now."

"This is my vacation. I was in Detroit visiting one of my sorority sisters and I thought I'd run out and see if the place is the same as I remembered it."

"How long are you going to stay?"

"I was going back to Detroit this afternoon, but there's a room available at the Maggie house. If anyone tried to persuade me to stay over I might consider it."

"Consider yourself persuaded," I said. "Give me a half hour to get cleaned up and I'll meet you at the Maggie house."

We started out and finished at our little German place on the other side of Main Street. Everything about Jill was perfection. Her dark, striking beauty, her lovely, trim figure, and the way she wore her clothes made me forget those dark days when she'd left me for George Glass. Of course that long spell of being alone had something to do with what happened to me. I was in love with her all over again. I think there may have been forces operating on her, too. She was working in the office of one of the steel companies in Youngstown. I think the change from college life to workaday life had been something of a letdown for her. Several times I caught a faint trace of restlessness in her voice and in the things she said about her job. On our walk home that night, I talked to her about it.

"You know, Jill," I said, "you might just as well face it. Everything you're doing is just by way of marking time until you get married. That's the only career you're really interested in. You're made for it."

"I keep getting propositions instead of proposals," she said. "Everyone in Youngstown is a wolf. I've only had one real proposal in my life and I had to turn that down."

"I'll bet you're referring to George Glass."

"Poor old George. After all the hard work he put in, I couldn't marry him. I thought about it—seriously, too. He just didn't have any sparkle. I'd have been bored."

"I don't want to contradict you," I said, "but you had another proposal. It had something to do with dungeons for nineteen children."

"How deep a hole have you got dug so far, Brother Delta?"

"Not very deep, but I've been practicing every day. I've got holes dug all over the university golf course."

We walked along in silence for a time.

"I think you really mean it," she said finally.

"About what?"

"About the house."

"I do. I really do. Just keep the offer on file."

She took my hand then, and we walked along through the summer evening and came again to the Maggie house. She looked up at me and smiled.

"Dear Brother Delta," she said, "you've given me another wonderful day, You always do. Please come down to Youngstown to see me. I'm going to miss you."

She reached up and kissed me and then she was gone.

On the last Friday in August, 1936, I walked out of the registrar's office of the University of Michigan with a little slip of paper which certified that I had been awarded the degree of Bachelor of Arts.

(My actual diploma came in the mail two months later.) It wasn't much of a commencement, and in later years I never knew just which class I belonged to. At the moment I didn't care about any of it. I was convinced that I was about to begin life. For the first time in my life I could look forward to a steady job. It wasn't exactly the job I wanted, but at twenty-four I'd waited a long time.

Part IV

I

At some time while I was in Ann Arbor in the summer of 1936, the lumberyard gave up the ghost. I've never been exactly sure what happened. I think that my father just got tired of struggling to overcome the eternal financial squeeze. I suppose the impending foreclosure of the mortgage was the straw that broke the camel's back. At any rate, he quietly closed the doors and got a job selling lumber on the road. At the age of fifty-two he was starting out all over again. His prospects were bleak, but it turned out that he'd made the right decision. The long struggle to keep the yard alive had broken his health and had made a prematurely old man out of him. He had never been a good businessman. He was too generous. I don't think he ever collected one penny of all the thousands of dollars that were owing him. As far as I know, he never attempted to do so. Yet he was a superb salesman, blessed with the faculty of making friends wherever he turned. He had friends in the lumber business all over the State of Michigan, and it soon became apparent that they would rather buy lumber from him than from anyone else. What there was to sell, he sold. This wasn't apparent when I came home to teach in September, 1936, however. It looked, then, as if I was going to have to support the whole family on my teacher's salary.

Our family was somewhat smaller now. Grandpa was still there, blithely walking downtown and back every day at the age of eighty-five to serve on his juries. Glad was still there, complaining loudly every time a nickel escaped. But my two brothers were gone. Walter was married and living in a small apartment on the other side of town, working now for one of his wife's family. My youngest brother, John, was still peddling milk for Sam Hendricks at ten dollars a week. Because he had no car and no immediate prospects of getting one, he'd gone out to the Flexner farm to live and be near his milk truck.

I was optimistic about the future when I came home. What seemed like the eternal quest was over. I had a steady job. I hadn't been home for more than a weekend before I discovered my problems were far from solved. When I went to the school-board office, I learned that I had been assigned as a teacher of seventh-grade English at Longfellow Junior High School, about a mile from home. My salary would be $1,100 a year, payable at the rate of $110 a month for the duration of the school year. This broke down to about $27.50 a week, which was less than I'd made at Fisher Body the previous fall. When I sat down to figure out what I was going to do with all this money, I received a rude awakening. To begin with, I owed $300, the money I'd borrowed to go to summer school, and it had to be paid back at the rate of thirty-three dollars a month—or about eight dollars a week. That reduced my pay to nineteen dollars right there. Then, because at that moment my family seemed in need of assistance, I agreed to pay my stepmother eleven dollars a week for room and board. This reduced my net to eight dollars. (Although the family crisis was relieved very shortly, Glad never let me off the hook for that eleven dollars.) I was entering upon a profession that required a good personal appearance, and I came to it in sad shape, indeed. I had one good suit—the one I had squeezed out of the chain letter a year and a half before—one pair of shoes from the same source, now resoled for the second time, a darned and ragged old sweater, a ratty overcoat that dated back to 1930, almost nothing in the way of haberdashery, and ancient relics of 1929 like golf shoes and my Kemper uniforms. (The Kemper overcoat had long since been cut down to make a mackinaw.) Of course, I had that suit of tails, but I could scarcely wear that to school. Quite reluctantly, I went down and purchased two new suits, a pair of shoes, and an assortment of shirts, underwear, and other accessories. It came to $120 and I contracted to pay for it at the rate of four dollars a week. This left me slightly less than five dollars for myself. I hadn't gained much ground since my coal-shoveling days.

In spite of my genteel poverty, the fall of 1936 was a happy and an exciting one. Early in October I borrowed my brother's car and drove down to Fort Wayne, Indiana, where I served my fourth stint as best man—this time for the Squirrel. (Bonnie Higgins was at the wedding, incidentally, but she was paired off with someone else, and I had a hard time getting more than a sisterly kiss out of her, much to her amusement.) The teaching itself was a challenge and a joy. I was fresh enough from the School of Education to remember everything I'd been taught and to take it seriously. I loved the age group. The response of a twelve-year-old youngster is a gratifying experience when properly evoked, and my classes were fun. The little girls giggled, and the little boys laughed. For that one semester, I think, I was a superior teacher.

The most happy glow of all came from Youngstown. I was back in love again, and this time I had every reason to believe that my suit was going to be successful. After that meeting in Ann Arbor, Jill and I had settled down to writing each other twice a week. Her letters were warm and friendly. By reading between the lines, I could build all kinds of rosy dreams for the future. Early in November, when she said she missed me, I wrote her that I was thinking of coming down to see her over Thanksgiving. I got an answer by special delivery. "Please come," it said.

There was an auspiciousness in the air, and it seemed to me that the time had come to tell Jill exactly how I felt about her and to ask her to marry me. I wasn't thinking very clearly, of course. I didn't have any money. I was in debt. Had she accepted me, I couldn't have afforded a honeymoon, nor did I have any place to bring a bride. Still, the omens were all good. A day or two before I was to leave for Ohio in my brother's car, my father came wheeling into the driveway with a brand-new Buick. He'd sold ten cars of lumber the week before. It was the first good money he'd made, and he used it to replace the battered old wreck he'd been driving for seven years. To my great surprise he asked me if I'd like to use it on my trip, so I came driving up to Jill's house in a shiny new automobile. It was a little like Cinderella going to the ball.

Jill and her mother wouldn't hear of my putting up at a hotel. They moved me right into the family guest room. I liked the family. Like everyone else, I think, they had suffered some from the Depression. They lived in a rambling old house that dated back forty years or more. The furniture was quite similar to the furniture at home. As a matter of fact, the Ryans had gone through pretty much our own experience. They'd lost the fine new house they'd built in 1929 and had moved into one that had belonged to Jill's maternal grandfather. The money for Jill's education had evidently come from some aunt or other. Jill's father was a druggist, a jaunty man, tall and thin and handsome, full of corny jokes and goodwill. Her mother was a thoroughly modern woman, pleasant of manner and still quite attractive looking. There was a sister of high-school age and a brother of about fourteen. And because I arrived in time for the annual Thanksgiving feast, I had a chance to meet quite an assortment of aunts, uncles, cousins, and grandparents. I noticed that there was a good deal of curiosity about what I was doing there, and it was evidently established to everyone's satisfaction that big things might be expected of me. It was flattering and encouraging.

That first day in Youngstown was spent in the bosom of the Ryan family. There was the usual abundance of food, and after the table was cleared and the dishes washed, the games began. Everyone gathered around the table to play Monopoly, a new game to me at that time. Then, as the crowd began to thin out, I settled down at the bridge table with Jill and her mother and one of the uncles. Jill's father went to sleep in a nearby chair while reading the first issue of something called *Life* magazine. It was pretty much the kind of Thanksgiving that I'd been used to all my life, and I fitted right in with that crowd. Strangely enough, the one person who didn't fit in was Jill. I don't know how I got that impression, or where it came from, but on two or three occasions during the day I had the most peculiar feeling that this simply wasn't her milieu. It may have been the clothes she wore—a little more chic, perhaps. It may have been the way she entered into the games—with just a trace of superciliousness. It may have been that I was used to thinking of her against the background of the Maggie house—a more sophisticated and worldly one than this.

Still, there was nothing I could put my finger on. Jill was cheerful and gracious. She helped with the dishes. She moved about with a calm efficiency, trading jokes and helping to organize things. She treated me just like one of the family. It wasn't until the last straggler had disappeared out the front door or up the stairs to bed that I had any time alone with her. It was a brief moment. She'd gone about turning out the lights and had settled down beside me on the sofa.

"That was some day," I said, "and some family, too."

"You like them?" she said. "I hoped you would." There was something wistful and warm about the way she said it, and I put my arm around her shoulders and drew her over to me. It seemed to me that the time had come to pour out all the things I'd been saving up for so long. Alas! It wasn't to be. The front door burst open and Jill's brother stomped through the living room on the way to the refrigerator. Jill went out to help him and he came back to sit in the straight-backed chair opposite me, a turkey sandwich in one hand, a glass of milk in the other. He discussed my father's new Buick and Michigan's lousy football team, which had just been walloped by Ohio State for the fourth year in a row. After a number of hints from Jill, he finally went off up the stairs, and once more I put my arm around her shoulder. The front door opened again and Jill's sister came in. We went through much the same performance. When

Jill came back from clearing the scene, she had a big grin on her face. She didn't sit down. She extended her two hands to pull me up from the sofa.

"Brother Delta," she said, "I'm afraid this isn't meant to be. I'm so pleased you've come and I'd like to sit here and talk with you, but I'm not a schoolteacher and I don't get the whole weekend off. Tomorrow's just another working day and I've got to get to bed." She kissed me lightly and led me toward the stairs.

I spent the next day sightseeing. It was a dull, damp, and chilly day, and Youngstown kept reminding me of home. There were steel mills instead of auto factories, but the rest of it was much the same. In the winter light the city seemed grim and dirty. When night came and I met Jill again, we went out partying. We must have gone to three or four different places. All of them could have been put right down in Flint. The people were the same. They talked about the same things and even told the same jokes. In all of this I felt right at home, but once again I noticed that Jill was different. It didn't worry me. One of the things about being in love with a person is a sense of pride in that person, and I was immensely proud of her. Her poise and beauty and the fact that she held herself a little aloof from the crowd were an indication to me that she was no ordinary girl, that she was something to be prized.

We didn't return to her house until early morning, and once more I didn't have a chance to talk with her. On Saturday, Jill's mother asked us if we'd drive her over to Pittsburgh so that she could do some of her Christmas shopping. It was a pleasant trip. We saw a movie and had dinner at the William Penn hotel. Everything was white linen and crystal glassware and elegant service, and we sat over the table until after ten so that it was well after midnight before we got home.

When I woke up that Sunday morning, Jill and her mother and sister had gone to Mass. Her brother and I sat at the kitchen table while Mr. Ryan delivered sausages and pancakes to our plates. After breakfast I went up and packed my suitcase for the trip home. I was just finishing this task when Jill came quietly into the room and sat on the edge of the bed.

"I'm afraid you're a little disappointed," she said. "I haven't given you much chance to talk. I have a feeling you wanted to."

"I did."

She looked down at her hands shyly and then looked back up at me.

"I wanted you to talk. I asked you down here because I hoped you would talk to me. You see, dear Brother Delta, I think I know what you want to say and all fall I've hoped you would say it. I'm really very perverse and unkind. After you drive all the way down here, I get cold feet. There must be something the matter with me. Maybe it's because I don't know you well enough."

I went over to her and took both her hands in mine.

"I don't think you're very perverse or unkind. I wanted to come down here. Just seeing you and being with you is enough for me. I've never told you I loved you, but I think you know, by now, that I do love you. I've loved you since the first day I saw you. I want to marry you and I think we will get married some day. In the meantime, maybe you're right about not knowing me well enough. Maybe you ought to come up to Flint."

"I'd like to come. I could stay with Helen."

"That wasn't exactly what I had in mind. If you had a job in Flint or Detroit, so that we could see each other oftener, I think things would work out better."

"It might. I'll try a visit first. We'll see."

"When do you want to come?"

"Whenever you want me to come. Write me."

II

On that November day when I drove back home from Youngstown, the Depression was seven years old. Very few people who had lived through those years were conscious of the fact that they were living through a revolution. There had been some pretty basic changes in the way the average American faced life, and those changes were now affecting his surroundings, his government, and his everyday living philosophy. Those of us in Flint were about to have the full meaning of this revolution revealed to us.

I had only recently been granted a college degree. I have refrained from commenting upon the academic content of my education, but I had not struggled through all those years without acquiring some learning. Among the courses which I had taken were two economics classes in labor. I had read Marx and Engels—I had a copy of the Communist Manifesto in my room at home—and I was thoroughly acquainted with the philosophy and the history of the labor movement. Unlike many of my fellow students at the University of Michigan, I had emerged from these studies neither a radical nor a champion of labor. The same professors who set a good many of my classmates to making speeches on the steps of the university library left me largely unmoved. On that day when Fred LaBeau suggested I join the union in the Fisher Mill, he was talking to the wrong man. Even though I was well aware that there were injustices in the mill situation, I wouldn't join. I was a product of my environment much more than I was a product of my education. One of the reasons why intellectuals have always had hard going among the masses is because of this domination of the environmental background and the acceptance of basic attitudes from childhood, which are ingrained in the majority of people. Until pure thought is itself transformed into emotional impulse, it does not get a hold on the people. I was a product of middle-class parents and I was brought up in a world that solidly embraced a middle-class philosophy. It was a relatively small world where everyone knew everyone else. There had never been a labor union in that world, because most people didn't believe one was needed. On of the basic tenets of my world was the belief that each man stood on his own legs and fought his own fight. His success or failure depended upon how strong he was and how well he fought. It was a world in which bullies existed, but it was also a world in which there was always going to be the triumph of righteousness. Someone could always be depended upon to come along and knock the bullies down. This philosophy was pounded into me in early childhood, and by the time I reached college it was as much a part of me as belief in God. It was a viewpoint that was incompatible with the theories of unionism. Had one of my father's truck drivers ever joined a union instead of taking his grievances straight to my father and putting them on the table like a man, I would have thought he was pretty sneaky. This attitude survived college and knowledge. I never thought of myself as a laboring man, not even when I was driving a coal truck or filing fenders in the Buick factory. If and when the barricades were manned, I knew which side I belonged on.

To bolster my basic attitudes, I had the results of personal observation. I'd worked at Buick, AC Spark Plug, and Fisher, and I had never seen a man pushed beyond his endurance. I felt that working conditions in the factory were good and that management was reasonable in its expectations of what a man could do. At some time during these years I had gone to see Charlie Chaplin's *Modern Times*. I thought that the antics of Charlie's little man on the assembly line were hilarious and I laughed at them, but when one of my college professors implied that these working conditions actually existed in industry, I bridled. I told him it was all right to exaggerate in the interests of comedy, but when the exaggerations were used to make political capital, it was something else again. No factory that I had ever seen would ever think of pushing a man to those lengths. I suggested that the professor go and work in a factory and see working conditions at first hand.

Prior to getting involved with Fred LaBeau and the embryonic union in the Fisher Mill, the only union man I'd ever known well was Guy Mudge, a motorman on the Flint streetcars. I'd become acquainted with Guy in those years of my adolescence after we first moved to Flint when I briefly changed my allegiance from locomotives to streetcars. Sometimes, in those days, I would call Guy's house and find out where he was working, then go board his car and ride back and forth from one end of the line to the other. I was much more interested in the way he ran the streetcar than I was in his union concerns, but he was often preoccupied with the affairs of the Amalgamated Electric Street Railway Workers Association, and he liked to converse with me on the subject. In time I came to know quite a lot about working rules and I was well aware of how much power the union had, but Guy Mudge was never able to make the union come alive. All the struggles over rules and money had taken place in far-off towns, waged by other locals in other times, and Flint had never had a streetcar strike. I came to think of the trolley workers' union as a lodge of some kind, a little like the Odd Fellows and Masons. That was the way I thought a union should be.

As we approached 1937, there were three main working groups in the city of Flint. The aristocrats of Flint labor were the men who worked for Buick. They were not necessarily the highest paid workers, but they were the senior workers—the stable ones. Some of them had already worked for Buick for thirty years, and there was even a second generation of Buick men. The average Buick worker owned his own home, his own car, and stock in the company. He had raised a family and in many cases he had educated them, as Lou Norris' father had. He had accumulated things. When the Depression came along, Buick workers suffered layoffs and hard times along with everyone else, but as a group they had more resources with which to weather the storm. They had to tighten their belts, but very few of them were in desperate straits.

The Chevrolet workers comprised the second working group in the city. Everything about Chevrolet was younger than Buick. Although Chevrolet had been manufacturing automobiles since 1912, it had not become a major factor in the growth of Flint until after World War I. Its greatest years of expansion were between 1918 and 1926. Its workers were still raising families and still paying on their houses when the Depression came. They were less deeply rooted, and they had fewer resources. To them the Depression became a bitter struggle to hold on to what little they had. Not all of them succeeded.

The key to what happened to Flint in the winter of 1936 and 1937 was the third working force, the men who worked for Fisher Body. They were relatively new to Flint. Of course, almost all of Flin't population came from somewhere else. People had streamed in, looking for work in the factories. In the early days they came from the surrounding countryside and from the small, nearby towns, but as the auto plants grew and needed more and more men, the workers came from further afield. There had been a big change in autos in the early twenties. The old touring cars disappeared in favor of closed models. The cost of transporting auto bodies up from Pontiac, where they had always been made, became too great, and when the chance arose to acquire a plant in Flint, General Motors established its first body factory in the city. This was in 1926. In order to staff this new plant, recruiters were bringing in workers from as faraway as Arkansas, Missouri, and Tennessee. They came in such large numbers that there wasn't adequate housing for them. The same phenomenal growth that I had observed in my own neighborhood as a boy was taking place all over the city, but the houses that were being built in the south end of town, near the Fisher Body plant, weren't very substantial ones, most of them being nothing but hastily constructed garages with no basements, plumbing, or central-heating facilities. They were slums before they were even occupied. The people who lived in them were poor before they came to Flint. They had nothing after they got there except what they earned in the factories. This does not mean that they were shiftless; on the contrary, from the very beginning they worked hard to improve their lot. One of the reasons why my father had located his lumberyard in the south end of town was to take advantage of the business that was bound to come from these people. During summer vacations while I was in high school, I worked for my father and I hauled a lot of lumber to families who were adding upper stories or rooms or basements to those little homes. I saw an awful lot of them transformed into pleasant houses. In most cases the improvements were made by the men after they came home from putting in a full day's work in the plants. They were hard workers and they wanted the good things in life and they struggled hard to get them during those first years in Flint, but they'd hardly begun to achieve anything when the Depression came. As the years passed and they averaged four months of work a year, they not only could not improve their lot, but their situation became truly desperate. These were the workers who were first driven onto the welfare in our town. The Depression came before they had any resources to sustain them. I noticed one thing about them quite early in the Depression. When they talked about "home," they were referring to those faraway places from which they had come. None of them had been in Flint long enough to put down any real roots in the city. They certainly had no affection for a place in which they were undergoing such hardships.

Flint was not a company town, but General Motors was its only manufacturing entity. I say this because General Motors was not imposed upon the city; it was born in Flint. The corporation had been organized by a Flint man, Billy Durant, and the first fifteen years of its corporate history is the story of the rather bizarre struggle of Billy Durant to control the company he had founded. Even after the ownership passed to Eastern interests in 1920, General Motors was managed by Flint men or by men who had lived there long enough to be considered local in origin. The list of men who learned their trade in this little city includes Walter P. Chrysler and Charles Nash, and as late as 1935 it was almost impossible to find a man in an executive capacity in the auto industry who had not served an apprenticeship in Flint, a fact in which the community took great pride. There was something of the old small town about a city in which the two principal executives, Harlow H. Curtice and William Knudsen, were still affectionately referred to as "Red" and "Bill" by most workers. It was an accepted practice for most of the old timers to drop around and get personal advice from their bosses both during and after working hours.

One qualification must be made of this view of Flint. It held true in the north end of town where the Buick workers lived. It was true to some extent in the west end where the Chevrolet workers lived, but it was not true in the south end. None of the more recent arrivals in town had ever heard of Billy Durant. Harlow H. Curtice was only a name they read in the newspapers. To them the auto industry and the city constituted an impersonal world, if not a hostile one.

The General Motors Corporation had always taken a paternal stance toward its employees. I do not think there was a single doubt in the mind of any General Motors executive that the workers in the Flint plants were treated fairly and paid well. Even Al Moriarity thought of himself as a model boss. His arbitrary attitude toward the men under him was simply a defense against a group of unruly men who weren't playing the game according to the rules.

The biggest single institution in Flint reflected the paternal and fair view which the General Motor executives had of themselves. This organization was known as the Industrial Mutual Association. It had built the big field-house type auditorium where I had gone dancing for so many years. The IMA was originally designed as a recreational organization, and in that field it had done wonders. It maintained a lake, golf courses, bowling alleys, and parks for its members. It supported a complete sandlot sports program, provided excursions for factory workers, and instituted various night-study programs. The twice-weekly dances, always featuring big-name bands, were part of the regular schedule of events. Membership in the IMA was not compulsory, but most Flint factory workers joined it. If the organization had one big drawback, it was the fact that it was dominated by the Buick workers, the most conservative element in Flint labor.

There had never been any labor trouble in the Flint plants of General Motors. Except for small groups like the one in the Fisher Mill there had never been any union movement in the shops. Despite the hard times there had been no publicly voiced dissatisfaction with conditions. When the National Recovery Act was passed in 1933, it contained provisions guaranteeing the right of collective bargaining for all workers. Shortly after this law went into effect, the IMA was designated as the collective bargaining agent for all Flint workers. It was announced in one of those small boxes that interrupt a news story in the daily paper and it appeared way back in the middle reaches of the Flint *Journal*. I was not concerned at the moment and I paid little attention to it. I don't know whether the designation came about as the result of an election or whether the directors of the IMA simply decided to fulfill the role. I have always assumed the latter. It wasn't important at the time, anyway. The year 1933 was an extremely poor time to raise any questions about wages or working conditions or representation. Before conditions changed and before anyone had a real chance to test the question of whether the IMA was a legal bargaining agent or not, the NRA was declared unconstitutional and the whole business of collective bargaining was forgotten, by all but a few. It appears that certain individuals were willing to test the IMA, however. At some time during the NRA period, a group of men in Fisher Body had applied for and received a local charter in the United Auto Workers of America, which was then an affiliate of the American Federation of Labor. I do not know who the original officers of this local were, but it seemed to be strongest where there were highly skilled workers as in the wood mill. Whatever the case, the union movement had not made much headway at the time I worked at Fisher in December, 1935. As far as I know, no progress had been made at all in the other General Motors plants in Flint, if any attempts had been made to organize them.

The year 1936 saw the passage of the National Labor Relations Act. Once again the right of all workers to engage in collective bargaining was guaranteed. And, once again, it was announced that the IMA had been designated as the collective bargaining agent for Flint workers in General Motors. The main result of the passage of the National Labor Relations Act was the organization of the Committee for Industrial Organization by John L. Lewis of the United Mine Workers. He announced that the automobile industry would be one of the first targets for organization. Able and competent organizers were sent to Flint in the fall of 1936. Using the original Fisher local as the nucleus around which to build, and with the help of adequate resources made available by the CIO, the organizers were able to recruit a considerable number of new members in both Fisher Body plants. It is quite obvious that the union's organizers knew that the Fisher Body workers presented the most vulnerable target for any drive of this sort, for they had no long-term allegiance to either the corporation or the city of Flint. A lot of them had real grievances, as I well knew. I have no idea what the actual membership figures in the Fisher local were on December 30, 1936, but I doubt if they amounted to even 50 percent of the workers in either plant. They may have run as low as 10 percent, but even using the more optimistic figure, the United Auto Workers' membership consisted of a very small part of the total Flint General Motors work force.

It was on December 30, 1936, at the close of the day shift, that workers in both Fisher Body plants sat down at their jobs. The sit-down strike was a new and novel strategy at that time. It was plainly dictated by the fact that the union had less than a majority of the workers in the two plants. There may have been a majority at a later date but most certainly not on December 30 when the strike began. When one considers that the real union target was the ultimate representation of all the workers in Flint plants, it is easy to see why some radical strategy was needed. Any strike under ordinary conditions would have failed. At that particular moment, for the first time in seven years, it appeared that the auto factories might run for six months or longer, and there weren't very many auto workers in a mood to jeopardize this chance at sustained employment. Furthermore, Flint was a city in which there was no tradition which would have caused a man to honor a picket line.

The only way a union with a small membership could bring management to a bargaining session was to stop work in the factories. A picket line wouldn't do that, but a plant seizure would. The big risk that the union ran lay in the fact that a plant seizure was patently illegal, and by using it they opened up side issues which could defeat them. The tactic of the sit-down strike hit at the very core of Anglo-Saxon jurisprudence: the right to own and control private property. The union leaders were well aware of this, and I believe that most of them subscribed to the principle of private property, and—it should be emphasized—not one of them ever advocated the abolition of these rights. That had absolutely nothing to do with the sit-down strike in Flint, although many of the main actors in the drama were later accused of being Communists. The sit-down was simply a stratagem aimed at bringing about one result—the achievement of union recognition. Even that was a modest goal, for the UAW did not ask to be recognized as the *sole* bargaining agent for General Motors workers in Flint, or even for Fisher Body workers. It simply asked to be recognized as a bargaining agent for its own membership.

The strike was brilliantly conceived. The timing was important. December 30 was a Wednesday. The next day, Thursday, was New Year's Eve. Friday, January 1, was a legal holiday, and the plants would normally be closed for the weekend on January 2 and 3. Nearly everyone had made plans for the long holiday weekend, and there was a natural reluctance to upset these plans, combined with an obvious confusion about how to change such things as court hours. There was also an understandable tendency to underestimate the significance of events. On the morning after the strike began, there was a flurry of moves. Lawyers went to court and argued. Conferences were held. Invectives were hurled, and the community waxed indignant, but the novelty of the situation and the lack of precedents contributed to a confusion that resulted in a kind of paralysis. The last day of 1936 passed without any resolution of the situation, legal or physical. People drifted away for the weekend. There was almost an air of calm. The opinion of the majority seemed to be that if the sit-downers wanted to give up their New Year's Eve celebrations, the holiday meals, and the football games, it would serve them right. And so five days passed in inaction. By January 4, the sit-down had become an established institution. The union had the initiative, the logistics for supplying the men had been worked out, and some very effective propaganda had been disseminated. On New Year's Eve, among the people of Flint, there seemed to be a general belief that the strikers were already tired of the whole thing and that they were sneaking out of the plants and going home. By Monday none of them would be left. When the plants were still held on Saturday, the rumors had changed. It was said that the people in the plants weren't workers at all. They were outsiders from Toledo and Detroit. By Sunday, the rumors had changed again. Not only were the sit-downers outsiders, but their numbers were being augmented hourly by carloads of people from all over the United States. There would soon be a sizable army in Flint to protect and help the strikers.

I have no idea where these rumors came from. I don't think any of them were true. If they were put out by antistrike forces, they backfired, for they tended to make for caution. Instead of acting in a rash manner with resultant violence, the authorities and the people tended to look twice before they made a move. If, on the other hand, the rumors were put out by the strikers, they were effective. It has always been my belief that the union followed a double-barreled course of action. One part was waged in the courts. Whenever a legal move was made the union lawyers launched a counteroffensive. All kinds of side issues were raised that obscured and delayed any effective action. During the second week of the strike, for example, a court order demanding evacuation of the plants was issued by Judge Edward Black, the highly respected, ninety-four-year-old dean of the Genesee County Circuit Court. No one in Flint held the esteem of his fellow townsmen like this old man. He had a reputation for probity that stretched as far back as anyone could remember. The union wasn't in the least awed by the old gentleman. They had discovered that he owned a sizable block of General Motors stock. This indicated that he was guilty of bias and that the order was illegally issued. Not only that, the old man was in violation of judicial ethics and, therefore, unfit to sit on the bench, The people of Flint were thunderstruck. Practically everyone in town, if they owned any stock at all, owned General Motors stock. I don't think it had ever occurred to anyone that this could prejudice a man's action. Everyone jumped up to defend the judge, and in the wave of widespread indignation, along with the legal hearings on the matter that followed the charges, actual proceedings against the sit-down strikers were delayed for several more days and almost shoved off the front page. In the first four weeks of the strike a good half dozen injunctions, writs, and other kinds of orders were fought on grounds of legal technicalities. They never resulted in anything. In some cases the points made by the union lawyers were valid. Sometimes they weren't, but it all added up to delay. The sit-down continued and the work stoppage continued. That's what the union really wanted.

The second half of the double-barreled union offensive was something else and it struck a lot closer to most residents of Flint. In effect, the organizers created a reign of terror in the city. The rumors about outsiders would have been a part of this. It is not a pleasant thing to contemplate one's city being taken over by invaders. There was also a threat of a general strike in support of the sit-downers. In retrospect, I don't think there was enough union strength in the city to make good on such a threat, but at the time no one was sure whether there were other unions willing to go along or not. And just to give some credence to the rumors right in the middle of the whole business, my mild and inoffensive little lodge man, Guy Mudge, led his Amalgamated Association of Electric Street Railway Workers out on strike. They remained on strike for the duration of the sit-down. Sound trucks were everywhere, taunting, urging, and using "unspeakable language." All this was a form of pressure designed to protect and support the strikers. The atmosphere was charged and tense.

It was impossible for any resident of the city of Flint to remain neutral. I was no exception, for the most meaningful years of my life had been spent there. And living in the north end of town insured the fact that I would take a narrow view of things. Within a radius of two miles of our house were the homes of all the more conservative elements of the Flint population. My schoolmates, friends, and neighbors were all indignant about the strike and what was happening to the city. The only two newspapers we ever read in Flint—the Flint *Journal* and the Detroit *Free Press*—attacked the strike and the strikers. The teachers in the school where I taught were up in arms. Even the children in my classes were against it. This last item may not seem very significant, but it had meaning for me. Only three months before, at the time of the Presidential election, I'd listened to these same children discussing Mr. Roosevelt and Mr. Landon, and I knew a month beforehand that Mr. Roosevelt was going to carry Flint by a large margin. In the aftermath of the election I'd told a friend that if he ever wanted to know exactly how things were in a given locality, all he had to do was poll the seventh graders. A twelve-year-old youngster repeats exactly what he hears at home and he usually believes implicitly whatever his father and mother tell him to believe. Out of 190 seventh graders in my classes at the time of the sit-down, only two were in favor of the strike, and I'm pretty sure that taken altogether, they mirrored the general feeling in the city. Under the circumstances, it couldn't be expected that I would take any other than a disapproving view. To me the sit-down was an attempt of a very small minority to impose their views on a large majority. Yet I had sense enough to know that I was being overwhelmed by a massive preponderance of rumors and propaganda, some of which might not be entirely accurate. I was guided, furthermore, by the sage advice of both my father and Grandpa Perry. They reminded me that I was not a General Motors employee, that the struggle was not my struggle, and that until it directly affected me, I would be well to stay away from it. I voiced my opinions forthrightly enough, but I stayed out of the incendiary actions in which the town seemed to be drifting. In the school where I taught, the gymnasium teacher had gone so far as to organize an action committee which was to all intents and purposes a vigilante committee. I refused to join it. I also refused to sign any of the numerous petitions that were being circulated against the strikers. I stayed away from the plants and I took no part in the parades or indignation meetings that marked the latter stages of the strike.

The situation in Flint built slowly. There were several crucial points. The first of these came about two weeks after the strike began. At that time the Buick and Chevrolet plants closed down, not because the workers joined the strike, but because automobiles could not be made without bodies. This action polarized sentiment. The Buick and Chevrolet workers took sides *against* the strikers. Very shortly, thereafter, the Flint Alliance was formed.

The Flint Alliance was the brainchild of a Buick factory worker —and former mayor of Flint—by the name of George Boysen. George was a forward-thinking, forceful man who had come off his bench a few years before to serve a brief term in politics during which he had been responsible for cleaning up and reorganizing the city government. Above everything else, George was a community booster and he took considerable umbrage at the news stories being sent out about the city by the newsmen who had been sent to cover the strike. These stories seemed to indicate that Flint was some kind of a backwater community that refused to accept the twentieth century. If the world wanted to know what the city was like, George would show them, and the best place to start was to get an expression of opinion about how the workers really felt about John L. Lewis and his organizers. He set out to get the signature of every Flint worker on a petition which he intended to send to Franklin D. Roosevelt asking the President to call off the union men. He got thirty thousand signatures within a week, each signatory claiming to belong to an organization of community boosters called the Flint Alliance. He fired the petition off to the White House and then he called a series of mass meetings and staged a mammoth torchlight parade through the downtown district to show the support of the workers for the city's leaders and authorities as against the union leadership. The petitions sent to the White House were studiously ignored by Mr. Roosevelt, but they weren't ignored by the union. Boysen was assailed as a stooge of General Motors, and it was claimed that all those signatures had been obtained by coercion. There was some indication that the out-of-town newspapermen believed this. It became necessary, in George Boysen's own mind, that the world be shown that the Flint Alliance was a spontaneously organized group, and so more public meetings were held and another torchlight parade was organized.

The main thing that the Flint Alliance did was to bring the tension to the breaking point. In spite of the apprehension in the city, there had been little violence in the first weeks, but after the second of those torchlight parades, the atmosphere became ugly. In the fourth week of the strike there were several clashes. One union member was shot and killed in a street fight. One antiunion member was killed in a bar brawl. The vigilante committee organized in our school was only one of several that had sprung up around town, and members of all these committees now began to appear outside the plants. The demands became shriller and the threats became more ominous. Barricades were thrown around the plants so that food and water could not be brought in to the strikers. The lights and heat in the factory were shut off. The scene around the plants began to take on all the aspects of a siege.

All during January the legal maneuvers had been going on to get the strikers out of the plants. The failure to bring any of these maneuvers to a meaningful conclusion was frustrating to those not in favor of the strike. To the average Flint resident it seemed like a simple case of trespass and he couldn't understand why it wasn't treated like that. All that was required was a court order drawn up in clear, unmistakable terms for the strikers to get out. If that order was ignored, then the strikers should be thrown out bodily. There were indications, however, that some people didn't think it was all that simple. The White House had ignored the petitions. Most irritating of all was the reaction in the state capital at Lansing. Michigan had inaugurated a new governor—Frank Murphy—on January 1, 1937, the third day of the strike. Mr. Murphy seemed determined to remain aloof from the situation in Flint. The only public statements he made during the first four weeks were pleas for calm. In his private statements he made it quite plain that he considered the sit-down to be just another strike, and in taking this attitude he completely ignored the illegal-seizure aspect of the case. Toward the end of the fourth week, when the battle in the courts came to its long-drawn-out conclusion and a court order was issued and served on the strikers ordering them to get out of the plants, and when these orders were ignored, the mayor of the city of Flint asked the governor to send in the National Guard to evict the union members. In response to this request, Governor Murphy made his famous statement to the effect that there were human rights as well as property rights and that sometimes those human rights transcended property rights. He had no intention of using the National Guard of the State of Michigan to shoot down citizens of the United States in cold blood. This was a courageous statement for a governor to make in 1937, an era that was still tied to the traditional attitudes of the past. In the long run, it cost Frank Murphy his political future in the State of Michigan. It also brought things to a head. The mood in Flint had grown ugly. Many people are prone to attribute this mood to agitation and propaganda on the part of General Motors, but in doing so they ignore the most basic element —the nature of the people. In spite of all that had happened to them in the previous ten years, the average citizen was still a conservative, grass-roots-oriented individual who accepted the traditional views of what was right and wrong. What had happened in Flint was plainly wrong. They were indignant about it and it had become plain that if any move was going to be made at all it would have to be made on the local level. Preparations were made for that move. Under the direction of Sheriff Thomas Wolcott of Genesee County and James V. Wills, the Flint chief of police, a sizable force of men was organized. On Monday, at the beginning of the fifth week of the occupation of the two Fisher plants, this force appeared at Fisher No. 2, just as it was getting dark. Sheriff Wolcott called for the men to come out of the plant peaceably. If they did not, he was prepared to evict them. The strikers did not come out, and there began the bloodiest battle in the history of Flint. In six hours of bitter fighting two men were killed and more than a hundred were injured. The strikers fought back with every weapon they could find. The amount of damage was awesome. Automobiles were wrecked, several fires were set in the factory, machinery was destroyed, but when the battle was broken off at midnight, the strikers were still in possession of the plant. Sheriff Wolcott promised that he would be back with a larger force next day and he warned the strikers that he would deputize every man in Flint if that was necessary. (Some indication of how the people of Flint felt about the sit-down strike can be gathered from the fact that Tom Wolcott became something of a folk hero during these events. For as long as he lived, almost twenty years, he was regularly reelected sheriff by overwhelming majorities.)

At this point, and as a direct result of the bloodshed at Fisher No. 2, Governor Murphy ordered the National Guard into Flint. He did not order them into the city to evict the strikers from the plants. He sent the Guard in to preserve order. He plainly stated that if there was any more violence on either side he would put the city under martial law. He thus forced peace on the city, but in doing so he ignored the fact that one of the "either" sides was the duly constituted authority of the city—elected by the people. For the rest of the week, armed troops patrolled the city streets. At the end of that week Governor Murphy called the executives of General Motors and the union leaders into his presence and insisted that they sit down and talk. Inasmuch as the sole issue in the strike was recognition of the union, the governor, in effect, decreed a victory for the sit-downers. When the two sides sat down to talk, the strikers marched out of the plants. The most significant victory for union labor in the history of the United States had been won. It opened the way for unionization, not only of the auto industry but of every other mass-production industry as well.

Like most other residents of Flint, at the time, I was resentful of the imposition of outside force on the community in the face of overwhelming sentiment against both the strike and the strikers. The significance of what had happened was a long time dawning on me. I was seeing a lot more than a union victory in a strike. I was seeing a way of life disappear. The small world with small problems was gone. The rural viewpoints that people had carried with them into the cities in the first three decades of the twentieth century were gone. The General Motors Corporation was no longer a local concern managed by local men with a kindly regard for the workers. The men at Fisher Body knew this. They'd seen it long before the rest of us did and their strike was against an impersonal entity, cold and hard. Something else had become apparent, too. The idea that each family and each community could take care of its own and exist like a small island in a great sea was no longer valid. The crisis of the Depression with its poverty and its hopelessness had long since proved too much for cities like Flint, for counties like Genesee County, for states like Michigan. The forces let loose by industrialization and urbanization, and the centralization of power in the hands of big corporations, were forces that were too great for one man or one small community to face alone. The Depression was a time when Americans ceased to be an inward-looking, isolated people. The whole essence of the New Deal was the abandonment of this small, individualistic outlook in favor of the bigger, stronger, national government and the immense power it could bring to bear on the solution of the pressing problems that faced us. Having turned to the place which could help, the individuals and the communities also came to accept the wider viewpoints held by the national government. Just how rapidly Americans can adjust to changed thinking can be seen from the fact that within months after the sit-down strike all of the General Motors plants were unionized. What is more, the workers were not coerced into the union. They joined willingly and enthusiastically. I changed myself. I came to believe that unions were a good thing but I came to believe in a lot of things in those years. It was a truly revolutionary world we lived in.

III

Revolutionary world or not, the everyday problems of existence continued to confront me as an individual. In the spring of 1937, as in all the other springs that had recently passed, the main problem was the Depression. It had a way of reaching into one's life in odd ways.

My career as a teacher of seventh-grade English ended abruptly a week after the sit-down strike. On the day I turned in my final grades for the first semester, I was handed a note from the superintendent of schools. I was to report immediately to Northern High School where I was to teach the second semester. Although this was a welcome testimonial to my success as a teacher, I have always regretted it. The seventh grade and I were made for each other. Things just weren't the same in senior high school.

In reporting to Northern I was returning to the school from which I had graduated eight years before. Although I was twenty-five years old, I soon found that there was a tendency on the part of the faculty to treat me as though I were still a student. Most of the teachers at Northern were the same teachers who had taught me. This accounted for some of the attitude toward me but not all of it. I was not the first graduate to return to the school. That honor had gone to Hank Feller, and Hank had promptly disgraced himself. He had always been partial to very young girls and at Northern he had scandalized the whole school by marrying one of his tenth-grade biology students. I think some of the faculty were afraid that this might signal a trend, and it took me a long time to gain the confidence of everyone. The peculiar part of it is that some of the suspicions of me proved well founded, although this did not immediately become apparent.

My first semester at Northern remains hazy to this day. I was not a good teacher. Because I was the most junior member of the faculty I was given all the odds and ends to teach. Among other things, I had classes in bookkeeping and salesmanship. The main thing that made me a poor teacher that spring, however, was my outside interests. From the beginning to the end I was intensely preoccupied by other things. As an apprentice teacher, I benefited from one important rule of the Flint school system. I did not have to undertake any extracurricular activities. Instead of sponsoring some club or activity, I supervised study halls. This gave me the opportunity to prepare my lesson plans during school hours and left my afternoons and evenings free. It was a good thing it worked out that way.

The primary source of my preoccupation was Jill Ryan. Immediately after my return from Youngstown, I had made arrangements with Helen Tarkington for Jill's visit to Flint. We had all settled on the Easter weekend which came the last Sunday in March. The sit-down strike had put off the final arrangements, and so I had only five weeks to make my preparations. The key to everything, it seemed to me, was to get Jill up to Flint to stay, and in order to accomplish that she had to have a job. During the whole period before she arrived I scurried around town arranging interviews for her. I used every friend and acquaintance I had, and by the time Jill arrived I had appointments for her at all the General Motors plants. This was all done with her knowledge, and the fact that she was excited about the prospects indicated that I had a lot to hope for.

I met Jill in Detroit on Good Friday morning. She had always been a striking girl, but in preparation for that trip out to Flint she had bought herself an entirely new wardrobe. When she came walking down the station platform toward me that bright, sunny morning, she was something to behold. She had on a severely cut, gray traveling suit, but the skirts were cut much shorter than most girls were wearing at that time. We started out that morning in a holiday spirit, laughing and making jokes and talking a blue streak. On the way up to Flint we stopped in a roadhouse and had a cocktail which made us all the happier. At one thirty she went to the first interview I had arranged for her. In her happy mood and those stunning clothes she could have had the whole town. She had four job offers, and we talked them over during dinner. She decided to take the one at Buick. There didn't seem to be a doubt in her mind about it. It has always seemed ironic to me, incidentally, that whenever I needed a job for myself I'd never been able to find one, yet I'd found four of them for Jill without any trouble at all.

Helen Tarkington had taken over the social arrangements for Jill's visit. Dinner was at her house that evening. Afterward we were all going to the country club for the Easter formal. I got into those tails of mine and George French picked me up. The Depression seemed to be over for him. He'd finished his course at General Motors Tech and was now a foreman in one of the plants. He'd been in love with Helen for two years now and had come increasingly under the influence of Judge Tarkington. All those old ideas of his about the proletariat had gone down the drain along with old cars he'd always tinkered with. When he arrived to pick me up that night, he was wearing white tie and tails and was driving a brand-new Buick. He reminded me of Maurice Chevalier somehow. We weren't boys anymore.

On that trip to Youngstown, I'd been struck by the fact that Jill was different from the people who surrounded her. I soon discovered she was different from the people in Flint, too. She'd bought a new black-lace evening gown for the occasion. It had a high neckline and long sleeves and clung closely to her figure. All the other girls at the dance were still wearing the uniform of the Depression—strapless satin evening gowns—and they all had their hair heaped on top of their heads in great masses. Jill's was cut short in a severe bob. She was almost a new kind of a girl and she stood out in that company. I was proud of her as I watched the heads turn. The evening went off wonderfully, and it was almost dawn when she put her arms around me and gave me a long, warm, good-night kiss. I had reached the high point in my love affair with her.

It is sometimes impossible to say what causes a love affair to founder, but I know pretty well what caused this one to collapse. It was primarily because there had never been any love affair at all. Oh, I loved Jill Ryan all right, but she didn't love me and she never had. If she'd been left to herself, way back there in the days of Howard Ehrmann's class, I don't think Jill would have noticed me, but she had because I'd taken the trouble to see that she would. Almost immediately, I had placed myself in the position of a court jester. I amused her, and she kept waiting to see what I was going to come up with next. Nothing I did produced any basic change in our relationship. It only caused her to speculate. Such a campaign as I had waged could have continued indefinitely, perhaps successfully, as far as marrying her was concerned, but in the end I would probably have had to douse myself in kerosene and launch myself across the sky like a comet. The only big question in the whole matter was just when I was going to stop amusing her.

The facts of life in the Depression were also a factor in the course of the affair and accounted for whatever success I'd had. Things didn't work out well for Jill. At the time George Glass had taken her to Detroit for the alumni football bust, the two of them had been treated like visiting royalty. She probably thought that prominent people were always going to make a fuss over George and she'd made a deliberate choice at that time, and she hadn't even bothered to give me an explanation—not that she'd owed me one. Then George Glass had turned out to be a dud. She went back home to Youngstown and got a job. Youngstown was an industrial city. It was dull and cheerless and dirty and it must have seemed like a prison to her. She'd spent four years in the lush green pastures of a university during the worst part of the Depression. She'd been much admired and was the center of things and because her education seems to have been more than adequately provided for she missed much of the meaning of what was going on in the outside world. I think she had been spoiled. When she graduated she may even have thought that she was entitled to the kind of world she'd come to know. Youngstown was a bad letdown. That seeming aloofness I'd noticed was a symptom of what was the matter with her. She was not getting involved with anyone. She intended to escape when she could and when she saw me in Ann Arbor the previous August she must have decided that I was better than Youngstown. After all I'd spent my whole career with her trying to be clever and witty. I certainly didn't disillusion her. Her first visit to Flint had been of one day's duration, most of it spent in Helen Tarkington's luxurious house. Then I'd come down to Youngstown to see her driving my father's brand-new Buick. Her second visit had started out with a sumptuous party at the country club. I think she honestly thought that I was the member of some kind of social elite. The whole business was about to turn back into a pumpkin.

There was one side of Jill that I'd never seen. She was Irish through and through. Somewhere in her makeup was a tendency to become moody, to withdraw into black depressions. If she got moody enough, she could be mean. Special handling is required for a person like this, and I wasn't equipped for it. I had never run up against it before.

Helen Tarkington had arranged for a private party on the second night of Jill's visit, inviting several of the sorority sisters who lived near Flint. It wasn't supposed to begin until eight in the evening, and I had planned to spend most of the day taking Jill around to meet my friends and some of my family. During the morning the weather turned bad. It began to rain and the day was dark and dreary and chill. Flint was a manufacturing town, and under the best of circumstances it had little glamour. On that March day, at the end of the long winter, the city seemed stripped naked. The lawns, which would soon be green, were still gray, and there were traces of the winter snow, dirty and black. The trees, not yet in leaf, were gaunt skeletons that accentuated the bleakness of the landscape. The factory buildings and the downtown streets were cloaked in winter grime and soot. If Jill had indeed come to Flint expecting to find a new world, one that was lovely and full of life, she was bound to be depressed by a city that was as drab and dispirited as the one from which she was trying to escape. To make matters worse, the friends she met were affected by this dreariness. It was a moment when everyone could have used a bright, sunny day. It was just another spring in the same old Depression. Most people were still broke and uncertain of the future, a condition that was aggravated by the fact that all of us had just come through the sit-down strike. A sunny day might have accentuated hope. The gloomy day simply emphasized the same old unpleasantness that we'd been going through for so long. On almost any other day people like Nick Woods and Bugs Huntley would have been amusing and they could have helped sustain the holiday mood so necessary for my success with Jill. They were pleasant enough. They were polite, but something more than pleasantness and politeness was needed. I didn't help matters any. From the very moment that Jill emerged from the Tarkington house into the drizzle and looked around her, she was dispirited. I did everything I could think of to cheer her up and I tried too hard. Finally, when my efforts failed I began to get down in the dumps myself. It was as though I'd started out to help a lady across a swamp. About halfway to the other side I had to start thinking about how to save myself. I could see both of us sinking right out of sight. I finally gave up calling on friends and steered Jill into a new Carole Lombard movie. Everyone else in the theater was laughing. Not Jill. We came out of the movie and went to Flint's best restaurant for dinner. Jill pecked at her food and made no attempt to converse with me. The ship was sinking fast and I knew it.

We were late getting to the party. It was held in that same lovely room that had so enchanted Jill on her first visit to Flint, two years before. It would have been better if there had been a bright fire. The room needed something to take off the chill of the steadily falling rain that dripped in the floodlights outside. Alas! Helen had put a bar across the front of the fireplace. Off in a corner, soft dance music was playing on a phonograph, but no one was dancing. It was that kind of a day, that kind of a night. Nothing worked.

When we got there, Jill headed straight for the bar, climbed up on a stool, and asked for a good stiff drink. She didn't get off that stool for three hours. There was something determined about her. The party jerked to life, but she didn't become a part of it. I had sense enough to stay out of her way and I noticed that even her sorority sisters weren't spending any more time with her than they could help. She was sullen and snappish. Eventually, when she began to show the effects of her drinking, I suggested that it might be a good idea if we got a little fresh air. She came along without a word. The rain had stopped by then, and I walked her several times around the block in the raw wind. On the last time around she pointed at George French's car and indicated she wanted to get in. She lit a cigarette and sat there on the front seat, staring straight ahead. After she put the cigarette out, she turned to me.

"It's no use," she said. "It's no damned good at all. I don't love you. I never will love you. God knows, I've tried."

"You don't have to try to love somebody," I said.

"Well, that's the way it is and that's the way it's going to be," she said grimly. "I've had enough of this and I'd appreciate it if you'd forget the whole thing." She put her hand down and opened the door and began getting out. By the time I caught up with her she was ready to let herself into the house. I put my hand on her arm. I thought I should make some attempt to soften things.

"Maybe you'll feel better about it tomorrow."

"I doubt it," she said, and went in.

Jill didn't do any more drinking, but she stayed away from me all the rest of that long night. She even excused herself and went to bed without saying good night to me. We had planned to go to church together on Easter, then have dinner with my family before George and Helen drove us back to Detroit. Early in the morning, however, Helen called and said that Jill wasn't feeling well and wanted to be excused. There was nothing I could do about it, but I hadn't quite given up yet. I walked over to George French's house and talked to him. He knew that something had gone wrong and he was of the opinion that Jill and I ought to be left alone to patch it up so he lent me his car. I was to drive Jill back to Detroit by myself. I picked her up about three thirty in the afternoon. We had no sooner pulled away from the curb than she withdrew into the far corner of the front seat and folded her arms.

"If you think I'm going to talk any more about this, you're mistaken," she said. "I just wish you'd let it lie."

I let it lie. It was an awkward ride. When we got out of the car, she hailed a redcap before I had a chance to get her bag out of the back. She marched stiffly through the station, and although it was still half an hour until train time, she scarcely halted at the gate.

"Good-bye," she said, holding out her hand.

The second big love of my life was over.

IV

That moment, as I watched Jill Ryan flounce off down the station platform, was a crushing one. I didn't stay crushed for very long—about five minutes, I'd say. I turned away and stumbled back to the car, my mind flailing out in all directions trying to find something I could do to reverse what had happened. I sensed that Jill had no understanding of me whatsoever. I'd played the fool with her for so long that she'd never had a chance to see the man underneath. On that long-ago night in Ann Arbor, Bonnie Higgins had asked me what I would be like if I ever stopped scintillating. I wasn't a natural scintillator and I knew it but I did think I had a few qualities that were worthwhile. Somehow I had to let Jill know what those qualities were and I also had to let her know that my love for her was not going to suffocate her. On the contrary, it could be a happy thing, and she could draw strength from it. The question was, how could I tell her all this?

My inspiration came just as I opened the door and slid behind the wheel of the car. I've never had another moment of inspiration quite like that in my whole life. I've had ideas, but most of them have grown from a small glimmer, and I've had to fumble my way along until things became clear. I'd been telling myself for a long time that I was going to be a writer and I suddenly knew that the time had come to prove it, The thing to do was to put my love on paper—lay it out so that Jill could see it and understand what a great love could do for two people. I sat there, leaning forward, my arms wrapped around the steering wheel, the door of the car still open, staring off into space. I not only knew what to do but I knew exactly how to do it. I wrote a whole novel in my mind in the short time before a redcap came along and advised me to close the door of the car. I knew who the characters were going to be, what they were going to do, and what they were going to say. I've never had anything unfold itself to me like that. The peculiar thing about it is that when I came to put it down on paper I didn't change it. It all came out just the way I saw it the first time.

It had taken me almost two hours to drive down to Detroit that afternoon. It took me one hour to drive home. I drove like a madman. It's a wonder I didn't smash the car up or get a ticket for reckless driving. My mind wasn't on the road at all. It was moving down that novel, page by page. I drove into George French's driveway, jumped out of the car, and started home at a trot. I didn't even thank George for the use of the car. All I could think about was getting up to my room to start putting things on paper. I came in the house, slammed the front door behind me, and jumped up the stairs, two steps at a time. I sat down at the old typewriter with my overcoat and hat on. I took the overcoat off at some time during the evening, but at midnight I was still sitting there with my hat on, pecking away. By then I'd finished the first chapter. It had gone without a hitch.

I started that novel on March 28, 1937. I finished the third and final draft of it on May 15, just a little more than six weeks later. While I was working on it, nothing else existed for me. I didn't sleep for more than three hours a night during the whole period. As I've said, I had no extracurricular obligations at school. On the first day of classes after Easter, I walked into the principal's office and blurted out that I was writing a novel and that it was important for me to finish it as soon as possible. I asked if I could be excused from school as soon as I finished my last class each day. It was a good thing I'd gone to school at Northern. At least, the faculty all felt kindly toward me. Otto Norwalk, the principal, put his arm around my shoulder in a fatherly fashion and told me that what was important to me was important to him. I was excused. I arrived at school every morning at eight o'clock. At a little after three-thirty in the afternoon I would be home again, sitting in my room, pecking away at the typewriter. I didn't go anywhere. I didn't see anyone. I barely spoke to my own family. I took my meals standing up in front of the refrigerator where I rummaged around for whatever I could find when I got hungry. It was no wonder that I couldn't remember much of what happened during my first semester at Northern High School.

The novel that I wrote—I called it *Reward on Saturday*—was

based roughly on one of Flint's better-known tragedies. The hero was the rector of a big, fashionable Episcopal church, who fell in love with one of his parishioners, a very beautiful woman who was notably cold of heart, very ambitious, and not a little selfish. She wanted something more than an Episcopal minister for a husband and in order to get her the hero had to leave the church. He went into politics, was elected mayor of the city, and inaugurated a crusade that swept the corrupt politicians out of office and into jail. He was well on his way to the governorship and God knows what else when he was framed by the machine, tried, and sentenced to prison himself. In the meantime, his nobility had won his wife's love. She learned the true meaning of love and what it could move a person to do. When her husband was sent to prison, she died of a broken heart. When he emerged from prison, his world in ashes, his great love dead, he died of a broken heart, too. I was the noble minister, of course, and Jill Ryan the woman who didn't learn the meaning of love until too late. This was pretty sticky stuff but it was just the kind of tragedy I was in the mood to write at the moment. Whatever else it was, it was a powerful love story. It moved me to tears while I was writing it and it moved almost everyone else to tears who had a chance to read it.

It is almost impossible for anyone who throws himself into a work of creation, as I did in those six weeks, to explain to others what happens. There is almost complete immersion. A writer is apt to become so obsessed with his idea that he ignores everything that is not concerned with it. He resists every extraneous influence around him. "Preoccupation" is not a strong-enough word to describe a world in which letters go unanswered, newspapers go unread, dishes unwashed, and bills unpaid. "Mania" would be a better word. When I finished *Reward on Saturday* I had the strange feeling that I was emerging from a dungeon. I was aware that things had happened while I was closeted up there in my room, but they had no impact on me whatsoever.

The first thing I had to face was the fact that school had closed. It had closed on the ninth of May because the money in the school system's treasury had run out. I don't know why it should have been such a surprise to me, for Flint schools had been closing from four to six weeks early ever since the Depression began. It was a major catastrophe for me. That salary of $1,100 had suddenly shrunk to $925. When I had gone into hibernation, I still had my March check uncashed. While I'd been writing I'd received my April check and a partial one for May. This amounted to about $250, but by the time I paid off the balance of my bank loan and finished paying for the clothes I'd bought and gave Glad the back room and board, I only had ten dollars to my name—and it would be almost five months before I got another paycheck. I'd struggled through college to get a degree and a teacher's certificate because I thought it would bring me some kind of security, and there I was, just as badly off as though I'd been working in the factories. I began to have the feeling that I was going to spend my whole life muddling through to nothing.

As I paid off the bills and the scene around me came into focus, my main concern was the manuscript I had just finished. I had made an original and two copies and I spent part of my last ten dollars to have them bound. I sent the original off to Professor Roy Cowden in Ann Arbor. Professor Cowden was the director of the Hopwood Prizes at the university. He'd been on sabbatical the year I entered the contest, but during the previous summer, when I was taking my degree, I had elected the second half of that creative writing course and he had taught it. He had liked my work and he had made me promise to let him see anything else I wrote. Now I thought he might know what to do with it.

At the same time I sent the original to Roy Cowden, I sent one of the copies off to Jill Ryan. After all, I'd written it for her. There was one thing that I didn't quite realize at the moment, however. I hadn't thought about Jill since the five minutes after she walked away from me down that station platform. I was under the impression that I'd been thinking about her, but it was the novel that really took control of me, and as I went along, the heroine of the novel became someone else than Jill—a person who had all the attributes that I wanted Jill to have. She was a different person entirely when I was finished. Without understanding what I'd done, I'd written myself right out of love with Jill. It was as though I'd had therapy.

I didn't have to wait very long for a reaction to the manuscript. Four days after I put it in the mail, my telephone rang late one night. It was Jill. She was weeping. She had just finished reading the book. She told me she loved me and she wanted me to come down to Youngstown at once. That was a moment of great triumph. I was going to have the one thing I wanted more than anything else in the world.

The very next morning, almost before I was out of bed, the telephone rang again. It was Roy Cowden. *He* had just finished reading the novel. He wanted to know when I could come down and see him. With the two dollars I had in my pocket at the moment, it was easier to get to Ann Arbor than it was to get to Youngstown. By one o'clock that afternoon I was being ushered to a seat on the glider on Roy Cowden's front porch. We settled there in the heat of the May afternoon, surrounded by the scent of lilacs, and Professor Cowden said, "This is the best novel written by a Michigan student since I've been teaching here."

Those were pretty heady words for me, and I think I would have listened more closely to Roy Cowden's suggestions if my head hadn't been swimming from the even headier words I'd heard the night before. He wanted me to come back to Ann Arbor in the fall and enroll in the university to study for my master's degree in English. When I finished it, he thought, he could promise me a job on the faculty. What he really wanted me to do, of course, was to enter that novel in the Hopwoods.

"You understand that I couldn't possibly promise you that you'd win because I don't know what would be entered against it," he said, "but I should think it would be worth a gamble."

Roy Cowden had given me the key that would lock up Jill Ryan for all time. She was depressed by the Youngstowns and the Flints and here I was being offered a chance to bring her back to the place she missed so much. Unfortunately, I'd been conditioned too well and too long by the Depression. All I could think of was the fact that it had taken me $500 to get through college for a year, even with a board job. I had two dollars in my pocket, and where was I going to get $500? Furthermore, if I married Jill, I'd need two or three times that. The thought actually did occur to me that Jill and I could live in Ann Arbor quite nicely *after* I'd won the prize and *after* I had an instructorship, but that meant postponing any marriage for a year. I wasn't quite ready to do anything like that. I wanted to talk to Jill first. I told Roy Cowden I'd give him an answer within a few days. As I hitchhiked back to Flint that afternoon, one thing escaped me completely. I wasn't thinking of Jill in the same terms at all anymore. I was like a rat running a maze. I was making all the right turns, but the thought of the reward at the end of the run didn't make my mouth water anymore. I would take it, all right, because I had earned it, but I couldn't even remember what it was going to taste like.

Little things began to happen that brought this home to me, but I needed one more crusher before the process was done. The minute I got back to Flint, I began the task of getting the money and the transportation together to get to Youngstown. I borrowed a little money here and a little there, and then I went to see George French to see if I could borrow his car. I hadn't seen George since the night I left his car in the driveway and scurried off home to start my writing. When I knocked on his door, I never got a chance to ask about the car. He had some news of his own. He had just proposed to Helen Tarkington and they were going to get married. (I seem to recall that George had done his proposing on the telephone just before I arrived, which probably accounts for the fact I suggested we see the bride in person and celebrate.) We picked Helen up and drove out to Fenton for a few drinks at the cocktail bar. Toward midnight, it had been settled that I would be the best man and that Jill Ryan would be the maid of honor, and Helen rushed out to a pay phone and put in a long-distance call to Jill. I strongly suspect she was thinking of a double wedding. When she came back, she announced that we were *all* going down to Youngstown over the Decoration Day weekend, then ten days away, to discuss plans for the wedding. I made no complaint. Ten days had suddenly become as satisfactory as ten hours. But an even stranger thing had happened without my noticing it. I hadn't even gone to the telephone to talk to Jill. Two months before I would have been standing at Helen's elbow, waiting to hear that dear voice. I went about my business in a normal fashion while I waited for the ten days to pass. It didn't disturb me that I hadn't received a letter from Jill. I hadn't written her, either. What I didn't know was that our on-again, off-again love affair was off again as far as Jill was concerned. She'd been having more of those second thoughts.

We made the trip to Youngstown, all right. It was a very short trip. Decoration Day was a three-day holiday in 1937, and we arrived at Jill's house after midnight on a Friday night. Jill ran down the steps and gave Helen a big hug and a kiss. Then she reached up and pecked George on the cheek. When she came to me she held out her hand in a very formal fashion. I knew what the score was. If I'd been alone, I'd have gotten back in the car, then and there, and driven back to Flint. As it was I only managed to get through a few hours. After we'd carried our bags into the house that night, Jill bustled around cheerfully putting a snack on the table for us, but she made such a point of ignoring me that it was noticeable. When George and I got upstairs to go to bed, I sat there on the covers, staring at the opposite wall.

"I'm going to get the hell out of here," I said. "I think the Tigers are playing a doubleheader up in Cleveland Sunday. I guess I'll see if I can get tickets."

"You can get one for me, too," George said. "If a girl ever treated me like that, I'd knock her on her ass."

I don't know what excuses Helen made, but on Sunday morning we all packed our bags and were ready to go. Once more Jill came into the room as I put my things away.

"I think you're at the bottom of this," she said.

"At the bottom of what?"

"Going home early. I wanted to talk to Helen about the wedding and I wanted to talk to you. I haven't had a chance."

"What do you want to talk to me about?"

"The novel. It was pretty good."

"You already said that on the phone. Or don't you remember?"

"I wanted to explain about that. I'm sorry the way things have turned out. I really am, but I tried."

"You've said that before, too, Jill. Look, all I want to do is forget the whole business. There's nothing to be sorry about and I won't bother you again."

V

One major problem had been solved. I didn't have to worry about getting married anymore. I was almost cheerful when I arrived home in Flint, for my future seemed to stretch out ahead of me unclouded and plainly marked. All I had to do was find the $500 to go back to school, after which I could look forward to collecting the money from the Hopwoods and teaching at the university. I started out with some determination. I went down to Ernest Potter's bank where I'd borrowed the money to go to summer school. Mr. Potter told me that he would be glad to loan me the money, but that small loans were limited to $300. He suggested that I get a summer job to earn the other $200 I would need. And there I was again! It was summer and the factories were closed down until fall. The retail business in Flint stores was consequently in the doldrums and no one was taking on any summer help. I went from friend to friend and with every step I took I realized that I was still in the same old Depression, the Depression that I thought had ended for me the year before. There wasn't a job to be found anywhere. Within a week I was following the same old procedures with the same old results. I got the classified section of the paper every day. I tramped the streets from morning until night. I stood in lines.

At some time early in that search for a job, when I was still optimistic, I dropped in at Northern High School to see Otto Norwalk, the principal. It was my intention to warn him that I wouldn't be back at my job in the fall. To my surprise, he wasn't pleased with the news. He thought I was being very unwise. I had taught my first year under a provisional teacher's certificate. Under Michigan law I could not receive my permanent certificate until I completed my second year. Otto thought I should get that permanent certificate before I considered taking a year off. It was the only thing that would guarantee me any security. Of course, he was in favor of my getting an advanced degree.

"We have several teachers working on their masters," he said. "Most of them are going to summer school and I think that is the best idea. We pay three hundred dollars extra to a man with a master's degree and we are authorized to encourage people to get them. If you go back to summer school this year, I think I can get you an additional seventy-five dollars to go with your annual increment."

Up until the time I had talked to Roy Cowden it had never entered my mind to take a master's degree at all. The only reason I was considering it now was to go back and get that Hopwood Prize, which I couldn't do without spending a year in residence at the university. Even after talking to Otto Norwalk, a master's degree didn't mean much to me, but the germ of an idea had been planted. The Depression did the rest. As I plodded around Flint looking for that nonexistent $200 job, I became increasingly frustrated and I soon found myself back in the same frame of mind I'd been in two years before. The word "job" kept hanging in the sky in front of my eyes like some Holy Grail to be pursued until it was safely tucked away. My ultimate decision, when it came, was born out of pure disgust.

On the last Monday morning in June, 1937, I was on the trail of a busboy's job in a downtown Flint restaurant. Although I got there long before the manager arrived, I found a line of twenty men ahead of me. As the restaurant manager pushed through the revolving door on his way in to work, he beckoned to the man at the head of the line to come in with him. Just like that, within three minutes, the job was filled. I was boiling mad. I went over to lean against a lamppost and unfolded the paper to look through the classified section again. As I stood there I happened to glance up and across the street and I found myself staring at the facade of Ernest Potter's bank. I stood there for another five minutes and then I slowly wadded up the paper, stepped over, and threw it in the nearest trash can. Within ten minutes I was filling out a loan application. By eleven o'clock I was home packing my things. By one in the afternoon I was on the road, hitchhiking to Ann Arbor.

I entered the 1937 summer session at the university in a completely sour frame of mind. It stayed with me through the summer and into the early fall. I think that I was feeling a little sorry for myself. I resented the Depression and everything about it—the job insecurity, the constant scrabbling for money, and my inability ever to get anywhere. I lived a hermitlike existence—sulking, I suppose. I didn't want to see anyone or talk to anyone. Everything I did, I did all by myself. I didn't know the names of the other roomers in the house where I lived. I didn't drink a friendly beer with an acquaintance all summer. I got up in the morning and went to classes. Every afternoon I went out to the university golf course and got in my eighteen lonely holes of golf. On Saturdays and Sundays I spent the whole day out there. In the evenings I studied. I accomplished a prodigious amount of work. I carried ten hours of course work—two more than normal. I wrote my master's thesis and had it accepted. It was on the Pontiac conspiracy, of course. I even improved my golf game. I started the summer shooting around 100. By the end I was consistently in the low 90s. On one memorable day I shot an 88, the best round of golf I'd ever played until that time.

One of the first things I did that summer was to go over and see Roy Cowden. Having decided to attend summer school, any chance that I would enter my novel in the Hopwoods was gone. Professor Cowden was quite disappointed, but he seemed to understand the reason for my decision.

"What would you like me to do with this novel?" he asked me. "Would you like me to send it to a friend of mine at a publisher's in New York?"

"I'd be very grateful," I said.

I heard no more about the novel until fall. In October, Professor Cowden forwarded me a letter written by Maxwell Perkins at Scribner's. Mr. Perkins said that he would have liked to have published the book and had so recommended, but he'd been overruled. Others didn't think it would sell. It was too sentimental. Nevertheless, Mr. Perkins said, he thought I had a great future as a writer and he wanted to see anything else I wrote. I kept that letter around for years and every time I got down in the dumps I would take it out and read it.

My second year of teaching, except for the loss of the seventh graders, was considerably happier than the first. I wasn't any better off financially. I began the school year owing $300. I had to buy an overcoat to replace the one I'd been wearing since 1930 and I had to buy another suit, and there was the usual list of odds and ends of shoes and other accessories. It all added up to about the same payments I'd had to make before. I received a salary increment that increased my weekly pay by about five dollars, but this was used up by a change in my living arrangements.

There had been some shifts in the situation at home. My brother John had given up his milk route to pursue an apprenticeship with the telephone company and had moved back in with the rest of us. Grandpa Perry, approaching eighty-seven, was beginning to go downhill. He was still trying to do all the things he'd always done but he wasn't succeeding very well. He would get up and start to walk downtown in the morning. Most of the time he made it, but there were days when it took him five hours to walk that two miles. Some days he would get halfway and have to sit down on someone's steps to rest. We'd receive a phone call and one of us would have to go down and bring him home. He was getting increasingly absent-minded, too, and we had to keep close watch on him all the time. Soon after school started my father suggested that it might be easier for all of us if Glad didn't have me to look after. The house was crowded and Grandpa was becoming a burden. I went up the street and got a room with the Smithsons, an elderly couple. They were glad to have the money for the room, but Mrs. Smithson didn't feel up to giving me board so I had to eat most of my meals out in restaurants. That used up the extra five dollars I was getting every week. I was still netting about five dollars a week, after all those years.

At school I was lucky. I was no longer the junior member of the faculty so I got rid of the bookkeeping and salesmanship. My whole teaching schedule consisted of classes in economics and civics, subjects in which I was adequately prepared. I had lost my immunity to extracurricular activities, however, and I was expected to bear my share of that burden. Indeed, at the first faculty meeting of the year, Otto Norwalk indicated that I would be in charge of the school paper, but before I started that Jim Barclay, the basketball coach, took me to one side to inform me that there would be some changes in the athletic department. He wondered if I'd like to help out. In the years since I went to school there, Northern High School had produced one of the most phenomenal records in Michigan high-school-athletic history. There had been several state championships in both football and basketball. The principal architect of this success, Guy Houston, had always been a kind of godlike figure to me and Jim Barclay, who was only a few years older than I was, was a remarkable man in every way. They ran a close-knit little group that was, in effect, a very exclusive little club within the faculty. They were high-principled, competent men who were close friends in and out of school. They played golf together, met each payday to play poker, helped each other out, in and out of season. In the summer time they all managed boys' camps or served as golf pros. I jumped at the chance to join this group and Otto Norwalk assigned me there. My first duties weren't very exciting. I coached the cheerleaders, took charge of athletic eligibility, and became assistant equipment manager. About a week after school started, however, Jim Barclay asked me if I'd like to ride along up to Bay City while he scouted their football team. On that first evening he began teaching me how to scout an opposing team and he continued his teaching on subsequent weekends. About the middle of October he told Guy Houston that I could handle a scouting assignment all by myself so Guy sent me down to Pontiac. It was a lucky chance. I discovered a weakness in the Pontiac line, and as a result Northern scored three touchdowns against an otherwise good Pontiac team. From then on I was a full-fledged scout and scouting led to other assignments, such as helping Harold Reynolds coach the junior varsity. By the time the football season ended, I was already an accepted member of the club. I played golf on Sunday with one of the foursomes into which we habitually separated. I attended the regular poker sessions. I was invited to go along to the annual meeting of the Michigan High School Coaches Association. When basketball started Jim Barclay gave me all of his scouting assignments and I began learning how to be a basketball coach.

In that fall of 1937 I moved out of the little world in which I'd circulated all my life and joined a new circle of friends. It was just as well, because the old gang was breaking up. Nick Woods suddenly threw up his job with General Motors. He and Flo packed everything they owned in the back of their car and drove off to Tennessee where Nick entered medical school. Bugs Huntley was promoted to be manager of another car-repossessing operation in Ohio and moved off to live in Cincinnati. And then, of course, there were the marriages.

The biggest wedding of all that fall was George French's. He did pretty well. His wedding took place on a Saturday night in a big downtown church and not a single member of the United Auto Workers' Union crashed the gate. It was a most peculiar affair from one standpoint. It may have been the only wedding in history at which the best man and the maid of honor weren't speaking to each other. I didn't even think Jill was beautiful anymore. That's how far I'd come since Decoration Day.

A month after George's wedding I served another stint as best man, this time for Lou Norris in Detroit. The wedding was notable for what happened afterward. While I was standing around at the reception, Bonnie Higgins came marching up to me and planted herself squarely in front of me to give me a big kiss.

"It's getting so I never see you anymore unless you're the best man at some damned wedding or other. How come?"

"This is my profession," I said. "People rely on me."

"Can I rely on you?"

"Sure. When are you getting married?"

"I wasn't thinking about that. I'll let you know when the time comes. I was thinking about right now. Are you tied up with any of these girls?"

"Nope. The maid of honor happens to be the matron of honor at this wedding. I think she has a husband."

"That's good. I want you to take me dancing somewhere. You're dressed for it and I'm dressed for something. Let's go."

I didn't get back from *that* wedding until Monday morning. If I'd got back much later I would have had to teach my classes in white tie and tails. Of course, Bonnie was bound to get married and she did. In the middle of next February, at the beginning of what turned out to be one of the worst blizzards we ever had, I received a telephone call from Toledo, Ohio. Bonnie was getting married in a wedding at her aunt's house and she wanted me to come. I couldn't miss anything like that so I got in my car and drove for eighteen hours through a howling storm, getting stuck every few miles. I arrived two hours late but I got there and Bonnie held things up until I changed into those tails and took my place beside her husband-to-be. It was another of those peculiar weddings. On the way down to Toledo, with the temperature down around twenty below, I had taken a stiff shot of whiskey every now and then to ward off the cold and when I got in the house and the heat hit me, I soon became slightly intoxicated. It wasn't until I got all the way back to Flint the next day that I realized I didn't even know what Bonnie's married name was. I had to write to the Squirrel to find out whom I had been best man for.

That car of mine, incidentally, was one of the worst investments I'd ever made. When I came back from summer school the previous fall, I went down to the IMA to look over the new 1938 Buicks. I picked out my dream car, a black convertible with red-leather upholstery that sold for $1,058. I couldn't buy it but I promised myself that when the Depression was over if that time ever came, I was going to have a car just like that. As the fall progressed and I had to go on scouting trips, I was borrowing cars from everyone and I knew I'd have to get something even if it wasn't a new Buick. I was in a penurious mood and I resolved I wouldn't go in debt. Right after Christmas I had sixty-five dollars in my pocket and it seemed to me that I ought to be able to do pretty well for that amount of money. The Depression was still the era of the twenty-dollar jalopy and some of my friends, notably George French, had owned them. If twenty dollars would buy a car that would run, then sixty-five dollars should buy one that would run pretty good. I found what I was looking for, a 1932 Chevrolet Victoria, selling for exactly my price including sales tax. It seemed to have had good care. The outside of it had been polished until it shone. The motor sounded good. It had 72,000 miles on the speedometer and reasonably good-looking tires. I paid the salesman my money and drove proudly off the lot. The 1932 cars had come out at the bottom of the Depression and in their anxiety to sell them, the manufacturers had put all kinds of gimmicks on them. The gimmick on my car was free wheeling. There was a big black button on the dashboard that could be pulled out, allowing the car to coast whenever anyone let up on the accelerator. Free wheeling endowed Chevrolets with certain weaknesses; they were subject to a long history of malaise in the rear ends. The only person in my acquaintance who had ever owned one of those cars when they were new was my dancing partner, Gretchen. Now and then, when we went to the IMA, I got to drive it and I soon became used to unaccounted-for noises and jolts as something failed to mesh. Gretchen had a rule that no one was ever to touch that free-wheeling button. It wasn't until I drove my car off the lot that I remembered the faults of that model and my attention was forcibly called to it by a steady clicking sound from the rear. I drove it three blocks and took it back to the salesman.

"Don't worry about it," he told me. "You know how these thirty-two Chevvies are. You just have to expect a little noise now and then. The car runs all right."

The next morning I got in it to go to school. I drove a few blocks and the clicking changed to a grinding ripping sound and the car went dead in the middle of the busiest intersection in the north end of town. I had a broken rear axle. I got some people to push me over to the side and walked on to school. I called the used-car lot and told them to come and get the car. I'd be down after work and get my money back.

"We don't give guarantees with sixty-five dollar cars," the salesman told me.

Jim Barclay had a friend in the garage business who agreed to repair it. I could come and pick it up at the end of the month on payday. I finally got it back during the first week in February. As I drove it out of the garage, there was a *cluck-cluck-cluck-cluck* in the rear end. I drove it right around the block and back into the garage again.

"Look, son," the garage man said patiently, "I did the best job I know how. There's a new rear axle in there, but let's face it, it's never going to be completely right. I've seen some of these thirty-two Chevvies that have had seven or eight rear axles in them. Just take my advice, don't ever pull out that free-wheeling button and don't ever drive anywhere you can't walk back from."

It was only a day or two later that I had to rush to Bonnie's wedding. I couldn't borrow anyone else's car. I couldn't hitchhike because of the storm, and the buses that ran to Toledo were on strike. There was nothing to do but take a chance on that car. I don't know how I ever made it the 120 miles down to Toledo through that drifting snow and bitter cold, but I did. I made it back, too, but not without some temper abrasions. I was poking along up the freshly plowed highway toward Flint when I came to a dry part of the pavement. I'd been doing twenty-five on the ice, and I decided to step up my speed a little. I stepped on the accelerator and the car moved faster. The minute I hit thirty miles an hour, the front end began to shake and shimmy uncontrollably. When I settled back to twenty-five, everything was all right. I tried it two or three times, but at exactly thirty miles an hour the shimmying would start again. I was boiling. It was bad enough to have a car with a bad rear end, but this Chevvie had a bad *front* end, too.

When I got home that night, after my 240 mile trip, I parked the car at the curb in front of the Smithson house. The next morning, a Monday, I went out to drive it to school. The temperature was down below zero and the motor was sluggish so I reached over to pull out the choke. I must have been thinking of something else, because I suddenly became conscious of the fact that my hand was on the free-wheeling button. I was horror struck, and I had reason to be. When I finally got the motor going and put the car in gear, there was a loud crack. The rear axle had broken again! I just left the old wreck sitting there in front of Smithsons' until June. That one trip to Bonnie's wedding was the only time I ever drove it anywhere.

VI

Much of the old life was now behind me. About a month after Bonnie's wedding, Guy Houston called me up to his office one day and asked me if I would like to be his assistant track coach. This job was originally supposed to go to Hank Feller, but when he had married his tenth grader, he had forfeited any chance he ever had of joining the athletic staff. Although I didn't have any firm background in track, I think Guy Houston remembered that I had been the student manager on that first track team we'd had in 1928. I was flattered by this gesture of recognition and I entered the new job with enthusiasm and in that first year I was gratified that Northern became a power in state track circles for the first time. It had a great deal to do with my outlook and in my course of action.

A lot of people have broken down the decade of the 1930s into periods such as Depression, Recovery, and Recession. As far as I was concerned, at the time, it was all the same. Things were a little better in the spring of 1938, but not much better. In Flint, where the economy was tied to the automobile, everyone judged things in terms of model years. The 1936, 1937, and 1938 model cars had been good ones. The factories had run five or six months instead of the four months that had been the rule in previous years, but six months was a long way from being a full year and there was still no effective form of unemployment insurance to take up the slack. The only way to get through the long period of layoff was to tighten one's belt. The casualties were still coming but in that year they began to affect my generation. The dairy business that Sam Hendricks had tried to salvage from the wreckage of the Flexner enterprises went bankrupt. Poor Sam never had a chance. In the four years since he'd come to Flint, he'd literally worked himself to death. After a summer of driving a taxicab, he died, leaving Molly a widow with three small children. Bugs Huntley had gone off to Cincinnati the year before and now he died of a stroke. Bugs had graduated with a degree in business administration and he'd never gotten beyond being a bill collector. When I wrote to the Squirrel to find out about Bonnie Higgins, I had a depressing letter from him. He'd long since had to give up his dream of becoming a doctor. He was working as a clerk in the International Harvester Company at Fort Wayne. All that wonderful insouciance that had made him such a delight was gone. Marty Williams, my other ex-roommate and a graduate engineer, had ended up as a meter repairman for a gas company in Independence, Kansas. It had begun to seem as though no one in my generation was ever going to get a start in life and I had reached the conclusion that none of us was ever going to be able to do the things we wanted to do. In the world in which all of us had reached maturity, security and a job had become the important things in life. Most of us had taken whatever we could find and we were hanging onto it. I wasn't much different from the others. I still didn't think of the teaching profession as my permanent occupation, but it was the only thing I had, and it was necessary to hang onto it. The only thing I could think of to do was to pursue a course that would make me better at my job. That meant getting my master's degree. I didn't really think of any other course of action except going to summer school in 1938.

As usual, I had financial problems. School closed six weeks early and I had to use my last paycheck to pay off all my debts. Then I promptly borrowed back that same tired old $300 to go back to Ann Arbor. I even made things a little worse for myself than usual. When it came time for me to leave for summer school, that old 1932 Chevvie was still parked in front of the Smithsons and I had to get it out of there. It seemed to me as though I ought to try to get some money out of it, but the only way to do that was to trade it in. I got that old expert, George French, to help me from getting stuck again and he turned up a 1934 Chevvie that looked pretty good. It cost $170. I got twenty-five dollars for the old car as a trade-in and I made up the rest of the down payment—twenty-five dollars—out of my summer-school money. The balance would be paid at the rate of twelve dollars a month, beginning in September, an agreement that practically guaranteed my ending up another year flat broke. The car turned out to be a good one, except for one thing. The 1934 Chevvies had a gimmick, too. It was called knee action and my car had weak knees. Every time I hit a bump, the front end would bounce along for a mile or so. It was like riding a rowboat in a stormy sea. Still, I never had to put a penny in the thing for repairs and I drove it for a year and a half.

The summer was an uneventful one. I played my usual game of

golf every day and twice on Saturdays and Sundays. I was no longer a recluse. I went drinking beer now and then and I took up with a trio of psychiatric case workers from the university hospital who offered me female companionship of a pleasant, platonic sort. I became friendly with a young couple who lived in the same house. They were from Bowling Green, Kentucky and they were studying for an advanced degree in music. They were forever organizing expeditions to go over to Detroit to the horse races and each evening we had a chamber-music recital or a jam session on our front porch. I learned quite a lot about Sigmund Freud and music.

When I went back to Flint in the fall, I had to find a new place to live. Pat Smithson had died during the summer and there still wasn't room at home. The place I found was charming beyond words. Jim Barclay's assistant basketball coach, Les Ehrbright, had a room available. Les and his wife, Beth, were just a year or two older than I was. They had two very small children. Les and I spent three hours or more together at basketball practice each day. We belonged to that poker club that met each payday. We played rummy in the basement at the school during lunch hour and we played golf together on weekends. Beth was a completely outgoing person with an infectious sense of humor and a hearty laugh and she got great delight out of putting me to changing the baby's diapers and spooning food into the little boy. It was a new side of life to me and I enjoyed it.

The year was almost completely taken up with athletics. This was the beginning of Northern High School's greatest athletic period. We won three state championships in a row in football and two in basketball and one in track. I was part of all this. I took tremendous pride in those teams and in the coaches with whom I worked, but it was hard work and I had little time for any social life. I was now doing all the scouting and assisting regularly with the junior varsity in football. In basketball I acted as scout, trainer, and referee at all scrimmages. When the track season came around, I began officiating at track meets around the state. One weekend I would be in Grand Rapids, the next in Lansing. At the state finals that year I was a field judge. I usually got fifteen dollars for each of these jobs and I used the money to buy a set of matched golf clubs from Guy Houston.

The days whizzed by. Usually, I would drag myself up the Ehrbrights' front stairs about nine thirty in the evening and sit down at my typewriter for an hour and a half. I'd never given up that dream, but I didn't have any good ideas. Strangely enough, *Reward on Saturday* was still alive. After it had been rejected by Maxwell Perkins in the fall of 1937, Professor Cowden sent it off to Donald

Elder at Doubleday. Mr. Elder was a good deal less than enthusiastic about the book and sent it back by return mail. This discouraged Roy Cowden and he withdrew from the picture. I sent the book out twice myself and both times it came back with rejection slips. Just as I was about to give up on it, in January, 1938, I happened to pick up a copy of *Atlantic Monthly*. It carried the announcement of a novel contest with a $10,000 first prize. I promptly wrapped the book up and sent it off. Nothing happened. Spring and summer passed. Shortly after I moved in with the Ehrbrights I received a five-page letter from Ted Weeks, the editor of *Atlantic*. He informed me that the novel had been one of the final three in the judging for the prize. He had voted for it, but the editors at Little, Brown had outvoted him on the grounds that it wouldn't sell. It was too sentimental. Mr. Weeks went on to say virtually all the other things that Mr. Perkins had, too, but he did add one nice little touch. He asked me to come to Boston and have lunch with him.

I didn't have enough money to go all the way to Boston for lunch, but the letter did set me to thinking about going somewhere. The thought kept nagging at me all fall that I hadn't had any kind of a vacation since I went to the Chicago World's Fair in 1933. That was five years. On Thanksgiving Day, after Northern won its final game of the season to cinch its state championship, I had to hurry away from the locker-room celebration because I was going to serve my eighth stint as a best man. One of the poker-playing Riley boys was marrying Lou Norris' sister—I had introduced them. I got into my tails and repaired to the First Presbyterian Church. After the ceremony, we all moved out to a private club on the southern outskirts of town for the reception. It lasted until two in the morning. As I drove home, I came to the Grand Trunk railroad tracks that crossed South Saginaw Street. I could see a locomotive sitting in the station. It was a big, shining thing and I stopped to look at it. It belonged to the International Limited, the crack passenger train that ran between Montreal and Chicago. I parked my car and gawked up at the engine, then wandered back along the line of sparkling Pullmans. When the train pulled out, I stood there on the platform watching until the two red lights disappeared from view.

I was still thinking about that train when I woke up the next morning. I got out of bed and counted my money. I'd just cashed my November paycheck and after paying all my bills I had fifty-five dollars left. I didn't hesitate. I got out my old suitcase and began throwing things in it. As I reached the front door, I shouted to Les and Beth that I'd see them Sunday night. At ten minutes to two I was aboard the Maple Leaf Limited, headed for Chicago.

I stayed at the Stevens Hotel, the only place I knew in Chicago. I saw two stage shows—one of them was *You Can't Take It With You*. And, quite by accident, I stumbled across the Chicago Civic Opera. I'd never seen an opera before and it seemed like a good idea to try it out so I bought a ticket. Without even knowing what I was looking at, I sat through a performance of *Tannhäuser* with Lauritz Melchior and Kirsten Flagstad. I don't suppose that anyone could have had a better introduction to opera than I had. I'd always loved good music, but as I sat there listening to those glorious voices I forgot where I was and who I was, and everything else in the world. When I emerged I was an opera fan. One short afternoon had added a whole new dimension to my life. It did more than that. It restored all of those dreams that had faded away during the Depression. I knew there were a million things that I'd never seen or experienced, and I promised myself that someday I was going to do everything. Everything about that two-day trip contributed to this mood. Both nights I sat in the bar and drank drinks and dreamed dreams. In the whole weekend I didn't see a person I knew and I talked to no one. It was a lonely weekend but it was a soul-satisfying one.

VII

When the summer of 1939 came, school closed five weeks early as usual, and I ended up virtually broke again. I borrowed my money and went off to Ann Arbor for the third summer of study and golf. On the day that I came back to reoccupy my room at the Ehrbrights', Germany invaded Poland and World War II began.

For most of the years of the Depression, Adolf Hitler had marched and blustered in a far-off world. In Michigan, we had been isolated physically from the events in Europe. Very few people I knew had ever been to Europe. With hard times and the time and money involved in making such a trip, it was almost an impossibility. Most Americans in our part of the country were traditionally isolationist, anyway. None of my friends had any relatives or acquaintances who were victims of the Nazis. As a graduate of the university and a holder of a degree in history, I understood quite well what was involved in the various moves—reoccupation of the Rhineland, rearmament, and Anschluss. Several times during those years I had cast anxious glances toward Europe, but that was the extent of my involvement. I knew that the strength of the United States Army was only 175,000 men as late as 1938, but I didn't worry. England was still rich and powerful and its empire was still intact. France waited behind its Maginot Line with what was reputed to be the best army in the world.

If there was one event in that whole sorry chain of events which woke Americans up, it was the Munich Pact and the subsequent betrayal of Czechoslovakia. I think I realized, then, that Adolf Hitler had to be stopped, and that he would be stopped—that a war was coming. Nearly everyone I knew stopped muttering about those "damned foolish Europeans" and started agreeing that it was now time to stop Hitler. In retrospect, I don't think Americans realize, even today, how indelibly the Czechoslovakian fiasco marked the Americans of my generation. It was the key to all future American foreign policy. Both Korea and Vietnam had their beginnings in the fall of 1938. Those of us who witnessed Chamberlain's surrender to Hitler quietly resolved that there would never again be an abject knuckling under to tyranny in any form.

Still, when I came home from summer school in 1939, the Depression preoccupied most Americans. The 1939 model cars had not sold at all well and the factories had gone through their shortest production season in three years. The 1940 cars had just been introduced when the war started, and people were worried about how well they were going to do. The Depression ended on the day the war began, but it did not become apparent to most of us for some little time. I started the school year with the same old problems. I owed money to the bank. I had no ready cash. I needed the usual new clothes. And I was faced with one new problem. My weak-kneed little car was showing signs of giving up the ghost. Little things had begun to go wrong with it. The battery ran down twice in one week which indicated there was probably a short circuit somewhere. The windshield wiper stopped working. The timing went off and the engine began backfiring, blowing out the muffler. The tires were wearing thin and I knew I'd have to get new ones soon. On the first day of school, Guy Houston gave me the fall scouting schedule and I learned that my first trip would be across the state to Muskegon, 150 miles away. I wasn't sure the old car would make it there and back so I decided to trade it in. I couldn't buy my dream car, but I did find a nice clean little 1937 Chevvie with less than 25,000 miles on it. I had to pay $375 for it, of which $300 was to be paid at the rate of thirty dollars a month. Although my salary was above forty dollars a week now, the various obligations that I had assumed would keep me strapped for most of the year and I still had the feeling that I wasn't getting anywhere.

School and athletics kept me quite busy during most of the year, but just before Christmas I undertook another venture that used up whatever spare time I had. The British navy had cornered and sunk the German pocket battleship *Graf Spee* in the Rio de la Plata, and for some reason or other this sparked my imagination. From it I got an excellent idea for a novel. It was the first good idea I'd had since *Reward on Saturday* and I went to work on it. When one considers that I'd never been to sea, that I'd never seen the ocean, a novel about ships and the sea was a pretty audacious undertaking. I didn't do badly with it. When it came time for knowledgeable people to read it, no one found any fault with the sea part at all. Of course, there was one major fault with it. I made the hero a German sea captain. I was still in a very early stage of development as a writer and to me the only important thing was to tell a good story when I found an idea. I hadn't learned yet how to change identities, situations, and locales to fit the exigencies of the times. I finished the book in 1941 and sent it off to Barthold Fles, a New York literary agent who had been recommended to me. Mr. Fles was a Jew and in March, 1941, Jews were pretty sensitive about heroic German naval officers. To say that Mr. Fles was insulted was the understatement of the year. I think he believed I was a member of the German-American Bund. He wrote me a long, vituperative letter about the novel and I didn't come off very well as a writer or an individual. There followed a long correspondence during which I managed to mollify him and prove that I was not a Nazi sympathizer, that I was only interested in telling a good story. It then came out that he thought the novel was a good one if I could just rewrite it and make the hero a Frenchman or an Englishman. I was quite willing to do this and asked him to send the manuscript back to me. He did. Unfortunately, during most of the correspondence I was in the United States Army, and at the time he sent it back to me I was stationed in New Orleans. Before it ever arrived there I was shipped overseas. As far as I know, the novel is still sitting in the Railway Express office in New Orleans.

Mr. Fles needn't have worried about my having any leanings toward Nazism. It was because I was anti-Nazi that I got into the only serious trouble of my whole teaching career. When I reported to school in the fall of 1939, I found that I had been assigned to teach United States history for the first time. One of the older teachers had retired and I had inherited her classes. It was the first opportunity that I'd had to teach in my field of major interest. It was doubly enjoyable because my classes were composed of pre-college students, all of whom were in the higher IQ range. Because of their responsiveness and lively interest in things, I became a better-than-average teacher again.

I had no trouble until we approached the end of the school year. By then we had reached the twentieth century in America and we were studying the Congress and the evolution of the committee system in that body. Wherever possible, I always tried to tie subject matter into contemporary themes and our investigation of Congressional committees came just at the time when the Dies Un-American Activities Committee was much in the news. It also came shortly after the invasion of Norway by the Germans and Quisling had become a byword. It was a good moment to take up the subject of both Martin Dies and patriotism, and I felt we could have an intelligent discussion of Americanism. As a culmination of our study of the Dies Committee, I told my students to go home and talk the matter over with their parents and come back the next day with a definition of just what Americanism was. I told them we would study these definitions and see if we could find one that everyone liked. When the students came in with their definitions, I picked out ten of them at random and had them written on the blackboard where we could all see them and discuss them. In one of my classes, a definition was put on the board by a pretty little dark-haired girl by the name of Frances Ratterman. Frances was the daughter of Frank Ratterman, president of one of Flint's American Legion posts.

I had come to know Frank Ratterman well over the years. He was one of the directors of the American Legion baseball program in the city. Most of the boys on our varsity teams were involved in the Legion program at one time or another, and I'd had to consult with Frank on various questions of eligibility. Our relationship was not good, primarily because of an incident that had recently taken place. Ratterman had passed out jackets to members of the city championship team at the end of the 1939 season. According to Michigan high-school eligibility rules, no boy could accept any gift with a value of more than five dollars. The jackets were plainly worth more than that, and I made all our boys return them to Ratterman. After two months of argument over the matter I won my point, but not until there had been some violent scenes, during one of which Frank had called me a son-of-a-bitching, God-damned stick-in-the-mud.

When Frances Ratterman went to the blackboard, she put a stock definition of Americanism on the board. One could almost see the flags waving and hear the bugles blowing. I was pretty sure that Frank had made it up himself, although he could have copied it out of one of the Legion publications. We discussed all the definitions at some length and finally took parts of several of them and put them together to make a single definition that we all liked. The only one we didn't discuss and use any part of was the Ratterman definition. I'd steered attention away from it very deliberately because I wanted to make a point. As I hoped, some student raised his hand at the end of class and asked why I didn't like it. I stepped triumphantly over to the blackboard and erased the words "United States" wherever they occurred and then wrote "Germany" in place of them. In place of the words, "our country," I wrote "the Fatherland." When I read the definition aloud, with these changes, it sounded exactly like an excerpt from one of Adolf Hitler's speeches. I said so. I also said that I didn't think most Americans wanted the United States to be that kind of a country, that I thought we could do better than that. I also thought that the Dies Committee could find better things to do than hold witch hunts. I carefully pointed out that this was only my opinion and that I had expressed it only because the students wanted to know it. I told them that I hoped they would form their own and not be influenced by mine. That was why I had let them spend the whole hour trying to arrive at some acceptable definition.

Frances Ratterman lost no time in getting home with the news. At nine o'clock the next morning the phone rang in my classroom, and Otto Norwalk asked me to step down to his office. When I arrived there I found myself confronted by Frances, her father, and three legionnaires in their blue caps. Frank Ratterman did all the talking for his side. The minute I sat down in a chair he jumped to his feet and pointed a finger at me. I was a Communist, he said, and I was teaching subversive theories in my classes. He wanted me fired. He wanted me fired then and there, before I had a chance to contaminate anyone else. Then he sat down. He had not said one word about what had happened in class. He had simply made an accusation and a demand.

Otto Norwalk was a tousle-headed, stoop-shouldered man with an innate gentleness about him. He usually spoke in a voice that was just above a whisper and I never knew him to be ruffled about anything. He was the epitome of calm that morning. He leaned back in his chair with his hands clasped behind his head and looked at each of us, then smiled a peculiar lopsided smile. When he started to speak everyone had to lean forward to hear what he said. He told Frank Ratterman that he had known me since I was fourteen years old. I was not a Communist. He'd known every Communist the school had turned out in the last eleven years and I wasn't one of them. He wasn't going to fire me, not only because I wasn't a Communist, but because he didn't have the power or the inclination to do so. However, if Mr. Ratterman wanted to take his problem to the school board he was welcome to do so. If he did such a thing, he'd better present some proof. So far, all he had made was an accusation, and it was a scurrilous accusation. Having said this, Otto Norwalk walked around his desk and opened the door. With a gesture of his hand, he indicated that the interview was over. Ratterman sat there, scowling, his face a deep, dark red. Suddenly, he jumped to his feet and this time he pointed at Otto Norwalk. He said he had not come up to the school to be insulted. We hadn't heard the end of this. With that, he stalked out of the office, followed by his brigade, none of whom had taken his hat off through the whole thing. After they'd gone, Otto Norwalk nodded at me and told me to go back to my class and not to worry. He didn't even bother to ask me what had happened.

It didn't take long for word to get around school about that meeting. I suppose Frances Ratterman discussed it with her friends. Just at the close of school that day, as I was getting ready to go out to track practice, I received a note from Otto Norwalk asking me to drop by his office again.

"Do you have a student in your class named Martha Collins?" he asked me.

"Yes, I do," I said.

"She came to see me this afternoon. She'd heard rumors about what happened here this morning and she was quite upset about them. She insisted on telling me what happened in your class. I must say, she had better control of herself than Mr. Ratterman did. She asked me if she could go to the school board and testify in your behalf. I told her I didn't think it would come to that, but she made me promise to let her know if it did."

"That was nice of her," I said, "but I think I can defend myself."

"You might bear in mind that the testimony of a disinterested party can be valuable. Just how well do you know Miss Collins?"

"Not very well. She's been in my class all year. She's a top-notch student."

It was almost two weeks before we heard from Ratterman again. When the message came it arrived in a letter from the office of the president of the school board. I was requested to appear before him on a Monday afternoon before the monthly meeting of the full board. It was a formal letter, probably written by some assistant, and at the bottom of it was appended a paragraph to the effect that I could bring an attorney if I so desired. When I showed the letter to Otto Norwalk he told me he would represent me.

Frank Ratterman and his squad of legionnaires, along with Frances Ratterman and one other girl from my class, were in the office when Otto and I arrived. As soon as everyone was seated, Ratterman jumped up and began a long harangue to the effect that war had broken out in Europe. The United States was in danger and it was about time we started defending ourselves from our enemies, both from without and from within. The best first step was to clean the Communists out of the school system. The president of the school board was increasingly irritated as this speech progressed and he finally stopped it and asked Frank Ratterman if he had any evidence that there were any Communists in the school system. For answer, Ratterman pointed his finger at me and spoke my name. The president looked at me over the top of his glasses with some interest. Well he might. He happened to be Ernest Potter from whom I'd been borrowing $300 every year for four years. I'd just finished talking with him a few days before to make sure I was going to get my loan for that summer. Of course, that wasn't all the dealings I'd had with Ernest Potter. He lived about a block from our house and I'd known him quite well since the days when he was my boy scoutmaster. He seemed to consider me for quite a long time before he quietly asked me if I'd like to answer the charges. I'd been carefully briefed by Otto Norwalk and I said that Mr. Ratterman had made an unfounded accusation. Until we heard the evidence, we'd have nothing to say. Ratterman then said he'd like to call on his daughter and another member of my class to tell what they knew. Frances Ratterman then gave her version of what had happened in my class that day. Both she and the other girl who followed her gave a badly twisted account of my conduct. According to them I'd made some very traitorous remarks about the United States. When they finished I jumped to my feet to sputter out a denial, but I'd only uttered a few words when Otto Norwalk signaled for attention. He said that he thought Mr. Potter ought to hear another version of what had happened and with that he stepped over to the office door, looked out, and beckoned to someone. In walked Martha Collins.

It was a very hot May afternoon and all of us had been perspiring freely, but Martha Collins wasn't perspiring. She had on a pink cotton dress and very high heels. Her dark brown hair was swept straight back to a bun in the back. She was calm and cool and spoke in a level voice, addressing herself directly to Mr. Potter. She told him exactly what had happened, even quoting Frances' definition with the changes I'd made in it, and repeated the remarks I'd made afterward. It was an impressive performance and when she finished both Otto Norwalk and Ernest Potter looked at her admiringly. There was a silence and then Mr. Potter asked me if that was what had happened. When I said it was, Mr. Potter quietly said he guessed it wasn't necessary to pursue the matter further. He would consider the matter closed.

That ended the incident of the definitions. There was still Martha Collins to take care of. I wasn't quite as lucky there—although I may have been luckier than I knew.

VIII

From the time I first went to teach at Northern I had been scrupulously careful not to get involved with the young ladies in my classes. The example of Hank Feller had been held up before me constantly. There had been other Northern teachers who had married girls out of their classes, but any teacher who committed this mistake suffered for it. If he wasn't shipped off to teach in some junior high school or other, he was treated like some dunce sitting in a corner wearing a pointed cap. The code was plain, but my particular friends such as Guy Houston and Jim Barclay were dead set against anything of this sort. With them it was not simply a question of propriety. It was a matter of being mature. A mature man picked on someone his own size.

It wasn't as easy to live within this code as one might think. By the very nature of his position, a teacher is a leader and the focus of some attention. I wasn't especially handsome, but I was young, I was single, I had a job, and above all I was there for everyone to see. The biggest trouble arose from the fact that one couldn't treat these young ladies as little girls anymore. By the time they were seniors most of them were fully developed women and not a few of them had developed sexual appetites. They could be dangerous. Above all else, in each high-school class there were a few really beautiful girls—real head turners. From the time I taught my first class, I came to recognize the fact I always had two or three girls with crushes on me. If I was in one of my vintage years, I would have more. If one of them happened to be one of the lovelies, it was hard not to look fondly at them and conjecture about what they might be like under ideal circumstances. I wouldn't have been human if I hadn't. Yet I had maintained strict control over myself all those years—until Martha Collins.

Martha was smart—an all-A student. She was talented. Above all else, she was probably the most beautiful physical specimen who ever attended Northern High School. Her face was classic in its regularity. Her eyes were violet colored—big and innocent. I don't think I ever saw eyes quite the color of hers. Her figure was eye-popping. She was high busted, she had a tiny waist, and her legs were symmetrically rounded, long, graceful dancer's legs. She was perfect in almost every dimension. She was well aware of what she had to offer. She chose to display her lovely figure at all times. She wore full-skirted dresses drawn tight about the middle so that the curves of her breasts and hips were accentuated. Everyone knew exactly what was under her dresses.

As anyone can imagine, Martha was no ordinary school girl. She had been modeling long before I first saw her. She danced professionally. In both her junior and senior years she had sung the lead in the school operetta. All of this had lent her a sophistication far beyond her years. She looked down at the school and the students. She never dated any of the boys and except for the operettas she never took part in any of the school activities. Because she always dressed in stunning clothes—she even had a fur coat—and because she drove to school in a Buick sport coupé everyday, I had suspected for some time that there was a man lurking in the background somewhere. She certainly didn't get all these things from her father. He was a shop steward at Fisher Body.

The relationship between Martha and me had been the normal student-teacher relationship right up until the time those definitions were put on the board. It may have been even more formal than usual because Martha sat in the back of the room and she rarely entered into class discussions. I had expressed myself quite accurately to Otto Norwalk when he asked me how well I knew her. The relationship changed abruptly because I had a little idiosyncrasy. All through my own years in high school the teachers had seated us alphabetically and Paul Lovegrove always ended up sitting behind me. Paul tickled the back of my neck with his pencil for three years until I finally got up and hit him over the head with a book just before graduation. (I suffered my only expulsion as a result of that.) I had a phobia against alphabetical seating and I never used it. Each year at the beginning of classes I would put all the names of my students in a hat and draw them out one by one, assigning them to seats in the order their names came out of the hat. Then, at the end of each marking period I'd shuffle them around, using the same method. Everyone had a change of scenery.

Although my students rarely sat in the back of the room through a whole semester, Martha had by the luck of the draw. Just a few days before the definition incident, I had staged my last seating shake-up and it brought Martha to sit in a front-row seat right in front of my desk. There was one direct result. Whatever degree of anonymity there had been between us was shattered. It was just at the beginning of this awakening that I got in trouble with the Rattermans. In the two weeks that passed between the meeting in Otto Norwalk's office and the hearing before Ernest Potter, the situation changed completely. I shudder to think what kind of a lie I would have told if Otto Norwalk had asked me how well I knew Martha in May. By then I felt as though I was having carnal knowledge of her. I already knew that I was headed for trouble.

It all began innocently enough. Martha was Phyliss Hahn—my tenth-grade flapper—all over again. She had a habit of hiking her skirt and crossing her legs, and from the first day she sat down facing me, I was treated to a first-class peep show. I did my level best not to pay any attention to it. I could keep a pretty good poker face, but I'm afraid I couldn't control my blushing. It only took a few days until Martha discovered the cause of it. I think it amused her to see my discomfiture and it was typical of her that she would decide to go on with her little joke. The display became somewhat more deliberate and a good deal more satisfying. There was more to it than that, however. Martha wasn't joking. She was serious about things as time passed and I began to sense that she was inviting me to do something about the situation.

On that afternoon when Mr. Potter dismissed us from the meeting in his office, I stopped briefly to thank him for his confidence in me and we stood there for a few minutes talking about when I would be down to the bank to pick up my summer-school money. When I got outside the office, Martha was gone. I hadn't had a chance to thank her. I went back up to school for track practice, then had dinner, and came on home to Les Ehrbright's. It was a warm May night with a big full moon. My room looked out over the street. When I entered I took my tie off and walked over to my typewriter which sat on a desk facing the window. I had just put some paper in the machine when a car—without lights—glided silently up to the curb in front of the house. There was a short, almost tentative, toot of the horn, obviously designed not to attract too much attention. I knew, as soon as I saw it, that the car was Martha's. I jumped up from my chair and went down the stairs, quickly and quietly. Martha was sitting behind the wheel and she motioned for me to get in. It was my intention to just sit there for a moment and thank her for what she had done, but the minute I sat down she put the car in gear and we moved silently down the street. She didn't turn the lights on until we swung the corner at the end of the block.

"Are you kidnapping me?" I asked her.

"I want to go someplace we can talk," she said.

I fished a cigarette out of my pocket, lit it, and settled back to watch her drive. She was a competent, businesslike driver who gave her full attention to what she was doing. She still had on her pink dress. The breeze blew a wisp of hair over her forehead and it occasionally fluffed the hem of her skirt back over her knee. She drove silently for ten minutes, never so much as looking my way. We left the city behind and abruptly turned off into a rough dirt trail that bumped off across an abandoned subdivision, eventually pulling up under a huge tree. She turned off the lights. Only then did she turn to look at me. I knew what was coming. I had no excuse. It was like Adam and Eve.

That first frantic embrace lasted only a few seconds and then she heaved a big sigh and pushed away. She asked for a cigarette and drew deeply on it.

"I knew it would be like that," she said. "I love you. I want to marry you. What are you going to do about it?"

Her words were sobering. I certainly wasn't in love with her. I knew exactly what I wanted from her and it wasn't marriage. I also had no illusions about what would happen to me if I took what I wanted. All the lights in my private warning system were flashing red. I made the proper response.

"Martha, whatever gave you the idea that you wanted to marry me?"

"In three more weeks I'll be graduated. What else is there to do but get married?"

"You've got four years of college yet."

"I don't intend to go to college. I know what I want to do. I want to get married."

"You're too young to get married. You ought to wait until you get older. Your tastes will change. By the time you're twenty-five all the things you like now will bore you to death."

"You sound just like my father. I'm not going to wait until I'm twenty-five." From far behind us a pair of headlights flashed as a car turned into the lane. Martha slid over behind the wheel and stepped on the starter. It took only a moment to get the car rolling.

We bumped on down the lane, turned a corner, and headed back to the highway. In ten minutes we were home.

"I just wanted you to know how I felt," Martha said. "I'll come back soon. You'd better be ready. I will."

Things changed for the worse—or better. The next morning when Martha came to class, she lifted her skirt high, crossed her legs, and gave me a long, slow wink. I couldn't take my eyes off her. I knew that if she ever drew up in front of that house again I was a gone goose. She waited three days. In the midst of a gentle spring rain, I heard the horn blow. I'd been talking to myself for three days, trying to tell myself to have some common sense, but I was like a zombie who had no control over himself. I got up and grabbed my raincoat out of the closet and walked down the stairs and was whisked away to the trysting place under the big tree.

Martha knew what she wanted. She had thoughtfully left all her underwear at home. From the moment I touched her I was possessed. So was she. We rolled around in the front seat for ten minutes in complete abandon. We were like two animals. Finally, when it became obvious that there was only one thing left to do, she tumbled over into the back seat.

The raincoat saved me. I had to get out of the car to take it off. As I stood there in the rain, a car came gliding silently up behind us with the lights off. A flashlight beam landed squarely on me, then switched quickly to the back seat where Martha was reclining. The car hesitated only long enough for that one brief probe, then moved on down the lane. Martha jumped up and climbed out the door to peer after it.

"Kids!" she said contemptuously, then climbed under the wheel and started the motor. We stopped, briefly, before reentering the main road, and once more she was in my arms, but she remained there only a moment.

"Tomorrow," she gasped. "I know a better place."

Les Ehrbright was waiting for me in the living room when I got home. He was very cool.

"Son," he said, "you're heading for a peck of trouble. I saw you drive off with that girl. You ought to know better than that. What are you going to do about it?"

"I know. The next time she comes around, you'd better go out and tell her I'm not here."

Martha came back the next night and Les went out and told her I'd gone away for the weekend. We had now reached the final two weeks of school, and it looked to me as though I might be able to escape with Les Ehrbright's help, but the damage had already been done. On Monday morning I met a grim-faced Jim Barclay in the hall and he asked me to step up to his office in the gym.

"I understand you've been having a little fling with one of the girls in your classes," he said.

"Did Les tell you that?"

"No. I overheard two boys in the locker room this morning. One of them told the other he caught you out beyond Civic Park with the Collins girl. He seemed to think you had her pants off."

I told Jim about the whole thing then.

"I don't think it's entirely your fault," he said, "but it doesn't make any difference whose fault it is. It's got to stop and I don't think you're going to stop it simply by having Les go out every night and tell her you're not home. She's too smart for anything like that. You've got to tell her you can't see her and you've got to tell her why you can't see her. You can't mince words."

Jim was right. Martha came to the house again that night, and Les told her, once more, that I wasn't home. The next morning when she came to class she marched over to my desk with fire in her eyes.

"You're avoiding me," she said.

"Martha, this is no place to discuss anything."

"If you won't talk to me outside of school, then you'll have to talk to me inside."

"All right," I said. "Pick me up at my father's house, tonight, not Les Ehrbright's."

When she arrived that night I went around to the driver's side of the car and opened the door.

"This is my boyfriend's car," she said. "He wouldn't like it if I let you drive it."

"I don't think he'd like it if he knew I was in it," I said. "Move over."

I drove out onto the main highway at the south of town and pulled off on the shoulder a half mile beyond the city limits.

"Can't you find a better place than this to park?" she said. "There must be a hundred cars going by here all the time. How can we do anything?"

"I didn't come here to do anything. I parked here so we wouldn't do anything. I came here to talk."

I was brief and I was blunt. I told her what Jim Barclay had overheard in the locker room.

"This kind of thing can really hurt," I said. "It can lose me my job and it will lose you your reputation."

"I don't care about my reputation," she said, "but I never did think about you and I'm sorry I didn't. It was pretty selfish of me. I'll make you a promise. I won't bother you any more until school is out. That's as long as my promise is good for. After that, no one can say anything."

When she let me out of the car, she blew me a kiss.

"So long. I'll see you on graduation day," she said.

Martha kept her promise—or she nearly did. She never so much as hiked up her dress in class. During graduation week, among my other duties, I had to attend the annual dinner dance. Long before I got there I was craftily planning my escape from Martha. I intended to run away. If she couldn't find me for three months during the summer, I was sure her ardor would cool off. In order to take up the month between the end of school and the beginning of the summer session in Ann Arbor, I decided to take a trip. Among the other small miracles that had happened, I was coming down to the end of the year with a surplus of $170. I wasn't quite sure how this happened, but to make matters even better, my father gave me thirty dollars for taking care of the fires and shoveling the walks at his house during the winter. I decided to use the two hundred dollars to finance the trip—I was planning to go to Boston and collect that lunch from Ted Weeks. I already had enough money coming from Ernest Potter to go to summer school.

The dinner dance was a lovely affair, as usual. It lasted until two in the morning. Right at the close of it, one of the parents asked me if I'd like to come back to his house for a little breakfast party. I accepted. I had seen Martha briefly at the dance, but I stayed as far away from her as I could. She had come in the company of a young man who was at least twice her own age and I didn't like his looks. There was never any drinking at high-school parties, but Martha's boyfriend was drinking and he was obviously giving Martha drinks because she began getting quite tipsy in the final stages.

The breakfast party was pleasant. It was held in a large home not far from my father's place. There were two other teachers there, three sets of parents, and about ten couples of students. The students retired to the basement recreation room, put some records on the phonograph, and danced. The older people sat up in the kitchen, eating, drinking coffee, and discussing the war in Europe. At a little after four o'clock, I made my excuses and bade my host and hostess good night. As I was standing in the doorway, the daughter of the house came running up the stairs and whispered something in her mother's ear. I saw a look of dismay cross the woman's face. She quickly beckoned to her husband and started for the recreation room. Scenting trouble and desiring to be of some help, I followed along behind. I was halfway down the stairs when I heard Martha's voice. I hadn't known she was at the party. As a matter of fact, she hadn't been until ten minutes before. She had just come walking up the driveway to let herself in the basement door. I suppose she had found out I was there, but how she got to that house I don't know. She couldn't have driven for she was quite drunk.

When I was halfway down the basement stairs I stopped to duck my head so that I could look down into the room. There, in the middle of the dance floor, gyrating to the music, was Martha. She was in the middle of a striptease. Her dress was already gone and she was just about to unhook her brassiere. The host and hostess hadn't hesitated on the stairs as I had—they'd swept right out onto the floor. But Martha saw them coming. She gave a little whoop and darted by them, toward the stairs. It wasn't until she reached the bottom step and started up that she saw me.

"Lover!" she screamed. In one big lurch she reached me and threw her arms around me. The hostess was right behind her, trying to pull her away. I had my arms up, trying to pry hers from around my neck.

"You'd better give us a little help here, John," the hostess shouted to her husband. Martha turned on her.

"You leave me alone," she said. "I want my lovin' teacher. He'll know what to do with me."

"You'd better take her up and put her under a shower and get some coffee in her," I said.

"Not goin' to take a shower," Martha said stubbornly.

"You've got to sober up," I said. "You're in no condition to drive home."

"Not goin' to drive home. You're goin' to take me home and I'm goin' to get in your little beddy-bye and you can take care of me for the rest of my life."

I managed to signal the host and we each grabbed her by an arm and hustled her up the stairs and through the house to the second floor, followed closely by the hostess and two other women. We plunked her down in the bathroom and hastily backed out while the women took over. When I got downstairs I lit a cigarette.

"If you don't mind," I said to the host, "I'm getting out of here before she comes out of that bathroom."

He was looking at me in a peculiar fashion.

"Is there anything between you and that girl?"

"No. I don't know where she got this idea, but I'm not having any of it."

"I should hope not," the man said. "I don't think it would be a very good thing."

I left. The women eventually got Martha straightened out and took her home.

We were now at graduation day, the last day of school. Martha didn't show up in class that day, for which I was thankful. I thought she'd missed her last chance. I felt safe. The scene at the commencement exercises that night was a happy one. The IMA auditorium was filled with seniors in caps and gowns and proud families in all their finery. I was in my assigned place, ushering people to their seats near the back of the room. Just before the processional, I felt a tug on my sleeve and I turned around to find Martha standing there. She looked me straight in the eyes with considerable self-assurance.

"This is graduation day," she said. "I just came to remind you that in one hour I will no longer be one of your students and my promise ends."

I knew she meant business, but I had beaten her. The minute the orchestra began to play for the seniors to march in, I would be gone. I had one more night to get through, but I wasn't worried about that. The first note of music sounded and I waved my hand at the head of the ushers and streaked for my car. I drove all the way out to Fenton, seventeen miles away. There was a cocktail bar there and I knew Martha would never look for me in it. I intended to sit there until it closed. By the time I got home at two o'clock, there would be no more danger. I wasn't staying with Les and Beth. They were closing their house the next morning, anyway. I had packed everything I would need for the summer in the back of the car and I had taken the rest of it over to my father's where I intended to stay for the night. At eight in the morning I would be on my way.

There was one major error in my thinking. The good side of me had been in firm control ever since Martha made her promise to me. I had made good resolutions and I had kept them. Unfortunately, more good resolutions go down the drain in cocktail bars than anywhere else. I had four drinks that night. I had a happy glow when it came time for me to go home. As the evening progressed I had been thinking some pretty fond thoughts about Martha. When I got behind the wheel of my car, all my good resolutions got in the back seat with the other belongings I wouldn't be needing for a while. Even then, I might have escaped, but when I drove into the driveway at my father's house, a figure got up from the steps of the front porch and walked over to my car. It was Martha, still in her cap and gown. She opened the door and got in the front seat.

"I suppose you thought you could hide from me."

"How did you know I was going to be here?" I asked.

"I had a friend call Mr. Ehrbright's house and Mr. Ehrbright told him." She motioned for me to back out of the driveway. "This is no time to park in any old car," she said. "I'll tell you where to go."

She directed me across town and into the parking lot beside an apartment house. She led the way up some stairs, took some keys out of her purse, unlocked a door, and turned on a light. She stood there, just inside the door and took off the mortarboard, fluffed up her hair, and then sailed the cap across the room where it landed in a corner. Then she reached up to the little clasp at the front of her gown and unhooked it. The gown fell open and she shucked it back off her shoulders and let it fall to the floor. There she stood, absolutely naked, except for her high-heeled shoes. She held out her hand to me.

"We have some unfinished business, teacher," she said. "Let's get at it."

We got at it immediately. My sex education was completed that night by an eighteen-year-old girl with long lovely legs and an exquisite figure. She was the most sensuous person imaginable and an absolute delight. I've often wondered where she learned to do all the things she knew how to do. We were together for three hours and Martha ended it almost as abruptly as she'd started it. The radio was playing on the bedside table and she suddenly sat up and put her feet over the side of the bed and slipped into her shoes.

"Twenty minutes," she said. "We've got twenty minutes to get out of here."

"How come?"

She pointed at the radio. "That was my boy friend. He's the radio announcer and he just signed off. If he doesn't stop for coffee, it takes him twenty minutes to get here."

While I got up and put on my clothes, Martha scurried around the room in the nude, straightening things up and making the bed. In the course of this activity, she retrieved her cap and gown, folded it up and brought it over to me.

"Would you do me a favor and turn this in for me? I never want to see that old school again."

"Sure," I said, "but what are you going to wear?"

"Oh, I have a dress over there in the closet. I left it here yesterday because I was so mad at those women who gave me a shower." She went over and took a flimsy little thing off a hanger, slipped it over her head, and straightened it out.

"Don't you ever wear any underwear?" I asked.

"Sometimes, but not when I feel nasty. I didn't wear any yesterday. All I wore was that cap and gown."

"Good God! Supposing you had tripped or stumbled while you were walking across the stage to get your diploma?"

"Oh, I thought of doing something like that. Just think, four thousand people would have dropped dead."

As we drove off in the car, she sat primly beside me.

"What time does the marriage license bureau open?" she asked me.

"Martha, I'm not going to marry you."

"Not even after all *that?*"

"Not even after all that. I don't love you and I don't think you love me, either. Be honest now. Do you?"

"Why do you think I did what I did?"

"I don't know. You were no virgin."

"I haven't been a virgin since I was twelve years old."

"How many men have you known?"

"Six, now."

"The one who owns the car?"

"Yeah, but not much lately. He's always trying to get me drunk. After this, I won't have anything more to do with him."

"Why did you do it with him?"

"I don't know. It seemed like a good idea at the time. He's pretty good looking. I guess I fell for him."

"But you're tired of him now and you'd be tired of me after a while."

"No, I wouldn't. Honest I wouldn't."

I drove on across town and she directed me into the alley that ran along in back of her house. After I stopped the car she smiled a peculiar little smile.

"I guess I don't really care whether we get married or not. All I care about is seeing you. We can do that."

"I'm going away. I have to go to summer school. Why don't you go out with some boys your own age this summer?"

"I don't want any boys my own age. They don't know anything. I'll come down to Ann Arbor and keep house for you. I want to get out of this jerky town anyway."

"I can't have you down in Ann Arbor, Martha."

"Why not? I could go to college. You want me to go to college."

"No," I said firmly.

She shook her head and smiled to herself.

"Kiss me, teacher," she said.

I kissed her. The trouble with kissing Martha was that it always led to something else. After a few moments she looked up at me. "Do me a favor?"

"All right," I said.

"Do me again?"

"Right here in the alley in broad daylight?"

"Nobody's up yet and nobody can see us with all these garages around. Please!"

After a while she sighed and sat up. "How wonderful," she said. "When are we leaving for Ann Arbor?"

"You're not going to Ann Arbor."

"We'll see. Anyway, we're going someplace." She opened the door and got out and ran around the front. As she rounded the corner of a garage she blew me a kiss. I put the car in gear and moved thoughtfully up the alley. I hadn't gone fifty yards when I happened to look to one side. There, standing beside his garage, smoking a pipe, was Frank Ratterman.

IX

The last morning at school was a brief session at which teachers turned in keys and school property. I had taken care of all this the afternoon before and I had intended to rush in, pick up my paycheck, and get on my way. I was really on the run, now. Before I was just trying to get away from Martha. Now I was running away from Frank Ratterman and everyone else. I had no idea how long Ratterman had been standing beside his garage and how much he'd seen, but I feared the worst and I suspected he'd be on the phone to Otto Norwalk with the news any minute.

There was bad news waiting for me at school, all right. The hall was teeming with seniors turning in caps and gowns and saying good-byes. Otto Norwalk was standing near the entrance talking to two teachers when I walked in the door. He looked up and raised his finger and asked me if I would step into his office. He would be along in a moment. When he finally arrived he was very solemn.

"I've just had a very disturbing report about you," he said. "It involves a very serious matter. It could put your position in this school system in jeopardy."

"Maybe you'd better tell me about it," I said.

"It involves a principle of conduct with a certain young lady. I don't have to mention names. This may be a figment of someone's imagination and for the moment I'm assuming that there's nothing to it, but I'm going to give you some advice. This whole business must not go any further. I hope you will use every resource at your command to see that it does not. If there is so much as a breath of suspicion that this is going beyond what has already happened, I might have to recommend your dismissal."

"Mr. Norwalk, I want to know exactly what you've been told," I said.

"I'm referring to the incident that took place after the dance the other night. It doesn't speak well for your past relationship with the young lady."

I was about to protest but I couldn't. The whole business had already gone further than that, quite a lot further, and I was almost certain that the phone was going to ring—maybe even while I was standing there—revealing the rest of it. It seeemd to me, right at that moment, that my whole life had been thrown away. I'd struggled and fought to get through college to get a degree so I could get a job. I could see all those long lines of unemployed looming before me again. I didn't even think there was any sense of going back to Ann Arbor to get my master's degree. Otto Norwalk got up from his chair and opened the door to indicate that our conference was over. As I passed by him he put his arm around my shoulder in a fatherly fashion.

"Now you go back down to Ann Arbor and get that master's degree," he said. "Come back in the fall and go to work and do the good job you've always done."

I picked up my check and got in my car. For most of the rest of that day I stumbled along blindly, scarcely knowing what I was doing. It was eleven o'clock that night before I began to feel better. By then I was a long way from home. As I have noted, the trip I had originally planned was to the East, but before I ever reached the city limits of Flint, I discarded that. I'd told everyone where I'd be and in my panic it struck me that Martha or Otto Norwalk or someone could worm it out of people. I decided that if I was going to have any fun at all I didn't want any bad news dogging my footsteps, so I simply went off in the other direction. Instead of going northeast, I went southwest.

I didn't have any goal during the first few days of the trip. One could say that I just wandered along from golf course to golf course, playing some new and inviting layout each day, and stopping to see the sights that cropped up along the road—including Mammoth Cave. My general route carried me through Indianapolis, Louisville, Nashville, and Memphis. On a steaming hot day I rolled into Hot Springs, Arkansas, where my father had often gone in the days before the Depression. I did everything there was to do there. I took the baths and drank the water and played golf. After three or four days, when it began to pall on me, I got back in my car and headed southwest again, toward Texarkana on US 67.

I had now arrived at one of those moments in my life which has become a milestone to me. It wasn't an important event. It wasn't even an event. I noticed on the way down to Texarkana that the traffic was very heavy. There was an aura of busyness everywhere and I had to thread my way in and out of the little towns I passed through. About five o'clock in the afternoon, as I approached Texarkana, the road climbed some hills and ran along at a slight elevation. I could look out over a plain to my left. There was a railroad marshaling yard on that plain. It was a vast place, stretching for two or three miles. I was impressed by it and I pulled off the road so that I could get a better look. There were literally thousands of tank cars in the panorama below me. Several switch engines were shunting them back and forth. As I shifted my gaze to take in the whole plain, I could see several refineries. Everywhere I looked there seemed to be high stacks with orange flame at the top. I couldn't remember ever seeing such a busy scene. Then, when I tried to pull back onto the road, I had to wait five minutes for the traffic to thin out. I said to myself, "My God, the Depression must be over." The minute I said it I knew it was true. Every city I'd hit all the way down from Flint had been busy like this. Even at home things had been flourishing. On the day I'd left, when I stopped downtown to cash my paycheck, the parking lots had all been full. And the factories hadn't closed down yet after the 1940 model runs. They might run right through. I shook my head and said the sentence again, changing it a little this time. "My God, the Depression is over." Then I said quite simply, "The Depression *is* over." And so, on that bluff near Texarkana, in June, 1940, eleven years after it began, the long hard pull ended for me. It was a fine and heady moment. I sensed that all those years of discouragement were behind me. For the first time in my whole adult life I could look ahead with some hope and confidence.

I came into Texarkana singing. It wasn't a very prepossessing town. The heat was oppressive and I had to wait three hours before I got a room in a hotel. I loved the place anyway. I kept saying, over and over, "The Depression is over." Everywhere I looked I saw proof of it. The town was full of shirt-sleeved men bending over blueprints.

I hadn't come to see Texarkana. I was in full flight when I arrived there, but as I lay awake in the hot room that night I told myself that it didn't make any difference what Frank Ratterman told Otto Norwalk. If I lost my teaching job I could get something else. There wouldn't be any more lines and want ads. I decided to turn around and go back home. Instead of going on further to the west, I headed north the next morning. Later in the afternoon, as I came down into Fort Smith, I had a flat tire. When I finished changing it, I was soaked through with perspiration. At the service station where I stopped to have it repaired, I asked the attendant if there was a cool place nearby where I could spend the night.

"Fayetteville," he said. "Ninety miles north of here. Coolest place in Arkansas. Look for the Mountain View Inn."

I was entering the Ozark Mountains and I traveled along something called the Boston Road. I'd lived all my life in relatively flat country and I was entirely unprepared for the breathtaking beauty that I saw about me. The lush green valleys that stretched out at my feet completely captivated me and, of course, that little chant I'd been repeating all day enhanced my pleasure. Time after time during that ninety-mile drive I stopped the car to stand and look down at the panoramas spread out before me. The station attendant had been right. Fayetteville was 20 degrees cooler and the Mountain View Inn was a gem. It was on the side of a hill and when I woke up the next morning there were birds singing in a tree outside my window. Far below me, in a valley, I could see a lovely green golf course. I never budged from Fayetteville for ten days. To me it was an Eden and in it I had the one perfect vacation I'd ever had.

On my way home from Fayetteville, I came to Boonville once again and I went back to look at Kemper. It hadn't changed a bit since I'd left it. I didn't feel any kindlier toward it so I got back in my car after one brief look and streaked for Chicago and late one night I checked in at the old familiar Stevens Hotel.

Once the worm turns, it seems to stay turned for a while. I had fully intended to drive on through to Ann Arbor the next morning, a Saturday, but when I counted my money in the Stevens that night, I was amazed to find that I'd spent only $150 of the $200 I'd allotted for my trip. I decided to stay in Chicago for a day and have one last fling. One of the things I wanted to do was go to the horse races at Washington Park. I was no longer a neophyte in that department. I'd been to the track many times with the Squirrel or with the couple from Bowling Green whom I'd met at summer school. They were native Kentuckians and had horse racing in their blood. They had taught me quite a lot. I'd never been as lucky at the track as I'd been that first time, but I'd never been unlucky, either. I was inclined to be cautious and stick to two-dollar bets on reasonably good horses.

When I got up that Saturday morning in the Stevens, I had breakfast in the coffee shop and then bought a morning paper and went to sit in the lobby. I had no more than opened to the racing page than I became conscious of a roly-poly little man with a shock of white hair who had come over to sit beside me on the sofa. He fidgeted around, trying to get a look at my paper, and he was so persistent that I finally folded it up and handed it to him. He was very apologetic. He didn't want the paper. He'd only been trying to find if a horse named Gallipolis was runing that afternoon. I looked and told him that Gallipolis was running in the third race. I asked him whether it was a good horse and whether I should bet on it.

"Oh, Lord, no!" he said. "Don't do that." He looked all around to see if anyone was within hearing distance. "The race is fixed."

I knew, immediately, that the man was setting me up for something and I was curious enough to find out what it was. I asked the obvious questions. He set me up for them like the straight man in a vaudeville act and I soon realized that I was being asked to contribute to the oldest badger game in the business. The man was trying to get a substantial bet down on every horse in the third race. He knew a man who knew Gallipolis' trainer and the horse was going to be pulled up so that another horse could win. He wouldn't tell me the name of the horse that was supposed to win—he never told his suckers that. We were supposed to go to a bookie and he would whisper the name of the winner in the bookie's ear, I would put down my money, and he would collect the ticket and hold it. At the end of the day I would meet him at the bookie's and we would collect our winnings and split them. Of course, when it came time to collect the money, he wouldn't show up. If, by chance, I ran into him, he could always claim that Gallipolis had done his part by not winning, but that some third horse had sneaked in to beat the one who was supposed to win. I contributed two dollars to the man for giving me his little educational lecture—he wanted me to put down fifty—and I came away thinking that he was working harder for his money than most ditchdiggers.

When I got to the track I bought a racing form and began doping the horses. I didn't come within five lengths of winning either of the first two races. Naturally, when I came to the third race, I looked first at Gallipolis. His form was terrible. He was the one horse in the race who couldn't possibly win it. The handicappers felt the same way about it as I did. "Forget this one," one of them said. "Doesn't belong here," was a second verdict. "A real money burner. Stay away," said another. I sat there thinking back over everything that had happened and one thing bothered me. I couldn't understand why my little tout had said that Gallipolis would be pulled up. There wasn't any need to pull him up. It looked like they'd have to push Gallipolis over the finish line in a wheelbarrow. The answer was obvious, of course. The little man *had* to be able to say that Gallipolis had gone through with his part of the bargain. It wasn't his fault if some other horse hadn't played the game. In other words, the one sure bet in that race was that Gallipolis would *not* win.

The longer I sat there, the sorrier I got for Gallipolis. Everyone was being real mean to that horse. By the time I started for the betting windows, I had made up my mind to bolster his self-respect by putting a little bet on him. As I stood in front of the two-dollar window, some kind of a bug bit me. Instead of shoving two ones through the wicket, I tossed a twenty-dollar bill at the seller and asked for ten tickets on Gallipolis' nose. At the time I made the bet, the odds were 20–1. Before he went to the post the odds had gone up to 25–1.

I'll say one thing for Gallipolis. He didn't run like any 25–1 shot. It was a six furlong race and there were eight horses in it. Gallipolis had the pole. He must have started running just before the gates were sprung open for he flew out of his stall as though he'd been shot from a cannon. Before he'd gone fifty yards he was three lengths in front. At the far turn he was eight lengths in front. That was when he began to run out of steam. Yet when the horses reached the head of the stretch he still had a lead of five lengths. I knew it was just a question of how long it was going to take those other seven horses to catch him. He came wobbling toward the finish line so tired he could hardly keep his feet, with the whole field gaining on him at every jump. They caught Gallipolis right at the wire. Five of those eight horses flashed across the finish line in a long row spread across the track. I couldn't tell who had won.

The photo sign went up. The placing judges took an unconscionably long time trying to figure it out. At long last the photo sign flashed off and the numbers went up. Poor old Gallipolis was second, beaten by a nostril. I reached in my pocket for my tickets to throw them away, but as I did so, there was a gasp from the crowd. Another red light had flashed on. It said, "Objection." Several minutes passed before the public-address announcer said, with a note of disbelief, that the rider of the fourth horse was claiming a foul against the rider of the third horse, and the rider of the third horse was claiming a foul against the rider of the first horse. There may have been another foul claim there, somewhere. It seemed like everyone was claiming something. The stewards looked at pictures and argued for half an hour. When they finished all the lights on the board flashed off. When they were turned on again, good old Gallipolis was up there in first place. I collected $546 for my winning tickets. The Depression was *really* over for me.

X

The world had changed. The summer of 1940 was bound to be anticlimactic after Martha and Texarkana and Gallipolis. I paid strict attention to business. I finished my master's degree and played golf. Just before school was out, Howard Ehrmann, my faculty adviser, called me into his office. We were old friends now and I had great respect for him. He thought I should go on and take my doctorate in history and he was prepared to offer me an instructorship so that I could continue my studies. I thought about it for several days and then declined the offer. With my master's degree completed I could look forward to a salary of $230 a month in the Flint schools. I would start the year with money in the bank and I wouldn't owe a cent. A lot of things I'd always dreamed about would be within my reach for the first time. If I pursued the doctorate I might be going to school until I was forty years old and I was just plain tired of school.

On the last Saturday night in August I left Ann Arbor for the last time. I drove home to Flint in a very leisurely fashion, wondering what I'd find there. There was a postcard waiting for me. It was from Martha in New York. She had a part in a musical comedy.

She told me I'd been right about not getting married. She'd fallen in love with her dance director.

The news relieved my mind a little, but I still didn't know whether Frank Ratterman had ever called Otto Norwalk. I went up to school to check in on Monday morning. Guy Houston and Jim Barclay were in the athletic office and they welcomed me with warm handshakes. Guy asked me if I could come in the next day and help sort the new equipment. At least I still had a job. From the gym I went down to the main office to pick up the keys to my room. Otto Norwalk was standing there with his usual solemn face and he beckoned me into his office. This was the moment I'd been worried about all summer. He pulled a sheet of paper out of his desk drawer and slid it across to me.

"I think this will please you," he said.

It was an official notice that I was appointed to the rank of assistant coach of the track team and as such I was entitled to an extra $300 a year. My salary would be $260 a month. I was going to be rich.

"I think I should tell you that we've been guaranteed a full ten months of school this year," Otto Norwalk said. "I have also recommended your appointment as a teacher in the system's summer session for each of the next two years. Your salary will be six hundred dollars for ten weeks. You've gone to a lot of expense to get your master's degree this last four years. You'll probably welcome a chance to make a little extra money."

I welcomed it. I decided to spend it. The first thing I thought about doing was to find my own apartment. I was tired of living with other people. I began looking around, but before I found anything, my father called me downstairs one morning for a little talk. There had been one very sad event in our family that last year. On the morning of January 10, 1940, on his eighty-ninth birthday, Grandpa Perry had passed away in his sleep. It was a fittingly peaceful end for Grandpa, that gentle, kind old man who had meant so much to me all my life. In a way his going had ended us as a family group. In the summer while I was at Ann Arbor, my youngest brother, John, had completed his apprenticeship with the telephone company and had moved away from Flint. Our once-large household now consisted of only my father and Glad. I should add that, by now, my stepmother had acquired a considerable affection amongst all of us. She still pinched pennies and lectured to us about money, but she'd been more than good to us and for us, and we all knew it and appreciated it. Now she was beginning to show her age a little and my father was worried about her. He was on the road a lot of the time and he felt that there ought to be a man around the house to take care of the fires and to shovel the walks in the winter and to do the other chores that only a man could do. He told me that he knew I wanted a place of my own, but he wondered if I would mind living at home for Glad's sake. If I would do it I could have my room and board free. This was too good a windfall to let go. I lived at home.

School was much the same that fall. We embarked on our third straight undefeated football season. Toward the middle of September, I again drove over to Muskegon on a scouting trip. All during the trip over there and back I kept remembering that it was just a year before that I'd bought the car I was driving. It was a good little car and I was well pleased with it, but it wasn't that dream car that I'd always wanted. I'd been promising myself that when the Depression was over I was going to get that car. Well, the Depression was over. On the next Saturday morning I went down to the salesroom and marched in. Within twenty minutes I'd purchased my car with the red-leather upholstery and the white sidewall tires. I'd have to pay thirty dollars a month for two years and a half, but the prospect didn't frighten me a bit. The salesman told me he'd call me when the car was ready for delivery.

The call came to me at school on the afternoon of Tuesday, October 15, 1940. We were getting ready for the Muskegon game and on that particular day we had scheduled a chalk-talk after practice. This would keep me at school until after nine o'clock. The car salesman assured me that would be all right because he had to work until ten. I arrived at the salesroom at quarter of ten and hastily transferred my belongings from the old car to the new. I drove out of the place in such a state of excitement that I didn't stop for dinner on the way home. I would have liked to have done something to celebrate the arrival of that new car—perhaps driving out to Fenton for a cocktail—but it was so late and I was so tired from my long day that I put the celebration off until the next night. Nevertheless, because it was a warm, moonlit October night, I had a good time. I parked the car in the driveway and sat on the front steps with a sandwich and glass of milk and admired it until midnight.

I had to get up early the next morning in order to keep an appointment before I went to school. I went out and got in that beautiful car and backed it out of the driveway. I drove it just one block and turned into another driveway. This second driveway belonged to the Cook Elementary School and my appointment was in the gymnasium there. It was the morning of the sixteenth of October, 1940. The first place to which I drove my new car was to the draft-registration board.

I guess that is the story of my generation. We graduated from school into the Depression. We graduated from the Depression into the armed services. Early in January, 1941, I was called to the National Guard Armory for a physical examination, along with five hundred other fellows. I could look around and see a lot of people I knew. There was Hank Feller and Jim Wiesner and George French. All three of the poker-playing Riley brothers were there. So was Lynn Parker, one of the boys I'd been instrumental in pledging during that year of the Squirrel. Even Martha Collins' radio announcer boyfriend was there—and Harold Reynolds, my fellow assistant coach, and Jim Gallardo, the center on our last state-championship football team. Some of us would be back to our Depression level salaries of twenty-one dollars a month—about five dollars a week—very soon.

It took some a little longer than others to go, but most of us made it within a year. My draft number was the third one out of the goldfish bowl, but I was a teacher and a coach and I could have been deferred until the end of the school year. I *was* deferred until the end of the basketball season, but I was uncomfortable about it because each month I had to go down and stand, hat in hand, before Frank Ratterman. He'd missed the show in the alley that morning, but he was still a factor in my life. He turned out to be the chairman of my draft board.

The first fellow to go from my immediate circle was Jim Wiesner, who was just beginning to get back on his feet in the plumbing business. Early in March, when we played a game against Port Huron High School, Bonnie Higgins and her husband came and sat on the bench with me. Bonnie's husband was leaving the next morning. Two weeks later, when our team was knocked out of the state tournament, I ran my wonderful new car into my father's garage, put it up on blocks, and took the wheels off. It had 1,600 miles on it. I patted it an affectionate good-bye and went down to catch the train for Fort Custer. I expected to be gone a year, but it was five and a half years before I came home again. The car was long since gone, and I was thirty-four years old.

More than nineteen million young men and women of my generation had the same deferred start in life. They went through more or less the same frustrations. I was luckier than some. Some of my friends never did come back. Harold Reynolds was a fighter pilot in the Navy and he lost his life in 1944. Bonnie Higgins' husband died at Omaha Beach. Larry Downey, the boy who studied chess problems in the lobby of the Union on the day I first met Bonnie, died in New Guinea. Dave Rock's son was killed at Remagen. Jim Gallardo was hit on Guadalcanal and never walked again. One of the Rileys lost both feet in the Bulge. The list is almost endless.

Yes, I'm moved to stand up for my generation. We are accused of materialism. It may be true, but it should be remembered that very few of us had anything before we reached the age of thirty. With the start most of us had, I doubt that we'd be normal if we didn't pay some attention to the material things. As to another charge made against us, that we never come to grips with the problems that face the nation and the world, I believe this is patently false. The young generation that came of age in the 1930s was the first truly liberal generation in the history of the United States. We are presently engaged in another revolution—a revolution for human rights. It is an important one and it must be won, but it should be borne in mind that this didn't have its beginning in the 1960s. It had its beginnings in the 1930s. It was then that the young people first began questioning the old beliefs and attitudes—and discarding them. And it was that same generation—now the older generation—which first brought an open mind to problems.

Way back there in 1929, on one of those summer evenings when I thought my father had a million dollars and before Molly Flexner came into my life, George French came over one evening to play croquet on our newly manicured backyard. After it got dark, we retired to the swing where Grandpa Perry was puffing away on one of his big cigars. Sometimes Grandpa could be inveigled into telling us stories about the days when he was young, just after the Civil War. On that night, however, he chose to give us some advice.

"Boys," he said, "the savings-bank interest rate went up to five percent this morning. If you've got any stocks, you'd better unload them quick. All hell is going to break loose in the market."

His advice was good. Unfortunately, he gave it to the wrong people. Neither George French nor I owned any stocks. It is doubtful we knew then what he was talking about. I understood later, though, and these days I always keep an eye on the bank-interest rate. Life is a good deal like that. Most people go along from day to day, meeting each problem as it arises, trying to cope with the things that concern them most. They are apt to brush aside advice from the outer world because it has no direct or immediate bearing on their lives—sometimes because they don't understand it. I'm still not sure where all my own ideas came from, nor am I sure how long it took for some of them to change me. All I know is that the changes were thrust upon me during those long years between 1929 and 1940, and by the same token most of the forces that changed the country to what it is today grew from that period, too. I think I was pretty lucky to have been young then, but then some people have all the luck.